The RAMBLERS

BY AIDAN DONNELLEY ROWLEY

Life After Yes

The RAMBLERS

A NOVEL

AIDAN DONNELLEY ROWLEY

wm

WILLIAM MORROW

An Imprint of HarperCollins*Publishers*

HarperCollins books may be purchased for educational, business, or sales promotional use. For information please e-mail the Special Markets Department at SPsales@harpercollins.com.

FIRST EDITION

Designed by Leah Carlson-Stanisic

Hummingbird art courtesy of Eva_Mask/Shutterstock, Inc.

Endpaper art by sokolova_sv/Shutterstock, Inc.

Library of Congress Cataloging-in-Publication Data has been applied for.

ISBN 978-0-06-241331-4

16 17 18 19 20 OV/RRD 10 9 8 7 6 5 4 3 2 1

For Bryan and the Rowlets

Sunday, November 24, 2013

CLIO ELOISE MARSH

If we expect to suffer, we are anxious.

—Charles Darwin,

The Expression of the Emotions in Man and Animals

There is grandeur in this view of life, with its several powers, having been originally breathed into a few forms or into one; and that, whilst this planet has gone cycling on according to the fixed law of gravity, from so simple a beginning endless forms most beautiful and most wonderful have been, and are being, evolved.

—Charles Darwin, *On the Origin of Species*

BEST OF NEW YORK 2013

Best Stress Reliever—Birdwatching with Clio Marsh

City stress getting to you? (Be honest: of course it is.) Wander over to Turtle Pond on Sundays at nine a.m. for an invigorating amble through the Ramble with bird enthusiast Clio Marsh. A curator in the Department of Ornithology at the American Museum of Natural History and an adjunct professor in evolutionary biology up at Columbia, Marsh has a knack for spotting theatrical avian displays—and for communing with nature-seeking New Yorkers. Nota bene: Forget the wilderness of online dating; turns out a Central Park sojourn can lead to love. Marsh herself met her current amour, hotelier and Northern Irish import Henry Kildare (who will open his fifth boutique hotel, the Here Inn, on the Upper West Side this fall) after one of her walks.

12:03AM

"People will see us."

Clio sits alone at the hotel bar.

She traces her fingertip around the rim of her empty champagne flute and surveys the aftermath of the party. The lobby and bar are littered with wineglasses and crumpled cocktail napkins, evidence of exuberance and good cheer. Wooden skewers with clinging shreds of chicken satay are tucked here and there. A crimson scarf has been left behind on a velvet chair. Towers of plates wait to be whisked away.

Henry's staffers dart about with a quiet efficiency, attacking the mess, transforming chaos back to order. All will be pristine in no time and the Here Inn will sparkle for the first guests, who will check into their new rooms in a matter of hours. Henry has done this four times before, and he swears this is the most fun part, when real people arrive toting their literal and metaphorical baggage.

In the beveled mirror above the bar, Clio catches a glimpse of herself and barely recognizes what she sees. The pin-straight hair; the dramatic eye makeup, now smudged; the twinkling silver dress. She crosses and uncrosses her legs on the leather bar stool, kicks off the brutal, borrowed heels, massages some feeling back into her toes.

For a sublime second, a sentence floats through her head unsolicited, an impossible thought.

I am happy.

Can this be? Is it too soon? It hasn't even been a year.

She feels a smile take over her face. Not one of the artificial, fake-it-to-make-it smiles she's perfected over the years as a matter of survival, the smile she flashed so many times tonight in an abiding effort to pass muster, but a real-deal smile.

Jett, the platinum-haired bartender, returns from hefting bags of empty bottles out back. A recent Juilliard grad, he harbors dreams of Broadway.

"I can't believe how quickly this place came together in the last month," Clio says, looking around and taking it all in. It's all so perfectly Henry: the pressed-tin ceiling, dark wood moldings, vintage chandeliers and mosaic floor. There's a real Christmas tree with tiny white lights by the wood-burning fireplace and the room smells of oak and pine. "When I left town, it was still a construction zone."

"The crew worked around the clock. You should have seen Mr. Kildare—he was right in there, screwing in lightbulbs and drilling holes . . ."

"Well, that must have been a sight," she says, smiling at the image. "It doesn't surprise me. Henry lives for the details."

"That he does," Jett says, filling her glass reflexively. "Where were you anyway?"

"South America, for work," she says, stretching her arms to stifle a yawn. Jett seems intrigued, so she continues. "My department has a grant to study Andean hummingbirds." Jett's eyes glaze over a bit. "I just flew in this morning so I could be here for the party, and I'm not really seeing straight. Can't tell if the champagne is helping or hurting."

"In my experience, champagne helps until it really doesn't," Jett says through a knowing smile. "So what's better? Chasing down birds or rubbing elbows with fancy New Yorkers?"

"The former," she says. "By a long shot."

"Thanksgiving plans?" Jett asks as he wipes down the bar.

The mere mention of the holiday makes Clio stiffen and sip. She needs a few days to fortify herself before she thinks about Thanksgiving. "I'll be in Connecticut, with my father," she says quietly, her eyes clouding. She finishes her drink in one swift gulp, tips her glass out to Jett for more. "And what about you, Jett?" she asks. "Big plans?"

"Oh, I'll be right here," he says, slapping the bar. "Another VIP night at the hotel. But tonight was the big one. I think it went well. Seemed like a great party."

She nods, takes a too-big sip of champagne. "It *was* a great party," she says, her voice light and drifting. Jett disappears into the kitchen and she flips through the pages of a leftover book. *Here Is New York* by E. B. White, Henry's literary hero and the inspiration for the hotel. It had been Henry's idea to give each guest tonight a copy as a parting favor.

A blast of cold air hits her. Clio turns toward the front door and sees Henry stumbling in from the street, alone. He ducked out not long ago for a cigar with the last of his guests, two nattily turned-out *New Yorker* editors and the etiquette columnist from *Town & Country*. His cheeks are rosy and his fedora threatens to topple. He spots her and sidles over, flashing a dazzling smile. She slips back on her heels and slides off her stool to stand as he approaches.

"Warm me up, m'lady. It's absolute winter out there," he croons, loosening his bow tie. The booze has brought out the dregs of his accent, which is all but gone after two decades in America. His blue eyes are unusually bright. He lifts Clio to sit on the bar top and presses himself between her legs. The marble, white with gray veins, is cool on her bare thighs.

"There's poetry in the wreckage, eh?" he says, looking around at the postparty disarray.

"Indeed there is."

"God, I've missed you, my Bird Girl," he says, tucking her hair behind her ears, kissing each lobe. "I'm so happy you're back. That you're here."

"I've missed you too," she says, running a hand through his hair. It's grayer than it was even six months ago.

Jett reappears to check on his boss.

"Pour me a nip of Jameson, will you? Neat," Henry slurs over her shoulder.

"Yes, sir," Jett says.

"Oh, laddy, no. Lose the 'sir' stuff. I know I'm old as dirt, that I've got years on you young things, but let's just pretend for the evening, shall we?"

Clio watches as Jett unscrews the bottle and pours, the brown liquid glistening in the crystal tumbler.

"Well, well," Henry says, taking Clio's face between his cold hands. "We bloody *did it*."

"*You* did it," she says, correcting him.

"*We*."

"*You*. All you," she says, pulling him to her. Tonight's success was not a stroke of luck or the aligning of a mysterious assemblage of stars. In the six months Clio's known Henry, she's barely seen him sit still. It's been an inspiring blur of long nights watching him squint into a glowing computer screen, a flurry of contracts and certificates and architectural floor plans, mad dashes around Manhattan to curry favor with investors and expeditors and media players, elaborate furniture and art sprees, all leading to this moment, the realization of a dream and a lot of hard work.

"You, me, tomato, tomahto, never mind. We did it and it's time to *move on*," Henry says, and kisses her again. It's not a delicate peck appropriate for public, but real and almost rough, magnificently forceful. He knocks her glass over and the remaining champagne spills, pooling on the bar. He puts his mouth on her ear, his breath warm and laced with tobacco. "I thought they'd never leave. All that schmoozy-dooze kissy-kissy bullshite and all I could think about was you, getting you upstairs . . ."

"You're *drunk*, Henry," Clio whispers, stating the obvious. She contorts her arm behind her to blot puddles of champagne that soak through to her skin.

"Drunk? Is that the best you've got, Professor Marsh? I'm miles past drunk. I'm bollixed. Gee-eyed. Langered. Plastered. Rat-arsed. The list goes on."

"I'll make a note to work on my Drunk and White lexicon," Clio says, and grins, proud of her timely levity. It's never been her strong suit. "I found you a Christmas present, you know."

"Did you now?" he says, and there's a boyish excitement in his face. "Is it under the tree?"

"Calm down, Mr. Kildare. All good things in time."

"How in the world did I get so lucky?"

"You and I both know I'm the lucky one."

Henry shakes his head, finishes off his drink. He wipes his face with the back of his shirtsleeve, then kisses Clio's bare shoulder.

"Oh, Clio, it's crazy . . . it's stupefying, really. Nearly fifty years on this good Earth and suddenly I'm a joyful bloke."

"After tonight, you deserve nothing less," Clio says.

"Yes, yes, because tonight was a massive hooley and this fine joint is up and running, but it's beyond that, you know," he says, grinning, tapping his finger to her nose. "I'm plain elated and my Lord, it's *you*. You are to blame for this. You and your clever friend Jameson, I reckon. In cahoots, you two."

A whiskey-soaked soliloquy. A tumble of feeling, of words. Clio flushes with embarrassment and puts her hands to his lips to quiet him. He laughs and slides a hand up her dress, high up her thigh, buries his face in the nape of her neck. His eyelashes tickle her skin as he blinks.

"I have no idea what happened to my suit jacket," he confesses through laughter, his mumbled words wet on her neck. "Could've used it out there in the Arctic. Ach, it's bound to turn up."

"It will," Clio says as he stands again. She places her hand on his chest. A button dangles from his vest. His shoes are untied. His hair is mussed from the wind. That mischievous, messy twinkle, camouflaged briefly by nerves and decorum tonight, is back. Clio traces the shape of his hand in hers, the edges of his badly bitten nails.

"What about *you*? How are *you*? You've been off sleeping in tents and chasing your birds and here you are, right before me, a bloody vision. How are you feeling, my darling? You must be exhausted."

"I actually feel great," she says, remembering her revelation from moments ago. She nearly whispers the word: "happy."

The music that's been playing in the background all night seems louder all of a sudden. Bono's voice bellows around them. "*And all I want is you . . .*"

"Yes, I want you. Tell me you want me." He lifts her chin with his forefinger, pulls her face to within inches of his. He kisses her again, then pulls away, awaits her answer.

"I want you," she says putting her hand on his cheek. "Oh, do I want you."

And she does. It's unlike anything she's felt before, this anticipatory burn. Time can't move fast enough.

"You know what I think?" he says. "I've behaved myself all night long. I've been a good and rightful boy. I've jumped through my hoops and done my deeds, but now I'm free to let you in on my plan. You know very well how I fancy a good plan."

She nods. He's a planner, this Henry.

He places a hand on each of her knees, presses his body into her again, flicks off her shoes. His voice dips deep into his nighttime growl. "Close your eyes."

She does.

"This is how it will go: We will make it only as far as the elevator. In we'll waltz, all manners, and the doors will close and I will push you against that back wall because I know you like a bit of rough-and-tumble and back you'll go, and I will lift this little frock that's driving me bloody mad and I will drop to my knees . . ." His hand inches up her leg.

"Keep going—"

"The best part," he whispers now, in her ear, "the clincher, my dear, is that tiny little camera tucked into the ceiling. *People will see us.* Tell me the thought doesn't get you wet. I dare you, tell me."

"Let's go," Clio says, looping a finger through his belt, yanking him closer. "Now."

He lifts her, floats her down to the floor, and as he does, she feels him stiff against her.

She drops to the ground to collect her heels. When she stands, she locks eyes with a man she doesn't know.

"Not so fast, you two," he says.

12:35AM

"Don't worry."

The man wears a dark suit. His eyes are a blazing electric blue. Has she seen him before? He's strangely familiar and Clio can't figure out why. Does he work at the museum? Is he a fellow professor at Columbia? He stands there, just staring at them with a look of sharp disapproval, until his face splits into a censorious grin. Then he tackles Henry in a hug.

"Well, Hanky. Sloshed again, I see. Fitting."

"Bloody hell, Patrick," Henry says, returning the exuberant embrace. "What on earth are you doing here?"

"You know exactly what I'm doing here," he says, grinning, winking at Clio. "I finagled a last-minute client meeting in the city to surprise you. Then the bloody flight was three hours delayed, but what the hell, better late than never. And this fresh-faced vision must be Clio? You said she was younger, Henry, but good God, robbing the cradle, are we?"

"Settle down, Pat. She's thirty-four. Your age," Henry says, pulling Clio between them. "Meet Patrick Kildare, my baby brother. Pat, meet Clio."

Ah, that's it. She's seen pictures of Patrick, the youngest of Henry's three brothers. He's the one who lives in Silicon Valley and works for Google. Married, two little boys whose toothless grins are all over Henry's iPhone. With one hand, Clio straightens her dress and extends the other to shake Patrick's. The resemblance, she appreciates now, is staggering. They have the same eyes, the same long lashes and unruly brows, the same inky black hair. The same straight nose and square jaw and cleft chin. But Patrick is conspicuously younger, hasn't yet grayed at his temples. His skin is still smooth, free of lines. He's slimmer, missing that slight paunch that's come from years of working hard and living well. It's startling, really: she's looking at Henry fifteen years ago.

"How was the party?" Patrick says. "What all did I miss?"

"Oh, it was just brilliant," Henry says. "Couldn't have asked for a better turnout. Who's who from *Condé Nast Traveler* and the *New York Times*. Graydon Carter from *Vanity Fair.* That funny young gal everyone's always raving about. What's her name again, Clio?"

"Lena Dunham," Clio says, wincing as she slips her heels back on.

The guest list was indeed something of a coup—tastemakers (oh, terrible word) from all over the city, media heavyweights, names from the targeted literary, restaurant and hospitality worlds.

"How long will we have the pleasure of your company?" Henry asks, his arm slung around Patrick.

"Not long, don't worry. Will squeeze in some face time and cocktail nonsense with my clients here and then be on my way. I'm afraid the wife will have my head if I'm gone much longer."

"We're booked pretty solid, thank the Lord, but I think I can finagle a room for you. Come, let's get you a nip of something to warm you up," Henry says. Jett stands by, waits for orders, but Henry dismisses him for the night and slips behind the bar himself, squinting to study the bottle labels. "Ah, the good stuff, here we go." He pulls down a bottle from the top shelf.

"I'm going to head up," Clio says. "You two catch up. I'm spent."

"Stay for *one* more drink, won't you?" Henry says, tugging at her hand.

"Yes, one measly cocktail with the miserable fellow who came all the way across the country to meet you?"

A real flatterer, this one, Clio muses, but she can't help but be touched. She wonders what Henry's told him about her.

"I think you two will do just fine without me," she says, starting to go, her exhaustion setting in. "It's really wonderful to meet you, Patrick."

"Likewise, dear," Patrick says, squeezing her hand. "I'll see you in the morning."

Clio stands on her tiptoes to kiss Henry's cheek. As she cuts through the dimly lit lobby, she glances back and sees the two brothers on opposite sides of the bar, hunched over rapidly disappearing amber cocktails, their foreheads almost touching. It's a tender scene; they seem quite close.

She presses the elevator button and waits.

The elevator arrives and Clio steps in, takes deep breaths. As the doors close, an arm reaches through and pulls her out. It's Henry, breathless, visibly undone. He nibbles his nails, then encircles her waist, looks right into her eyes. "I'm so sorry about this, Clio. I had no idea Patrick was going to show up. I'm glad he's here, don't get me wrong, but I'm desperate to get you out of that dress and . . ."

"It's fine, Henry," she says. "He's your brother. Spend time with him. I'm not going anywhere."

"But I haven't seen you. God, who knew three weeks could be an eternity? And then you're leaving me again on Wednesday, damn you."

"Trust me, I'd rather stay here with you." And suddenly the idea of being with her father alone in her childhood home for the last time fills her with dread. She hadn't even known the house was for sale when he e-mailed her two days before she left on her research trip to tell her he'd accepted an offer on it from a young family who wanted to move in right after Thanksgiving. *Don't worry about coming home*, he wrote in the e-mail, the words a well-worn refrain. *I just wanted you to know.*

She pulls away from Henry, crosses her arms in front of her.

"Promise me you'll wait up for me tonight? I know you're wiped, but I have something for you."

"What is it?" she asks, her stomach clenching.

"Don't worry," he says. "I know you don't like surprises. But trust me. You'll like this one."

He calls the elevator again, and she steps inside, turns to face him. The doors close between them and she is alone.

12:52AM

"Come."

And there it goes, Clio thinks as the elevator ascends. The happiness she felt earlier falls away. She feels her pulse quicken. Her temples ache; her shoulders tense.

A surprise? What kind of surprise? The racing after her, the cryptic insistence that she wait up for him . . . This is all so strange, so unlike him. She's grown accustomed to Henry's thoughtful gestures—inventive dates around the city, small trinkets, near-daily overtures of affection that she's come to expect and enjoy as part and parcel of what's been an almost old-fashioned courtship—but everything about tonight is different and this behavior unsettles her.

When the elevator doors open on the hotel's top floor, Clio staggers out. *Just get into the room,* she thinks. *One foot in front of the other.* It's late after all. She's been awake for almost twenty-four hours. She had a few too many glasses of champagne. She probably just needs water and rest. She peels off her heels again, the awful toe-tangling stilettos that have left her feet feeling fuzzy and numb, and walks the length of the quiet hall, a honey-hued runway mottled with light that spills evenly from crystal sconces. Framed *New Yorker* covers line the wall. She notices for the first time that the rich wooden plaques are up, hanging by each closed door, colossal room numbers etched in the handsome font she helped Henry select.

At the door to Henry's suite, she waves her keycard in front of the sensor. A red light appears. She tries again. The red light again. Shit. She looks around, suddenly wondering if it's the right door, if he's changed the lock. She tries again and the green light blinks and she hears the familiar click of the door unlatching. Inside the room, she drops her shoes by the door and tosses her clutch on the bed. The bag flies open and her phone tumbles out. The screen is lit with a text.

Smith: So sorry I bailed early. It was lovely and: Lena!! Squeeee! Need to focus on self-care this week and rest. Hope you understand. Xx PS—You were luminous tonight. So glad you let me play stylist. And so glad you're home! I missed you.

Smith. Her closest friend in the world. They met sixteen years ago as freshmen at Yale and have lived together since, those four years on campus and the last twelve in Smith's apartment in the San Remo, on Central Park West.

Clio laughs at the self-care bit. She can't help it. Such a Smith-ism. Ever since she started talking to this new life coach, there's been a lot of "self" talk (self-esteem, self-care, self-compassion . . .). Ordinarily she'd tease Smith about it, but Clio has to cut her friend some slack this week. Smith's younger sister, Sally, is getting married on Saturday and it's a miracle that Smith is still vertical. It will be a big, extravagant affair at the Waldorf and Smith insists she's okay with this, that she's "delighted" for her sister, that she simply "adores" her sister's suitably dull fiancé, Briggs, but Clio knows better. Smith was meant to go first. Smith had the emerald engagement ring, the ethereal vintage lace dress, the dashing Pakistani neurosurgeon, the first baby's name all but chosen.

Clio will never forget the day it all fell apart last December: how puffy-eyed Smith sulked around the apartment in a daze, how Clio followed in her wake, helping her eliminate all traces of the man who had just blindsided her. They threw out his organic peanut butter, his electronic toothbrush, his favorite Harvard sweatshirt. Then they sat in the bay window in the living room for hours, sipping wine and trying to decipher his cryptic parting words: *I love you too much to continue this.*

Clio responds to the text.

Clio: No worries about tonight. I survived. Sleep tight. xo C . . .

She sets down her phone, stands and scans the space for clues, but the room appears just as it did three weeks ago when she left town. She's grown fond of this cozy haven with its faux-fur throws and crisp white linens. Sunday nights in this room are her favorite by far; she and Henry have started a tradition of room service and robes and marathon television watching.

She pulls Smith's dress over her head, drapes it carefully on the chair by the window. In her bra and underwear, she studies herself in the full-length mirror next to the bed. Her body is fuller now, the curves of her hips a bit softer; she's gained some of the weight back.

She walks to the closet and takes out her ivory robe. Henry had the lapel monogrammed with "BG," short for "Bird Girl," his nickname for her. She slips it on and walks to the window. The night sky is a soothing chalkboard black. The stars are hiding, but the moon is big and bright. An airplane dots the sky, and she finds herself thinking of all the people inside it, strapped to their seats, surrendering to what will be, floating between here and there.

She glances down at the street. Three flags—an Irish tricolor (a nod to his Dublin-born mother), a Union Jack and an American flag have been hung above the hotel entrance and now duke it out in the howling wind. People are still out and about even though it's late and bitterly cold. They pass by in electric droves, bundled and determined, leaving glass-muted puffs of laughter and conversation in their wake.

Clio loses herself for a moment but comes to feeling foolish and inexplicably sad. She's dizzy. Her head is light and aches subtly. Doubt wraps her, disorients her.

It's still not clear how any of this happened, the successful older man, the glittering New York City existence, the cocktail dresses and late-night champagne. This is the stuff of fairy tales and she knows this, the makings of other people's outlandish dreams. This isn't Clio. She's worked hard all of these years to focus on her career, on securing grant after grant for her departmental work. She's been fine without a man. She accepted that her life would be one of research and being on her own, but here she is, waiting and deeply uneasy, anticipating what might come next.

Clio should have known something was amiss when she didn't immediately jump on the chance to join the expedition to the Ecuadorian Andes, to study a rare species of hummingbird that lives in the oxygen-deficient, snowcapped Antisana volcano peaks, a miracle of adaptation that they say would have impressed Charles Darwin himself. Arthur, her museum department head, a cantankerous genius with a bite far softer than his bark, chafed at her reluctance. "This research is your *baby*, Clio. And a priceless opportunity to rub elbows with the Chimborazo Hillstars? You'd be crazy to pass this one up." The expression on his face said it all: *What's gotten into you, Clio Marsh?*

And he was right to be perplexed. Field research has always been her favorite part of her work, but this time she felt hesitant, even slightly resentful. She was anxious about leaving Smith alone before the wedding, yes, but more than that she didn't want to abandon Henry, particularly during the stressful weeks before the opening, and her ambivalence bothered her. Never before had anyone or anything competed with her birds.

But Smith assured her she'd be busy with a few new clients, not to mention her maid-of-honor duties, and Henry was anxious and preoccupied in the final weeks before the opening, so off she went, though she insisted on three weeks instead of her usual six or eight. The team included ornithology colleagues from the museum, a team of UC Berkeley geneticists and a scruffy young photographer from *National Geographic*. Arthur's granddaughter, Angie, one of Clio's most promising students at Columbia, tagged along too as a fresh-faced and eager apprentice, her eyes permanently wide, her little notebook always open, her unending questions riddled with keen detail and enthusiasm. Angie went wild when they caught a close glimpse of the White-tufted Sunbeam, *Aglaeactis castelnaudii*. Clio will not forget the look on Angie's face in that moment, the purity of her awe.

The first few days of the trip were grueling. They ascended too quickly from Quito to their high-elevation field site located just above the tree line near the Antisana Ecological Reserve and did not have enough time to acclimate properly. Clio lost her appetite and struggled to catch her breath; she huffed and puffed while setting up the delicate mist nets and snagged her backpack on one, breaking the very fine nylon threads, a rookie mistake she hadn't made in more than a decade. But she pushed through and soon enough slipped into her Zen-like concentration, becoming so absorbed in her work of collecting tissue samples that she came to ignore the constant throbbing headache that was her companion throughout the entire trip. At dawn, when the birds danced around her in the hazy morning light, twirling in the air like tiny acrobats, Clio thought she might never come home.

But at night as Clio tossed and turned on her cot in the freezing-cold tent, her mind slipped first to images of her father alone in their house, surrounded by moving boxes, the guilt flaring inside of her, a familiar fire. But then she would leap, with a speed and effortlessness that startled her, to Henry. She imagined him, his crooked smile, his hearty laugh, but mostly his touch. She pictured the two of them together walking through the park or around the Upper West Side, but she also closed her eyes and saw the two of them together in the hotel bed, her body loose and ecstatic under the weight of his. She ached for him. She missed him in a way she'd never missed anyone except for her mother, and with an intensity that unnerved and embarrassed her. Each day Clio was gone, Henry seemed to vaporize a bit more. Doubts simmered; what if she was just imagining this other glittering world so many thousands of miles away? The human mind, she knew all too well, could play the cruelest tricks.

Walking into the hotel lobby earlier this evening, Clio caught a glimpse of Henry for the first time in three weeks and felt an enormous surge of relief that he was a living, breathing person. She watched him for a few moments before he noticed her. He appeared elegant in the new tweed jacket she'd helped him pick, the silk bow tie he practiced tying on his thigh through fits of hiccuping Guinness-soaked laughter, the fedora like the one E. B. White wore on the little book's front cover. He leaned against the bar, his dark brow furrowed, eyes darting as he nervously scanned notes for his welcome speech. When he looked up and saw her, he lit up and bounded over, arms outstretched. He swallowed her in a hug and kissed her neck. *Christ, Clio, I've been a bloody wreck*, he said, his eyes shining. *But I'm better now that you're here.*

He was real.

Is real.

But now what? Now he says he has a surprise.

Clio considers the possibility that the surprise is a ring, that he wants to marry her. *Shit shit shit*. She's never consciously wanted this, she never allowed herself to want this, at least not in any concrete way. She thinks of her parents. Married at seventeen because they were in a bind, Clio being the bind. She thinks of her father hunched in defeat over her mother's grave almost a year ago, his eyes hollow and wet.

There's so much about her that Henry doesn't know. So much that she hasn't been able to tell him.

She looks around for a hidden box. It's a small room, and there aren't many hiding spots. She runs to his bedside table and throws open the drawer, but it's empty. That would be too obvious anyway. She checks the marble shelves in the bathroom but finds only fresh towels. She rifles through the pockets of his jackets and pants. Looks through his briefcase. Nothing. What's wrong with her? Snooping like this? This is not who she is.

She casts her gaze back around the room, the plush cream carpet and the impossibly large bed dressed neatly in white linens and topped with an excess of plump white pillows.

The bed. All she can think about now: their first time. She made him wait even though she didn't want to. Two full months, months of rich conversation about hummingbirds and hotels, charming jokes about bottled lust, electric brushes of the hand, longer and longer kisses in front of the big shadowy building, and then she couldn't wait another minute. *Meet me now.* Daytime in this room, sunlight bold through pristine glass. A fumbling prologue. A careful undressing. The welcome weight of his body on top of hers. Soft skin. Sandpaper stubble. A laboring for breath. A biting of pillow sham, futile attempts to muffle the scream.

She looks up now, catches her reflection in the twin mirrored bedside tables, fruit of a Sotheby's estate sale. Earlier, she marveled at how together she looked for once, how coiffed and perhaps glamorous, even, but now she looks tired and worried. Her sandy hair, so sleek before, is now full of static. Her mascara has left dark circles around her eyes. Her cheekbones are sharp, jutting from her face. She figures it out, what's haunting her; she looks just like her mother.

She looks away.

She shoves her hands in the deep pockets of her robe. Her right hand closes around something jagged and hard.

A key.

She pulls it out, studies it. It's an old-fashioned brass skeleton key. Along its side, a single word, all caps: HOME.

She holds it up in the moonlight. Turns it over in her hand. What in the world?

She hears something and startles.

A cacophonous banging followed by song. Verdi. Henry belts out *Falstaff,* his favorite of all, and fumbles with the door. Light falls in from the hall and he crashes through, all six feet two inches of him tumbling in a fit of laughter to the carpet. He crawls over to her, an impish grin splayed on his face. He pulls up on her knees, his blue eyes ablaze.

"No stoicism tonight. No *thank you,*" he slurs nonsensically. "When I saw you I fell in love, and you smiled because you knew."

"Okay, Don Juan, how many more drinks did you have?" she says, nervous laughter escaping her.

"Oh, my bird nerd . . . *When I saw you I fell in love* . . . such brilliance is Arrigo Boito's. That libretto of his was downright divine," Henry says, then spins and falls back onto the bed.

She holds up the key, dangles it over him. "I found this in my robe."

"Ha! Just as I planned!" he says as he stands, swaying like a tree in deep wind.

"What's it for?" she asks, aware now of her rapid-fire pulse, the sweat on her palms.

"Come," he says, waving her over, but she stays put.

"*Come,*" he repeats.

His hands tremble.

"Are you okay, Henry?" she says, studying his face.

"You know something? I'm bloody keyed up. Fine all night but now I'm right shredded."

"Henry, what's going on?" she asks, but she's not sure she wants to know. She senses it now; something big is about to happen. Everything is about to change. She swallows and waits in the darkness, watches as

Henry places both hands around the left side of the big white bookshelf, the bookshelf that was until hours ago stuffed with hundreds of copies of *Here Is New York*. He squats slightly. Steadies himself on the carpet. He uses his whole body to pull. The shelf slides over along a thin metal track. Inch by inch it goes, tucking neatly in the corner of the room.

And there it is.

A door.

1:03AM

"Where are we?"

Her hands shake. She tries to fit the key in the door and finally manages. When she turns the key, she feels the door budge. She pushes it open, walks through. Henry follows close behind.

On the other side of the threshold, Clio pauses. Her feet sink into deep, succulent carpet. It is quiet and dark, but in the distance she spies moonlight through drapes, a spiderweb of shadows on the floor. Her eyes are quick to adjust and she can make out certain shapes: two low-profile couches that face each other, something floating in between.

In the far corner, a table and chairs.

"Where are we?" she says.

"Where do you think we are?"

He punts her question back at her, like a shrink would. This feels strangely like a game. She doesn't answer him.

"How about *home*?" Henry says.

Home.

One word and her nausea flares.

"How about *our home*?"

She says nothing. Looks back at the door.

"When did you do this? When did you put in that door?"

"You've been gone *almost a month*. Felt like a bloody eternity, really. A lot happened when you were off frolicking in the mountains," he says, flipping on the light.

Now she can see more. Yes, couches. Between them, a coffee table, its surface stacked high with books. An ice bucket with a bottle of champagne. In the corner of the room, a glass table glistens with six chairs around it. A trio of windows overlooks West Seventy-Ninth Street. Opposite the windows is an empty bookshelf.

Clio can't bring herself to speak, but her feet press forward to explore the place. She walks past the living area and into a kitchen. The countertops are a deep green marble. The tiles of the backsplash are rose gold. She opens the fridge and sees a few rounds of cheese from Murray's, strawberries. She passes a stacked washer-dryer opposite the kitchen and turns into a small room. There is a window and a desk.

"Clio, come with me," he says, and takes her hand. They walk back into the living room and he pulls her to sit with him on one of the couches. "You haven't said a word. What do you think? I realize it's a bit on the spare side but we can fill it with all the things we love. Your books about Darwin. A marble bust of E. B. White, if we want one. Fuck it, whatever, just please. Clio. Tell me what you think?"

What does she think? She *can't* think. She can barely see. She can barely breathe. With each passing moment, the room grows blurrier around her. She feels her body tensing, her breath growing shallow. "It's just that this is . . . a lot."

"Yes, I see that, but hear me out. I thought I was one way, Clio, that certain woebegone workaholic way I am. Good or bad or bloody indifferent, I figured it was who I am and that I would never in a million years change, but now I feel myself *changing* and *wanting* things and you are the thing I want. I want us to be together, I think . . . I mean I look at you and I even think about becoming a father. Having a family. Jesus, those are words I never thought I would say—"

Clio's eyes drift down and then to the ceiling. She feels herself swaying and grabs on to the edge of the couch for support.

"—and I was pretty bloody certain we were on the same page, but now I'm looking at you and you're ashen and seem as if you've seen a ghost, but I love you, I *do*. I need *you*. I love you, Clio. I want a life. *With you*."

Is she hallucinating this? Is this really happening? He's drunk but also strangely clear. Making no sense. Making perfect sense.

Clio squints and looks away, at the door through which they walked minutes ago.

"Clio?" Henry says, shaking her, attempting to snap her back. "What's come over you? What's wrong?"

"Is it hot in here?" she hears herself say, stalling.

"I don't think so," he says. "I can check the thermostat though." He gets up and stumbles over to the wall. "Oh, bollocks, where is the bloody thing? I built this damn room, I should know."

Suddenly, she's very aware of her body, of its movements, of each strained, staccato breath. Questions ricochet like a pinball inside her: *Will I faint? Will I throw up? Do I have a dangerous, life-threatening fever? Will something horrific happen to me before I'm able to get out of here?*

It takes her a moment, as it always does, but now she knows exactly what this is, that this has likely been building all night: another panic attack. There have been too many to count, but not a single one since Henry. Her internal chatter rises rapidly from whisper to roar: *Calm down. It's just another panic attack, Clio. Breathe. Calm down. You'll be fine. Breathe. But what if this time is different? What if it's not a panic attack at all, but something grave? What if something is fatally wrong?*

What if this is a heart attack or an aneurysm? Stop, Clio. You know what this is. Breathe. Believe that you're fine. Be calm. Pick a neutral spot in the room and focus on it. You're okay. Just wait it out. But what if this time I'm not okay? You're okay. Every time you've been okay, right? Okay. Breathe. In and out. In and out. Think of still water. Think of blue sky. Happy, floating clouds. You are okay. *But what if . . . But this time might be different. I have to . . . I have to . . . escape.*

She jerks up to stand and feels herself teetering. A gossamer veil hangs between her and the room; everything is now muted, filtered, faded. Sweat spills from every inch of her body. Her fingertips and hands and arms tingle and then go completely numb. She struggles to swallow. Her chest tightens, locks. The light pouring in from the street spins and flashes. She squints. Objects in the room shift ominously about. She fears that she's about to fall. Henry's face is glazed with horror and alarm, but she can't think about Henry right now.

Her sole focus: escape. She must get out—out of this room, out of this hotel, out of this situation. She runs back through the door into the other room. She grabs for her bag and Smith's heels, and keeps flying out the door. She turns just long enough to see Henry jogging after but stopping outside the room. His eyes blaze with confusion. He says something, words that trail her, echoing in her buzzing ears.

"What the hell, Clio? What's wrong with you?"

She eyes the elevator, but it's too far and too risky. The fire door is closer and she bolts through it, scurries barefoot down eleven flights.

By the time she reaches the ground floor, she can barely stand. The pain in her legs is now razor-sharp, stabbing.

She might just die.

The motion detectors work, thank God, and the door to the street automatically opens as she barrels toward it. Outside, the cold air stings her cheeks. Wind threatens to blow open her robe, but she manages to hold it closed over her bare body. She steadies herself long enough to step back into the heels and hobbles toward the street, where she comes dangerously close to being hit by a car. She throws up an arm to hail a cab. Mercifully, one is quick to pull over. The driver, a young guy with bleary eyes, turns all the way around and peers worriedly through the divider.

"Everything okay, miss?" he says, concern plain in his voice.

"The San Remo, please. Central Park West between Seventy-Fourth and Seventy-Fifth," Clio says, forcing the words out, scrambling to find the lone Xanax that floats in her purse.

8:27AM

"I lied."

"Oh my God. You scared the living crap out of me, Clio. What are you doing here?" Smith says, perching on the edge of her own bed.

Clio sits up and rubs her eyes, looks groggily around Smith's bedroom. She vaguely remembers entering the apartment, eyeing the bed in her own room, but then climbing into bed next to a sleeping Smith, a comfort habit she's had for years. The events from last night play in a steady, sickening loop in Clio's head. Did she really run off like that in the middle of the night?

"Do you even remember texting me last night? You said the hotel has a hidden door? Were you drunk?"

"Slow down . . . wait . . . oh, my head. Whisper . . . ," Clio says. Her body is leaden; the

Xanax she popped in the cab knocked her out hard. And then it all comes rushing back. "Henry told me he had a surprise and the surprise was an *apartment*, Smith. The poor guy. He was wasted and waxed poetic about wanting a *life* together. And what did I do?"

"Please tell me you didn't—" Smith says, shaking her head as if she can't even bear to hear the rest.

"I did. I ran for the hills. Shit."

"See, I told you this was more than a casual fling," Smith says. There's a discernible edge in her voice, a hint of accusation.

"Apparently, he's more serious about this than I thought," Clio says, scanning the room, which is painted a dusty saffron yellow, a color Smith has used around the apartment, one Clio's come to associate fondly with the last decade-plus of her life. Being in the room now feels strange, different.

"An apartment? But are *you* serious about him?" Smith asks.

"I don't even know," Clio says. Clio thinks of the nights in Ecuador, of how she longed for him. Yes. But what good is this knowledge now that the façade she's erected is falling away? Her calamitous meltdown last night has no doubt changed everything. She saw it on his face, that wincing glimmer of recognition. *This woman is unhinged.* Soon he'll have to know the truth. And then she'll be alone again.

At first, it's true, Clio was more than willing to be Henry's latest flavor. She'd thought it through and decided that it would be good for her to fill some of her time with pleasurable experiences. Surely, going out with an attractive, intelligent and worldly man was healthier than hibernating and crying into her bird books or trolling the grief chat boards she rustled up online. How many times could she read another punctuation-free paragraph saying that getting over the loss of a loved one takes *time*?

He wanted to see lots of her and she agreed. He took her to see *Madame Butterfly* at the Met, to sip Guinness at his favorite city pubs. They had picnics in Central Park and spent a night at the quiet Sheeley House bed and breakfast in the Hudson Valley, rode bikes up to the

Cloisters, went to see Shakespeare in the Park's *The Comedy of Errors*. Henry even became a regular on her Sunday birding tours, disappearing after to work so she could have her time with Smith.

To say that it wasn't the right time for her to jump into anything serious was an understatement, but never did she let herself think this would lead to something lasting. Well, that's not entirely true. More than once, she'd be sitting in her office at the museum or up at Columbia and she'd catch herself daydreaming, imagining a future with this most unusual man, but then she'd put an end to the nonsense; people like her did not end up with people like him outside of the movies. People like him did not end up with anyone. His whole existence was predicated on change, on hopping around from one hotel to the next, on working feverishly hard at the expense of a personal life. There were women, but they were exquisite, disposable accoutrements to his busy life. Models. Actresses. Socialites. Not ornithologists.

"He mentioned maybe even having a family," Clio says quietly, aware of the tremble in her voice. The moment the words are out, she wishes she could retrieve them. This is a delicate topic for Smith.

"But he's so old. I mean, he's almost fifty," Smith says.

"I know," Clio says, looking down. "But he's youthful. Sometimes, I forget that he's so much older . . . I'm not sure it matters."

"Do you think he actually *wants* kids? He somehow doesn't strike me as the playground type, you know."

"I have no idea. We've never discussed it. We've never discussed any of this." Clio swallows and feels herself bristling at Smith's comment.

"And might I remind you that *you* don't want to have kids?"

"I never said that," Clio says, fixing her gaze on the Picasso lithograph Smith's parents bought her when she turned thirty. "I mean, not exactly. I said that people like me perhaps *shouldn't* have kids. That I need to consider the risks. There's a difference."

Smith straightens a stack of books on the bedside table, puts her hands on her hips and lifts the shades, looks out onto Central Park West. Clio sighs.

"Listen, don't be upset. None of this matters anymore, Smith. I went full-on psycho in front of him. You should have seen the poor man's face. Pure horror. I hightailed it out of there like the room was on fire. So now I've gone and wrecked it all. It's over. He's a practical man with a reputation to uphold. I've unwittingly given him an out. I'm pretty sure he's going to take it."

The retelling brings back the nausea. Mere hours later and it all seems like a harrowing dream. When the cab pulled up downstairs, Clio was alert enough to catch the doorman's reaction to her frightful state. There she was, arriving at one of the most elite buildings in Manhattan in the dead of the night, pale as a ghost in nothing but a hotel bathrobe and glitter heels, a total loon.

Like the cabdriver, the doorman asked if she was okay because it was clear she was not, but she breezed past him.

"God, Clio, why didn't you wake me up when you came in?"

"I wanted to, but you have such a big week ahead with the wedding and everything—and you know I've been through this before. It's always a matter of waiting it out. Anyway. Enough about me. I was worried when you left the party so early."

"Oh, I'm basically fine," Smith says, turning back to Clio. "Anyway, as Life Coach Laura would say, I must *act as if* . . ."

"Fake it until you make it?" Clio says, quoting a Laura-ism.

Smith hits Clio with a pillow. "Seriously, I've missed you. How was the trip? We barely talked about it last night."

"It was good," Clio says. "Tiring. I'm happy I'm back at sea level. The altitude was killer. Angie hardly noticed, of course. Must be nice to be all of twenty-three."

"Well, I'm happy you're back," Smith says. "You know I can't deal when you're off the grid. The truth is, Sally is driving me *mad* and I have no one to bitch to but you."

"You know, I actually missed your bitching," Clio says. "I can't believe the wedding is this weekend. How's the toast coming?"

"It's not," Smith says, sighing. "Not even a trickle. I'm completely blocked, which is bizarre because you know me, I'm rarely at a loss for words. I'm sure it has to do with Asad somehow, some unconscious resentment that's tripping me up. Fucker. I'm still having dreams about him."

Clio reaches out and touches her friend's hand. "I'm so sorry, Smith." Smith pulls her hand away and straightens.

"Whatever. It is what it is. I'm not going to hide in the corner and cry that my little sister is getting hitched before I am just because I got dumped by the guy I was supposed to marry. Life Coach Laura says envy is poison and I refuse to have any part in it. It sucks, but all of this is old news, Clio, and now you have this grand gesture from Henry and you know what? I'm so thrilled for you. You two will figure out a way to move past last night and it will be great. After everything you've been through? Clio, you *deserve* this."

Clio listens to Smith's words, words laced with the very thing she's denying—envy. Her adamant, Life Coach Laura–fueled positivity isn't convincing this time. When Smith says, *You deserve this,* Clio can't help but wonder if what she really means is *I deserve this. This is meant to happen to me.* And both of them would have agreed that Smith was supposed to be the first to make the foray into a more settled life. This, the way their respective lives appear to be unfolding, is no doubt a shock to them both.

"I'm not sure I agree I deserve this, but next time I lose my mind, I will wake you up," Clio says, attempting to lighten things.

"No," Smith says. "No, no. There will not be a next time. We need to find a way to fix this *panic thing*."

Clio nods, but a familiar resentment builds quietly inside her. Her best friend is a fixer, a tweaker, a professional organizer of other people's lives, but how many times does she have to explain to Smith that not everything is a matter of fixing and tweaking? There will most certainly be a next time, and a next time, and a time after that. This is who she is. This is who she's wired to be. It's not a matter of having a perfectly arranged closet or talking to a life coach or seeing a therapist or meditating, of ingesting copious amounts of Rumi and kale and green tea. She's spent years doing her own research and still she's left without an answer to the one question that's plagued her since she was a girl, since she knew enough to ask. *Am I okay?*

"I just can't stop thinking about the fact that . . . well, about the fact that I lied to him, for one thing," Clio says. She doesn't meet Smith's eyes.

"What do you mean, you lied?" Smith asks, tilting her head with interest. Clio has been dreading this and now it's out in the open. She has always been so big on honesty, on how vital it is. After all those years of her parents lying to her about her mother's illness, her violent mood swings and sudden disappearances, after all those years of going to bed hungry because her mother had promised to make Clio's favorite meal but had instead left Clio to discover a bare kitchen and her mother locked in her bedroom, it's been a soft spot.

"He still thinks Eloise died of cancer when I was a little girl," Clio says quietly.

"What? You still haven't told him?"

Clio shakes her head.

"So he doesn't know anything about her? I mean, why does he think you're going home on Wednesday?"

"I told him my dad sold the house and I'm helping him move."

Smith gives her an exasperated look.

"Smith, stop! I feel guilty enough as it is. I didn't think I'd ever see him again."

And she didn't. She goes back over it in her head as she has a hundred times before, the day they met in Central Park last May.

It was after the tour, after her group had scattered, and there he was, a damp and dashing man on the bench. A look. Blue, tear-glossed eyes. A conversation between strangers. A New York City moment that would, against all odds, grow to be something more.

I'm fine all year long, but this day is hard. It's the anniversary of Mum's death. She died ten years ago and I reckon it should get easier, but here I am, a mess.

Silence. A siren in the distance. A stroller rolling by.

I understand, she said. *I lost my mother too.*

I'm so sorry, he said. *When did she die?*

We lost her a long time ago.

What was she like, your mum?

She was . . . Clio paused. How to explain Eloise to a stranger? *She was eccentric.*

How so?

Well, let's see. She read me every work by Darwin before I was six.

Ah! She sounds charming.

She was. I mean, she could be. She's the reason I love birds.

Clio thought of her beautiful, wasp-waisted mother barefoot in the backyard, twirling about in one of her long flowing hippie dresses, her wild, tangled hair tied up in a precarious bun, loose strands falling artfully over her gaunt face, obscuring her soft hazel eyes. Eloise worked hard to attract birds to their small yard; she put out sugar-water feeders and mixed her own birdseed and collected guides to help them identify the species that would visit. She gave Clio her first pair of binoculars, fruit of a nearby yard sale. She even came on one of Clio's bird tours that last April before she was too sick to leave the house. Clio had braced herself, as she always did, for a scene, but her mother had surprised her by listening intently as Clio described the patterns of spring migration and pointed out the Northern Parulas, Ovenbirds, Common Yellowthroats. Afterward, they went for lunch at Alice's Tea Cup, where they nibbled on tea sandwiches and cookies amid groups of little girls wearing fairy wings and talked about Clio's latest discoveries in the lab. It was Clio's last happy memory of her mother.

She sounds colorful, Henry said that day.

And what about you? What was your mother like?

Ah, well. My mum worked at the Grand Opera House in Belfast. I sup-

pose I have her to thank for my love of Verdi. She loved Shakespeare, too. Especially the comedies. Midsummer Night's Dream. Twelfth Night. *I miss her. God, I miss her terribly. Was your mum sick for a while too?*

Clio thought about this.

Yes, she said. *She was.* And this was nothing but true.

That's when he said it. *Bloody cancer.*

And Clio nodded. That's all she did; she nodded. She never explicitly said that Eloise had had cancer, she offered no elaborate lie, but simply went along with things, and he connected the dots he wanted to connect and she didn't correct him.

"Oh, Clio," Smith says, taking Clio's hand. "If anything, it was an innocent omission. He heard what he wanted to hear. You two only met six months ago. Plenty of people wouldn't even get this deep in six months, especially in this town."

Maybe Smith is right. Maybe she's being far too dramatic about this. It's true, it wasn't as if she lied outright, but what troubles her is that she's been consciously withholding something significant, editing herself around him to play it safe. It's just that it's been so nice to get swept up in this other world, the dates and the romance, and plus, she was so sure it was just a fling anyway. She saw no reason to burden this unsuspecting man with her dark childhood tales. But now something has shifted, and she can't shake the feeling that they really don't know each other. They've skipped over some important steps.

"I have to tell him. I need to tell him everything, lay all my cards on the table." She says this almost as if to reassure herself, but the very thought of this panics her.

"You should. Henry's a grown-up. He's not some immature asshole who can't handle real life. He'll understand, Clio. It might even bring you closer. Think about that." It's as if Smith can read her mind. She looks up at her friend, who appears pensive, like she is thinking very hard.

"Let me ask you something simple, okay?" Smith says. "What do you want?"

"That's something simple?"

What does she want? The problem seems to be that she has no idea what she wants. The problem seems to be that she's never quite believed that she's allowed to want anything at all. She didn't grow up in Smith's charmed world where desires were voiced, dreams trumpeted. What she wants? She wants to stop worrying so much, to stop having these crippling attacks of anxiety, to live her life. She wants to see her mother one last time. She wants to sleep soundly at night and wake up each morning and do her research and give her lectures and lead her tours.

Does she want to commit to a man who is so much older, who lives in a *hotel*, of all places? Isn't that alone strange enough? Who lives life in a hotel? Eloise, a character from a children's book who also happens to share her mother's name, that's who. A fictional creation. And everyone knows that women outlive men by an average of five years. What if he gets sick? She's survived one loved one's illness; she doesn't know if she can handle it again. Wouldn't it somehow be easier to cut her losses now and be alone? All these years of throwing herself into her hard work at the museum and at Columbia and coming back here night after night to fall asleep reading her research have brought her immense satisfaction, yes, but they've also been years of avoidance. As long as she's stayed busy, she hasn't been able to consider this question.

The truth: she doesn't know what she wants.

"You love him, Clio," Smith says. "In all the time I've known you, I've never seen you like this. You're a different person with him. You're glowing. You smile more. You love him. You are in *love* with him."

I am, Clio wants to say, but she stops the words before they can fall from her. She's never felt this way about a man. Yes, there was Jack, the boy next door in New Haven, but that was friendship, not love. There was that one night in her bedroom, but he was practically a brother to her. And then there was the handful of men she dated after college—well, slept with a few times and then cast off for one lame reason or another. But even in the relatively brief time she's been with

Henry, she can tell how different this is. She wakes up each morning thinking of Henry, goes to sleep wondering about him, conjuring up a list of questions she hopes she will get a chance to ask. Her fascination with him is not wholly unlike her passion for hummingbirds, how they hover and eat and sleep. She wants to know everything about him: Does he remember his nightly dreams? Has he always preferred vanilla to chocolate? What places must he visit in his lifetime? But with love comes fear. She knows just how invested she is because when she pictures a life without him she feels miserable, terrified.

"Just tell him," Smith says, determination spiking her words. "No one on earth has a perfect family, Clio. You and I both know that firsthand."

Funny for her to say, Clio can't help but think. Smith likes to fuss about her family, how overbearing they can be, how materialistic and entitled they are, but Clio has a hard time feeling too sorry for her friend. Yes, her father, Thatcher, can be imperious and controlling and has always made Clio feel uneasy, but Bitsy, despite her sometimes meddling ways, is a devoted and mindful mother. She brings chicken soup when her daughter has even a whiff of a cold and happily stocks the fridge with Smith's favorites from Zabar's—smoked salmon and herring and peppery rotisserie chicken; mini black-and-white cookies and rounds of brie—when she's busy with clients. All four of them—the parents and both sisters—live here in this building and gather at least once a week for dinner. Smith talks to her mom and sister several times a day. Clio is willing to concede that every family has its issues, but the situation with the Andersons has always been pretty enviable to her. All she wanted growing up was one ounce of the consistent attention and affection Smith continues to receive on a daily basis.

"I know you don't believe this, but you're a catch, Clio," Smith says as they walk together toward the kitchen. "You're smart and fascinating and, well, I mean *look* at you. Let's just say you've come a long way from your *college look*."

"My college look?" Clio says, laughing.

Smith disappears for a moment and returns clutching a photograph of the two of them in their caps and gowns on graduation day. "Evidence," she says, placing the frame in Clio's hands.

Clio looks at the image of her younger self, pale, thin, her round eyes hidden behind big plastic-framed glasses. Smith's right; she has evolved.

"I saw the way Henry looked at you last night. The man is smitten. He could have anyone, Clio, and he's chosen you for a reason. Because you're special. Give the guy some credit that he will accept *all of you.*"

As Smith retreats to the kitchen to get the coffee started, Clio ducks into the laundry room and eyes a pile of dirty clothes. Instinctively, she begins separating it into lights and darks, like she used to. In their first years here, when Clio couldn't contribute much financially, she'd do their laundry to feel better about the situation.

"Stop, Clio. You don't need to do that," Smith says insistently, as she always does, but Clio continues. "You should at least let Henry know you're okay. He's probably worried sick."

"I texted him when I got here to tell him that I'm alive." Clio pauses and smiles. "Do you remember that night after our first date when we Googled him?"

Smith nods. "Of course. We stayed up forever."

I met someone, Clio said that night when she returned to the apartment. She'd tried to sound nonchalant. For a moment, Clio thought she saw Smith flinch, as if she'd been punched in the stomach. But then Smith reached for her laptop so they could Google him. At first Clio felt a flare of resistance to this idea; part of her wanted to stop her friend, to put off the information-gathering and just let this play out. But she said nothing and sat by Smith's side as she clicked her way through Henry's past.

All they had to do was type in *Henry Kildare Ireland hotel* and they learned quite a lot. Of his birth in 1963 in Stranmillis, a suburb of Belfast; his graduation with honors from Oxford, where he studied business. The names of his hotels in Northern Ireland and here in the

States. The awards he'd collected for his professional and philanthropic greatness. A profile of him in *Vanity Fair* revealed that he moved to the United States in 1994. Two sentences in this article popped: *I'm not looking to get married. I'm married to my work.*

Sound bites. A cliché. At the time, all of it an immense relief. Reading this about him, Clio felt hopeful and encouraged. On the topic of marriage, she was not indifferent. The fear in her was real, jagged. Possibly a bona fide phobia, she learned. It had a clinical name even: *gamophobia*. While friends like Smith giddily anticipated this step in their lives, the idea of it petrified Clio. She was willing to feel love, to commit to a point, but the concept of forever, of a legal binding to another person, haunted her. Henry, with his five decades of bachelorhood and demanding professional life, seemed a safe bet, a man who wouldn't push her toward something she wasn't ready for.

And then there were pictures. Images of Henry, always appearing slightly disheveled in his quirky, tweedy finery, old-fashioned suits and hats, those old Dubarry boat shoes, always the same subtly crooked smile, a litany of swan-necked socialites draped on his side. Also: a younger Henry with his banker father, Declan Kildare, and with his late mother too, Dublin-born Aoife Kildare, an administrator for the Grand Opera House. Clio could see that Henry had her almond-shaped eyes. At the flurry of images, Smith grew excited. *Look at you, finding a blue-eyed George Clooney.*

The details had a funny, almost dizzying effect on Clio. The more she learned, the less real he seemed. The image in her mind of this bedraggled, intelligent man on the park bench began to recede as she took in image after image of the same yet different man. The hours spent searching made her feel like what happened in the park was fiction, a footnote that would be lost.

But then she read *Here Is New York*, the little book that he'd clutched in his hands and raved about. When she finished the book, a piece of paper floated to the carpet of Smith's guest room and she scrambled to retrieve it. *You might just be my thing.*

Clio checks the time, sees that it's coming up on nine. "Oh no. I'm going to be late for my tour."

Clio scrambles to get dressed. In the bathroom, she splashes water on her face and wipes away some of last night's makeup, which still lingers. She pulls her hair back in a ponytail. Back in Smith's guest room, the room she's come to think of as hers, she looks around at all of her books and boxes of papers, her small collection of binoculars.

Will she leave this room and go live in a hotel with Henry? Staying here was always meant to be temporary anyway. The plan had been to find her own place, but this was never in the cards; all those years working on her PhD at Columbia, doing research at the museum, and this was the only way she could afford to live in Manhattan.

Clio felt guilty that she wasn't contributing enough, but Smith insisted she not worry, that she wasn't paying either—her parents were—and besides, she wanted Clio around. It would be a continuation of college. But Clio did worry and worry some more, then and particularly now that she's still here after all these years. She's wired to worry, to fret, to feel shame. It comforts her that after several years of not being able to contribute anything at all, she's now paying half the monthly maintenance, but she wishes she could do more. Quite simply, she can't; she has her college loans to repay. She knows Smith understands, but it all continues to make Clio feel uneasy even though Smith's been nothing but generous. Even when she was with Asad, when he was here all the time and Clio was concerned that she should get out of their way, Smith made genuine efforts to involve Clio, to have her around.

Smith reappears. Hands Clio her favorite stainless steel travel mug, a gift from Jack from years ago, filled with hot coffee. "Extra sweet. Just how you like it."

"Thanks, you."

"Clio?"

"Yes?"

"Look, I know it's scary, but if you open up and let him in, it will bring you closer. And if it doesn't, Clio, I hate to say this, but maybe that means he's not the right person. You deserve to be with someone who loves all of you, even your messy parts."

"I know," Clio says. "Either way, I'll survive."

And she will. She's survived much more than this.

"I'll see you after your tour," Smith says.

Clio smiles weakly at her friend, grabs her binoculars, and slips out the front door.

9:04AM

"It's too late."

It's a bitterly cold morning. It will no doubt be a quiet day of birding, but Clio doesn't mind. Quiet is fine. Quiet is better on a day like today when she hasn't slept much and her mind is far away. She shivers and pulls the collar of her jacket up over her mouth. All these Manhattan winters and she still hasn't invested in a proper parka, one of the puffy sleeping-bag coats everyone seems to live in as soon as the temperature drops. She wears the ski jacket she's had since high school, a cheerful cherry red, and layers it over a thick wool sweater. The coffee Smith made does the trick, waking her up just enough to function. She approaches the dock at Turtle Pond, where the week's group waits for her. She waves.

She slips her phone from her pocket to check it one more time as she heads over to join them. Still nothing at all from Henry. Just a lonely *Okay* in response to her texts in the middle of the night telling him she had a panic attack but that he shouldn't worry because she was fine and safe and needed a bit of space. *Okay.* That's it. Her exhaustion is thick like fog and it's hard to tell what she feels most right now. Fear that she's irrevocably botched the one romantic relationship she's had in her life. Disappointment that he didn't race after her, down those steps, out onto the blustery sidewalk. Anger that she can't react normally to a romantic gesture.

Clio wears her dark glasses, a pair she's had forever, the lenses scratched and earpieces subtly bent. She feels safer behind them today, like she's hiding from the world.

At the dock, she scatters hellos and answers questions about her trip to the Andes. There are a few new people today who read about her in *New York* magazine, but at this point in the season, most of her birders are her regulars, the only souls who would venture out in this breed of cold.

There's Bob, probably seventy, a retired environmental engineer, and Jewel, fifty-five or so, who teaches high school English, and Sophie, a slight woman in her eighties who had a big career in fashion, and Jackson, a fourteen-year-old boy. His mother came for the first walk and pulled Clio aside and told her that her son was on the autism spectrum and that he knew an impossible amount about birds. This has proven to be true. Jackson is often the first to identify the birds they encounter. Oh, and Lillian, in her sixties, who is a widow and a breast cancer survivor, and Victoria, a sophomore at Columbia and one of Clio's former students.

She scans the cast of characters, and though distracted, she smiles. Never does she lose perspective about how wonderful this is, coming here and doing this, spending time with this cluster of eccentric binocular-wielding New Yorkers who arrive here each Sunday. The details of these folks are not lost on her—the tattered too-short khakis and orthotic walking shoes, the little dog-eared copies of Sibley's bird guide clutched in gloved hands, the misshapen baseball caps emblazoned with company names, the plain faces—no makeup, no masks.

Everyone is on the same page: eager to see birds and have a peaceful morning outdoors. Even today, she appreciates this. Or tries to. As she waits for a few late stragglers to join the group, her mind wanders. She imagines what Henry might be doing now. It is the hotel's first day and he's no doubt down in the lobby greeting guests. But surely he's hungover after last night, and this brings her some solace, it does, the idea that he's suffering too.

Jackson asks if she's heard the rumblings about the five Long-eared Owls spotted nearby, and she has and answers robotically in the affirmative, wondering if Henry is thinking about her. It's entirely possible that last night is troubling him as much as it is plaguing her. But it is just as possible that he has already moved on, written her off as unstable. The male brain is highly specialized, wired to compartmentalize these things, a neurological trait she once admired but now resents. Clio shakes her head to make these jumbled thoughts disappear.

"Okay, gang, let's get going," she says. "I'm so happy to be back. It's certainly chilly, but that shouldn't stop us."

Clio leads the group toward the Ramble, her very favorite thirty-six acres in the world. It's a magical oasis, with its rocky outcrops, wooded hills, serpentine paths, peaceful coves around the lake, a pond, and a stream called the Gill. Over two hundred species of birds have been identified here, particularly during spring and fall migrations. Standing in the middle of the Ramble, she can even forget she is in Manhattan.

She didn't even know the Ramble existed until she came to New York, and it wasn't until she discovered it and started visiting regularly that the city truly felt like a place that could one day be her permanent home. Like so many New Yorkers she's met, Henry didn't even know about the Ramble either until she gave him a tour through it last May during the peak of spring migration. It was the best kind of day, having rained in the morning, the wind blowing from the south, and Clio pointed out bird after bird—a Cerulean Warbler and then a Golden-winged Warbler too, both relative rarities, and then the Gray-cheeked Thrush and an American Redstart. It was clear on his face that Henry was quickly becoming enamored with this spot in the park. Predictably, he found a way to tie it all back to E. B. White, digging up a piece the author had written about the city's attempts to "unscramble the Ramble." He did his own research on the sly, coming up with odd trivia about the Ramble and its designer, American landscape architect Frederick Law Olmsted. *Did you know that he was supposed to go to Yale, but then he abandoned his college plans when sumac poisoning hurt his eyes?* No, she did not.

She quickly checks her phone again. Again, nothing. When she looks up, she sees someone striding toward them, a tall, broad-shouldered man wearing a familiar knit newsboy cap. Her heart lifts—Henry. But as he approaches, Clio sees it is Patrick. Henry's brother.

In the daylight, he looks different. Tired. His eyes, warm last night, hold worry. Clio knows that he's not here to see birds.

"So! This is the famous Ramble." He flashes an unconvincing smile. "Sorry I'm late for the tour. May I join?" he asks, hands in his pockets.

"Of course, of course," Clio says, panic building inside her. "So, yes, this is my little corner of paradise."

"I'm sure it's lovely in the summer," Patrick says, looking around at the stark trees against the sunless sky.

"Hey, Northern Ireland isn't exactly a tropical paradise."

"But I live in *California* now," Patrick says. "So, where are the hummers? Henry says they're your favorite. Will we see any today?"

"No, sadly," Clio answers, nervously kicking the ground. "It's too late in the year. They've all migrated south for warmer climes."

"Ah, so they're smart birds, too." Patrick assumes his spot at the back of the group.

"A Varied Thrush!" Jackson says, pointing at the bare branches of a nearby tree. He tilts his head skyward, lifts his binoculars. Others follow suit, including Clio. She sees nothing. She's missed it.

"Could be," she says. "Good eye, Jackson."

She continues to walk, looking hard at the bushes and trees, willing herself to spot something, eager to make it up to her group, who have but the dregs of her attention. She reminds herself to breathe, to keep going, but Patrick's presence is more than unnerving. How much does he know about last night? Is he here to conduct due diligence on his brother's crazy girlfriend?

They walk east along the double-arched bridge and she sees it, a Hermit Thrush balancing on a thin, delicate branch.

"Look!" she says in a forceful whisper, but loses the bird. She trains her binoculars on the branch, waits for the slightest movement to find the bird. She does find it, and a faint and familiar sense of victory pulses through her. "Up there! See how her feathers are puffed up for insulation?"

Clio feels something lift inside, but then her phone buzzes, pulling her from the moment. She sneaks a peek and it is a text from Henry. Relief and apprehension rush through her.

Henry: We should talk tonight.

Clio: Okay.

She writes that one weak little word and waits for a follow-up text, something more affectionate and reassuring, but it doesn't come. She turns off her phone and puts it away. She looks over at Patrick, studies him for clues, but his poker face is enviable. He catches her staring and she turns away.

The rest of the walk tumbles by in a blur. This is typically the highlight of her week, the hours during which she's most present, most attuned to the world, but she's a shell of herself today.

In the end, they have some good sightings—the regular wintering White-throated Sparrows and Dark-eyed Juncos, but also the less common at this time of year Gray Catbird and year-round Carolina Wren. It's also a fine day for ducks; they spot Mallards and American Black Ducks and Northern Shovelers, Buffleheads and Ruddy Ducks. A solid morning, particularly given the cold, and Clio tries to convince herself it wasn't a total bust, but she can't shake the shame she feels, the knowledge that she has fallen short, that she has let these good people, virtual strangers she's grown inordinately fond of, down. She leads them south along a park drive and back up to the Humboldt statue across from the museum. The pine dinosaurs flank the entrance, evidence that the holidays aren't far off. Steel bleachers are being erected along the avenue for the Macy's Thanksgiving Day Parade. When the floats go by, Clio will be home in New Haven packing. The movers come in just a week. She can no longer avoid thinking of all that this means.

"Thanks, everyone. Have a great Thanksgiving and I will see you the weekend after next," she says to her walkers, her eyes suddenly wet with tears.

The air is crisp, vaguely damp, and smells faintly of roasted chestnuts. Clio shakes a few hands. Lillian lingers and embraces her in a hug. Maybe she can tell something's wrong. "I would love to hear more about the Andes sometime. It's my dream to get there."

"Oh yes, I'd like that very much," Clio says, and means it.

Everyone scatters, but Patrick remains.

11:21AM

"I know all about this bench."

How about a coffee?" Patrick asks.

"I'd love to but my friend Smith always meets me over by the Gill after my tours—it's a kind of ritual we have. But maybe we could sit down for a bit?" Clio asks, her voice shaking.

They walk back into the park, through the Ramble, and sit on what she has come to think of as her bench. Patrick is quiet while she takes a moment, before she forgets, to quickly jot the day's findings in her journal. When she finishes, she tucks her notes away and looks over to him.

"That was something," he says matter-of-factly, "though I certainly felt out of step with the others. Those folks seem to know what they're doing. That kid is amazing. He might know more about birds than you do."

Clio laughs. "Jackson is by far my best student."

"He made me miss my boys."

"I'm sure you're excited to get home. But I know Henry is so glad you came," Clio says. "And I love that you asked about hummingbirds. Have you ever seen one?"

"I can't say that I have," Patrick says.

"They are the most amazing creatures," Clio says. "Like flying jewels. So tiny and colorful and fierce."

"Well, I'll be sure to add 'see a hummingbird' to my bucket list, then. How many years have you been doing this?"

She thinks about this. "Let's see. A little more than twelve. I started right after 9/11. That was a tough time, but doing this each week helped."

It was more than a tough time. Clio had just graduated from Yale and was new to the city, still harboring a tremendous amount of guilt about not returning home after graduation to be with her parents, who needed her. Her mother had stopped taking her medication and would call Clio at Smith's apartment at odd hours, telling her to come home. She'd send disturbing e-mails about government conspiracies and hummingbird deaths and Clio would torture herself, reading her mother's words again and again, committing her nonsensical musings to memory, etching them forever in her mind.

They're watching us, again, Clio, I see the red lights blinking in the windows! Did you know a hummingbird's heart beats over 500 times per minute and then shuts down almost completely at night, Clio? Many hummingbirds die in their sleep, Clio. Did you know that did you know that? IN THEIR SLEEP?

And then the attack on top of it all. She felt like the world might actually end on that impossibly gorgeous morning. When it happened, she was up at Columbia, waiting for her phylogenetics lecture to begin. She remembers her professor arriving a few minutes late, gripping the lectern as if he might fall, his face ashen, his voice shaking, as he made the cryptic announcement into the microphone. *Because of this morning's unfolding events, class is canceled today.* He offered no details, but they swirled about her, bits coming from fellow students who were late to class, students who'd seen television coverage or heard something on the radio.

She stumbled back to the San Remo in a traumatized daze, inhaling the terrifying smell of destruction that would linger over the city for weeks. When she got to Smith's apartment she tried to call her parents to tell them she was all right, dialing the numbers over and over again for hours until she finally got through. Her mother went back to the hospital the next day and stayed there for weeks. Clio herself didn't sleep through the night for months, and that's how she found herself clutching her first prescription. Prozac. "A tiny dose," her doctor said, "like nothing at all," almost nonchalantly. Clio filled the prescription. Held the little bottle in her hands. When she took the first pill, swallowing it down with water from Smith's tap, she cried. This wasn't nothing for her.

After a few weeks, the medicine kicked in and she felt a new softness, a haze folding over her. The world seemed lighter and kinder, muted almost. She slept soundly. She stopped dreaming of falling buildings and plunging bodies, of dark plumes of smoke, of strangers' faces, of swollen eyes, of her mother sedated on a hospital bed in New Haven. When she did wake up in the night, she wasn't throttled with fear.

But she didn't feel like herself. Before this, she didn't even know what this meant—*feeling like herself*—but when it was gone, it felt like a loss. She missed the intensity, the rawness of the world, the ups and the downs. She even missed the panic attacks that had plagued her since the beginning of college. After many months, she called her doctor and said she wanted to wean off, and she did. Her doctor prescribed Xanax and told her to take it when she felt particularly anxious. This seemed to work, but sometimes it was difficult to catch the anxiety before it blew up. But one thing helped most. Wandering here, to the park, specifically to the Ramble, the tangled wilderness at its center. When it was too cold and she was feeling panicky, she'd take refuge in the dark, damp halls of the ornithology collection at the Museum of Natural History instead. In these places, she felt she could breathe.

"I think back to the beginning," Clio says, smiling, "and I was so intent on knowing every little thing about the Ramble and I prepared all of these notes, a cheat sheet almost, and I came up with all these ideas about the virtues of getting lost, about the wilderness of the world, and it was so unnecessary because I realized that these people could do their own Internet searches and collect all the information in the world, but they would come on my walks to find some quiet. They come to see birds and to escape, to breathe, not to be lectured. You know, I met Henry right here on this bench after one of my walks."

Patrick nods. "Yes, I know all about this bench."

"You do?" Clio says, incredulous, thinking again about that day last May.

It had rained that morning. It was a quick, furious pour and in its aftermath, the park was a glistening green. Clio and her walkers had ducked into Belvedere Castle for the thick of it and then resumed, soon serenaded by the Warbling Vireo's sweet songs. A Baltimore Oriole flitted back and forth from a nest in an oak tree.

After the tour, there he was, Henry, then just a curious stranger, a man with black hair sitting on the bench she'd come to think of as hers. From the short distance, a few yards at most, he struck her as pristine and professorial; he wore a tweed jacket more fitting for fall, a pair of gray slacks. He was hunched over, his head cradled in his hands, his elbows resting on his knees. She wondered if he was crying or sleeping or drunk.

Her first instinct was to find a new spot, but the moment she began to turn away, the man lifted his head and looked at her. Oh, that first look. It was not the look of a stranger. There was nothing perfunctory about this inaugural glance. There was so much packed in there—warmth, sadness, curiosity, desire. His eyes were the ticket. A blazing blue in the post-rain noon sunlight, they shone from behind heavy, sleepy lids. His cheeks, she saw now, were wet. There was no question he had been crying, but about what? He drew a handkerchief from his jacket pocket and wiped his eyes and sniffled and smiled. And, again, this smile was rare, not run-of-the-mill, not a conciliatory, casual thing, but edged in mystery and meaning. He nodded toward the bench and uttered one word. A question.

Sit?

And the crazy thing is she did. She sat down next to him. Looking back, it makes little sense. She'd spent her life in self-protection mode, cultivating a safe distance from others, but there was something about this man. He was strikingly handsome, and Clio wondered vaguely if she was supposed to know who he was, if he was a movie star. Whatever it was, she responded to his simple, odd question and walked over, clutching her binoculars and bag and small notebook, and she sat next to him on the bench. The world went on around them.

He was very different up close, from this proximal vantage, leagues less polished. There was a keen scruffiness to him, an aura of unraveling; this relieved Clio, and her relief surprised her because this meant somehow that she already cared. His dress shirt was woefully wrinkled, stained with drips of coffee. His slacks were too short and tattered at the hem. His socks were a bright green with small white shamrocks. His shoes looked as if they might fall apart. One was untied.

I got caught in the rain, he said, his voice deep and smoky, hints of an accent cutting through.

They talked. In staccato bursts at first, but then with an ease that seemed to startle them both. They talked about the park and the birds and the rain, about the fact that they'd both lost mothers, that he was opening a hotel. Hours went by. Clio felt thankful that Smith was occupied at a baby shower downtown. Otherwise, Clio would have run off long before to meet her friend.

"Henry called me that afternoon, you know," Patrick says. "Told me about you. Before your head swells, I should mention that we talk on that particular day every year, the day Mum died. I usually call him, to check in. He took it the hardest of all of us, was always quite the mother's boy, but this year he phoned me instead."

"What did he say?" Clio says, curious, biting her bottom lip.

"Oh, I don't know, that he was off brooding in the park and he met the most becoming and unusual girl, that he blabbered on about our mum, that it just so happened that this girl had lost her own mother. He said he saw this as a sign. And I gave him a hard time for this foolish sign nonsense. I told him to ask you out. He said he already did."

"Yes, he was pretty quick to do that," Clio says.

"You don't understand how this shocked me, Clio. My brother is all about work. There have always been women, flings, yes, but he's never much cared about anyone. I pester him about settling down sometimes because he's so wonderful with my sons, but he's been adamant that marriage and a family aren't part of his plan. He's always had this thing about sticking it to our old man, showing him that he could come here to the States and make a name for himself, and I think he's become addicted to the grind, to the success, but then he calls me up that day and goes on and on about you and frankly it didn't even matter what he said, because I could detect this change in my brother and I had this good feeling."

He pauses, looks over at Clio, but says nothing. She feels her body continue to tense, the tears rising. She blinks, willing them to stay put.

"What a sorry sight he was this morning at breakfast. All puffy eyed and wrecked. He had me to the room because he wasn't quite in the shape to show his face. You'd think with Henry's size he'd be able to drink us all under the table, but not so. He's always been the lightweight in the Kildare clan. So he was struggling mightily this morning and looked like shit. He's very worried about you, Clio."

Clio nods and stares out at the Gill, the calm surface of the water shiny with sun. The two towers of the San Remo stand proud in the distance. The tears she's tried so hard to hold back rise now, pooling in her eyes. A single droplet snakes down her cheek. She doesn't wipe it away.

"He's right to be worried, Patrick," she says. "I'm a mess. He shouldn't waste his time on me. There are so many other women who—"

Patrick gently grabs her arm and she stops speaking.

"He only cares about one," Patrick says firmly, fixing her with his eyes. "Trust me, Clio, this is all very new. He's scarlet for you, but he's shaken. As it seems you are. I'm not even sure what I'm doing here."

Clio swallows and nods, looks down at the leaf-strewn path.

"I'm not so sure I deserve him."

Patrick considers this and as he does a sinister silence takes hold. But then he shakes his head. "Nobody's perfect, Clio. Not even our Henry," he says, his face easing into an earnest grin. "My mum had horror stories of what Henry was like as a little boy. She said he was an utter rascal. Apparently, he used to unscrew all the jars in the fridge, and he'd bury Mum's favorite silver necklace in the garden, and he once put ice cubes in my bed in the middle of the night while I was in the bathroom. The truth is, as the baby I idolized him, but he was certainly strange. Always reading books about faraway places. Always involving me in these elaborate and imaginative games. He's brilliant with my sons, I must say. They talk about Uncle Henry all the time."

Clio imagines Henry goofing around with Patrick's little boys and the picture delights her even though it's somewhat difficult to conjure. She's never had the chance to see him around kids. Her mind wanders. What if . . . She stops herself from going too far with this.

Speaking of, Clio looks up and sees Smith approaching now on the path. The sight of her friend brings with it a wave of comfort, of relief. She wears her mother Bitsy's big sable fur and a pair of heeled boots. Something's up.

"Oh, I'm so sorry, I lost track of time," Clio says. "That's my friend Smith coming to meet me."

Smith walks up and throws her arm around Clio and kisses her hello. "God, it's freezing out here."

"Smith, this is Patrick, Henry's brother. He flew in from California to see the hotel."

Smith extends a leather-gloved hand and Patrick shakes it. "Well I can certainly see the resemblance," Smith says, smiling flirtatiously. Smith has always known how to turn it on for attractive men. "The Kildare eyes."

"A pleasure to meet you, Smith. I just had the fine privilege of following along with Clio on her bird walk. Learned a thing or two. In my estimation, a morning well spent, but I should get going and leave you two to do your catching up. Clio, if I don't see you again, I do hope you stay well."

If I don't see you again. Stay well.

A lump forms in Clio's throat as she watches him go. Will she see him again? Was that it?

"He just showed up on my walk," Clio explains. "Came to make sure his brother's highly questionable girlfriend is not a total mental case, and I'm not sure I've convinced him of that. How was your morning?"

"Good. Fine. Did a little client prep and ran a few miles on the treadmill and tidied up. I know that things are going to go haywire in a few days with Thanksgiving and all the wedding hoopla, so I need to be on my game." There is a tension in Smith's face as she speaks, an unmistakable stiffness to her jaw. She stares out over the water.

"The wedding will be fine, Smith," Clio says. "I'll make sure you survive it."

Clio too must survive it. Yet another party to make her anxious. And by all indications, the wedding will be in keeping with all things Anderson: tastefully extravagant. Sally and Smith's parents, Bitsy and Thatcher, have been unfailingly kind to Clio, in their own Waspish way, and Clio will always have a special softness for Bitsy, who drove Smith to New Haven the night that Clio's mother died, but Clio's never felt totally comfortable in the family's presence. She knows that in their eyes she'll always be Smith's quirky college roommate, Smith's pity project. Smith checks her watch, seems anxious.

"Hot date?" Clio says.

"Soooo . . . ," Smith says coyly. "I invited Tate to join us."

"Tate?"

"Tate Pennington? From the game yesterday? Jesus, Clio, do you remember anything from last night?"

"Oh! Tate! Of course," Clio says. This was one of the first things Smith mentioned when she arrived at the hotel's opening party. That she'd run into her old friend Tate at the Yale-Harvard tailgate that morning; that they laughed about being the only "pathetic singletons" there.

"I hope you're not upset that I invited him. Thought we three could go abuse Thatcher's tab at the Boathouse?"

"Yeah. Sure," Clio says, but the truth is that she is slightly annoyed. She was craving time alone with her friend, eager for Smith's take on Patrick's appearance, for some timely optimistic gloss. They've met like this almost every week for years now, and it's become a ritual of sorts, a bookend to each week, their Sunday date. Typically, they sit here for a while and then walk through the Ramble and find their spot in the grass by the Gill.

"I guess Tate built some kind of photography app with another guy from our class and they sold it about a year ago," Smith says breathlessly. "He just got separated . . . from a girl in our class. Olivia Farnsworth, long dark hair, Silliman, field hockey team? Remember her?"

Clio shakes her head no as Smith pops up and waves. "There he is!" she says.

He's still tall and thin and fair, endearingly disheveled. Though she never got to know him well, her memories of him are sharp and enduring, in contrast to the rest of the red brick and ivy blur. Smith likes to point out that Clio never made much of an effort to get to know most of their classmates. Throughout college Clio cultivated an air of aloofness. She wore the same plain uniform every day—faded jeans and a sweater—and threw her hair back in a ponytail. She worked hard to seem like she didn't care, but underneath it all was a simple, gnawing sense of inferiority, that everyone else fit in and she didn't. During the week, she kept to herself, diligently attending class and studying hard, working various jobs to help with tuition, spending time with Smith and making phone calls to Jack. On weekends, while Smith flitted around from party to party, ever the well-bred social butterfly, Clio hid in the hushed stacks at Sterling Memorial Library or went home to run errands for her overwhelmed parents, stocking the fridge with her mother's favorite yogurt, her father's Heineken and Canadian bacon, running to the pharmacy to refill a prescription. *They'll figure it out without you*, Smith said insistently. But Clio wasn't so sure.

She has come to realize over the years how foolish this façade was, that everyone else was no doubt just as lost and insecure and confused as she was. But Tate made an impact and she remembers him fondly. He was a bit of an oddball like she was, effeminate or maybe just artsy, an outsider who had never been to Nantucket or Paris, who didn't smoke pot at prep school or know how to handle a lacrosse stick. He carried a Polaroid camera everywhere, even to his shifts at the campus laundry, where he and Clio worked together freshman year, at first quietly side by side, but soon dipping into cathartic conversations about their new privileged peers, kids who didn't have to work to subsidize their tuition like they did, kids who went out for expensive sushi dinners instead of eating in the dining hall, kids like Smith, who were essentially members of a different species.

"Clio Marsh," Tate says, throwing his arm around her a bit awkwardly. "Wow. It's been a while. You look great. Different."

Clio smiles. The flattery does little to distract her from the fact that she's very likely losing the one man she's cared about, but she does what she's learned to do. She pretends, pushes through, reaches out to hug this classmate she hasn't seen in more than ten years. "You too, Tate. How have you been?" she asks.

At this question, he laughs. "Oh, you know, a combination of amazing and miserable. I'm ready for a Bloody Mary. After last night, my head's in revolt. The hair of the dog might do the trick," he says without missing a beat.

"On to the Boathouse then?" Smith says, looking at Clio.

Clio shrugs. She feels faint, as if the wind is passing through her. She's here, but she's not. She finds a word, a single word, all she can muster: "Sure."

"Ah, the famous Loeb Boathouse. Designed by revered park architect Calvert Vaux in 1872," he says, suddenly slipping into tour guide mode. "Built to provide a covered spot for docking and storing boats. Victorian details. Demolished in 1950 after falling into terrible disrepair and the new Boathouse opened its doors in 1954. Unofficial headquarters for birders who jot their sightings in a notebook inside the building."

Smith looks over at Clio and smiles. "Clio here is one of the city's most celebrated birdwatchers. I imagine you know all about this famous notebook, Clio?"

Clio nods yes but wishes Smith would pick up on the fact that she's not up for chitchat. Sure, she knows about the notebook, but she can't shake the feeling that she's participating in some kind of bizarre theatrical game. Still, she plays along because she cares about Smith, because each word spoken takes her out of her catastrophizing head.

"So how do you know so much about the Boathouse?" Clio says.

Tate smiles. "I'm working on an image-recognition New York City architecture app. That, and applying to grad programs in photography. I'm kind of all over the place, to be honest, but trying to be cool with the fact that I really have no fucking clue what I'm doing."

This is the Tate she remembers. The guy who's quick to admit his own ignorance. Yale was a glittering place, intimidating at times, and how refreshing it was to encounter a kindred soul who didn't pretend to have it all together.

The three of them make their way to the bar and restaurant not far from them in the park. Despite the cold, there's plenty of activity.

Families. Joggers. Bikers. Dogs. When they enter the restaurant, the maître d' makes a beeline for Smith and kisses her on the cheek hello.

"My Napoleonic father's a regular in these parts," she whispers to Tate. "Lots of client meetings. You know how it goes."

They sit at a table by the window. The waiter hands them menus and Tate is quick to order his drink. Smith follows suit and Clio orders a drink too, though she will not drink it. Her head is already too light. When the cocktails arrive, Tate plucks an olive from his and tosses it in his mouth. He drains his glass quickly, as if on a mission, and looks up at Clio. Smiles. "We used to have some pretty good talks while we were busy doing glamorous tasks like cleaning the washers."

Clio nods. Thinks back. "We did."

Clio remembers those months, how she looked forward to seeing him during their shifts. He lacked the pretension she glimpsed in so many of their classmates. He was on the quiet side, but everything he did say felt real in a way. His comments on their shared new culture were interesting, if somewhat antiestablishment, and made her feel less alone.

"Look at you two," Smith says. "Bonding over dirty laundry, literally."

Tate grins. "Clio, not sure whether Smith's given you the scoop, but by way of background, I'm a minor-league wreck at the moment. Going through a divorce. Stoked to be back in New York City, though. California was never for me."

"Love troubles abound," Smith says before Clio has a chance to get a word in. "Clio here is dealing with a situation with her boyfriend. Tell him, Clio. How great to get a male perspective."

Clio stares at Smith, trying to figure out why she would put her on the spot like this. She knows how private Clio is. She considers standing up, leaving. The fresh air outside would be a balm and she'd feel better, but she can't do that to her friend. Nor can she just sit here and ignore Smith's invitation to speak. "Um, so, I've been dating someone and I thought it was casual but now he wants me to move in with him," she says, as if the story's really this simple.

"Wow, that's great. You love him?" Tate asks earnestly, fiddling with his ice. His gaze is steady.

Clio stares down into the depths of her drink, a Bloody Mary that's growing watery as the ice melts. It startles her how easily he throws the word out. Love. It's a simpler thing for other people, she thinks.

"Um, well, I've never been in love before," she says, forcing a shaky smile. "So I'm not sure I know." She catches Smith's eye and can see that her friend is catching on, that she's concerned. Clio's seen this look many times.

"Is he a good guy, at least?" Tate says, glancing toward Smith.

Clio nods. So does Smith.

"He's old as the hills," Smith says. "But he's extremely charming in this kind of vaguely paunchy Pierce Brosnan way. And he adores Clio. Yes, he's a good guy."

"Old as the hills? Smith! He's *fifty*," Clio says, grateful for the sudden dose of levity. She pretends to hit Smith with her napkin.

"He's ancient! He'll keel over at any moment!" Tate says.

"Okay, fine, he's not ancient. But he's not a sprite like us either," Smith says. "And I say cheers to that."

"And I say go for it then. I know I should be advocating restraint after the crap I've been dealing with, but hell, that's not the way to live life. You've got to risk it. What's the point otherwise? Play it safe and then die alone?"

"So depressing. I liked you more when you were talking about the campus laundry," Smith says, nudging him playfully.

Smith orders another round of drinks and tucks her hair behind her ear. She's flirting again, something Smith does expertly, but also something Clio hasn't seen her do in a while. This lightness has been missing. Even with Asad, there was a frank seriousness to Smith, a detectable caution in her dress and mannerisms, a palpable undercurrent of fear that Smith would lose him. But here she sits, sipping a daytime cocktail in this sun-blanched restaurant, a true smile on her face. Still, Clio can see it in the dark circles under Smith's eyes, the melancholy that lingers.

"What Clio failed to mention is that he doesn't just want her to move in. He *designed* a full apartment on the top floor of his hotel for them to live in. All she has to do is move her things a few blocks from my place and, voilà!"

Voilà.

Smith's words are like cuts, each one sharper than the next. Clio knows she means well, but she can't do this. She can't sit here at this fancy restaurant and drink vodka and carry on like her life is some Hollywood movie, inching toward some simple, saccharine happy ending. She must get out of here.

She stands abruptly. Smith grabs Clio's arm. "You okay?"

Clio nods quickly. Assures them both she's just fine even though that's a lie. She's not fine. She's coming apart, bit by bit, her body growing weak, her mind addled with images of Henry's smile, with his triumphant laughter, with the last words she heard him speak. *What's wrong with you?*

"I need to run," Clio says, "I need to get in touch with Henry." She pushes her drink to the center of the table; she hasn't taken a single sip. "This one's up for grabs. You two can fight over it."

"We'll duke it out," Tate quips, the concern in his eyes quickly fading.

Clio finds a twenty in her bag and hands it to Smith, as she always does. Smith bats it away. "Stop. It's Thatcher's pleasure."

"It was so good to see you again, Tate," Clio says. He gives her a knowing look, a comforting nod, as if to say, *She's in good hands; I'm still that quiet kid from freshman year.*

At the door of the restaurant, Clio looks back. The two of them are deep in conversation, laughing.

As she exits the restaurant, she nearly stumbles. Her exhaustion is thick and throttling. It's unclear what awaits her, but she can't put it off any longer.

5:07PM

"You barely know me."

Clio wanders out of the park and pulls out her phone. She dials Jack. When he picks up, one of his daughters cries in the background. "Hang on," he says. "Let me sneak into the bathroom."

As always, the sound of his voice soothes her. She hears a door close and then it's quiet. "I have so much to tell you," she says. "I think I screwed things up with Henry. I'm no good at this, Jack. And now Smith is off drinking with this guy from college and I'm worried she's falling apart and I'm dreading coming home to my dad. It's just so sad."

"Have you called your dad, Clio?" Jack says.

"Not yet," she says, and is suddenly defensive with guilt. "I just got back yesterday."

"You've managed to call me twice since you've been back," he says.

"Because it's *you*," Clio says.

"Call him," Jack says. "Let him know when you're coming home. Call me later and tell me everything, but go call your dad. There's a small human banging on the door anyway. I've got to go."

Clio laughs. "All right, Mr. Conscience. Say hello to the small human."

She hangs up and stares at the screen. She promised her father she'd call to discuss Thanksgiving as soon as she got home, but yesterday was a flurry of activity from the moment she touched down at JFK. She'd hoped to catch up on some sleep after her trip, but Smith had other plans: a makeover.

This was a big night, Smith argued, and Clio needed to look the part. She insisted that Clio borrow a dress and heels, that if she took the train home that evening from the Yale-Harvard game in New Haven and found Clio wearing her melancholy navy shift dress to the party, she wouldn't forgive her.

So instead of spending the day sifting through her field notes from Ecuador, Clio, flattened by fatigue, floated from salon to salon, where Smith had booked appointments for her, being pampered. She sipped mint tea and nibbled on almond cookies and allowed herself to be transformed from angst-ridden ornithologist to well-heeled ingénue. It was all an act, a contrivance, but Clio delighted in not fighting it; it was, oddly, just what she needed. And when she stood in front of Smith's full-length mirror ready to go in her glittery dress and heels, her dark-blond hair smooth and straight, makeup flawless on her pale skin, she felt a surge of confidence.

The day had slipped by and the party began and, well, she never called her dad.

She loves him, she reminds herself of this, but talking to her father inevitably brings her back. All those years of the three of them—Clio and her mother and father—in that small house weathering the hibernations and disappearances and outbursts, the empty fridge and thrown dishes, the visits from the police, the tears and rants and apologies, the endless sinister storms Clio would understand only when she was older and finally learned the truth.

She reaches the museum steps and sits, hands deep in her pockets, her breath leaving white wisps of condensation in the air. From her perch, she spots a trio of pigeons near the curb. They peck at a twist of pretzel and this makes her think of her mother, who was always full of odd facts about Darwin. One such fact was that he studied pigeons, obtaining skins from around the world, tucking into pigeon treatises, befriending fellow fanciers and joining London pigeon clubs. *Say hello hello to the pigeons,* Eloise would say when they spoke on the phone.

She dials. Her father answers on the second ring. She can picture his movements, his standing up from his TV chair and walking swiftly to the kitchen to the home's only phone. On Sundays he watches football, something Eloise gave him flak for. She thought it was a brutal sport.

"Marsh residence," he says. The mere sound of his voice and tears prick her eyes. Guilt spreads within her, a gnawing feeling that she's fallen woefully short as a daughter, that she's betrayed him somehow by getting on with her life, a life that doesn't really include him.

"Hey, Dad, it's Clio," she says, swallowing, a familiar lump forming in her throat.

"So you got back okay?"

"Yes," she says. "Last night was the opening of Henry's hotel. It went well."

"Good to hear," he says, his voice distant.

"I'd like for you to meet him at some point," Clio surprises herself by saying, and waits.

"I'd like that," he says, his words perfunctory, trailing off and giving way to a heavy silence.

The truth is that she's not ready for her father to meet Henry. She's never been ready to bring a man home. Not that there have been many men. Clio's chalked it all up to choice; after having a front-row seat to her parents' struggle, she hasn't exactly been eager to commit. But now there is a man in the picture and she cares about him and, no, she's not ready for any of this.

The silence now doesn't surprise her, but it does leave her crestfallen. When her mother died, she foolishly hoped that her relationship with her father would reset itself, that they'd learn to lean on each other, that they'd make efforts to get to know each other. Her hopes were high; she'd be dutiful about calling often, about checking in. She'd reach out several times a week even if only to talk about the banal details of their respective lives, her work with the birds, his construction jobs. It would be healthy for each of them to indulge in some of the normalcy they never had when her mother was around.

She willed an optimism that felt flimsy at times, a deep wish that things would magically transform, that he would find his voice in the precarious aftermath, and she'd find hers too, that they'd take greater interest in each other's lives, that they'd ask each other questions and make up for all those lost years.

They didn't. It hasn't happened that way. Instead, more distance. More silence. Clio has rationalized it all, has worked hard to assuage her own blooming shame, soothing herself with stories likely fictive; maybe this is what her father prefers.

He's always been quiet, a man of few words, never one to examine or explore life too deeply, the strong silent type who never really seemed all that strong—though who is she to judge, there's no saying she would have had more fortitude in his unfortunate spot of essentially babysitting a time bomb.

He's stayed in New Haven and she's stayed here. They talk from time to time, their calls strained and halting and full of hurt that neither of them seems to be able to unpack. She can't shake the feeling that she's abandoned him.

"I'm going to catch an early train on Wednesday," she says.

"I told you I can handle the house," her father says now. "You don't need to come. I know you've been busy with the travel and with Henry. I can handle it and I don't want to burden you with—"

"Dad, *stop,*" she says, aware of a trace bitterness in her voice, biting her lip. "I'm coming home. I want to, okay? If you can pick me up at the station, great. Otherwise, I'll catch a cab, or call Jack, or something . . ."

"I always pick you up," he says.

"You didn't last year," she says quickly, immediately regretting this unnecessary barb. Why must she always bring up the past?

"I have to work on Wednesday, but if you get in before eight or eight thirty, that'll work."

"I think there's a 5:57 or 5:47. I'll be in before eight. We can have dinner together, or—"

"Good then."

"How are the Giants playing?" Clio asks. It's a foolish, insipid question, but it's all she's got. They've perfected a collective cowardice, grown skilled at talking about everything other than what matters.

"Oh, not so well. Nice to take a break from the packing, though. Having myself a Heineken that Jack brought by. I'm looking forward to seeing you," he says. "It's been too long."

It's been too long. A dagger. Always.

"Yeah, you too, Dad," she says before hanging up. She looks down at her phone and then up at the trees, the sky, city strangers out and about, doing their Sunday stuff. A bolt of determination hits her: This time, things with her father will be different. She will go home and see him and they will talk. They will get somewhere.

Clio stands and walks down to the sidewalk. She begins her well-worn route back to the hotel, cutting through by the Hayden Planetarium. She walks by the Nobel statue and heads west along Seventy-Ninth. When she reaches Amsterdam, she feels herself slowing. A surprising sense of calm falls over her as she takes in this little corner of the world that's become so familiar. She's come to recognize certain people and certain dogs. Down the way, ruddy-faced men stumble euphorically from under the neon harp of the Dublin House, the charming sliver of a pub where she and Henry had drinks on their first date after he walked her through the construction site for the hotel.

That night. She remembers it so clearly, how easy it was to talk to him, how he was a gentleman but also fun. He walked her back to the San Remo and handed her his very own copy of E. B. White's *Here Is New York*, telling her: *Read this and you will understand*. She wasn't sure what she was meant to understand and didn't ask but it was all very clever; this ensured that she would see him again because she'd have to return his book. She promised to read it, and this made him smile and he took her face in his hands, bent down and whispered words she wouldn't forget. *Just think, days ago, I didn't know you. Time is a funny thing.*

And then their first kiss. A simple kiss, a wispy tease, barely there at all. He pulled away and stood quietly, his tall silhouette stark against a wallpaper of trees and spring night sky. And Clio just stayed there on the sidewalk, smiling. He walked away into the night, making it only as far as the corner before turning back to see if she was still there. She was.

He's it, Smith said later after all the Googling. Clio fought her on this. There was no *it*. *It* was a fiction, a fairy tale, a fallacy. *It* was what got people in trouble. But Smith wouldn't budge. She held firm. *It, I tell you.*

She stayed up and read *Here Is New York*. She read carefully but quickly, and when she got to the final page, the part he'd underlined about the beleaguered willow tree . . . *Life under difficulties, growth against odds, sap-rise in the midst of concrete* . . . she felt tears filling her eyes.

When she closed the book, a scrap of paper fell out and floated to the floor, a scrap of paper she's saved. *You might just be my thing. —HK.*

Goodness, he liked her. Even then. From the very beginning. Enough to call his brother. Enough to write a love note. Last night was not good, there's no way to make it good now, but they will talk about it like they have talked about nearly everything and move on; she will make it right. Determined, Clio picks up her pace.

At the entrance of the hotel, she pauses and peers inside. Through the glass, she beholds a new scene: a hum of activity, vitality, life, the first guests.

She walks inside. The concierge greets her warmly. "Welcome back, Ms. Marsh. He's in the garden," he says.

Nerves come as she walks past a boisterous crowd gathered at the elevator bank, toward the glass door to the courtyard. She grabs the handle and pushes her way out.

Henry is sitting on a bench and turns toward her. A tired smile overtakes his face, but there is distance in his eyes. Things are different now.

"I needed some air," Henry says, standing. "I've been a disaster all day."

"Me too," she says, nodding.

He wears his favorite ivory cable Aran sweater, his heather-gray Irish flat cap, an old pair of Levi's. He hesitates for a moment but then comes straight at her, eyes steady and tired, and wraps his whole body around her. He lifts her up, carries her to the bench and holds her on his lap. She stares up at the white sky.

A fleck of cold brings her back to the moment.

"Snow," Henry says. "I have a thing for snow."

"I didn't know that," she says.

"Now you do."

With the two of them, there's been little silence. All those years, both of them alone, saving up stories. They've packed their time together with words. But here and now: silence. Clio wants to believe that there's something peaceful about this snowy quiet.

"Come on," he says. "Let's head up."

They ride up in the small elevator with an older couple who's just checked in. Henry shifts into work mode, turning on the charm, welcoming them to his hotel, but Clio hangs back and takes in the rich detail of the tiny space. The wallpaper—made of recycled strips of old *New York Times*. The lantern that once hung in the Algonquin Hotel, where E. B. White wrote *Here Is New York;* the round vintage buttons with numbers in an antique font. The red light of the ceiling camera reminds her of his words last night: *People will see us*. The memory arouses her, fills her with warmth. All she wants is for everything to be fine, to fast-forward through the hard parts. All she wants is to kiss him, to feel his weight on top of her again.

When Henry opens the door to his room, Clio sees something that both saddens her and makes perfect sense: the bookshelf is back in its place. The door is hidden once more, gone, as if it were all a dream. Empty room service platters rest on the bed. Newspapers are strewn everywhere. Clio drops her bag to the carpet, takes a deep breath.

Henry unzips her jacket, peels it from her and marches it to the closet, where he hangs it.

"What happened last night?" he says, nibbling his nail, pulling her to sit beside him on the bed. "You scared me running off like that. Tell me about these panic attacks. What do they feel like? Why do they happen?"

His questions are fair. Straightforward. She's answered them before.

"Have you ever had one?" she asks.

He shakes his head. This does not surprise her. He's not wired that way.

"They're so awful, Henry. You feel like the walls are closing in, like your lungs and your heart are just going to stop, like you're going to die even though you know that it's all irrational. I had them in waves since college, sometimes two or three a week, but I haven't had one in a while. Since before I met you." Henry smiles at this.

"Last night was a lot, Henry. The party was wonderful and I had a really fine time, but I think I was more anxious than I realized and then the apartment and your saying all of these incredibly meaningful things about the future. I just—"

"Look, Clio," he interrupts, a hint of anger in his voice. "It wasn't right of me to put all of this on you, to catch you off guard like that. You were exhausted, and I had far too much to drink, and believe me when I tell you I'm feeling my share of shame today. I'm typically a bit more cautious in my dealings with you. You know that."

"I do," Clio says meekly. "I don't want you to have to be cautious with me, but it just felt so out of the blue, that suddenly the world was moving so fast. I feel like you barely know me."

He pauses. Considers this.

"I'm not sure that's fair. I think I know a good deal about you," he says. "I know that you do this soft, hiccuplike thing when you sleep. I know that you walk to the window when you have an idea for work or are feeling overwhelmed by something. I know that you would prefer having your nose in a book to doing most anything else. I know that your favorite color is red and that you drink your coffee extra sweet and that you love raw cookie dough and have never in your life tried calamari. I know that you love subtitled films and that your movie snacks are Milk Duds and extra-buttery popcorn. I appreciate that there is far more to you, Clio, and I want to learn it all, but you can't say that I don't know you."

He's been paying attention. Each detail lifts her. She reaches for his hand. He laces his fingers in hers.

"Look, Clio. Before you, there were affairs. Nothing more. And I was surprised at how different I felt when I met you. Truth is, I was going to wait. I know you're going home this week to pack up the house, and it's all loaded emotionally, and I vowed to myself to wait until you were back and the hotel was moving and grooving, but then I saw you across the bar for the first time in three weeks and you looked so beautiful. And I was just overcome with something I've never in my life felt, something I can't explain, and I just couldn't wait. I love you and I want this, Clio. I'm afraid I was rather under the impression that we were on the same page, that this was mutual."

"It is," Clio says. "But there are some things I need to tell you, Henry. Things about my past. About my family."

"Then *tell me*," he says, his blue eyes wide and pleading. "Tell me everything."

"I will," she says. "But you've got to give me some time."

"Okay," he says, nodding, looking down. "If that's what you need. Has it even occurred to you that I might be scared too?"

And this, this question, for some reason, it stuns her and changes everything. Because, no, it hasn't occurred to her that he might be scared. What in the world does he have to be scared of?

"You are?" she says. "You're scared?"

"I am," he says. "I'm old, Clio. I'm getting on in age and it suddenly occurs to me that I might want more than a bunch of hotels and I guess I'm scared that maybe I've missed the boat and it's too late, or maybe that I'm terrible at all of this. I know how to open a hotel with my eyes closed, but I'm not sure I know how to do *this*."

Clio looks into his eyes. There's so much hope there, mixed in with the blue.

"Your brother showed up on my walk today," she says.

"I know. He confessed when I saw him earlier."

"He loves you a lot."

Henry smiles a weak smile. "It was good to see him. Made me realize how much I miss him and his kids and the rest of my family. You really are so lucky to have your dad so close. A mere stone's throw, really."

Lucky. She's never thought of it this way. That she's lucky to have her father so close. She's spent so many years now trying to put distance between herself and her parents, herself and her past, but maybe she is in fact lucky on some level. She thinks of her father all alone in that decrepit house, swimming in a sea of cardboard boxes, eating dinner after dinner alone, all of the times she felt she should hop a train and be with him but couldn't bring herself to. It was all too hard.

Henry orders another round of room service.

The food arrives quickly and they quietly tuck into a sumptuous feast. Clio tastes everything, savoring the range of flavors—the nutty smoothness of the pumpkin gnocchi, the tang of the blue cheese burger, the earthy tones of the papery vegetable terrine. Henry does what Henry does, presiding over it all, passing her a beer.

"So, how was the first day?" she says.

"Oh, I think as first days of hotels go, it was pretty grand." He laughs.

When her phone rings, it startles her. A number she doesn't recognize appears on the screen, stirs anxiety. She doesn't answer. It rings again. The same number. Henry asks if she needs to answer it, but she shakes her head no. Who keeps calling her? There's no voice mail when she checks.

"You know what?" he says, cutting the quiet.

"What?" Clio says.

"I think everything will be just fine." It's as if he can read her mind, as if he knows how desperately she needs this assurance. And maybe, in a way, he *can* read her mind. Maybe this is how it works when it works: someone begins to know you, not perfectly, never perfectly, but well enough to look you in the eye and guess what you need.

Everything will be just fine.

It's something a mother might say. A mother other than the kind Clio had.

Clio's been waiting far too long for someone to say this.

She's waited far too long to believe it.

"I know it's my turn to choose the show, but let's do a little *Downton*. You, my Bird Girl, have had quite the twenty-four hours."

She leans over and kisses him and burrows her face into his chest, listens to the defiant thrum of his beating heart. When she pulls away, she knows what she wants to do, what she must do. She thinks of the Andean hummingbirds she saw up in the mountains, their tiny bodies evolving so that they can survive at higher and higher altitudes. She can't hesitate. If she does, she might lose her nerve.

"Come home with me, Henry?" she says. "I want you to meet my father."

SMITH MAE ANDERSON

Start where you are.

—Pema Chödrön, *Comfortable with Uncertainty*

SMITH ANDERSON

THE ORDER OF THINGS, LLC

theorderofthings.net

MINDFUL ORDER FOR A MINDFUL EXISTENCE

As founder of the Order of Things, LLC, I believe that organization and tranquility in the home lead to organization and tranquility in the head and heart. I tackle each project with comprehensive, tailor-made innovation, streamlining the homes, schedules and daily lives of my loyal and discerning clients. Without fail, my no-nonsense approach yields exceptional results and enduring change. With a BA in psychology and physics from Yale University and an MBA in management from Columbia University, I began my career as a management consultant with McKinsey, a profession in which I thrived due to my innate passion for detail and efficiency. Today I apply those skills and passion to train my clients to clear their homes of burdensome clutter, simplify overbooked days and improve quality of life. I've gained a reputation for imagining solutions that are unique, practical and aesthetically superior. I transform the entire essence of each space. From powerful executives to time-strapped parents, my clients celebrate my incomparable mix of Ivy League intelligence, resolute confidentiality and abiding devotion to design. I have appeared on the *Today* show and *Good Morning America* and am regularly featured in the *New York Times* and *New York Post, Psychology Today,* and *O, The Oprah Magazine,* among other publications. I am at work on my first book on clutter theory, cognitive dissonance and the butterfly effect.

Smith Anderson

7:31AM

"Shit. Shit. Fuck."

Smith opens her eyes. The world is sideways.

This can't be happening. But it is. Oh, fuck, it is.

She's on the floor of her bathroom. Curled into a fetal ball, her left cheek pressed to the statuary marble, that perfect slab she painstakingly picked from a stone yard in Queens. She blinks, rubs her leaden eyes and wonders if it's possible she's dreaming. She sure as hell hopes so.

But no.

This is very much real.

All is blurry for a moment, but then two alarming details snap into focus: One, her brand-new iPhone sits on the edge of a pond of brown, lumpy liquid that can only be vomit. Two, she is for some reason wearing her bridesmaid dress.

Shit.

She sits up slowly. Looks down at the diaphanous dress, a bold sapphire with a portrait neckline fit for one of Henry VIII's fucking wives, picked to match the blue art deco ceiling of the Starlight Roof at the Waldorf. The Valentino fall 2013 ready-to-wear season, Sally explained with considerable animation—fashion is a near-pathological hobby of hers—was inspired by the private sensuality depicted in serene portraits of women. *Think Vermeer,* she said.

Fuck Vermeer.

Smith surveys the damage. There's plenty. An enormous crusty stain snakes down the front. In the center of the stain, a noodle dangles. She removes it and is suddenly hit with the odor of two things she utterly deplores: Chinese food and bourbon. For better or worse, she's always had a keen sense of smell.

Too nauseated to stand or to do anything at all, Smith sits for a moment and indulges in a stream of punishing thoughts. *What the fuck?*

Time passes. It can't be said how much, but eventually she uses the edge of the tub to pull herself to stand, and as she does, she wipes the side of her face with a shaky hand and peeks down into the toilet. The evidence is pungent, a muddy and mocking yellow brown. More noodles—chewed and intact—float on the surface of the water. Lo mein, she presumes. It's all too much to behold; she gags, comes close to losing it again. She flushes the toilet, bends down and fishes her phone from the floor, dabs it dry with a hand towel. She walks it to the vanity and plugs it in. The screen lights up, but she sees now that it is woefully cracked.

Shit.

To add punishment to punishment, Smith studies herself in the Venetian mirror that hangs over the bathroom sink. Her eyes are as puffy as they feel, bloodshot and shame glossed, the blue of her irises hardly visible through small slits. Dregs of makeup are caked on her wan face. Her long dark hair is a tangled bird's nest. She opens the medicine cabinet and grabs two small bottles. Shakes a vitamin D capsule and an omega-3 supplement into her palm. Washes them both down with a gulp of filtered water from the faucet. Just when she thinks things cannot get any worse, they do. One earlobe is bare; she's missing one of her two-carat diamond studs. A business school graduation gift from her parents.

Fuck.

Pieces of last night come back in fierce, unsettling flashes. Dots connect. A picture takes shape. Tate. He's to blame for this. Or, perhaps, to thank? Interestingly, even this morning, even immersed in this nightmare Kafkaesque scene, the thought of him stirs a smile. Is it possible that she likes him? She's almost forgotten what these flutters feel like; she hasn't liked someone new in so long.

What happened last night? She remembers leaving the Boathouse around sunset. Tate was exuberant and animated. His arm linked in hers, he had a suggestion.

Let's walk around. Play Tipsy Tourist. I'm new to New York again. Come on. Let's go explore the city.

Malachy's.

Nothing like a tried-and-true Irish pub.

The 1 train downtown.

The exquisite grit of the underground. Those rats get a bad rap.

Margaritas at Caliente.

We need pizza.

Grimaldi's in SoHo.

Holding his hand—wait, they were holding hands?

One more drink . . .

The Dead Poet. Bourbon.

So, wanna come to a wedding with me Saturday?

Indeed. I dig a good boozefest. Who's getting married?

My younger sister.

Ohhhhh. Awkward silence.

Shit. Shit. Fuck.

She steps on something sharp and screams out, her shrill voice marring the quiet, and lowers herself to sit on the edge of the tub. She lifts her foot and sees that her diamond earring has pierced her heel. She pulls it out and blood begins to stream. All over her white skin and her white floor. And the train of the dress.

She hears a muffled noise in the distance. A slamming door. Then silence.

Footsteps.

The bathroom doorknob turns.

She's not alone.

7:41AM

"What's gotten into you?"

"What in the heavens?" Bitsy stands in the bathroom doorway, towering over her. She wears a pink robe, shearling slippers, a halo of curlers. She appears to be somewhat winded. "Why on earth did you choose to lose your dinner on the Valentino?"

"There was no choice involved, Mom," Smith says, looking down. She feels the pills in her throat, as if they are caught. She takes another sip of water. Tries to swallow.

"There's always choice involved," Bitsy says, a flash of judgment in her eyes.

"The good news is that I found my earring," Smith says, rinsing it under the faucet.

"Oh, is it silver-lining time?" Bitsy says, grinning, eyes twinkling, and steps behind Smith to unzip the dress. How did she zip herself into it last night? She has no recollection of trying it on.

"Whatever happened to knocking?" Smith says. Historically, this sweeping in unannounced, common in these parts, hasn't bothered Smith so much, but today she feels her blood beginning to boil. Is maintaining a modicum of privacy too much to ask?

"I've been knocking for twelve hours. I came to see if you were okay. You didn't show up for Sunday dinner, you didn't call, you didn't answer your phone, you upset your sister, you worried me. Your father is up in arms. None of this is like you, so I decided to pay you a little visit. Never did I expect such comedy. What in the world happened to you?"

"Suddenly you're worried that I'm okay? I've had the shittiest year of my life and you've been off in the pastures with Sally picking linens and china and now you're concerned? Better check in on the *other daughter* and make sure she's not going to *totally* lose her shit the week of golden girl's wedding. That would be highly unfortunate and reflect poorly on you and Thatch. We wouldn't want that."

"What's gotten into you?" Bitsy says. "If you must know, your father is very concerned about you. He's the one who insisted I come check in on you, but I was a bit delayed getting here because I had to chase poor Esmeralda down to the lobby. Your father fired her *again*. The week of the wedding! Thank the Lord, I convinced her to stay, but what an ugly spectacle. The doorman and that nice family from 12B were *staring*."

Smith hears something. It takes a moment to realize she's laughing. "Dad's an asshole, Mom. That's hardly a news flash."

Her mother laughs. "I suppose he is a bit *difficult*, but he loves you, Smith. And he's worried about you. I am, too."

"Because I didn't show up for one dinner? I was out, Mom. I lost track of time. My phone died. It's not a big deal."

"You know it's more than *one dinner*, love. You haven't been yourself recently and I know you're *busy* and you have your own life, but I'm your mother and I'm allowed to be concerned."

Bitsy fumbles around under the bathroom vanity for paper towels and cleaning supplies.

"Stop, Mom. I'll do it."

Bitsy ignores her daughter and gets down on the floor to clean. She holds her nose with one hand as she works with the other, capturing hardened vomit with several layers of organic paper towels, stuffing it all into a thick garbage bag Smith holds open. Smith then sprays a chemical-free room freshener again and again, but it does little to mask the stench. She takes the bag from her mother and carries it to the service entrance, placing it down outside the door. She wonders if the maintenance guy will be onto her.

Bitsy flashes a mischievous grin. "So, tell me, who was he?"

"He?"

How does her mother know there was a he?

"I know these things, dear, and trust me, I don't give a fig if you tied one on with some mystery ziff. Truth is, we were all talking about it just last night, that you need to loosen up and have a little fun after everything with . . . well, despite the mess, I'm pleased you've given it a go."

After everything with . . . Her mother can't even bring herself to say Asad's name. It eats at Smith, the way it always does when the subject comes up with her family, that while she's been devastated about the breakup all of this time, her parents have been *relieved*. Her mother's saccharine words, which she uttered again and again during that impossible time, repeat in Smith's head now, a sickening script: *It's for the best, Muffin. It's for the best. Marriage is difficult enough as it is without such an obvious hurdle.*

"I really wish I weren't fodder for family gossip," Smith says. "Don't you all have better things to talk about than my dating life or lack thereof?"

"That's what happens when you skip family dinner, love. Practically written into boilerplate of the Anderson Contract. We all talk about each other, always lovingly—well, mostly lovingly—and particularly behind backs. Speaking of which, your sister is acting like a space cadet and your father chooses *now* to dabble in insomnia and gobble up all manner of sleeping pills and I might just smack him upside the head because he hasn't lifted a twitchetty finger for this quaint little wedding that's *days away*."

"Oh, is it? I hadn't noticed. No one has really mentioned the wedding."

Her mother doesn't laugh. "Look, dear, can the sarcasm. It's not becoming. I know this wedding business must be incredibly hard for you. She's not just your sister but your *younger* sister, and she's getting *married*, and look at you this morning. A royal mess. And that's all right, my sweet. It's only natural that you'd be in a bit of an existential tizzy over this, but you can't take it out on your sister. She loves you and she thinks you're giving her the cold shoulder."

The cold shoulder? Smith feels her body stiffening and her face growing hot. Is her mother actually saying these things? One admittedly untoward morning and now Smith is a disaster? And this cold-shoulder business? Total bullshit.

"Need I remind you that I've spent the last year of my life acting as her proxy at wedding-planner meetings she was too busy to make, giving serious thought to floral arrangements and table linens and whether we should have one or two photo booths and what kind of artisanal cocktails we should serve? I've been at Sally's beck and call and I've been happy to do this, but I'm allowed to have my own life and last time I checked, one evening does not a cold shoulder make. And, for the record, Sally has been in another world with Briggs and hasn't exactly been making an effort to hang out with me, which makes sense. I get it. It's their time."

Smith remembers the prologue to her would-be wedding well. Those two months were, hands down, the best of her life, a breathless blur of sex and daydreams about their future. They agreed they'd try to get pregnant on their honeymoon; he was five years older and neither of them wanted to waste any time starting a family. She began to scour baby-name blogs. The fact that his family, tucked away in Pakistan, didn't know about her yet, and the fact that her family—the opposite of tucked away—had outright reservations, all of this obviously concerned her, but also added a hot, illicit edge to it all.

"For the record, dear, not that anyone's asking, but this hasn't been a cakewalk for me, either. Have you even thought about that? This wedding has been a lot of *work* and I'm not sure any of you appreciate how *taxing* this has all been on me. Not to mention, the thought of giving one of you away has me a speck rattled."

Smith chuckles. "Giving one of us away? You sound like I do with my clients when we're pruning a shoe collection."

Bitsy smiles. "Well, wouldn't that mean that you're the keeper? The one I can't bear to part with?"

"Yes, if this was all your doing. But it's not. Sally's the one who's moving on. And yours truly? Busy standing still and ruining gowns."

"Isn't that the truth? I will take that beleaguered thing to Marta at the cleaners, but even she isn't a miracle worker. Let's cross our fingers, shall we? Promise me you will meet us for the fitting later at Bergdorf's?"

Bergdorf's. The mere mention makes her wistful even though this is ridiculous. It's still just a store.

"Did I tell you? A four-bedroom is opening up on the fourth floor. Sally and I are going to look at it tomorrow morning. It looks like the owners on the other side of them won't budge, so a combination seems out of the question and two bedrooms aren't sufficient for more than one kid. Although you girls always did share a room. That was, without a doubt, one of the best decisions we ever made, keeping you two together. You two were always so close, Smith."

The past tense. All in the past tense.

"And we still are, Mom," Smith says, wondering if this is entirely true. The last year has brought distance, but that's only natural. They're at entirely different points in their lives. "Clio's probably moving out soon too. Henry renovated a full apartment for them on the top floor of the hotel."

At this news, Bitsy's eyes twinkle. "Isn't that something? An old-fashioned gentleman, that Henry. And, my Lord, I can't get over how beautiful Clio's looking these days. Just goes to show what love can do. She was an awkward thing in college, but my, how she's blossomed. And she looks so *young*. Not a day over twenty-five, I'd say."

"Okay, got the memo. Clio looks good. Gets better with age, unlike the rest of us mere mortals," Smith says.

Bitsy laughs. "I always thought you'd end up with someone older like Henry, some man about town, you know."

"Is that how you imagined things? Interesting," Smith says, aware of the edge in her voice.

How is this helpful? How is this remotely helpful? How about: *I'm sorry that your two best friends in the world are moving on. That must be difficult.*

"So," Bitsy says, "how's the toast coming?"

"It will come together," Smith says. "I'm trying to identify a few salient themes."

"I have no doubt that you'll say something wonderful and *appropriate*," Bitsy says.

"Are you worried that I'm going to fly off the handle and say something inappropriate? That maybe I'll use my soapbox to make Thatch squirm? Maybe I'll tell about that one time in the Hamptons when he got so ripped that he confessed to Sally and me that he'd rather have had sons. That would work because I could make some quip about how then he wouldn't have had to pay for this outlandish wedding."

"Don't even joke about that," Bitsy says, the slightest smile riding her lips.

"Calm down, Bits. You and I both know I will bite my tongue and say something perfectly controlled and disingenuous that makes you burst with pride," Smith says. "Relax."

"Ha. Isn't that a joke? Relax when this wedding is mere minutes away and my to-do list is a mile long? I will be elated when this whole thing is done and dusted. Anyway, a thought. In your speech, you could mention your minimalism and your sister's—what's the word . . . You've always been *neat as a pin*. Even as a baby, you'd sit there in your high chair, sorting your foods by category and color. Barely needed a bib. Your sister, on the other hand, was a revolutionary slob, always sporting a fetching sweet potato beard. And have you seen her apartment recently? I know that she's been spending the bulk of her time at Briggs's packing up his things, but her place is an untoward sty. I keep dropping hints that our housekeeper can come to her more than once per week, but she refuses."

"The illustrious doctor perhaps has more important things to worry about than keeping house," Smith says. "Such things are the dominion of us lesser folk."

Smith feels herself getting riled. The daily transcendental meditation has helped considerably but is clearly no silver bullet. Her mother must leave before she loses it.

Bitsy fixes her with a stare. "We're proud of you both. Period."

Bullshit, but she's too exhausted to go there. "I need some coffee," Smith mumbles to herself. She makes her way to the kitchen. Bitsy follows.

Smith flips on the light in the kitchen and startles. It's a mess. Chinese food cartons and chopsticks are scattered on the counter. Four empty bottles of Red Stripe beer are lined up by the sink, the other two in the cardboard carrier. She lifts a bottle to her nose and inhales. The sour smell brings her back to college, the last time she drank beer. A paper bag sits on the marble floor and Smith grabs for it and studies the delivery receipt. *The Cottage. 12:49 a.m.* She works to remember. Shards come back to her. The doorman calling up, the man at her door,

Tate standing in her kitchen cracking open the beers. His words: *Look at you, still on the parentals' golden leash.*

"Let's get some coffee into those veins then and perk you right up," Bitsy says, walking toward the Keurig machine. She pops it open and fiddles with it. "How do you even work this thing? Why does everything have to be so complex these days? What are these little cup jobs?"

"They're called pods, Mom. Let me do that."

Bitsy swats her hand away. "Not a chance. If I am going to keep up with you girls and all of your 'technology,' " she says, making air quotes, "I must force myself to learn."

Bitsy presses a button. The machine growls. "Success!" she declares, clapping her hands, ducking and squinting to watch the coffee drip.

"Just so you know, you missed quite the war over the seating chart at dinner last night," her mother says. "Your sister and I have *very* different ideas of how to do it. I was counting on you to be there to play peacekeeper."

"Um, I might need you to add a plus-one for me," Smith says sheepishly.

"My, my. Is it the guy from last night?" her mother says, grinning. "I knew you'd pull something off in the eleventh hour."

"Yes, Bits, the guy from last night," Smith says. She thinks back to college, marvels at the fact that she and Tate were on that campus together for four years but barely exchanged a word. They ran in different circles. He seemed quiet, brooding, artistic. All these years later, he has a conspicuous edge to him, an endearing pinch of cockiness. Is it the money? Smith doesn't give two shits about the money. She knows tons of people, of men, with money and not one of them has made her feel what she felt with Tate last night. Last night was about far more than money.

And now she wants him to come to this wedding, but what's to say this will actually happen? Will he even remember last night? She hopes so. They had fun. It can't all be in her head. If they weren't having such a good time, they wouldn't have spent all those hours together. There were plenty of opportunities for him to take off. What does he think of her? Will he even call?

Her head is cracked and all she wants to do is get into bed and sleep it off. She looks around the apartment and thinks of Clio, how nice it was to wake up and have her here yesterday morning like old times. But Clio's moving on. She says she's not sure, but Smith has more confidence that it will happen. She'll be near but far, in a new place, with a man, beginning a life. Just like her sister.

Smith thinks of the day ahead. Remembers that she has an appointment. A new client named Adelaide Loring. Smith recalls their brief phone call, how this soft-spoken woman mentioned right away her reason for calling: that her husband had died recently, and she was finally feeling ready to go through and purge her house of some of his things. Smith retrieves her phone from the bathroom and carries it back with her to the kitchen, where she plugs it in, and stands drinking coffee with her mother. She looks at her calendar for the day.

8:00 A.M. Meditate!
10:00 A.M. Client meeting
1 P.M. Sally's final fitting
4 P.M. Pick up takeout containers for jelly beans
5 P.M. Write speech!
7 P.M. Life coach

She checks her e-mail. It's all a bunch of junk—holiday promotions and other spam, which she dutifully deletes—but then she sees Asad's name in her inbox and her heart drops inside her. She's physically shaken; hot coffee splashes all over her, soaking through her robe, leaving angry red blotches on her chest.

Her mother grabs a dish towel and runs it under cold water, hands it to Smith, concern and judgment fighting in her eyes. "Really, Smith."

"You should go, Mom," Smith says. "I have to pull myself together for a client meeting."

"You will do it. You always pull it off. You're the eel's ankle."

Smith laughs. "Good one. I like it even better even than the oyster's earrings. I'm not sure I believe anything you're saying, but I'm too hungover to argue. Just need a few tea bags on the eyes and a shower and I'll be as good as new. Don't worry."

"Don't worry? Ha. That's what mothers do. Day and night. Night and day. We worry and then we worry some more and then we worry about our worrying. You'll see one day."

Will she?

"*Please* don't forget the fitting, though. It will break your sister's heart if you miss it."

Smith nods as her mother leaves. She knows all too well about broken hearts.

8:30AM

"I told him something I never told you."

Smith sits in the bay window of her living room and waits for the front door to close behind her mother. Her hands tremble. She hasn't seen Asad or spoken to him since that traumatic morning at the Time Warner Center when they agreed to meet so she could return the ring.

She opens his e-mail and reads.

To: Anderson, Smith
From: Rahman, Asad
Time: 7:12 a.m.
Subject: RE: 7 THINNGS

Smith,
I must say that I was startled to find your note upon waking up this morning.

Shit. She stops. Scrolls down. Sees that *she* sent him an e-mail at 1:19 a.m. She cringes as she reads her own words.

To: Rahman, Asad
From: Anderson, Smith
Time: 1:19 a.m.
Subject: 7 THINNGS

Asad,
You said you love me too much to continue this. I went along with it bc what am I supposed to do, pitch a fit & say noooo but the truth is I still don't understand what happned with us. One moment we were fine, no amazing, eating turkey and pie with my family, and you are distant and I ask why and then everything falls apart.

I also don't get how you can already be MARRIED to someone your parents fuckin picked for u. how does this work again? Anyway, I know you are moving on, fuck hate that—moving on—but now I think I am too. Maybe im finally ready?

At Yale game yestrday, I talked to this guy. We couldn't stop talking, like when you and I met. Remember that? And we went OUT and for the first time since we broke, I had FUN. I dodnt feel so melancholy. I think I like really like him.

Assy, I told him something I never told you. I was too scared to tell you. Is that strange? I don't even know why I'm telling you this now.

Sally is getting married on Saturday. I'm happy for them, but also pissed because they don't have fractioin of what we had. Angry because that should have been us. We wanted that, didn't we?

It still kills me tht I was your secret—for so long. Im better then beings someones secrt.

The good news though is that I'm OKAY. I just wanted you to know that. I know that morning at time warner was a disaster, but I'm okay now.

I made a lst because I know you like lists.. that u dont have the attention spn to read something w/o njmbers in it

Love, Smith

She might be sick again. She honestly might be sick again. She heads for the bathroom, hand over mouth, reading his response en route.

To: Anderson, Smith
From: Rahman, Asad
Time: 7:12 a.m.
Subject: RE: 7 THINNGS

Smith,
I must say that I was startled to find your note this morning.

I must also say that I was pleased. You and I both know that you don't just stop thinking about someone who has been such a big part of your life. I've been thinking about you too, about the good time we had together. I do still think it's best for us not to talk. You and I both know this is the way things need to be. I also must respect Kandira and her wishes. We have some good news: she's pregnant. We're expecting a boy.

It makes me happy to hear you are moving on, too. Enjoy the wedding this weekend. I hope it's a joyful time for you and your family. Please give the bride my best.

Asad

A baby. He's having a baby. A punch in the gut.

Kandira and her wishes? Smith knows it's not this poor girl's fault, that his newly minted wife had nothing to do with their demise, that she was just a pawn in Asad's mother's game, a nice Punjabi girl, far better suited for her perfect boy than Smith. Looking back, Smith feels foolish for thinking their plan would work, but oh how she believed that it would.

They met through Sally; Asad was a neurosurgery resident at Columbia while Sally was in medical school there and he came to one of Sally's parties. He stood quietly in the corner and Smith walked over and introduced herself. His eyes were dark and intense but with a discernible playfulness underneath. They talked for hours and Smith behaved herself, conversing politely, keeping her hands to herself even though she'd never in her life felt an attraction this intense. By the end of the evening, she'd had a few too many drinks and it took every ounce of restraint she had not to yank him next door to her apartment and run her hands all over his smooth, whiskey skin.

She learned that night that he grew up in Pakistan but came to the States for college at Harvard before doing medical school at Columbia, and he'd never gone back. They began dating. He worked endless hours at the hospital but would come over late at night in his scrubs with a good bottle of wine that they'd share in bed. Time meant nothing to them; they'd stay up all night having sex again and again. He was adventurous between the sheets, introducing her to new positions and porn and toys. He seemed embarrassed by his own creativity, but Smith encouraged him and was amply rewarded for her encouragement. They slept little and it amazed her that they could function at all during the day, but function they did, and beautifully, riding the adrenaline of new love.

Things became serious fast. Smith introduced him to her parents, knowing that they would startle at her suitor. He was far from the preppy country-clubbing banker they'd hoped for, but Bitsy and Thatch put on a good show and were outwardly gracious toward him, all gentility and manners and the pretense of open-mindedness, and he had gone to Harvard, after all, but behind the scenes, they expressed their grave reservations about Smith's and Asad's markedly "different backgrounds." Smith delighted some in seeing them squirm; she'd always derived some pleasure in playing the rebel to Sally's good girl.

It's true that her parents' objections only made Smith's desire for Asad more insatiable, but shit, she loved the guy in a way she didn't know was possible. He was unlike anyone she'd ever met. She'd been around smart people all her life, but his intelligence was in a different category. His mind, like his body, was downright exquisite. They met more than two years ago and spoke about marriage from the very beginning. After a year of dating, he proposed. She told her parents, but the news didn't seem to register. Bitsy, an old-fashioned romantic, barely made a fuss. Thatcher couldn't be bothered. It was as if they thought this was all a childish game of rebellion, that it would never happen, but Smith pushed on, determined to marry him. Sally was Sally, butterflies and rainbows of excitement; she talked of planning a bachelorette party.

Smith and Asad came up with a plan with regard to his parents: They would marry quietly at city hall before Christmas and honeymoon after. Only when they returned would he communicate the news to his conservative family, who he was certain would disapprove at first and then come around. They'd wait for emotions to settle and then have a big party in New York City in the springtime and travel to Pakistan over the summer for celebrations there. A year later, she would be pregnant.

Smith believed it would all work out. She looked into converting to Islam, even though Asad insisted this wasn't necessary. It was something she felt compelled to do, for him, to convey how much she cared and wanted this. She felt no real allegiance to Christianity and was determined to do what she could to ensure acceptance by his family.

When their engagement ended inexplicably right after Thanksgiving, Smith cried for days on end. She stayed in her big Pratesi-clad bed, where they'd spent all those passionate nights. She completely lost her appetite and canceled dozens of appointments with clients.

Everyone was terribly worried about her. She lost weight. Everyone said she looked great. Weeks blurred by and just as she was starting to function again, Sally phoned to announce that she was engaged. She and Briggs were in the Caribbean and he had proposed underwater on a scuba-diving expedition. The phone connection was bad and there was a bunch of static, but the unapologetic glee in her sister's voice was grating and all Smith could think was: *What the fuck? Are you kidding me?* A more extreme version of what Smith felt yesterday when Clio told her about Henry and the apartment.

Sally and Clio are wonderful people, her two favorite people in the world, and, yes, they deserve love and happiness, but it's just that Smith was sure she would be the first to lock it in and settle down. Is this jealousy or envy? What's the difference again? Either way, it's awful.

Smith drops her phone on her unmade bed. She walks to the window, presses her hands and forehead to the glass and stares out. The trees dance in the wind. Down below, dogs are walked and cars blur by, but it's the strollers that pop most vividly from the gray. She wills herself not to cry.

She pulls the covers down on her bed and climbs in, reaches for her phone and rereads the e-mail she sent, cringing at each typo and each hint of desperation.

I told him something I never told you.

She pauses and remembers just what she told Tate.

She's embarrassed, but it's more than this. She's confused. It's unclear why she would tell someone she barely knows something so private, something she was convinced she had moved beyond long ago. Why is this coming up now? It's also unclear, not to mention highly unsettling, why she sent a drunken missive to Asad. The timing of all of this is beyond troubling; the last thing she needs is such blatant self-sabotage the week of her sister's wedding.

It's one thing to go out and have a little fun, but this today is not fun.

She will delete the messages, pretend none of this happened, get on with things. She's always been good at doing this, dusting off, moving on, pretending, always pretending that everything is *fine*. Because, in the grand scheme, everything *is* fine. People send e-mails while drunk, people's exes have babies, people's sisters get married, people's roommates move out.

It's just that it's happening *all at once*. Thank God she's speaking with her life coach tonight. Hiring Laura was one of her more inspired ideas. She doesn't care if people roll their eyes or scoff, it's been one of the best things she's done for herself. She didn't need therapy, someone to sit and squint and ask her about her past and dissect her dreams and pinpoint some lurking pathology; she needed someone to give her a kick in the butt and help her piece her life back together in a proactive way. That's exactly what Laura's done.

Right now, she does the only thing she can think to do . . . She texts Clio.

Smith: Fuck. Drank a MILLION cocktails. Invited Tate to wedding. Told him what happened freshman year. I think I like him. Maybe. THEN e-mailed Asad ☹

Clio: Oh my.

Smith: Oh my is right. His wife is pregnant. I'm sick.

Clio: Shit. Are you okay?

Smith: Not remotely. Will call after meeting. How did things go with Henry?

Clio: Asked him to come home with me for tgiving, but not sure he can get away from the hotel. Anxious, but fingers crossed.

Smith: It will be fine! I bet he finds a way to come. He DIGS u.

Clio: Hope you're right.

Her instinct is to type one final text. Something sunny to end on, something upbeat and glass-half-full. *I'll be fine. It's okay. Don't worry about me*. But she doesn't. Because it's not even close to true. She has no idea if she'll be fine. She has no idea if any of this shit is okay. Maybe Clio *should* worry about her. Smith can't remember the last time she felt this low.

She looks around the room. It's all fucking wrong. The cream-colored couch she had custom-made floats in the center of the space, flanked by two antique end tables she found in Paris. Two powder-blue chairs she found at a Sotheby's auction. The surfaces are all clear, devoid of life. No knickknacks. Just two photographs. One of her family on a beach in Cannes. She and Sally have tanned skin and toothless smiles. Her parents perch behind them. The other photo is the one of Smith and Clio on graduation day at Yale, smiles so wide it hurts to look at them. Her mother's words ring in her ears: *She looks so young. Not a day over twenty-five.*

Fuck.

She checks the time. She has more than an hour, which leaves plenty of time to turn this around. She will meditate. She's become a decent meditator, though it's proven hard to clear the cobwebs of her busy life. She's learned to try to bring it back to the present moment. Meditating seems to help a little. Yes, that's what she will do. She sits up, flings her legs over the side of the bed, straightens her spine, closes her eyes, focuses on her breath.

In and out.

In and out.

It doesn't work this time. Instead of emptying out, her mind tangles with thoughts she can't control.

I will be alone.

Did he see me naked?

How much lo mein did I eat?

I'm fucking fat.

My father is a psychopath.

I hope his baby's ugly.

I'm an awful person.

Not a day over twenty-five.

How will I make it through my meeting?

Did I order enough jelly beans for the hotel bags?

He will never call. Why would he?

She opens her eyes. Stands up. This bullshit is making it worse. She marches to the kitchen, wipes down every surface, makes a pot of chamomile tea. She opens the fridge. It bursts with fresh vegetables she bought from the organic section of Fairway yesterday. Her plan had been to chop them all and store them in their glass Tupperware as she does every Sunday, but instead of chopping, she was out.

She grabs a big bunch of kale. Rinses it, dries each leaf thoroughly. She readies the rest of the ingredients for her vegan breakfast shake—cashew-nut butter and almond milk and frozen organic blackberries and a shot of sea buckthorn to strengthen her hair and nails. She tosses it all in the blender and turns it on. The sound is mechanical and soothing. Only now does she let herself cry.

Through the fog of her tears, she watches it all mix together. A thick pulpy froth, mauvy-green swirls. Rogue blackberry seeds dot the glass. Half-consciously, she reaches for the handle of the pitcher, yanks it off its electric base. Wide-eyed, she's hypnotized by the mad spinning of metal blades, and she throws the pitcher. She throws it with a force she didn't know she had, hurtling the precious and pricey Vitamix, the item she researched so carefully before purchasing, across the kitchen. It snaps against the gleaming white wall.

The glass shatters. Shards fly everywhere. Lumpy liquid splatters like angry art and snakes quietly toward the floor.

Smith stands frozen in place, her bare feet wreathed in shimmering glass, wondering what the hell's happening to her.

9:55AM

"We did not send you to Yale to become a housekeeper."

The doorman at the Beresford recognizes Smith and waves her in. Over the years, she's worked with many clients in this gorgeous prewar building and this continues to be a perk of her job: spending time in some of the most exquisite apartments in Manhattan.

In the elevator, she presses fifteen, pops two Advil, and wills her head to stop throbbing. On the walk here, she stopped at a newsstand, bought one of those little plastic pill packages and also a vacuous tabloid featuring makeup-free celebrities on the cover. She doesn't usually buy or read this garbage, but today she has a pass.

Despite the epic hangover and the Asad baby bomb and her alarming kitchen outburst, Smith feels it, the tickle of anticipation and excitement that comes before she meets a new client, a continual reminder that she in fact loves what she does, that her work is *meaningful*. It's not just about organization. Yes, she takes great pleasure in the physical act of sifting and sorting, it's always brought her immense satisfaction, but it's really about people she meets, about helping them. And it heartens her that as truly awful as this morning's been, as tempted as she was to cancel and clear her day, she's happy to be in this elevator, to have this opportunity to get outside of herself. If she can't have order in her own life at the moment, at least she can help her client.

Her phone dings in her bag and her first thought is: *Tate?* But no, it's a new e-mail from her father. This is never a good thing. She reads his words, ever economical, words laced with a subtle cruelty she's come to expect from the man. Resentment spikes swiftly inside her.

Your mother informs me that you've ruined your bridesmaid dress. I don't know what's going on with you, but for the sake of this family, please pull yourself together for this weekend. We love you, Smith, but you must stop acting like a child. Please.

Leave it to Thatcher to make a bad situation worse. His judgment and disapproval are as familiar to her as the Upper West Side. He wanted her to play soccer in school, but she ran cross-country. He wanted her to follow in his footsteps and go to Princeton, but she "rebelled" and chose Yale. With her impeccable undergraduate grades, she was supposed to follow him into the business world, but she dared to consider a professional path that might actually make her happy. Imagine that.

Her choice of career continues to be a sore spot, a nasty thorn. His hurtful words still ring in her ear, an awful, belittling anthem. *We did not send you to Yale to become a housekeeper. I'm not sure why you insist upon doing this to us*. His condescension has persisted despite her periodic efforts to convince him (and herself) of the importance of what she does. Even the name of her organization consulting company—

The Order of Things, a reference to Foucault's 1966 book of the same name—was conceived with him in mind, a transparent attempt to impress him, to lend some ivory-tower heft to her admittedly noncerebral work.

She didn't want to take his money to start her business. She wanted more than anything to refuse it, to do it entirely on her own, but she needed his help. He loves to remind her that he got her started. He loves to point to the investment as evidence of his affection, his support. But she knows better. Love is far more complicated than writing a check.

Smith puts her phone away and Thatcher out of her mind and walks down the hall to apartment 15BC. She pauses briefly before ringing the bell. At first, there is no answer, but she notices that the door is cracked open. She slips in. The apartment is quiet but for the hum of a dishwasher in the distance. Smith drops her bag to the white marble floor, kicks off her shoes by the door.

"Hello?" Smith calls out.

A petite woman in yoga pants appears. She is fresh faced and smiling, her blond hair cropped short. She holds out her hand and Smith shakes it.

"I'm Adelaide," she says. "So nice to meet you."

"Likewise," Smith says, taking a look around. The apartment appears tidy, but many do. The real work is most often hidden away, tucked behind closed doors.

"I must apologize in advance for the state of this place. I haven't stayed on top of things, particularly recently."

"That's why I'm here," Smith says.

"I've gathered all of his things here in the bedroom," Adelaide says, leading Smith through an open door. "I heard about you from my mother. I think she knows your mother?"

"Entirely possible. My mother seems to know the world. Did you grow up here too?"

"On the Upper East. Went to Horace Mann. You?"

"Brearley," Smith says. "What year were you? I had some friends at Horace Mann."

"Nineteen ninety-seven," Adelaide says.

"Me too. Where'd you go for college?"

"Wesleyan," Adelaide says. "That's where I met Rupert. Sophomore year. We were babies, but it all worked out. Fourteen years. Three boys."

Adelaide reaches for a photograph on the dresser, hands it to Smith. Three blond boys plopped in green grass. Pale blue eyes. Matching smiles.

"I wouldn't give up on having my girl," Adelaide says, looking down. "We agreed to try one more time right before he got diagnosed. They are wild, my little guys, but they keep me on my toes and they are getting me through this. They are so unbelievably strong. I wish I could bottle their strength. They are holding it together far better than their mother. My hope is that if I go through some of his things and put them away, I'll feel somewhat better. I owe it to them to start coming out of this."

"You'll get there," Smith says. "It's a process."

When Smith first started her business, these were the situations that tripped her up most. She was skilled at creating order, but how was she supposed to respond to moments of vulnerability like this? What was she supposed to say? She learned, though, and it took some time, that there was no right thing to say, that more often than not, her clients just wanted to be heard.

"I'm so sorry. For your loss."

"Oh, thank you," Adelaide says, a hint of a smile crossing her face. "It always strikes me as funny when people say that—'your loss'—and trust me, that's what everyone says, but it's as if I've misplaced my husband, as if it's just a matter of looking around. I'm not sure there's a better word. Anyway, given everything, the boys are doing remarkably well. They haven't missed a beat at school. They're keeping up with sports and their friends. It's truly inspiring, and if not for them,

I would *never* be hosting Thanksgiving. I didn't even do this when Rupert was alive. I'm your prototypical city takeout queen and I've avoided hosting holidays like the plague, but suddenly I have this urge to invite people here. I'm probably overcompensating. I don't know."

"How old are they? Your boys?"

"Six, eight, ten. We stair-stepped them. All my husband's idea. He didn't want to space them out too much because he wanted us to 'get our life back' while we were still young. He was always this big adventurer—climbing mountains and rafting down rapids. We always planned to go to Costa Rica for our fifteenth wedding anniversary. I'm thinking it would still be nice to go, to take the boys in a few years."

"You should," Smith says, but she's snagged on the fact that this woman is *her age* and she has had an entire family—a husband and three children—and, yes, she's young by New York City standards to have done this, but still.

Adelaide holds up a tuxedo jacket now. "He wore this to our wedding," she says, and Smith can almost feel the woman's nostalgia. "Wouldn't it be something, if the boys each wore this tux to get married? This same tuxedo that their dad wore when he married me? Is that a crazy thought? I keep doing this to myself, flashing forward to the big days, the graduations and the wedding days, and the fact that he won't be there just kills me."

Adelaide's face relaxes into a wondrous smile before the tears come.

"That would be incredible, Adelaide, if they wore this tux. We'll have it dry-cleaned and preserved and tuck it away in a special place."

A place where she cannot see it, or touch it, or sniff it, or cry on it. Over the years, Smith has come to appreciate how much of this process ends up being about thoughtful separation, about fashioning distance between people and things, people and the past. About moving things to their optimal resting places—whether a closet, a corner or Goodwill.

Adelaide hands Smith the tuxedo and turns her attention to a pile of dress shirts. Smith holds the tux up, scans the swath of black and notices a stain on the lapel. She can't help herself; she scratches at it with her nail.

"Wedding cake," Adelaide says, looking over. "Vanilla buttercream. He was always sloppy in his eating."

"My sister's having vanilla buttercream, too. She started off saying she wanted something low-key like doughnuts, but now she's picked this six-tier monstrosity. My mother had her heart set on German chocolate, but the bride won out."

"Oh, when's the wedding?"

"This weekend. At the Waldorf. My parents got married there and now my sister's getting married there. I think it's crazy to get married Thanksgiving weekend. It's like adding a layer of dysfunction to dysfunction and I think it's presumptuous to hijack a holiday, but it is what it is."

Adelaide chuckles. "You like the guy?"

Smith stands now, drapes the tuxedo on the bed. "I do. He's really . . . sweet. To be honest, I don't feel like I know him that well, but he makes my sister happy and they seem well suited. She's a doctor and he's this dopey but lovable former jock who's in finance now and they just kind of work together."

"That's good. I don't think my sisters ever loved Rup. They never said so, but I could feel it, you know? I think they believed that he tamed me or drained me of my ambition or something, that if I didn't marry him and have our boys, I would be running Congress or curing cancer," Adelaide says, cracking her knuckles.

Smith stares at Adelaide's ring, the sliver of platinum, the modest but brilliant stone.

"It's gorgeous," Smith says, pointing at the ring. She tries her hardest to stay focused, but it's hopeless. Her mind wanders to that afternoon eighteen months ago when they were lying in bed and he was holding her hand and *he* brought it up, not her. *Let's go shopping*, he said. She didn't have to ask what he meant.

"I don't even know what I'm supposed to do with it now," Adelaide says. "Do I keep it on? Take it off? I suppose if I ever get back out there, I'll put it away or wear it on a necklace or something. I can't even fathom that, though."

Smith told herself that she'd get out there again right away. That she wasn't going to be one of those pathetic souls pining away for some lost love, that she was stronger and more practical than that. She was on the other side of thirty and this was, after all, a numbers game. She wasn't going to meet anyone moping around her apartment in her mint mask and bathrobe. She asked friends to set her up, went on a flurry of dates, most of them horrific, not, in retrospect, because the men were that bad, but because it was simply too soon and she was still trying to figure out what the fuck had happened with Asad. Her head simply wasn't in the game. She thinks of Tate now, wonders if she's in any better place, if she's even ready to have a relationship.

"I find myself wondering if I'll get married," Smith says, out of nowhere. Her embarrassment is swift and acute; what in the world is wrong with her? Has last night compromised her professionalism as well? She's always careful to elicit confessions but never to give them.

Adelaide stops what she's doing and fixes Smith with a stare. "If that's what you want, what you really want, don't you think you will?"

Smith nods. "I don't know. I came close. I really want kids."

Did she really just say this? The kid thing? To a brand-new client? Her face burns as she thinks about last night. Snatches of her conversation with Tate come back. Her disclosure. His response. *You made the best decision you could at the time*. But was it? "Of course you want kids," Adelaide says, grinning. "Best thing I ever did."

"I'm so sorry," Smith says. "I'm not quite myself today."

"Don't apologize," Adelaide says. "I haven't been myself in months. And it's kind of refreshing to hear someone else talk. I feel like I've been so in my head and I get it, *I'm grieving*, and I have every right to be focused on myself and my boys, but the world goes on. There are stories other than mine. It's good to remember this. So, thank you."

"Well, I'm glad I could provide a brief detour then," Smith says, smiling, lifting a stack of shirts and resting it on the bed.

Adelaide holds up a Chicago Cubs T-shirt. "He wore this the day Charlie was born. I can see him now, sitting in that chair in the corner of the hospital room, biting his lower lip until it was literally bloody, scared shitless about what was to come."

"Another keeper," Smith says. "Another treasure. Okay, so we'll put everything you know you want to keep here. And then everything you know you want to store here. And then we'll put everything you want to donate here."

They begin emptying the closet and drawers, working in companionable silence.

"It will happen, Smith. Marriage. Kids. You have time," Adelaide says abruptly.

"I know I do," Smith says, forcing a smile, but does she really know this? She's read all these awful articles about how much harder it is to find marriageable men in your thirties, how fertility plummets in these years.

Time. It's something she thinks about often. Usually as she's lying in bed at night, alone, staring at the canopy that looms above. Where would she be in a year? Five? Ten? Twenty? Once, it was a fun, frilly exercise, to imagine what the future would hold, but recently she's felt panicked at the thought that she might grow old alone in the apartment her parents gave her.

In the room grow piles. Keep. Donate. Trash. Adelaide stretches her arms above her head, something like accomplishment plain on her face. Smith has done little but sit there and talk, and that's fine. Sometimes this is how it happens. Her role is different every day; today is about being here, a warm body in a room, a reassuring voice.

Adelaide reaches into the closet and hands Smith more shirts. "I think we can give these away. He never liked them much anyway. I was always trying to spiff him up and he humored me on occasion, but he was a T-shirt guy," Adelaide says as they pack the dress shirts in cardboard boxes bound for Goodwill.

"How many people are you expecting for Thanksgiving?" Smith asks.

"My parents and his. My two sisters and their families. His brother and his family. I'll do a buffet. It's going to be a packed house. What about you? Any plans?"

"My family is gathering at our place in Southampton with the groom's family. A rehearsal dinner for the rehearsal dinner. Should be interesting." Smith looks down at her watch and sees that their time's up. "I've got to get going. Off to my sister's final dress fitting."

"I'll walk you out. Any chance you can come back next week? This was really helpful," Adelaide says.

Smith pulls out her phone, ashamed of her broken screen. "How's next Thursday at ten a.m.?"

"Perfect," Adelaide says.

Smith slips out into the hallway and exhales. She made it through the meeting without getting sick or ruining her reputation entirely. Small victories. She checks her phone, feels those pathetic flutters in her stomach.

Nothing at all from Tate.

1:15PM

"Watch where you're going."

The problem with living where you grew up: everything is a memory.

The problem with being profoundly hungover: everything is depressing.

Smith makes her way toward midtown, noting all the ways in which the world is a dismal and sinister place. She knows she's dehydrated and exhausted and rattled by the Asad news, but her self-awareness is no elixir; it still sucks. She'd forgotten just how dreadful it is not to be firing on all cylinders, clear on things. She contemplates making a quick stop at the Apple Store to have her cracked screen looked at, but she's not up for the swarms of people. Facing a hip young guy at the Genius Bar would be too much.

"Watch where you're going, lady," a haggard-looking woman says. And this angers Smith even though maybe it shouldn't. She is, after all, stumbling like a zombie through a thicket of people, her eyes fixed on her phone, her mind miles away.

Oh, and fucking midtown. Predictably, a mess. The crowds are suffocating, swallow her in. She winds her way through floods of blank-faced tourists and holiday shoppers who wield big, colorful bags of stuff they don't need.

She arrives early at Bergdorf Goodman. As always, the place bursts with elegant objects. She takes a quick spin through bags and jewelry. The names of the featured designers are familiar, for better or worse, part of her vernacular—Balenciaga and Bottega Veneta and Céline and Goyard. She and her sister and mother have these bags, as do many of her clients. Thousands of dollars for an unremarkable tote just because of the name on it, because of the message it sends. Women swaddled in dark clothes bend over glass cases and all but salivate, drape handbags over their shoulders and pout fishlike into mirrors.

She does just what she knows she shouldn't do. She walks through the fine jewelry area of the main floor, back to the Kentshire section, and as she does, her heart picks up speed. She hasn't been back since that afternoon she came here with Asad. She tried on several rings, but she knew right away which one was her favorite, an antique cushion-cut diamond flanked by two emeralds, set on a thin rose-gold band. Asad beamed, took the clerk's card.

"Can I help you with something?" the woman behind the counter says.

"No, thank you," Smith says, shrinking away. "Just looking."

She snakes through the clusters of people and heads for the escalator. Since she was a little girl, she's always loved a good escalator ride, that moment when you must precisely time your first step so as not to stumble, the subtle thrill of being lifted, of seeing exactly where you are going, the more gradual ascent. Sally preferred the efficiency of the elevator, of being boxed in, of pressing a simple button and being shot up toward the sky.

Smith steps off on the seventh floor and wanders the home section. She winds through the maze of pristine items, pausing to finger the fine linens and towels, to study the delicate china patterns on display.

The small books section has always been her favorite. Bitsy raised the girls to revere books. From a young age, Smith and Sally knew how important it was to read everything, to stay flush with exquisite words, to have poetic sentences in the ear at all times. Grammar? Oh, a must. The English education at Brearley was top-notch naturally, but Bitsy did a little extra grammar work with them on the side after school. Bad grammar was a pet peeve and she made sure that her girls felt the same way.

Many evenings of their childhood, even through those demanding years of high school, the three of them would climb into Bitsy's big bed after dinner. More often than not, Thatcher was still at the office or entertaining a client, but this worked well because it was Anderson girl time. They read together for at least thirty minutes. For their birthdays each year, Bitsy always bought three copies of the books she deemed good enough and interesting enough for the girls. The tradition dates back to when they were toddlers. Bitsy was keenly loyal to the Corner Bookstore on Madison, where she knew the owner. They would lie there, side by side, reading the same book, and when they were all finished, they would discuss it. Sally seemed to *love* every book. Smith was always more critical, noting inconsistencies in the prose, flaws in pace and tone.

For Smith's birthday this year, it was *Let's Bring Back: The Lost Language Edition: A Collection of Forgotten-Yet-Delightful Words, Phrases, Praises, Insults, Idioms, and Literary Flourishes from Eras Past.* Many of the sayings in the book are ones Bitsy already uses, words and expressions Smith and Sally love to mock her for using. *Mom, you can't say things like bezonian*—"rascal"—*or bitchfoxly*—"woman of the night"—*and expect us to understand.*

In the past few months it's become something of an elaborate inside joke, a secret language, a competition. Which Anderson girl can pepper her sentences with the greatest number of antiquated gems? Smith has had grand plans to load up her wedding speech with perfectly plucked phrases. That is, if she gets around to actually writing it.

"Smith!"

The sound of her name snaps her back to consciousness. A dark-haired woman waves wildly from the entrance of the children's shop. Who is this? The woman, who's pushing a stroller, is only vaguely familiar. It takes her a moment to place her, but it's Francesca Slade, a classmate from Brearley. She hasn't seen her since Talia, another Brearley girl, got married five years ago.

"It's been *years*!" Francesca says, leaning over and capturing Smith in a hug. The hug is awkward, in no small part due to the fact that Fran (as they used to call her back in the day) is hugely pregnant. "Thank God for Facebook! I'm not sure I would've recognized you. You look so *good* as opposed to my fatty self. Twins, actually! We find out the sex in a few weeks and I'm gunning for girls after this tiny monster," she says, pointing to a towheaded toddler boy in her stroller.

Smith knows his name. Cooper. She shouldn't know his name, but she knows many random things about many people she doesn't actually know because of social media.

"What's Sally up to these days? Wait, don't tell me. Facebook trivia. A doctor, no? I've got to say that surprised me. You always struck me as the straight arrow and she always struck me as the rather bohemian one."

Is this a slight? Is she saying that Smith's work is bohemian? What does this even mean?

"Funny how things happen, huh?" Smith says. "She's getting married this weekend. I'm here for her final fitting. Pretty crazy."

"Oh, how wonderful! I got my dress here too, but that feels like eons ago. I swear having kids totally *fucks* the flow of time. I know, I know, this little guy's going to say *fuck* at his preschool interviews. I've got to watch it. I literally cannot remember my life before it was overtaken. I'm not complaining because obviously all of this madness is the best thing that's ever happened to me even if my body's a disaster and my husband doesn't want to come near me . . . oh wait, I *am* complaining. Anyway, I'm here trying to get a little early Christmas shopping done because you know how nutty this season can be. They actually have *toys* here, which I never knew, and they aren't quite as hideous as some of the others. I swear we spent this small fortune decorating this chic home and now it's in tatters and cluttered with rainbow plastic crap and all of our antique furniture has these hideous foam edges. I'm sure you know all about that with your organization work? I'm sure you see a whole lot of 'me's. I was just telling Michael last night that I've become a *type*, or an archetype maybe? Smith, I swear to God I was going to be the one holding out, working all night at Goldman, doing Sheryl Sandberg proud, leaning way waaaaay in, but it just hit me when I saw this little face. The instinct was all it took. And now look at me." She finally stops speaking, breathless.

"You look fantastic," Smith says. A generous and harmless lie. Yes, Fran looks puffy and tired, and yes, her monologue just now bordered on manic narcissism, but still, she looks *happy*, or is this just a grass-is-greener thing where here is Smith, in the best shape of her life by far, wanting something other than to fit into her skinny jeans?

"Where's the wedding?"

"At the Waldorf," Smith says. "The Starlight Roof."

"Oh, I love that space! So Gatsby!"

Smith went with Sally to look at several venues around the city, and though Sally fell in love with a raw loft space in SoHo, Bitsy argued fervently for the Waldorf, and it didn't take much for Sally to acquiesce. Sally has always been a pleaser, and good about picking her Bitsy battles, and it wasn't worth it to alienate her mother when she would be the one doing so much of the planning. They sent out save-the-dates almost a full year in advance, a thick ivory card with a black and white photograph of the Waldorf from 1971, the year their parents were married there.

"It was *so* good to see you," Fran says, taking Smith's hands. "I'm going to track you down."

"Do," Smith says. "But I must run. Can't be late for the bride. Good luck with everything."

Smith walks the length of the hall, pausing by the sleek restaurant, which hums with fashionable New Yorkers. They came here that day after they looked at rings downstairs. Asad wanted to celebrate.

Smith keeps walking and ducks into the bridal salon. The small space is hushed and smells faintly of lavender. A despondent-looking blonde perches behind a silver-leafed desk, her face lit by a computer screen. Wedding dresses hang near the entrance and Smith sifts through them. Plastic crinkles between her fingers. It's a mournful, mocking sound. She never got to the point of buying her own dress, but she'd found it in a tiny boutique. It was vintage, made of the most exquisite Chantilly lace, and had a high neck. Somehow, it was both demure and sexy. She'd wear this to the American party in the spring, and for the celebrations in Pakistan, she imagined honoring his family by doing a proper henna ceremony and donning traditional garb, one of the heavily embroidered red, pink or purple *shalwar kameez* she saw on Pinterest accompanied by heavy gold jewelry.

When Smith looks up, she sees Bitsy and Sally walking toward her. Their arms are linked and they laugh about something. Their laughter carries melodically and Smith feels a pang of envy at their lightness. They don't see her at first, but when they do, their faces change. Is it pity that fills their eyes? Is Smith seeing things?

"You don't look half as hungover as Mom described," Sally says, giggling her Sally giggle, kissing Smith on the cheek.

The three of them are ushered to the back of the boutique and into a small fitting room. The lights are dimmed slightly and a single votive candle flickers on a glass table. Three small bottles of water wait. In the hall, deferential staffers flutter around, speaking in ominous code, ducking their heads in.

Inside the room, the dress waits, a stationary cloud of white shrouded in thick plastic. A seamstress carefully removes the dress from its wrapping.

"Beautiful," she mutters reverently, studying it, running her hand down its length.

Sally is quiet and careful in her undressing and something like somberness fills the room. Sally has always been more modest than Smith and now she stands here in her underwear and strapless bodice, arms crossed over her chest. Smith catches a glimpse of Sally's body. Thin, but curvy.

"I can't believe *this is it,*" Sally says sweetly, staring at herself in the mirror, straightening the waistband of her white underwear. "I'm getting *married*?"

Her voice is high and cartoonish, grating.

The seamstress helps Sally into the dress. It's enormous, princess-like, precisely what Smith predicted her sister would pick. The seamstress zips it from behind.

It fits. It fits perfectly. There is no gushing, no giddy prancing around.

Just reverential silence.

"You look gorgeous," Smith hears herself say.

She would say this anyway, but it also happens to be true. Her sister looks like a dream—tiny waist, antique lace trimming a bodice that reveals the slightest peek of cleavage, a full ball skirt fit for fairy-tale twirling. It's now that Smith feels traces of what she's been waiting to feel, hoping to feel: happiness for her sister. But this happiness swiftly gives way to an almost eerie strangeness. There's something deeply disorienting about this moment and Smith feels light-headed, confused. They've always looked so much alike, have often been mistaken for twins. And so here she is, her mirrored self, in a wedding gown. It's like a preview of her own bridal self, a cruel image of what might have been.

"Pretty as a picture," Bitsy croons, clasping her hands in front of her.

"So, that's it?" Sally says to the seamstress. "It's finished. No more changes?"

The seamstress nods. Smith can detect disappointment in her sister's questions, a touch of defeat. After a year of hunting for the dress, for the location, for the perfect details to capture them as a couple, the day is almost here. Which also means it's almost over.

"You know my friend Callie from Princeton?" Sally says, stepping gingerly out of the dress. "She said that she felt this slight depression the day after her wedding. I can see that. This has all been kind of *fun*."

This makes no sense at all to Smith, but she bites her tongue. What Smith was looking forward to was what came after the wedding. The real-life part. Nights on the couch in sweatpants watching good television and bad television too, passionate debates about current events over fine restaurant meals, the milestones of pregnancy and childhood witnessed wondrously side by side.

At the front of the salon again, the three of them float saccharine good-byes to the girl behind the computer. Another bride waits with her mother now, stars in her young blue eyes.

"How's the registry looking?" Bitsy asks. "Tell me at least one thing is going smoothly."

Sally smiles, turns to Smith. "Mom's all bent out of shape because she was so proud of herself for using her French and taking over the table linens from the wedding planner and they came in wrong. Also, a few people have replied saying they are bringing uninvited plus-ones. I told her I don't give a shit, but she's got a nasty little bee in her bonnet."

"It's just that the French chickadee at the linens company is such a ne'er-do-well. We had the linens shipped from Paris, and they came in weeks ago. I just opened them and they're all wrong. For the love of God, they're *rose*. We ordered *blush*. And this little fluffer's bending my ear telling me that she actually prefers rose to blush—some nonsense about a new color trend. And then I'm sitting there, ostensibly on hold, but I can hear her, on her other phone, beating her gums in French for five solid minutes about this wretched cheapskate first date she's been on. I really don't understand your generation, girls. All those castles in the air. Tell me, whatever happened to privacy? Whatever happened to not airing dirty laundry in public? Whatever happened to maintaining some modicum of propriety?"

Smith nods, but her mind is miles away.

"Are you okay?" Sally says, grabbing Smith's arm.

"Not really. I found out this morning that Asad and his wife are having a baby."

She looks up at her mother and sister, waits for a reaction, some sympathy. Sally appears genuinely shaken, but a smile spreads over Bitsy's face. A fucking *smile*.

"Whaaat? I apologize if news of a *baby* makes me happy, dear," Bitsy says in a furious whisper.

"Are you kidding me, Mom? He was the love of my life and he dumps me with no explanation and I'm supposed to be tickled that he's about to become a father? Really?"

"Look, sweets, I know you've been having a rotten time, but you and I both know very well that he wasn't the love of your life. You took up with him to piss Daddy off. And it worked. You made your point, but don't pretend this fellow was something he wasn't. You're better than that."

"Am I?" Smith says, fixing her mother with a glare.

"Yes, you are. Look, I can't do this right now. I'm going to head home and fix a stiff one and take another stab at that darned seating chart. You girls should go have a cocktail and catch up. It'll be nice; you can commiserate about how insensitive your well-meaning mother is," Bitsy says, kissing both girls on the cheek, pointing to the restaurant.

"I'm game," Sally says, shrugging.

"Sure," Smith says, eyeing the restaurant. It's the last place in the world she wants to go.

Sally threads her arm through Smith's and leans on her shoulder, just like they used to do as girls walking down the sidewalks of their neighborhood. It's a small thing, and a familiar one too, and Smith feels it, *it*, that ineffable closeness that's evolved over time. The physical proximity to her sister is comforting and she finds herself longing for simpler times. Sally smells, as she always has, like lemon and sugar.

5:14PM

"What do you mean, you knew?"

"Bottled or tap?" the waiter asks. Smith and Sally sit in the banquette by the window, giving Smith a sweeping view of Central Park.

"Fizzy water, please," Sally answers for them with her near-childish ebullience. In moments like this, it amazes Smith that Sally is an actual doctor. That she wears the white coat and sees patients.

"Good old fizzy water. I love that you still call it that," Smith says.

"A relic. I've held on to a few of them. 'Borella' is so much better than 'umbrella.' Yes, I'll read a maz-agine during my pedicure. Sure, I'll have a sprinkling of Parsabom on my penne. Even Briggs has begun to dip into the sacred Smith-Sally-Bitsy fictionary. It's pretty sweet."

"Your hair looks good," Smith says. "I like the color. It will photograph well. And the fringe of bangs suits you."

"Thanks," Sally says. "I know it's terribly clichéd to say this, but I want to look like myself, but the best version of myself. Does that make any sense?"

"Perfect sense," Smith says, but she's barely listening. It's hard to focus. She fiddles with her phone, forwards her life coach her e-mail exchange with Asad so they can talk about it later. "Sorry, just had to do one quick thing. I'm all yours."

Sally flashes a nervous smile. "Do you remember that night when Mom and Dad went out and I convinced you that we should cut our hair? Remember how we took the scissors into the bathroom and locked the door and that poor sitter—what was her name? Cristin? Crystal?—didn't have a clue and we cut each other's hair short and tried to curl it to look like Betty Boop? How hilarious was that?"

Smith laughs. She remembers the scene differently, as far less than hilarious. She can see them now, her parents coming through the front door after one of their countless charity events. Her father stumbling and mumbling, lubricated with alcohol, her mother sharp as ever. When Bitsy saw the girls, sheepish and freshly shorn, and the quaking sitter in the background, horror filled her eyes. And then Thatcher, catching on to the transgression, flipped in an instant from affable bow-tied banker to aggressive taskmaster. *What have you girls done? Was this your idea, Smith?*

"And what was our punishment?" Sally says. "An appointment at the salon at the Waldorf with her guy to remedy the situation. Unduly harsh."

Smith looks around the restaurant and suddenly remembers why she's been avoiding it. Memories fire at her, but her sister says something.

"I knew," Sally says quietly, looking down.

"Knew about what?" Smith says, staring at her sister.

"About Asad and the baby."

Smith feels her entire body stiffening. Looks down at her lap, back up at her sister, who's visibly troubled. What the fuck?

"What do you mean, you knew?"

"Smith, calm down," Sally says in a whisper. "You know very well that Asad and I have tons of friends in common from med school. I heard a month or so ago and I didn't see what the point was in telling you. You're working so hard to move on, Smith. Why would I tell you this and set you back? You're doing so well."

"I'm doing so well? *This* is doing so well?" she says, aware of the inappropriate decibel level of her voice. "I'm coming apart at the seams, Sally. I went on a bender with a guy I barely know last night. I'm hungover as shit and this restaurant is about to make me sob because the last time I was here was with him and I'm doing so well? And who the hell are you to decide what I should know, Sally? I know you are the younger and wiser one, but don't you think I might like to know that the man I came very close to marrying is having a baby with someone else? Shit, Sally, what is this? I loved him. I was converting to *Islam* for him. He and I were talking about kids and now you're all carrying on like it was *nothing*, like what we had was a figment of my imagination."

"*Smith*," Sally says, dragging out the one syllable of her name. "*Smiiiithhhh*. I know you loved him. I know how hard the breakup was, but I also felt that it would be incredibly hard for you to hear this piece of news. You must see that it was a tough call for me. That I was trying to protect you."

"I don't need you to protect me," Smith says, wondering if this is true. Maybe her sister is right, her sister is always right, sunny Sally who has always gotten it. Maybe this is exactly what she needs, someone to protect her, a paternalistic shield from this unfurling nightmare. She feels sick. She sips her water but can barely swallow. "I can't believe you didn't tell me. We used to tell each other *everything*."

A tear snakes down Smith's cheek, but she doesn't look away. Instead she looks right at Sally. And here it is, a staring contest like old times. They used to sit on their twin beds, cross-legged, hair back in ponytails, all business, and do this very thing. They'd keep it up for a long while, but invariably it was Smith who looked away first. Sally was better, faster, more determined.

"Speaking of which, why didn't you tell me about this guy? Mom says he might come to the wedding?"

"Is that a problem?" Smith says, studying her sister's face for judgment.

"Don't be silly," Sally says sweetly. "I want you to have a date. Who is he? Do you like him?"

"I think I do, but then again I have no idea what's up and what's down. I'm not sure it matters if I like him because he hasn't called and I doubt he will and it's all just fitting. I feel *sick*."

"I'm sorry," Sally says. "I didn't mean for this to be this way. Especially this week."

Especially this week? What does that mean?

"Me too," Smith says, pushing her chair away from the table. "I'm really not feeling well. I think I'm just going to go. I have to pick up some things for your out-of-town bags."

"Let me come with you?" Sally says.

"No," Smith says. "I need to be alone right now." Her hands shake as she pulls out her wallet and fishes a twenty from the billfold. She attempts to flatten it on the table under her palm, but the wrinkles remain. She leaves it on the table and slips through the front door, sneaks through the elevator doors that are closing.

Outside, it's cold. The streets swarm with people and cars. She heads east to Lexington Avenue, to the Container Store. Before entering, she admires the place as she always does, her big glass haven, where he asked her to marry him.

She didn't expect anything, not that night. She met him after a long day of surgery in front of New York Hospital, where he worked. He wore his scrubs. It was a breezy night and they walked west. He led her down Lexington. It was late and the store was closed, but Smith noticed the flicker of candles inside. Asad walked to the entrance and motioned to a guard who waited inside. When the guard unlocked the glass front door, Smith knew. He proposed in the kitchen aisle, and per Asad's very particular instructions, after she said yes, the guard played Peter Gabriel's "In Your Eyes" from an old-school boom box just as John Cusack did in *Say Anything,* which was her favorite movie, quickly his too. The ring, the one they'd spotted at Bergdorf's just weeks before, fit perfectly, and she stared at it through tears as he changed out of his scrubs in the men's room. Asad thanked the guard and escorted Smith to Daniel, a famous French restaurant, where a champagne-soaked seven-course tasting meal awaited them. It was, without question, the best night of her life.

When Smith enters the store, the memories of her engagement night fill her. It's the first time she's been back here since the breakup. She's had items shipped or messengered, but these weren't options this time. She walks to the customer service desk, aware of her heightened anxiety.

"I'm picking up an order for Anderson," she says to the clerk, who then disappears into the back. The clerk, a heavyset, kind-faced woman named Dawn, returns empty-handed.

"I'm sorry, I have nothing back there for you. Could it possibly be under another name?"

Another name. For a split second, she thinks, *Rahman*. Smith Rahman. Almost. Shit, she needs to get a grip.

"No, it's Anderson. A-N-D-E-R-S-O-N. I called last week. It's one hundred translucent take-out containers. The polyethylene ones, BPA-free? I can find the product number on my phone if that would be helpful."

"No, I know what you're talking about. Let me look it up on the computer and see if we have some of those in stock here in the store," she says, tapping away at the keyboard, squinting at the monitor, shaking her head. "No, it looks like we have only eighteen. Would you like those?"

"Dawn, I'm sorry, but I ordered these items and I *need* them today and I'm not leaving the store without them, so you better come up with them, okay?"

The woman looks up from the computer, something like fear in her eyes. "Ma'am, it's showing that we have eighteen in stock upstairs if you'd like those. I can run and get them for you."

Smith feels her pulse quickening. "I do not fucking want eighteen. I want *one hundred*. Like I ordered. I need to fill these boxes with *jelly beans,* Dawn, for my sister's wedding, which is *this* weekend, and it will take me some *time* to fill these and I *need* them now. Do you realize how often I shop at this store, Dawn? How many clients I send here? Can I talk to your manager about this?"

Smith barely recognizes herself in this moment. This isn't who she is; she's kind and patient, slow to anger, but here she is being one of those abominable people who lash out. She's ashamed, but also notes that it feels strangely good to be standing her ground after being so acquiescent all the fucking time with her parents and her sister and her clients.

And yet she feels for poor, visibly shaken Dawn, Dawn who looks like she might cry, Dawn who nods and disappears. Smith knows very well that this is not about Dawn and missing plastic containers.

A man comes out soon after, clutching a stacked tower of take-out containers, which he hands over the counter. "Ms. Anderson, I'm so sorry about the mix-up with the order. I would like you to take these today, and we will have the rest shipped to you by Wednesday at the latest *all free of charge*. I know you are a good customer of the store and I apologize for this."

Smith takes the containers, containers that cruelly remind her of the Chinese food she scarfed last night; hugs the tower to her chest; and feels her eyes pooling with tears. "Thank you," she says. "I'm so sorry. Truly sorry. Wednesday will be just fine."

Back on the street, tears begin to roll down her cheeks as she heads for home. Poor Dawn. What was Smith thinking yelling at the unsuspecting woman like that? She was just doing her job.

As she walks, she pulls out her phone and runs her fingers along the shattered screen. She types in her password and begins going down the rabbit hole, checking everything—her calendar and her e-mail. Her Facebook, Instagram and Twitter. She looks up Tate and sees that he's spent the day exploring Battery Park City. On his Instagram feed is a photo of an old man with a cane and a mother pushing a double stroller. He also took a black and white photograph of a graffiti-laden wall. She remembers more from last night. Snippets of endearing booze-soaked wisdom. *Maybe it's clichéd, yes, it most definitely is, but I think the ugly and hard things are sometimes the most enthralling.*

The social media anesthetic is swift in taking hold; her mind grows blurry and numb. She nearly walks straight into oncoming traffic.

She checks everything again and again, to fill the empty space that's starting to expand within her, a deep, throttling loneliness. There's nothing from Tate. Not a thing. Two days ago she was fine with not having a date to the wedding, it didn't faze her, but now she dreads the idea of going alone. And she doesn't just want to go with anyone. She wants to go with *him*.

Fuck.

She walks on. At Central Park South, she stops for some reason and finds herself staring at the carriage horses lined up to take tourists through Central Park. They're dolled up, these immense and gorgeous animals, festooned with foolish jewel-toned feathers. She read an article once about these horses, about how poorly they are treated, and yet it's an industry that booms because people are blind to the truth and the misery, forking over bundles of cash and climbing on, settling into the clichéd fairy-tale carriage, eager for a tour of a heralded place that's shiny and new, a small adventure, but at what expense?

These horses break her heart.

Their eyes are dark and scared and sad. They wait because it's all they can do.

6:32PM

"Thank you for being human."

A nondescript brown paper bag sits outside her apartment door. She lifts it and is hit with the familiar, sweet scent of oatmeal raisin cookies from Levain, her all-time favorite bakery. She hasn't had one in ages. Slipped inside of the bag, Smith finds a sheet of Sally's new stationery with her soon-to-be triple-barreled name—*Sally Anderson McGee*. Words are scribbled on it. *I'm sorry, S. Forgive me.*

It's not that simple, Smith thinks tersely, walking inside, tossing the bag to the floor, grabbing a pen from her purse. This gesture is so incredibly Sally. The last thing Smith wants is to stew unnecessarily, but what happened at the restaurant hurt her. She saw a different side of her sister. Maybe the wedding's getting the best of her, she hopes that's all, but that Sally across the table was distant and distracted. Smith flips over the card and writes her own words: *Maybe you haven't noticed, but I don't eat these anymore*. She contemplates dropping them outside her sister's apartment just next door but stops herself. She doesn't want to be that person. She takes the cookies to the kitchen and places them on the counter and then retreats to the bedroom, where she changes into her Monday evening uniform: a ratty old Yale sweatshirt and a pilled pair of sweats she's had forever. She sits in her bay window, staring out at the treetops, and waits to dial her coach.

Talking to you, I'm sensing a power-strip metaphor, Laura said during their consultation call almost a year ago. *So many people plugging into you for a charge—your parents, your sister, Clio, your clients—but what do you do to charge yourself, Smith?*

Smith was dumbfounded. More than thirty years on this planet and it took this woman all of thirty minutes to come up with this? Who cared if she charged a hefty fee and she would never meet her in person? Worth. Every. Penny.

Smith did wonder at first if it was a bit strange to have these sessions by phone when she lived in a city teeming with therapists and experts and coaches, but she decided that there was something nice, and deserved, about curling up at home for these therapeutic calls. And she knew herself, too; she'd be more open and less self-conscious on the phone.

But what was Smith doing to charge herself, Laura wanted to know. Then, *nothing*. She was working eighteen-hour days, racing between clients, sleeping poorly, eating crap and gaining weight, trying and failing to hold it together after her breakup with Asad. Everyone was worried. *She* was worried. Worried enough to hunt down a life coach. Even ever-optimistic Bitsy suggested she might want to "see someone" and ever-practical Dr. Sally suggested she might want to "take something," but Smith wasn't going to be yet another New Yorker racing for therapy or pills for what she honestly believed was a fleeting moment of crisis. She was stronger than that.

But even Smith knew she needed help from someone objective outside her circle, someone who could offer some guidance. She got Laura's name from a client and though initially very skeptical, she did copious research about life coaching and found its core beliefs compelling: that people are essentially creative, resourceful and whole, that there is no assumed pathology. She got over her skepticism quickly and found its core beliefs compelling: that people are essentially creative, resourceful and whole, that there is no assumed pathology. She learned that the job of a coach is to listen deeply, ask powerful questions, challenge assumptions and evoke wisdom that the client holds inside herself within a space of nonjudgment, that coaching is an empowering, supportive process with tangible, transformative results. All of this was right up her alley. Still, Smith was a bit dubious and concerned. The profession was new and still largely unregulated. Anyone could call herself a coach without formal training, and "life coaching" had a bad name for many. You had to be careful.

Before their first session, Smith meticulously filled out an Intended Goals Sheet and a questionnaire, with questions like: *If someone was giving a speech about you fifteen years from now, what would you want them to say? Who would you be and what would you do if no one was looking?*

Laura told her she could just jot notes, but Smith treated it like a proper assignment and wrote and wrote, even editing her answers as if she were to receive a grade at the end.

Smith picks up the phone, stares for a moment at the receiver and then looks around her quiet home. She dials and Laura answers, beginning the way she does each week.

"How has the week been since we last spoke? Were you able to complete this week's goals?"

Smith doesn't answer.

"I'm noticing some silence, Smith. Can you try to explain that silence to me?"

Smith laughs. She *laughs*. The sound of her own laughter is a foreign trill, a near-cackle, edged in almost cartoon darkness. "I'm sorry, Laura.

I don't even remember what my goals were. Things kind of fell apart in the last twenty-four hours. I don't even know where to start."

"Start at the beginning. And remember, Smith, that this is a safe place, that I am granting you permission to not know the answers. There are no gold stars here. Just give me the quick and dirty version of what happened. No editorializing."

Safe place. Permission. Gold stars. These words, usually fine, seem like jokes today. What is she doing spending good money on this nonsense? Does she really think that speaking to a stranger on the other side of the country will fix this shit?

Smith forces a deep breath and begins. "Okay. Well, first I woke up on my bathroom floor in a bridesmaid dress I don't remember putting on. I'd gotten sick from drinking late into the night with a guy. Then I apparently e-mailed Asad in the middle of the night telling him how I didn't need him anymore and he responded telling me that he and his wife are pregnant, which was like a dagger. Oh, and Clio's moving out to live with Henry and I just got in a fight with Sally. Apparently, she's known about Asad having a baby and didn't tell me. I haven't written *a word* of her wedding toast. Oh, and for the grand finale, I made a poor woman cry at the Container Store a few hours ago. It's been a day."

"Wow. That's a lot, isn't it?"

Yes, Laura. It's a lot.

"Well, I'm hearing a lot of things coming up in what you're saying. Clio moving out. Your ex having a baby. Your sister getting married. All of these, Smith, are *huge* triggers. And triggers make all of us do things that might feel very out of character. I invite you to get quiet, to breathe and acknowledge yourself for everything you're dealing with, because it's a lot. Remember, it's okay to give yourself a little room for imperfection. Be *where you are* in terms of whatever feelings are coming up. You know that expression 'Wherever you go, there you are'? Just be there. Can you tell me what you'd like to focus on, what's most important to you to look at and get curious about today?"

Smith pauses. She's hit with an image. She and Tate on the couch, her legs draped on his lap.

"I told him a secret," Smith says.

"Who?"

"The guy."

"Who is this guy, Smith?"

"I went to Yale with him. I didn't know him that well then. We didn't run in the same circles."

"And you told him something, Smith? A secret? Are you willing to tell me what you told him?"

A secret. That's what it was, what it is, though it hasn't felt like a secret because she hasn't been thinking about it, about the fact that she's been hiding something from her family, from the world, even from herself.

"I had an abortion freshman year of college," Smith blurts out.

"Thank you for trusting me with that information," Laura says. "How did it just feel to tell me that, Smith?"

"I don't know. Kind of scary, I guess."

"It makes sense that it was scary. And did you tell anyone when it happened? Who was there to support you?"

"Just Clio," Smith says. "I barely knew her, but somehow I knew she was the person to tell."

It was Clio who asked if Smith might be pregnant, who walked with her to the pharmacy to buy the test, who waited outside the bathroom stall in the dorm and guarded the door so no one else would come in. It was Clio who sat with Smith on the bottom bunk in their closet-sized bedroom while a stunned Smith cried. It was Clio who listened, not a flicker of judgment in her steady blue eyes, as Smith marched rationally through her options and concluded that she would end the pregnancy. It was Clio who walked with her that damp morning to her appointment at the clinic and waited in the grim, fluorescent-lit waiting room for it to be over. It was Clio who hovered without intruding in the days, weeks, and years that followed, always asking if Smith was okay.

"How do you think you knew that, Smith, that Clio was the best person to support you?" Laura says.

"I don't know," Smith says. "I just knew."

From the moment Clio walked through the door of their dorm that first day, Smith sensed that there was something special about her. Bitsy and Thatcher were quick to judge when Clio arrived all alone, with no parents and few belongings.

Smith and her parents were already settling in the dorm. Bitsy was all aflutter, unpacking things Smith had urged her not to buy. Throw pillows and silver picture frames and bedding far too fine for a college kid. Thatcher paced in the background, huffing and puffing about sundry gripes, including that the dorms at Princeton were superior. When Clio walked through the door, Smith noticed how her parents' eyes drifted to her new roommate. Their judgment was conspicuous and embarrassing. Smith cringed when Thatcher asked Clio where her parents were, and even more so when Clio fumbled with her answer.

From the beginning, Smith felt an urge to protect her new roommate. Though it would take Clio several months to open up, it was immediately clear to Smith that this girl was a completely different breed from the girls she'd grown up with—that she'd been through hard times, that she'd survived something meaningful, that she had it in her to be a true friend. About all of this, Smith was very much right.

"She's always understood me better than anyone else. Far better than my own family. Not telling them was one of the best decisions I ever made. They would never have understood. Anderson girls are not the sort to get knocked up at eighteen. My father wouldn't speak to me for a week after I voted for Obama. Can't even fathom what my little freshman news would have done to him."

"It makes perfect sense to me that you didn't tell your parents, that you tucked it away. We've discussed how your parents cherish appearances, how you feel you must be Perfect Smith for them, right?

That sometimes you feel their support of you, financial and otherwise, hinges on you being a certain version of yourself?"

"Yeah," Smith says, thinking about this. "But it's exhausting, Laura. I live here in this apartment and I make sure not to upset them too much, but it's stifling. It's not healthy. And I've been carrying around this secret for all these years and maybe it's affecting me more than I thought and I feel kind of *angry* that I've had to hide this. And now Asad's having a baby. I was so stunned this morning. I literally felt sick, but now I'm not as upset, which kind of surprises me."

"I know you know this, but in terms of the abortion, you experienced something many college girls experience," Laura says. "Not to diminish what you've been through, but it happens."

"Yeah, that's what he said last night. Tate. He was just so cool about it. He asked me something I can't stop thinking about now. He asked me if I ever regret my decision."

"Do you?" Laura says.

"I don't think so," Smith says, noticing a catch in her voice that suggests that even after all these years, the topic is an emotional one. "I don't regret it, but when I think about it, it does make me sad. That it happened at all. That I had to go through that. That I didn't even feel like I could tell anyone in my family. And I *want* a family, Laura, and sometimes I wonder if that was my chance, if I blew it. But most of the time I don't even think about it at all. I had convinced myself that I was over it, that it was just this thing in my past, but then there I was last night telling Tate. And then I wake up to this baby news. It's kind of uncanny."

"Why do you think you told him?"

"Vats of alcohol?" Smith says, laughing, but her laughter quickly tapers. "I don't know. It just came out. There's something about him."

What is it, though? A lack of pretense, for one. Tate's been through hard things and he's honest. She's never seen a man be that vulnerable. Asad was a stoic and Smith thought she liked that, his macho toughness, but now she's not so sure. Tate was sweet last night, endearing and *open,* and Smith realized at some point in the night that she'd stopped trying to be her best self and was just herself, struggling and insecure about certain things. And, yes, the alcohol certainly pushed her along, but she just felt like even if she didn't see this guy again, she wanted him to *see* her, to know something about her. She felt safe.

"He was so open with me about his own life and I guess I just felt comfortable?"

"*Yes.* You felt comfortable. I want to hear more about that. Who were you being in that moment you told him, Smith?"

Who was she being? She was being an idiot. She was being everything she isn't—messy, carefree. But she was also being herself, the self she doesn't usually let people see, the self she's worked so doggedly for all of these years to control, to box up.

"Someone who was free? Imperfect? Alive?" Smith says, the words just tumbling from her.

"Exactly," Laura says. "Thank you for being *human.* How are you feeling right now?"

Smith takes a breath and thinks about this. She's been jittery all day, nauseated, on the brink of tears. Flitting between exhaustion and confusion and disappointment. But she feels a bit different now.

"I feel vulnerable," Smith says, well aware that she's using a word Laura loves. "I asked Tate to Sally's wedding and he said he'd come, but I haven't heard from him today and I'm feeling foolish and I don't know what's happening. I hate this. I'm just feeling stuck, Laura. He made some crack last night about me still being on the golden leash or something and I know he was joking around, but it didn't feel funny. I mean, let's be real: I'm living in the building where I spent my childhood; I've literally gone nowhere and suddenly, it seems the universe is intent on shoving my inertia in my face. I met with a client today and she was the most lovely woman who just lost her husband and she has three boys and we sat there going through her things and pictures and she's had this whole *life,* Laura, and it's obviously devastating that she's lost the love of her life, but I found myself oddly envying her because of all the things she's had. And then, lo and behold, I run into an old classmate from high school and she's pregnant and pushing a stroller and I felt it again . . . envious, like everyone is moving forward but me."

"I want you to know that I'm hearing you and I can sense how stuck you feel, but I feel it's my job to remind you how far you have come. Think back, Smith. Remember how hard it was for you to get out of bed when we first started talking? Remember how poorly you were treating your mind and body? Remember all the goals you set and how many you have met? You are absolutely moving forward, Smith, but it's work. It's not meant to feel simple. I'm proud of you. What I want you to tell me is what you want *right now*. Do you want this man to come with you to the wedding? Do you want to explore this person more, this *you* more?"

"I do," Smith says with a certainty that startles her. "But I'm not sure if it matters what I want."

"It absolutely does," Laura says. "Tell me. The wedding is this week, and how are you feeling about it, Smith? What are you most worried about?"

"My speech," Smith says quickly. "I want to say the right thing and be sentimental and funny and share the perfect anecdotes and I want my parents' friends to think I'm smart too, that just because I'm not the doctor it doesn't mean I'm stupid."

"Consider something," Laura says. "What if there is no right thing to say? What if the best thing you can do is get up there and be yourself and say something true?"

Smith thinks about this. What if it's this simple? "I guess I'm also worried that people will see me as the older spinster sister and that they will somehow notice just how much I'm struggling."

"And why would it be so bad for people to see that things aren't perfect in your life? What do you think would happen?"

What would happen? Smith can't answer this. "I don't know," she says.

"I don't know your parents. I've never met them and I don't need to. But I do know you pretty well at this point and I have tremendous confidence that you will stand up and tell the truth. *Your truth*. That's all you need to do."

"I just want him to come. I know it sounds so cheesy, but when I was with him last night, I was able to *let go* in a way I haven't in a really long time."

"That's not cheesy, Smith. That's wonderful. Now, I'm going to make a *request* for you to take really good care of yourself in the week ahead and I want to come to some agreements about what you need to give yourself permission for around the wedding weekend, okay?"

"Okay."

"First, if you are at the wedding and things get too hard, I want you to allow yourself to step away. It doesn't matter that you are the maid of honor. You are a person and you have needs and you must give yourself space if that feels right. And another thing: I'm going to ask you to try to limit your use of social media this week. You and I have discussed that there are certain times when it's not healthy for you and it makes you feel things you do not need to feel. This week is about *you* and not about all those people in your feeds. And with respect to Tate, would you perhaps give yourself permission to reach out to him after a certain time if you haven't heard from him? Just so you *know* what to expect this weekend, whether you will be there on your own or with a date?"

"I've never done that. I've always waited for the guy to call."

"How would calling him make you feel?"

Smith feels a slight smile coming on. "Vulnerable." That word again.

"Yup. I've said it before, but vulnerability is the true cornerstone to connection, Smith. We can't reach other people and be reached if we have our walls up all the time."

Smith clutches the phone and nods. "Intellectually, I know you're right, but walls sometimes feel easier."

"I know they do, and we've talked about how you were raised in a world of walls. Many of us were."

"Okay, I'll do it. I'll get in touch with him tomorrow morning if I haven't heard from him, just to find out about the wedding."

"That sounds like a solid plan to me," Laura says. "And listen, if you need to chat before our next session, please call me. Smith, I'm *here*."

"Thank you, Laura," Smith says, "but, one more thing."

"Yes?"

"I hurled a glass pitcher against a wall this morning. I've never done anything like that in my life. It kind of scared me."

A brief stretch of silence gives way to Laura's laughter. "Progress, I tell you," she says.

When they hang up, Smith feels a surge of motivation and positivity. She stretches her arms overhead and stands and lights a pine-scented candle on the coffee table in the living room. She turns on some holiday music, which, yes, she listens to year-round. Bach's Christmas Oratorio. The music fills the room, its dulcet tones stirring in her a deep nostalgia. For what? The halcyon hues of childhood? For those bright college days? She once listened to this CD in the library at Davenport College as she studied for finals.

In the kitchen, spotless once more, she brews some mint tea. Hydration is key, she remembers, and pours herself a tall glass of sparkling water too, and slices a small wedge of fresh organic lime on her monogrammed cutting board. Smith squeezes the lime and then drops it in, watches it sink to the bottom. She drinks the water fast, the bubbles burning her throat, and then pours another glass. She can do this.

She runs a bath. Laura is right; she must take good care of herself this week. She must avoid people and things that drain her and drag her down. As she waits for the tub to fill, she opens the cabinet and scans her aromatherapy collection, all those pristine bottles lined up. She chooses one, lavender, and squeezes a few drops into the water. She breathes deeply as the scent fills the room. She steps out of her clothes, folds them neatly and places them on the window seat, removes her underwear and bra, folds them too.

The bath does what it always does: it calms her. She towels off and lotions her body, pulls a comb through her hair. She wraps up in her robe and finds her Moleskine notebook. She will jot some notes for her speech.

Her phone buzzes. A text appears on her screen.

It's him.

Tate: You around?

A smile spreads across her face and her hands begin to tremble. She reads the two words again and again.

She can't bring herself to respond but sits there frozen.

Now she hears the lobby phone crooning in the distance, in the front of the apartment. She stands and runs to it. Picks up. It's Edwin the doorman.

"Ms. Anderson, I have a gentleman named Tate here to see you."

Panic fills her, but also something else. Joy. Relief. She looks down at herself, her bare body cloaked loosely in a robe. She runs her hands through her wet hair.

"Edwin, can you stall him for five minutes and then send him up?"

"Of course, Ms. Anderson."

Tuesday, November 26, 2013

TATE ROBERT PENNINGTON

All photographs are self-portraits.

—Minor White (1908–1976)

YALE ALUMNI MAGAZINE

SEPTEMBER/OCTOBER 2012

where they are now

PhotoPoetry for five million users—and counting

Tate Pennington '01 (economics) has, along with classmate Arun Vihal '01 (engineering), developed a digital application ("app") that marries Pennington's childhood passions of photography and poetry and Vihal's engineering skills. The passion project, PhotoPoet, was never meant to be more than that. Conceived by the classmates on a weekend surfing trip to Malibu, the product was built and rolled out to users by Pennington and Vihal in a swift six months. The application permits users to combine their own photography with classic and current poetry, poetry that is in the public domain and poetry that has been submitted by writers and curated by Pennington himself. The company, which boasts a social good component (for every hundred shares, $1 goes to PEN American Center and $1 goes to literacy programs in Vihal's home country of India), was recently purchased by Twitter for $40 million.

Yale: Why photography and poetry?

Pennington: When I was small, my parents gave me a Polaroid. I would take pictures of everything, including my family's feet under the dinner table. My father wanted me to be a baseball player, but I preferred staying inside and reading William Carlos Williams and Walt Whitman. No real training!

Y: Did you consider a photography or English major while studying at Yale?

P: I didn't really. I would have loved to major in these subjects, but I knew I needed to earn a paycheck. I went the more practical route of economics and thankfully I found my way back here.

Y: Why is PhotoPoet not just another app?

P: Well, I'm biased, but I don't think enough people have poetry in their lives. We live in a self-improvement and happiness culture full of fixes, but it's astonishing what a handful of meaningful words can do, particularly when combined with a telling image. I also think people have the desire to ***create*** things and this app allows that. There's also good quality control; you can't just post ***any*** words.

Y: Why the philanthropic component of the business?

P: Arun and I felt strongly about this. He and I have been privileged with a fine education and opportunities and share in a moral compulsion to help people who do not have the freedom we do to express ourselves, or the means to learn the way we've been able to.

Leon Truitt '81—This interview has been condensed and edited.

1:12AM

"A bucket of booze & some pussy."

A bucket of booze & some pussy will do you a world of good.

So went Jeff's opening line in the e-mail arranging tonight's guys' night.

They've been down here at the White Horse Tavern for hours now. Six of them, married and decidedly unmarried, scattered around the crowded bar, which is made from a single, seamless slab of mahogany.

There are white horses everywhere. Perching atop chandeliers, cantering along darkened ledges and shelves. The most prominent white horse stares down at them from the wall behind the mirrored bar. Tate looks up at it, this familiar creature, and drinks White Horse Whisky in the form of pity shots, one after the other, in an as-ever-futile effort to numb the hard shit. After five shots, he puts up his hand in protest, reminds the guys that his favorite poet, Dylan Thomas, *died* after downing a record shitload of whiskey shots—eighteen or something—at this very bar, but more shots arrive. He does them. Who is he to turn them down?

The guys take turns visiting the neon jukebox nestled next to the grandfather clock in the corner, to queue up songs old and new. Pharrell and Morrissey, Radiohead and Counting Crows.

Jeff, a friend from high school in St. Louis, always a stand-up guy, organized tonight, corralling a solid crew of his buddies for an evening of anesthetic carousing. Tate feels a vague gratitude for the gesture, but mostly he finds himself judging his company. His first instinct is that they are moneymaking dicks blitzed with beer and high on Investopedia lingo. It's all market-turmoil this and standard-deviation that, abandon rates and face values, and Tate feels a blaze of relief that he escaped this shit before it was too late. This could've been him. This *would've* been him. He's no better than these dudes.

Tate looks around, and though his mind is getting foggy, he fills with a mixture of awe and nostalgia. This place is a historic landmark for the alcoholic artist; it's been the cradle and grave of a slew of famous patrons he admires—Anaïs Nin, Jack Kerouac, Norman Mailer and Andy Warhol and Frank McCourt. Rumor has it that the night Belushi died in 1982, Dan Aykroyd arrived at closing time to shut the doors and buy the entire bar a round of drinks. That Thomas slipped into a coma and died days after his epic whiskey record is certainly a cautionary tale of sorts: Do not romanticize the boozing/creative life. It's just fantasy.

But now, for Tate, this fantasy feels oddly real. He can afford to fuck around and take pictures, live here in this swanky section of the city (his apartment, a newly renovated floor-through two bed, two bath, is, conveniently, around the corner) and still have plenty of dough left over to drink, and drink a lot. His mother is worried. She isn't even here to witness his aggressive unraveling, but maybe she can just hear in his voice how badly he's flailing. And she has every reason to be concerned, because he's always been the good boy, her good little Tater-Tot, straight-arrow sonny-son.

He didn't even drink much in college. Everyone around him seemed to be hammered at all hours, fumbling around with nascent freedom and acting like total delinquents, prideful about stupid shit and blank heads, but he derived a curious pride from being the clearheaded one, the one with no real interest in altering his mind. He dabbled, got drunk a couple of times, but was never sold. I mean, shit, it was *Yale* and he was supposed to piss it away? No thank you.

Now look at him: making up for lost time.

"Three o'clock," Jeff says now, gesturing to their right.

Tate looks. She is tall, thin, tan, blond and bland like the Barbie dolls his sister, Emily, used to decapitate when they were kids. The girl is with a flock of friends. They wear black, drink white wine, hypnotize themselves with glowing phones, tapping, scrolling, swiping, pouting their lips to snap pictures of themselves.

"Dude, they are *young*," Tate says. In their early twenties, maybe? Probably NYU girls. It's hard to remember being that young.

Jeff shrugs. "Just what you need. You're all up in your head about this Olivia shit and it's up to me as your friend to yank you down and shake you up and remind you that there are other snatches in the sea. It's my job, man. And you should appreciate that I'm working hard."

"I do appreciate it," Tate says, lifting his glass to clink Jeff's. "You want to know something crazy? I almost brought someone tonight. A girl."

Jeff rolls his eyes. "You almost brought a girl?"

"Yeah," Tate says. "Did my best but this chick's all class and I don't blame her because look at me, I'm a derelict at the moment. And look at this scene, man. She doesn't belong in a hole like this."

"Who the hell is she? There's not supposed to be a girl, Pennington.

It's supposed to be plural. *Girls,* okay? The last thing you need is another Olivia right now."

Tate considers this. Through this entire mess, Jeff has been the voice of reason, and maybe he's right. Maybe Tate's reaching for another girl because this is all that he knows. He was with Olivia since he was *twenty-one,* probably the age of those girls over there, and he doesn't even know how to be on his own. Maybe he needs to find out.

"Smith's the anti-Olivia, man. Cool as shit."

"Smith?" Jeff says, laughing. "Isn't that a dude's name? You swinging the other way now? This is all getting interesting. I always did wonder about the fitted jeans and the passion for frilly poetry. It's coming together now."

"It's her mother's maiden name, dipshit. I went to Yale with her but wrote her off as this blue-blood princess, but either I had it all wrong or she's changed. It doesn't matter, but she's pretty cool, man. And the things is, Jeff, I can't figure her out. We got sauced last night and went on this epic bender and ended up back at her place. This fancy pad in the San Remo, you know it? Gorgeous, two-towered prewar on the Upper West? She tried on a gown and showed me her drawer of sex toys but wouldn't kiss me."

"Fucking *tease,*" Jeff says. "And the last thing you need is another one of those after Olivia. I hope I don't have to remind you of all the times you called me frustrated that she was shutting you down and making you feel like a perv. You're a man. You need sex. Eye on the prize over there, okay?"

The sex thing with Olivia was tough. It certainly wasn't their biggest issue—the shock-and-awe infidelity takes the cake—but it was a problem. He wanted sex, sex of the frequent and adventurous variety, and she wanted almost no sex, sex of the boring, let's-check-this-off-the-list-and-keep-the-lights-off variety. He chalked it up to being married. *Maybe this is what happens when you're with someone for a while,* he decided, but his needs were his needs and he resorted to extra time in the shower and a smattering of surreptitious porn. None of it was good.

"Come to think of it," Tate says, gesturing toward the blonde at the bar, "she's not half-bad."

The words fall from him, but his mind is on Smith, who is leagues more beautiful than the girl. Smith was named by *The Rumpus,* the campus tabloid, as one of Yale's fifty most beautiful people, a detail they joked about Saturday at the tailgate.

It was just a few hours ago that he rang her doorbell and she stood there, hair wet and combed, face makeup-free, in nothing but a thin white bathrobe. Fucking sexy as shit, but he didn't say this. He played it cool even though it took every ounce of restraint. She flashed a coy smile and invited him in and they sat in her living room, the kind of living room old and important people have, and she kept apologizing for last night.

That wasn't me, she said again and again, and he wanted her to stop saying this. Finally, he cut her off.

Whoever that was, I liked her.

She said nothing at all about the wedding, so he brought it up, asked if he was still invited, and she nodded. He confessed that he had nothing to wear but his ill-fated wedding tux, which he kept as some masochistic memento, that he would shop for something new, and did she want to come? Again, she nodded. Then he asked her to get dressed and come downtown with him and he could see it in her eyes that she was considering it, that part of her wanted to go, but she said no, that she needed to work some more on her wedding toast and get some sleep. And then, like that, his buddy the doorman was hailing him a taxi.

"Look, Pennington, it's clear that I'm no expert on this, but methinks you need to take a breather from relationship garbage. You need to have fun. You need to shellac yourself in alcohol and bring hot girls home to that rad pad of yours. That Olivia screwed you up good and I get that it blows, but, dude, it's high time to move on. You need to kill that beer while I get you another and then you need to pick your pretty-boy head up and look around this joint and decide who it's going to be. Because I'm not letting you go home alone."

Tate laughs and obediently drinks up. His head is light, his body near numb. Maybe Jeff's right. Maybe he's fucking right. What he needs is a good mindless fuck. A release. To steer clear of melodrama and keep things simple, in and out, black and white. He takes the final sip and pushes the glass from him. It topples over. The sight of the glass rolling down the bar strangely delights him.

"Easy, tiger," Jeff says, sliding a fresh Guinness in front of him. "So, how's the new pad working out anyway? That place is ridiculous. Please tell me that you know that. I'm working my ass off and my place is nothing like yours. Not that I'm bitter."

"Good, man. Good. The place is good. Needs a little attention, but it's good."

Tate bought his new apartment sight unseen. There were pictures online and it looked fine. All he cared about was that there was an extra bathroom he could convert to a proper darkroom. He sent Jeff to take a look for him and the report was a solid thumbs-up, so he made an all-cash offer over the telephone. Initially, he'd planned to come and crash on Jeff's couch for a while, but then he worried he'd run back to her. Buying was a better anchor.

He looks over again at the cookie-cutter blonde and knocks back his beer. He knows better. He knows he's just short of blotto, that it's time to kill his tab and go. His mind is soft, scrambled. He needs sleep. But no. He will at the very least talk to her, prove some hazy, fucked-up point. He will extract her from her babbling minions. Butter her up with the dregs of his own Midwestern charm, which Olivia all but extricated. It will be good for him to do this, to man up, to follow through.

Go get 'em, Pennington, one of the asshole guys says as he stumbles over.

He's hovering now. It's almost too easy. Their bodies are already touching.

She's equally gone; her eyes are pickled and vacant. A ballerina, he hypothesizes. Maybe a model. Those legs. Twisting around and around.

Like magic, the other girls scatter. Tate and the nameless babe stand at the bar, leaning over its top.

Time blurs by. He switches back to whiskey.

"Dylan Thomas had eighteen whiskies here once. The record."

"Dylan Thomas?" she says.

"*Though lovers be lost love shall not*? The guy in the big black and white photo hanging in the other room?"

Nothing. Zip. Her face is blank and he finds himself thankful for her ignorance. What a fucking joke. They drink and drink, melt into each other.

"Let's get the hell out of here," he hears himself say.

She smiles yes, slides her hand into the back pocket of his jeans. He feels himself stiffening, adjusts his pants.

They waltz home, holding hands. The air is thick and it's fucking cold. He could use some California weather right about now. Her fingers are small, skinny things, noodle-like and limp. He yanks her along the charming, moonlit sidewalk he photographs by day, winds them around the corner through clusters of people pondering their next move. He leads her up his stoop, and once inside, he sees a package addressed to him. He grabs it, tucks it under his arm, and they seem to float up one flight. He trails her, his hand on her perfect ass. It takes a year to unlock the door.

"Beer?" he offers. The nameless girl accepts. He wonders if she has any idea that he has no clue what her name is, whether she'd care. In the kitchen, he pulls two bottles from the otherwise empty fridge, pops them open with his teeth. She's still in the other room, looking at his photographs, which lie around the room, some framed, some just prints on the floor.

"Did you take all of these?" she asks.

"Yes."

"They're beautiful."

That word. That fucking word.

"Who's that?" she says, pointing at the photo he shouldn't even have.

He hesitates. Keeps it simple. "A bride."

"She's beautiful."

The word again. Tate walks to the picture, studies it, studies her. Her dark tumble of hair and dark eyes. Abruptly, he flips the frame around to face the wall. He doesn't need her staring at him anymore. Yes, he's to blame for this pathetic flagellation. He slipped this in his suitcase on that last day in their apartment before he left for New York because it was one of his favorite portraits, told himself it was about art and not about denial. Even then, he knew this was total bullshit. When he finally unpacked days later, he saw it and cried like a baby and contemplated hurling it across the room, but instead propped it against a bare wall.

And now he's kissing the nameless girl. Her lips are minty. He takes her hand, leads her to the bedroom. They fall together onto his unmade bed. Disembodied, cartoonish laughter rises up from them like smoke. Hers, high-pitched and trilling. His, deep, forced, anger laced. She takes off her own clothes, sits cross-legged in the center of the bed, eyes glowing in the dark, waiting.

Her peach is bald, juicy, spread open.

He unbuckles his jeans.

A crashing sound comes from the other room. Tate startles.

"Shit. What was that?" she says, shooting up, pulling covers up over her, tucking her long, bleached hair behind her ears.

He jogs into the other room. The photograph of Olivia has toppled over, to the floor. Shattered. Shards of glass glisten everywhere. He kneels down. Glass pierces his palm, but he doesn't stop picking up the pieces. Even in the darkness, he can see the blood on his hand. He tastes it. Keeps going.

She stands behind him now, the nameless girl. Naked. Ready.

"Come," she says. "Do that later."

"You should go," he says abruptly, his voice firm, without looking up at her. He can see her face without seeing it. Humiliated. Confused.

Tate stays right where he is, hunched on the hardwood floor, frozen in place next to the broken picture of his pretty cunt of a wife—she's still technically his wife—his hands splintered with glass. He stays there until the front door slams, until it's clear he's alone. The guilt is immediate, a tidal wave. He feels sorry for this girl with her happy blond hair and black clothes and sweet body who had the shit luck of walking into that bar, of stumbling into him, his life, *this*.

He tells himself a little story: That she will be fine. She will get over this, this strange run-in with a fucked-up fuckup. She will meet her pretty little friends for pretty little brunch salads tomorrow and they will find a way to make it funny. And then she will do it all over again tomorrow night and the next. She will meet another guy. And another and another until one sticks and stays. And then he will marry her, this guy, and love her deeply and desperately, forget himself and follow her wherever she wants to go.

They will settle into a home, a life, a capital-F Future.

One day, she will turn to him and she will fucking say it as if she is saying something mundane like "We are out of milk": *I am not happy. I have not been happy. I want to be happy.*

And the guy, the foolish guy, will panic. He will promise to change, will promise to do anything, anything at all, to give her what she wants. But it will be too fucking late. What she wants, it will turn out, is something else, someone else. A brand-new life. She will move on to the Better Man, start over on page one. And the first guy will drink and drown and try but fail to fuck pretty girls, and get all cut up by shit like life and broken glass.

Fuck, he's a mess.

In the darkness, Tate stands. Through his drunken fog, he gazes down at the shards, shining like tears. He decides to leave them there. He pulls the photo from its matting, takes one last look, and rips it to confetti shreds. Sprinkles them, like ashes, over the hardwood floor.

In the bathroom, he blots the blood with the old Yale T-shirt she used to sleep in. He wraps his hand in photo-matting tape because it's all he has. He reaches down and grabs himself. He's no longer hard, but it doesn't take much and he's stiff again. He stands in the dark bathroom and strokes himself and thinks of her tonight. Shy in her bathrobe, her long legs crossed, traces of fear in her eyes.

He comes. He comes hard and fast.

Fuck it.

9:53AM

"I'm a grown man, Mom."

Tate shoots up in bed.

Dregs of his dream linger. In it, he stood naked in an endless cornfield just like the ones near his childhood home. The corn was high, flesh toned and phallic, ready to be harvested, and all he could see was the blue sky above. He heard a commotion, someone calling his name, and suddenly she was with him. She was a giant, all tits, twenty feet tall. She bent down to pick him up in her palm, stroked his head, his chest, his cock. He trembled, exploded, looked up and her face was a fitful hologram, old and new and old and new. Back and forth between Olivia and Smith. Both of them. Neither of them.

He lies back down. Stares up at the ceiling.

His head throbs. It occurs to him that he's probably still drunk.

He sits up, swings his legs over the side of the mattress, looks toward the window. It's light out. Morning. The bedside clock confirms this. It's not just morning but late morning. Almost ten.

Next to the clock, a Heineken bottle lies sideways, glowing green. Tate reaches out to feel the sticky surface, peers down its nose, decides there is a little left, one final drop. He holds the bottle up to his mouth. There is indeed a mini-swig remaining, enough to coat his tongue. The beer is sour now, punishingly warm.

He scans the room. He's lived here for a few months now and it looks as it did when he moved in. The walls are still bare, gray-white in hue. There are tiny holes in these walls, from the previous owner. Tate's real estate broker said they could make a fuss about this, have the walls patched before closing, but Tate told her he didn't really care. He just wanted to get on with his life.

He stands now, walks to the window, and peers out. There's still some snow on the streets. Shit, maybe he shouldn't have left California. Snow in November? His place is on the second floor, just above the ground. So close that he can see the tops of people's heads as they shuffle by, on their way to the coffee shop, on their way to work. Close enough that he can read the sinister headlines of their newspapers, see the bald spots beginning to come.

Tate turns around, peers back into his room. The bed floats in the center, a wide white square topped with a tangle of sheets he hasn't washed in weeks. On the other bedside table, he spots another beer, his bottle's twin, this one upright and full next to his little black leather bowl, a bowl full of matchbooks, names of bars printed on their backs. Relics of all the nights he's pissed away in the last few months.

She smoked sometimes. Said it was because she was anxious. Everything made her anxious—her work at the law firm, the nightly news, standard doctor's appointments, the traffic on the freeway. She kept a pack of Camel Lights tucked in her pocket at all times and Tate knew when she pulled one out that it was time to ask her what was going on. And he did this. He did this every fucking time. He asked. He listened. He talked her off a litany of ledges. And she seemed so genuinely thankful for him in these moments, these moments when she was crumbling and going dark. Maybe this is odd, but he found her most irresistible when her face was twisted with worry, when she really needed him.

After she passed the California bar exam, they traveled to Thailand and there was this one night where she started talking in her sleep. Just sat up, eyes closed, and started mumbling shit. That she never felt pretty enough, that her mother said it was a good thing she was smart. And she remembered none of it the next day, but it was the most brilliant clue, he thought, to what she needed, and so he told her all the time how beautiful she was. It was never a lie.

She was beautiful.

Is.

Was.

Fuck, that word again. The past tense haunts him. She never believed him when he told her this. She'd argue with him, tell him to stop lying, point to the evidence—pockets of cellulite on her thighs, the small bump on the bridge of her nose—but he wouldn't have it. She was not perfect, but she was stunning. He did all that he could to convince her of this, but in the end it wasn't enough. It seems she needed a different kind of affirmation in the form of an older, more powerful man. A knight in shining corporate armor to ride on into her desolate, document-strewn office and say: *You've been working so hard. Let's grab a drink.*

She told him exactly how it happened because he asked her to. Every detail, a dagger.

The phone rings now, sparing Tate from going further down the rabbit hole. The landline. This means one thing: it's his mother.

"Hello?" Tate says, finding a pair of pajama pants on the floor.

"Morning," she says. She calls every morning at this hour. He suspects it's because she's worried about him, wants to make sure he is awake and okay.

"Morning, Mom," he says.

"What's on tap today?"

"More of the same. I'll take some photos."

He doesn't mention shopping with Smith. His mother wouldn't approve. She's still holding out hope that he and Olivia will mend things.

"Do you think you should maybe find work, honey? To keep busy? I don't like the idea of you having all of this time on your hands."

"I'm pursuing photography, Mom. I consider it work."

The word grates. *Pursuing*. What the fuck does this even mean? It means showing up at B&H Photo and buying thousands of dollars' worth of cameras and lenses, most of which still sits in boxes and bags in the other room. His first camera, a Polaroid and an eleventh-birthday gift from his parents, sits on his bedside table.

"How was yesterday?" she asks.

"Like the days before it, Mom."

"Did you get my package?" she asks. She sends "care packages" every few weeks.

Her question jars his memory and he recalls the white package by the door downstairs, his name bold on the front. He brought it up but didn't open it.

"You can stop sending me underwear. I'm a grown man, Mom."

"Nonsense. You're more of a boy than ever. Just because you have money in the bank doesn't mean you're taking any better care of yourself. I bet you're still living out of a suitcase. I bet there is no food in your fridge. I bet you haven't done laundry in eons."

She knows him. She knows him well. And he bristles under the weight of this knowing.

He walks slowly toward the door, adjusts himself, feels that the cotton of his boxer-briefs is stiff. Shame fills him, but why the fuck should it? Tate stares at the mountain of laundry in the corner of the room.

"Why don't you let me come for Thanksgiving? I will spend a few days getting you settled and we can catch up. I want to lay eyes on you, son. And that fancy new place of yours."

"You and Dad are leaving for the cruise tomorrow. It's too late to cancel. And besides, you've been looking forward to it all year. You deserve it. Next year, Emily and Todd will be back from London and the baby will be here and we will all be together. This is your off year. And I need to try to do a thing or two on my own," Tate says. "Don't worry about me, Mom."

It's a foolish thing to say because he knows she worries, that she has always worried, that she's probably more worried now than ever. Just a year ago, his life was—*seemed*—settled. His company had been acquired and the money was due to come in, and he told his mother they'd probably have kids soon because this is what he hoped for. His mother was desperate for grandchildren. And it made him happy to make her so hopeful, her and his dad both. They were nothing but good parents, contented individuals who had an uncomplicated view of the world, a world that has been very good to them, giving them a son and a daughter both, hardworking kids who never caused much trouble. His sister, Emily, two years younger, lives in London with her husband. She is four months pregnant with their first child.

Olivia always loved Tate's mother, how she was always calling, always visiting, always sending packages. She said that when she became a mom, she wanted to be like Tate's mother. Her mother was okay but selfish, and she preferred Mrs. Pennington.

"Okay, but I just want you to be happy again, Tate," she says. She's been saying this at the end of every phone call.

"I know, Mom. And I will be."

It's what she deserves to hear. In truth, the words have him thinking. He was happy before, at least he thought he was, but maybe he took it for granted. He never came home from work at the start-up and said, *I am a happy guy*. He and Olivia never curled up in bed, kissed each other good night and said, *We're so happy, aren't we?* It doesn't seem like happiness is something you really talk about or think consciously about until it is threatened, slipping.

What would it take to be happy again? Tate's not so sure. He's bought this apartment. That's a step. A place of his own. A place he can transform as he likes. He can have lots of furniture or none at all. He can leave his dirty socks on the floor because there's no one to bug him. He can fill his fridge with alcohol and sausage. He can do whatever the fuck he wants. It is all up to him. But the thing that surprises him most, and maybe it shouldn't, is that the money doesn't seem to be making him happy. He became *rich* overnight and he figured this would cheer him up, but what were the fucking chances this would happen at the exact time that he lost his marriage? His hope is that it will just take some time to settle into this new normal, this life with funds and without Olivia, to embrace this Life 2.0, but even the thought of his new freedom is disconcerting. Olivia ran a tight ship. She had her ways of doing things and her ways organically became his. It took a while, but he learned to turn the water off as he was brushing his teeth, how to fold the towels the way she liked, how she liked her coffee.

He's stopped waiting for her to call, to write, to appear at the door of this apartment she doesn't even know about, to start gliding around tidying things up, mock-chastising him for his messes, for his temporary slip back into bachelorhood. And it hits him, finally, and hard: this isn't temporary.

After he hangs up with his mom, the day stretches before him. He will meet Smith in the afternoon at a tiny suit shop not far from here. Until then he will take his camera out and walk the streets in search of interesting people. He's gotten pretty good at approaching strangers and sneaking a shot or even sometimes asking them if he can take their photograph. It surprises him how many people are game; sure, some people say no and turn away, but many are willing to offer themselves, who they are, who they are striving to be, why they are here in this city that is so wonderful and so hard.

Tate pulls on a fresh pair of underwear and yesterday's jeans, which were still on the floor, then carries the beer bottles into his small kitchen. He places the bottles on the counter but then picks the full one back up, studies it. He sees lipstick. Takes a sip.

The living room is still dark, the shades drawn tight. Tate flips on the light and walks toward the mess. The shreds. The picture is gone, decomposed, in remnant bits, but he can still see it in his mind. There she is. Olivia. Looking back at him over her shoulder. It is their wedding day. They are in San Francisco at her parents' yacht club. They are in the suite where they got ready and would spend their first night as husband and wife. She said she didn't want to see him before the ceremony, that it was bad luck, but Tate convinced her that he needed to see her before everyone else saw her, that he wanted to take her picture while she was just his, that he needed a few moments alone with her, in that room. Without family, without makeup and hair people, without the hired photographer and video guy, without the world. And Olivia acquiesced. Humored him, and they had their time. She wore a big white dress. She wore her dark hair pinned back, swept off her face. He snapped the shot and it became his favorite.

He framed the photo and hung it up in their hallway. She hated it. Pointed out all the things that were wrong with it. One eye was smaller than the other, her nose looked big, she thought she had a double chin. But he didn't see these things. Even after she pointed them out, he didn't see them. He just saw a gorgeous, happy girl.

But was she ever happy? Was she even happy on that day? She was stressed, anxious about being the center of attention, eager for the whole thing to be over. There was fear in her chocolate eyes, in the shaky half smile she wore on her face. She was nervous. She was scared of something.

It's just you and me, *Liv,* he said to her, trying to calm her down. Did she know even then that it wouldn't work? That things would fall apart the way they did? That one day he would cry like a baby and cling to her, hold on for dear life?

He studies the shreds. Considers taping them back together but sweeps them up and floats them into the trash.

He sees the package by the door, walks toward it. He really doesn't need more underwear, but he knows his mom needs to send them. He feels a punch when he sees the return address. It's not from his mother. His stomach knots. Her lawyer. The papers. They're finally here.

He sits to open it. Two sets of paper, flagged for him to sign.

Part of him wants to grab a pen and just fucking do it. Be done. But, thankfully, he decides to read.

Mr. Pennington,

My client is eager to settle this matter as I know you are too. As we have heretofore agreed upon, pursuant to California law, my client is entitled to half of the community property, including, but not limited to, the proceeds of your sale of your company PhotoPoet Inc. in the fall of 2012. You built the company during your marriage to my client and she supported you and, more importantly, contributed her legal expertise and services during its establishment, and as such the company is considered marital property and should be divided as such. It should be noted that my client is additionally seeking 50% of the value of the stock options in Twitter ("Parent Company") that are at the present moment unvested. The valuation of said options will be calculated by a mutually arrived-upon method.

My client informs me that you wish to settle this matter quickly and that this stock option amendment to the agreement shouldn't unduly stall our progress on this matter.

Sincerely,
Ronald Berman
Attorney at Law

What the fuck? He checks his e-mail to see if there's anything from his lawyer about this but gets distracted when he sees the e-mail from Olivia. From late last night. Right about the time there was another girl in his bed.

He feels his pulse quicken as he clicks to read.

10:49AM

"You have every right to despise me."

To: Pennington, Tate
From: Farnsworth, Olivia
Time: 2:36 a.m. EST
Subject: Thanksgiving

T,
Thanksgiving is Thursday. I'm going to my parents', but you won't be there and this isn't right. I'm having all of these doubts. I'm worried I made a big mistake. I think I was going through something. 13 years. Are we really just throwing that away?

Remember our good times? They weren't just good, were they? They were magical. I keep thinking about the night we met. At that silly corporate recruiting event at Union League? How we started talking about how scared we were to graduate?

And the day you proposed. How the world had suddenly stopped, how we were cuddled up on the couch, glued to the television, scared out of our minds. I remember the moment you turned to me and you had this fear in your eyes, but there was hope there too. And you walked into the kitchen and came back and got down on your knee and said that suddenly everything was clear, that life was short, and we, Tate, were what mattered. We. I loved that it was your mother's ring, that there was suddenly all of this history there on my finger. I am so glad you wouldn't let me give it back because the truth is, I don't want to let go of it.

Every time something happens now, little or big, I think to pick up the phone and call you and I know that I can't do this anymore, that I've lost this privilege. And so they are building up in me, all of these things. I loved how we were always able to talk about anything . . . everything. Like when we talked for hours about whether each of us was more like our mother or our father? Or that conversation we had about the afterlife and ghosts? Or remember that time we got in a fight about the meaning of that Whitman poem you love?

Your mom tells me you're pursuing photography and this makes me happy because I know you've always loved it. I apologize that I never took it seriously, this passion of yours. I think I was envious that you felt so deeply about something. The only thing I've felt so deeply about is you. I hope that you are finally leading the life that you wanted to, but I'm heartbroken that it doesn't include me.

You have every right to despise me. You have every right to delete this e-mail without reading it. I know I told you I wouldn't contact you for a while, but it's been a while and I miss you, Tate. I am also writing because I'll be in New York in two weeks for work. And I would love nothing more than to have dinner with you. I want to see

your eyes and your smile and tell you something that I've been unable to say for some reason I'm still trying to understand.

I'm sorry.

These words are empty nothings, black smudges on a white screen, but I'm hoping that if I see you in person, there will be some life in them. Because I mean it, Tate. I've messed up in ways I know will haunt me. I know you are busy moving on and you should be doing just that, but please tell me you'll see me.

I saw this great quote the other day from Norman Cousins. He said: "Life is an adventure in forgiveness." I believe this.

You might have gotten something by now from my lawyer. Look, Tate, my lawyer insisted on this amendment thing, that I should get part of the stock because I was your wife and because I reviewed your contracts and business plan, and I told him to hold off, that I'm having doubts, but he sent it anyway. I hope we can talk about all of this?

Happy Thanksgiving, T.
Googolplex,
Olivia

Fuck her.

Fuck her.

She runs around under his nose with this other prick, serves him up months of radio silence and now this sentimental saccharine manipulative shit?

They always signed their e-mails this way, with the world's second-largest number with a name, a one followed by a googol of zeros. He wonders now why they didn't use the largest number instead. What was it called? Googolplexian? He can't recall, but he does remember every single thing she mentioned in the e-mail. The memories are cruel and endless.

As if it were yesterday, he can picture them standing together in their dark suits at a Goldman Sachs recruiting event. Twenty-one and clueless, she smiled at him, picked a dot of lint from the lapel of his suit. This was something his mother was always doing, grooming him, taking care of him.

She was from the Bay Area. This made sense; she had this breezy California coolness to her upon first impression, a bohemian, mellow charm. She was easy to talk to, artful in her self-deprecation about the predictable narrowness of her future plans. She'd recently taken the LSAT and done quite well. She was in the process of applying to handful of law schools—Columbia, Yale, Stanford—but her sights were set on New York. She wanted to spend a few years there before heading home.

She was also looking into banking and consulting. Covering her bases.

I'm boring, she whispered.

Me too, Tate whispered back even though he did not feel this to be true. He told her he was considering a career in finance because he needed a good paycheck, because he was toying with the idea of taking over his father's insurance business in St. Louis. But later that first night, he also told her that if he could be anything in the world, if money were no object, he would become a photographer. Back in his dorm, he showed her some of his pictures.

When Tate's father had a mild heart attack two weeks before graduation, Olivia insisted on flying home with him to St. Louis. She held his hand at the hospital, made his mother cups of tea. It was then, at some point during those blurry few days, that Tate decided he would one day marry this girl. Before flying back to school to graduate and pack up his dorm, Tate asked his mother for her ring. She cried when he asked, and smiled.

She is a very nice girl, his mother said.

He held on to the ring and proposed on September 12, 2001, almost exactly a year after they got together. They huddled in bed watching the news coverage. She finished school, sat for the California bar. They traveled to Asia for her bar trip and then he quit his job and they moved to San Francisco, got married in a small ceremony by the water. She began work at the law firm and he got a job at a photo software startup. In 2010, he and his buddy from Yale started developing their app. When the company was acquired last year, he found himself holding a check for millions of dollars. This all happened after everything began to unravel with Olivia, and at the time, he hoped the news and the money would patch them back together somehow. Olivia's reaction was not what he expected and oddly, it made him respect her more. She said she was proud of him, that he deserved all the success in the world, but that the money didn't change the way she felt about him, and them. They were over, she insisted.

I am not happy. I have not been happy. I want to be happy, she said that day, on the couch. She couldn't even look at him when she uttered this trio of sentences, these sentences that fell from her with a haunting, lifeless formality as if she were a child who'd memorized lines from a script. It struck him even then how slowly she spoke, enunciating each word, how she eschewed contractions.

I am not happy. I have not been happy. I want to be happy.

The words still mock him. They repeat on a loop in his head.

They are his words too now.

They sat at the dining table, an heirloom from her grandmother she'd take with her, and had a civilized chat. They agreed that they wanted to settle things quickly and amicably, that there was no reason for things to get nasty. They had each come into the union with not much of anything, just high hopes and the promise delivered by a fine education. They didn't own a house. Their possessions were commingled, but this wouldn't be hard to undo. It surprised him, and pleased him, that Olivia made almost no mention of the funds he now had. Naively, it didn't occur to him that she'd retain a high-wattage attorney who'd put it in her head to get her hands on as much as she could. It should have.

And now it all makes sense. She doesn't want him back, but she wants to butter him up and drag this out so he considers forking over a fortune.

Fuck her.

1:49PM

"Not today."

He's been wandering for hours now, stumbling along, lifting his lens again and again to capture things that strike him: an abandoned pacifier on a cracked square of concrete, an elegant old man reading *Moby-Dick* in the window of a coffee shop, a messy pyramid of trash bags waiting for collection. The details are endless and medicinal almost. They do the trick, anyway; he escapes thinking about Olivia for stretches at a time.

On Hudson Street now, he pulls out the list he made when he first got back to the city. It's a list of all the places he wants to see and photograph, places that are lesser known, tucked away, off the radar of most tourists and most New Yorkers even. Odd museums, specialty shops, secluded gardens. For him, it's never been about doing what everyone else is doing.

One thing's clear as fucking day: he's spent too much time thinking about Olivia. *Not today*, he thinks. He will put her and the papers out of his head the rest of the day. He will distract himself with pictures and Smith.

With purpose, he heads to number six on the list: Poets House in Battery Park City, on River Terrace at Murray Street. From what he's read, it's a literary center with two floors of sun-drenched spaces overlooking the Hudson, a library of more than fifty thousand volumes, an archive of poets' recordings and videos, a program hall for readings, an exhibition space and a children's library.

After about twenty minutes of exploring, he finds himself on the third floor . . . he reads every little plaque, each small explanation. The poet Stanley Kunitz, one of the founders of the house, purposely left off the apostrophe on *poets* because "some things must never be possessed but shared." The words spark something in him. He finds he wants to tell Smith about these words, to discuss them with her.

He looks down at his watch, feels a wave of anticipation that he'll see Smith soon. Ever since he got Olivia's e-mail, he's felt this almost physical urge to be next to Smith, because when he's with her, his mind behaves better. Is she just a diversion? He doesn't know yet, but he feels something.

How perfect that New York, the muse of so many, should have this place. He thinks of some of his favorite poems: Robert Lowell's "Central Park" and John Hollander's "West End Blues" and Amy Clampitt's "Times Square Water Music."

Outside again, he pulls up his own PhotoPoet app on his phone and takes a picture of the sun glinting off the Hudson, a sliver of the house itself in the right-most edge. And then he runs a search for Howard Moss and finds what he's looking for, a quote about New York poems as "histories of desperation or hope; note-takings of the phenomenal; musings on loneliness, connection, isolation, joy."

—

He loses himself in words, in ideas, in old volumes, in the familiar, in the new. When it comes time to leave, he snaps a few more pictures, pulls out his crumpling list and crosses it off.

He sets out for SoHo, with only a vague confidence about where he is going. He takes more pictures—of people on the street and in the windows of buses, of old, rusty bicycles and dogs tethered to streetlamps, of a cloud-mottled fall sky.

3:57PM

"Do you believe in second chances?"

At the store, a small, bespoke boutique called Seize sur Vingt on Greene, Tate waits for Smith. He read about the place in *New York* magazine, this menswear spot for the "young and well funded." The space has a relaxed vibe to it and smells subtly of leather and exudes a hipster masculinity. He chats with a guy who pulls out thick binders of fabric samples with wild names ("Immigrant Punk," "Can't Get Used to Losing You," "Pontius Pilate").

When Smith enters the store, the energy in the air palpably shifts, it literally does, and he feels himself come alive. What is it with this girl? He can't quite figure it out and the fact that he can't pin her down intrigues him. He's always been a quick reader, a swift and solid judge of character, but there's something exquisitely slippery about her, about her contradictions, about the fact that she toggles between being a snob and being a hippie, a wild child one night and a demure intellect the next, a mixture of safety and risk.

"Tell me something," she says by way of hello. "What is this place and why are there tits all over the walls?" She gestures toward the big photographs of women hanging throughout. She wastes no time, begins thumbing through square stacks of elegant, vibrantly colored dress shirts. There are indeed blown-up photographs of topless chicks everywhere.

Tits. One word and he's lit. She could have used any other word; he'd have expected her to say *breasts* or something more proper, but *tits*. Fucking *tits*. *Yes.*

"I read about it in a magazine," Tate says. "Come. I have some ideas, but show me what you like."

Smith makes her way through the racks of dress shirts and sport coats, a focused no-nonsense look on her face. He watches her movements, how she takes each garment in her hand and releases it and moves on to the next. Her brow furrows in concentration.

"What about this one?" he says, holding up a black-gray suit. "I can pair it with a skinny blue tie to match your dress."

"I can't believe I tried the dress on for you," she whispers as her cheeks grow pink. "Not sure that dress is going to be *the* dress. It's suffering at the moment."

Tate laughs. Thinks of that moment when she appeared naked beside him, hugging a plastic-wrapped dress. As he helped her zip up the back, he willed himself not to get hard.

"How was last night?" she says. "Did you have fun?"

He laughs. "It was a standard-issue shit show." He fights the urge to elaborate. It's strange, but part of him wants to go there, tell her about the girl who came back to his place, but he resists. He knows that the story hardly paints him in the best light.

With the help of the salesman, they pick several things for him to try and he slips into the dressing room. When he comes out, Smith looks up from her phone.

"I *like* it," she says casually. "Everyone else will be in a tux, but it's cool and it suits you." She grabs a handful of fabric in the back. "That's better. Can we have this tailored by Friday?"

The guy from the store nods. "Sure thing. It typically takes a few weeks, but we'll rush it. Next time, leave yourself some more time and we'll do something custom and send it overseas for the cutting and basting."

"Done then," Tate says.

"What about the other stuff? Do you want to keep looking?"

"I'd rather get out of here and grab a drink with you," he says.

Outside the store, Tate looks at his watch. "That took fifteen minutes, you know. When I shopped with Olivia, it would take hours. She would pick everything and perseverate over all the details. It was downright exhausting."

"I like to think of myself as decisive," she says, smiling. "I like what I like."

"You do, don't you?" he says. Yes, shameless flirtation.

They walk together to Balthazar, a French brasserie on Spring Street. It's an odd time of day, between lunch and dinner, but they take a seat at the bar. He orders a beer and oysters. She orders a glass of champagne and a shrimp cocktail.

"I've never liked oysters," she says.

"Why not?"

"The texture, I guess. I don't really know. Isn't it bizarre that there are things we do and don't do and we don't even know why?"

"Yes," he says, looking around. He's always loved the restaurant's jovial, quasi-Parisian atmosphere, the feel of the place with its high-backed red leather banquettes, tall tin ceiling, colossal distressed antique mirrors, beleaguered tiled floor, bleached saffron walls and front full of windows.

"I used to come here for brunch all the time in the years right after college," she says. "We'd gorge on fries and drink endless Bellinis. God, that was fun."

"I came here a bunch then too," he says. "I wonder if we were ever here at the same time. Bizarre to think about, right? Anyway, tell me something. Tell me about your work."

"Really?" she says, laughing. It's a fucking sexy laugh too, deep and throaty. "I'm sorry," she says, composing herself. "I just find it comical that I've burdened you with my deepest secrets, that you've witnessed me hunched over a toilet bowl, that we just speed-purchased formalwear and now we are dipping into the stiff get-to-know-you, tell-me-about-your-work chat."

"And, footnote, I've seen you naked," Tate says. "You forgot to mention that detail."

"What?"

"Yes," he says. "You didn't exactly sequester yourself to try on the dress. You just stripped down. I had no complaints. None. *None. Not a one.*"

Her face is red. Through her embarrassment, she simpers.

"Listen. You're totally gorgeous and you know you are, so let's skip the coy fretting. I'm just going to have to get that image out of my head as I fumble to have a serious conversation with you about our respective professional pursuits. Tell me this: The Order of Things? You a big Foucault fan?" he says, running his finger around the rim of his glass.

"Not really. Sure, I read the book. Not sure I understood a word of it, but I liked how he explored the relationship between power and knowledge. I pretty much just thought it was a fitting name for my business because, well, I deal with the order of people's things. And I figured it would impress the academic snobs like us who even know who Foucault is. I know that all of this still has something to do with trying to impress my father. He's never approved of my work. He thinks it's beneath me and horrifically noncerebral and he huffs and puffs, but he's also the one who tossed some seed money at me so I could get things going. I know I'm lucky to have their financial support, but it has its strings. Every now and then, he asks when I'm going to throw in the towel and do something real and it just makes me want to work harder. It's fucked up. Thirty-four years old and I'm still on a quest for parental approval. And now I'm writing a book and the truth is I have no idea whether I really want to be writing a book, but I know being a published author will impress him. It's messed up."

"Tell me about the book," he says.

"Who knows if it'll ever really happen, but I kind of love it. There's something really cool about taking my laptop to a coffee shop and chipping away at it. Being in the mix of all of these creative, quirky New Yorkers. It's about chaos theory and cognitive dissonance. And the butterfly effect, applying these principles to questions of domestic order."

"The butterfly effect?" he says.

"You familiar?"

"Barely."

"Okay, so the idea is that small differences in initial conditions yield widely divergent outcomes for dynamic systems, rendering long-term prediction generally impossible."

"Okay, Señorita Wikipedia, English please."

She laughs. Tries again. "Okay, think about this. A hurricane's formation might be contingent on whether or not a butterfly far far away flapped its wings weeks ago. Or maybe you'll do better with a pop culture example? Did you ever see that Gwyneth Paltrow movie *Sliding Doors*?"

"About a dozen times. Olivia was marginally obsessed with Gwyneth."

"Full disclosure: so am I. Anyway, think about it. A small thing like slipping through the sliding doors of the subway or waiting for the next train can make a huge difference in your life."

Tate nods. Now he understands. What if he'd never caught Olivia in the act with that bastard partner? Would he be sitting here right now? What if he never took that fateful surf trip to Malibu with Arun where they came up with the idea for PhotoPoet?

"I get it," he says. "Like what if I said fuck it and didn't head to the game last weekend. This conversation wouldn't be happening."

"Exactly. And I think there are really interesting applications in my work. People get so overwhelmed by all their stuff, by the clutter that accumulates, but what I try to teach them is that all they have to do is start very small. Pick one drawer or shelf and clear it. And then move to the next thing. Sorting through a pile of documents or clearing out your e-mail inbox can literally change your life. It's kind of interesting though because, sometimes, I have a hard time determining whether this book ambition is all fueled by an authentic desire to explore these things or whether I'm trying to convince myself, not to mention the parental units, that there is some academic merit to the work I've chosen, you know?"

"I do know," he says. "The whole parental approval thing sounds very familiar. My folks are thousands of miles away and yet I find myself wondering if they will ever approve of this photography thing. I can't tell you how many conversations I've had with my poor mom about it, trying to explain what I do each day, how important it is to me. But she's just a mom, worried that I'm lonely. Truth is, sometimes I am, but isn't that just the way it is?"

Smith nods. "I think so. I feel it too and I'm around people *all the time*. I wonder if it's all this social media stuff, you know? We feel like we're connecting, but we're really disconnecting, creating empty little dopamine rushes for ourselves."

"*Yes,*" he says. "The truth is that I feel less lonely than I have in years because I'm actually out in the world, connecting with people, looking at them, into their eyes, speaking with them sometimes. And I have this guilt because I actually created one of these apps that take people away. I love the product, that people can marry images and words, but they'd be better off putting the phone down entirely. I bet your work is really about the people too."

"Completely. I get this direct window into lives. It's never just about the home. There is heartbreak and happiness and love and loss. Just yesterday, I helped this woman sort through her husband's things. He died eight months ago. And we didn't just make piles. We talked. About her three sons, about Thanksgiving, even about Sally's wedding, and that was the perfect example of me being *affected* by my work, you know? I walked out of there being like, shit, even if you find the right guy, he might just die. Or here is this woman *my age* and she's already had a husband and three kids and I feel this stupid panic."

"But isn't panic so counterproductive? I mean, if we flip out because time's passing, aren't we poised to miss it? That's what pisses me off, you know? I'm telling myself that I want to get on with things, stop thinking about the past and forge this healthy new existence here, but then I drown in drink and get all fucking nostalgic and then I just feel like all kinds of shit."

"Cognitive dissonance," she says, nodding. "You tell yourself you will behave one way and then you do the opposite and then you feel this toxic internal inconsistency plague you. Believe me, I'm familiar. What you can do is change your outlook and cut yourself some slack about the fact that you are in no position to move on yet and just keep doing what you're doing, or you can change your behavior so it's more consistent with your goal, right?"

He nods, trying to understand this. She's fucking smart, this one. He orders another round of drinks. Smith grows quiet and shifts on her stool.

"Tell me something," she says, mischief flickering in her eyes. "Do you really like photography or are you doing it because you can?"

Who is this girl and how, in a few days, does she know just how to call him on his crap?

"What's that supposed to mean?" he says.

"You sold your company. You have money. You don't need to work. Trust me, I know the type," she says. "And there's nothing wrong with taking time and having a hobby, but a hobby is different from *work*."

"Shit, you sound just like my mother," Tate says, sitting up straighter in his chair, taking a long swig of beer. "I've been pulling long nights working on these insipid grad school essays. Not sure I'd be doing that if I didn't give a shit, right?"

She shrugs. "People go to school all the time because they can't figure out what else to do. I'm just saying you should figure out your story. Because if you have money, some people might assume that you're just having fun, just doing something to fill time, and it is up to you to *show them* that you are serious and that you want to be taken seriously. My work, for example, is just that—*work*. It's not some cute little thing I do to occupy myself. Despite what my parents think. Despite what I sometimes think."

He watches her get riled up and feels even more drawn to her. There is passion in this girl, anger of uncertain origin, vitality.

The waiter appears with the oysters, mumbles something about them, but Tate isn't focusing on the waiter.

"And as for the money thing," he says, picking up an oyster, letting it slide down his throat, "I've promised myself I won't let it change me, but what I want to know is whether it's actually up to me. I mean, here I am, in the middle of the day with a knockout drinking and scarfing five-dollar oysters? I suppose I'm eating my words."

She smiles. "I think it's at least partially a choice. I mean, I look at my father and he's done really well for himself and he's proud of that because he didn't come from a lot, but it's up to him whether he puts it away, or donates it to good causes, or spends an insane amount on his daughter's wedding, right? I mean, I love the man, I do, but he's doing everything in his power to make sure the world knows how much he's worth, which, for the record, drives my mother crazy. You just wait. This wedding is going to be off the hook and I'm pretty sure I'm going to feel really embarrassed by all of it, but then I'm also like, who am I to judge? What's to say there's anything wrong with any of that? I tell myself I have different sensibilities, that I'm far more down-to-earth than my father, but maybe that's bullshit, right? I mean, I live in the

San Remo. My clients have multiple homes. Anyway, you'll figure it out. Whether you want to be the low-key incognito rich guy or shout it from the rooftops. I look at you and tend to think you're in the former camp, but maybe I'm wrong. Maybe it's too soon to tell. Anyway, did you expect this? That your idea would lead to all this?"

"Never," he says. "I didn't even know enough to hope. And maybe that's why it worked out the way it did. It's funny, but I remember the day I had the idea. My buddy and I bailed on work and went surfing. It was a particularly rad day and the sky was insane and I took all of these photos on my phone and my mind filled up with all of these words . . . words from college, from things I'd read, my favorite poets. And that was that. I was jazzed, but I didn't know. I remember feeling *alive*."

Smith nods. "I got my MBA and worked as an organization consultant for a while. I did the whole traveling-Monday-through-Thursday thing. And I enjoyed it. I liked my colleagues and my clients, but it was a similar thing. I was at a client's office and I sat there mindlessly sorting through her stuff and she was so *thankful,* went on and on about how I had helped her. And it just clicked. That I wanted to do that, to work with people, but in a very different way. I returned to New York and gave notice immediately, began to brainstorm my business. In retrospect, I'm amazed at how confident I was about it all."

Confidence. That's it. She's confident even though she's seeking. It's what Olivia always lacked. She was smart and beautiful and had every reason to be confident, but she could never muster it, and despite his efforts to convince her, she was woefully insecure, and that insecurity was there even in her e-mail last night, a sense that she had made the wrong move, that characteristic backpedaling she did again and again. He didn't even realize how exhausting it was, how much his efforts depleted him, how unhealthy it all was.

"I think it's great," Tate says.

"What's great?" Smith says.

"That you knew what you wanted and fucking went for it," he says.

"You have quite the mouth on you," she says, sipping her drink.

"Apologies."

"No need," she says, smiling. "I'm not quite as delicate as I look."

A loud, chipper sound carries toward them and they both pivot on their bar stools. A toddler sits with his parents in one of the little bar booths. He plays with an iPad and his mother scrambles to turn down the volume. The mother and father are a hip duo, smartly dressed.

"See?" he says. "You *can* have a kid and still live your life. Look at them drinking their wine while he techs out and builds a French fry fort."

"That was my favorite book as a kid," she whispers, pointing over to the family's table. "*Goodnight Moon.*"

Sure enough, a copy of the famous children's book rests near the edge of the table, its green cover a familiar, happy sight. *Is she serious?* Tate thinks. This was his favorite story, too. He has so many memories of sitting on his mother's lap, flipping through those colorful pages.

"Mine too. Not making that shit up. I loved that little tiny mouse on the green carpet and that bunny grandma in the rocking chair."

"So, you want kids?" she says, her smile faint, her eyes shining.

"I do. A bunch. Though I would probably make a piss-poor father at the moment," he says. "How can you not want kids?"

"Clio doesn't want kids," Smith says.

Tate nods. "I guess there are probably valid reasons to forgo parenthood, but hell, I want a little one of those to take to the diner."

"Well, you better get to work on that. You're not getting any younger," she says, mock-lecturing him.

"Again, my mother. Are you her special agent or something?"

"You never know," Smith says, seeming melancholy all of a sudden. "I just found out that Asad and his wife are having a baby," she says. "I wish I could say that I'm cool with it."

"Wife?" Smith mentioned Asad several times during their late night out, making it clear that she was on the rebound too.

"Yeah, he got married just a few months after he left me. A quasi-arranged thing. A nice Pakistani girl. And now they're pregnant. Feels awesome."

"Shit. That sucks," he says. "I would probably lose my shit if I found out Olivia was having a kid."

With Olivia, he was the one who brought up having children. It seemed strange to him that all these years were ticking by and they weren't taking this step. Did she not have a biological clock? Did she not notice that all of their friends were beginning to post pictures of babies on Facebook, babies with fat cheeks and ridiculous preppy names? He began to wonder whether this was something she really wanted. She always said she did, that it was just a matter of timing, that she wasn't in it to play Stepford Wife, that she had legit career ambitions, wanted to establish herself at the firm, wanted them to establish themselves financially. *You can't just bring a kid into this world,* she said. And Tate nodded because this was what he had learned to do, to listen, to cave, but his head roiled with questions, with counterpoints, with concerns. *Isn't that exactly what you do,* he thought, *bring a kid into this world and then figure it out? Isn't it always a leap?* But each time they talked about it, he pussied out and kowtowed to her logic, a logic that seemed flimsier and flimsier each time they revisited it.

He looks up and sees Smith watching him in the mirror above the bar.

"You're thinking of her," she says.

Caught. "Just a little. Fucking settlement bullshit. But I'm thinking of her far less than I was a few days ago. Thanks to you."

"Glad I could be a distraction," she says.

"A pretty hot distraction, mind you."

She blushes. "Do you believe in second chances? Would you give her another shot if she asked?"

Tate thinks of the e-mail but doesn't mention it. There's no need for Smith to know about it. "I haven't heard from her in a while. It's over. No second chances. What about you? If he came crawling back, begging for another go at things, what would you do?"

"I'd let him grovel, but then I'd send him packing back to his pregnant wife. I'd try to get a little more of an explanation out of him, though. To this day, I'm not sure what happened. Everything was great and then it seemed to combust overnight. I'm thinking maybe you're lucky on some level that you have an explanation. I really don't."

"I do and I don't. The cheating was the final straw, but I can see now we were incompatible in a lot of ways. She's pretty linear, you know? Not in a bad way, but she just likes things to be a certain way and I'm realizing I need adventure, a little kink."

"Kink?" She blushes even more.

He nods. "Want my take?" he says, motioning to the bartender for another round of drinks. "I think we both loved people and had our hearts shredded, but in my ignorant opinion, it's good that we felt so deeply. I mean, fuck, there are some people walking around who don't even know what it is to love someone. And, hell, it's torture to be burned like we've been, but maybe it's good to be rattled like that. We're still young. We have time to figure it out. And what surprises me is that it doesn't scare me away from doing it again, even though perhaps it should. I just want to feel it again, you know? Does that make me crazy?"

"Maybe so," she says, laughing. "But I feel the exact same way."

Shit, what is this? What's happening? It's been *days* and all he wants is to take her home and ask her a million questions. A few hours of crash-coursing in each other's lives and then they'd spend the afternoon fucking in his bed, emerging only to pee and answer the doorbell for their delivery food.

"You're not thinking of her anymore, are you?" she says, flashing a naughty grin, stealing a sip of his beer.

"No," he says, smiling. "I'm not."

Her phone buzzes and she reaches for it. She reads the screen and then looks up.

"It's Clio. She wants me to come by the hotel and see the apartment Henry designed, the one that caused all of the drama. Come with me?"

6:31PM

"They had an epic sex life."

The bartender at the hotel, a young white-haired guy, refills their beers. Henry takes a sip, smiles. "Come," he says to Tate, standing. Tate follows him through the restaurant into the hotel's lobby and out through a door into a small garden.

"There's no Guinness that comes close to the ones brewed back home. Oh, do I miss the pubs—the Crown in Belfast and the Anchor near Oxford and Toners in Dublin near where Mum grew up. I hate to be the snobbish fuddy-duddy, but most of the pubs here are cheap copies. A few are tolerable, thank God. Have you been to the Dublin House down the way?"

Tate shakes his head, sips his beer. "I haven't."

"We'll all go one night," Henry says. "The bartender was my only friend on this side of the pond for a while. I'd go there, drown my sorrows, talk to him and get through to the next day. I was such a lonely bloke."

"And now look at you," Tate says, smiling, kicking the blue stone bench.

"Smoke and mirrors, my lad," Henry says, grinning. "I'm still that melancholy, scruffy thirty-year-old, but I've learned how to fool people and rub a few pennies together."

"You miss Ireland?" Tate says.

"Sometimes," Henry says, casting his gaze up at the sky. "Sometimes I feel as if I've lost my roots. My accent's nearly gone, I've been here almost twenty years. These young spuds in the hotel world call me Irish and years ago, I would have corrected them and told them I was Northern Irish and given them a talking-to about the Troubles, regaling them with stories about being stopped and checked for IRA bombs in the city center, but I've softened, which I suppose is good in a way. But I do miss it. I miss the pubs. I miss rugby. Every St. Patty's day, my brothers and I would go see the two top school teams play for the Ulster Schools' Cup at Ravenhill Stadium. I actually started playing again this past spring after I met Clio. On Sundays while Clio and Smith do their thing. It's been good for me. You should come play. We could use some young blood."

"I don't know the first thing about rugby," Tate says.

"Ah, you'd be a quick study. Far tougher and better sport than American football."

"I'm not sure how tough I am," Tate says.

"We're all plenty tough," Henry says. "Gotta be in this brilliant, messy city."

"I love it here," Tate says, sipping his beer. "San Francisco was a good town, but I never had that feeling of walking through history, you know?"

Henry nods.

"The architecture here is nuts. Smith and I popped out from the subway earlier and we stopped in front of the Dakota and it hit me.

John Lennon was shot *here*. There were all these tourists with cameras and people walking by, pulling their dogs on leashes, pushing their strollers, yakking into their phones, and that's why I love with this city, which is so fucking *strange* because I lived here after college and never saw the appeal. None of it made sense to me then. It was smelly and noisy and crowded and even though I was living the finance-dude-expense-account life, I just wasn't sold," Tate says, sipping his beer.

"It *is* smelly and noisy and crowded," Henry says, straightening his tie. "But it's also the best bloody place in the world. I've been here nearly twenty years and it still amazes me."

"It is, right?" Tate says. "The last year has been hell, but it got me here. That's something."

"A *big* something, bloke. Cheers!" Henry croons, lifting his glass to clink Tate's.

"I've spent all these years fretting over appearances, my résumé, worrying about what my parents think, and I feel like I'm starting not to care. It's bizarre."

"Let me tell you something, and I can only say this because I have a few years on ya, but the day you stop caring is the day life really begins. My old man had it all figured out for his Kildare boys. We would go to uni and then settle in Belfast and work with him at the bank. Coming here was the best thing I ever did, but shit, was it hard. I came here with nothing. I didn't know a soul. I worked my bloody tail off, but you know what? It was *fine*. It was worth it. Shit, I could go on and on about all of this, but let me ask you something, Tate, before the ladies get back," Henry says, the quality of his voice changing. "You and Smith? Tell me."

What's he supposed to say?

"Smith means the world to Clio," Henry says. "Been like a sister to her. She has a bloody heart of gold, and this is between us, but Clio's worried that Smith is fraying with the wedding and all, but I told Clio that we are all fraying, quietly or not-so-quietly fraying and patching; that's life for you. You were married, I understand?"

"Yes," Tate says, suddenly getting the impression that he's being interrogated. "Ironing out the settlement. Trying to figure out how much I care about the money I never thought I'd have in the first place."

"Ah, the money dance," Henry says. "None of my bloody business, but let me tell you something, okay? I've only known Smith for a short while, but she's something special, and she puts on a good show, a near-flawless one, but I can see it myself, she's as fragile as the rest of us. And you know what? In my admittedly ignorant opinion, she's scared, because if things work out as I'm hoping they do, her dearest friend in the world will be moving out. And her kid sister is getting hitched. And she's soft. And maybe this is inappropriate—I suspect it is—but I'm feeling protective."

"I get it, man," Tate says, nodding, sipping his drink, staring up at the sky. "What do you know about this Asad guy? It seems he did a number on her."

"I never met the bloke, but apparently he was a good one. Wickedly smart doctor, and from what Clio says, he was bloody head over heels for Smith, but then something switched and it all crumbled. Clio said he was very Westernized but in the end, he talked a lot about his family and his culture, how the marriage just wouldn't work. It remains something of a mystery, I suppose, as to what really happened, but what I do know is that they had an epic sex life; my poor Clio caught them in a number of compromising positions over at the San Remo flat and I'm not sure she's recovered. Anyway, it's old news. He lives in Boston now. Apparently some hotshot neurosurgeon at Mass General."

Tate sips his beer, nods. A highly sexual neurosurgeon. Tough act to follow. "What about you and Clio? Pretty serious, I gather?"

"I think so, yes," Henry says, but his words are edged in discernible doubt. "I hope so anyway. We'll see."

Tate looks up and he sees Smith and Clio on the other side of the door.

"So, what's the verdict, Andy?"

"Andy?" Tate says.

"My diminutive for the lovely Ms. Anderson here," Henry explains, smiling. "Get with the fine program, lad. So, did I do a passable job per your expert opinion, Andy? Do the aesthetics pass muster?" Henry asks as the girls walk into the courtyard.

"It's stunning, Henry," Smith says. "Truly."

Henry grins, raising his glass to clink Tate's.

"What have you two been chatting about?" Smith says.

"Rugby and beer and having the balls to say 'piss off' to our parents," Henry says. "You know, the basics."

Tate smiles.

"Thanksgiving plans, Tate?"

"My plans are pretty nonexistent. Flying solo this year. Maybe I'll take my camera out and shoot all the despondent, lonely folks on Thanksgiving Day."

"Nonsense," Henry says. "I think you should escort this lovely young lady to the Hamptons and ply her with enough liquor to stumble through the prewedding thicket. I'd do it myself if I didn't have to stay here and tend to the holiday rush."

He squeezes Clio. She buries her head in his chest.

"What do you say, Pennington?" Smith says. "The gift of Emersonian solitude or deep Tolstoyan Anderson dysfunction?"

"Tough call," Tate says, but he knows just what he will do.

9:28PM

"Onward."

Back home now. Tate is buzzed but not drunk. In fact, he's far clearer than he's been in ages. He opens his laptop and reads Olivia's e-mail again and writes his response.

To: Farnsworth, Olivia
From: Pennington, Tate
Time: 9:30 p.m.
Subject: I do not despise you

Liv,
I do not despise you. I could not despise you if I tried, and let me tell you, I've tried. I'm happy to be back here. I think New York City might be my place after all. When we were here, I don't think we knew how to love it. I think it was too overwhelming for us. It still is, but I find myself welcoming that. The material

is endless and as a rookie photographer, I'm a kid in a candy shop.

It's hard to believe that it's Thanksgiving again. I look back to this time last year and realize things were falling apart. I didn't see it, but I wasn't looking to see it either. Why would I? I think about how quiet you were in St. Louis, how you offered little in conversation with my parents, how you barely touched your food. You were beginning to slip from me even then.

I've been barely holding my head above water, Liv. I finally feel like things are looking up, but none of this is easy. It's the hardest thing I've ever done, forging a life without you. I'm just now beginning to remember what it is to have fun, to laugh, to be me. I know you know this, but you are fine. You do not need me to be fine. You have proven that to me.

I don't think I can see you when you come to New York. I don't think that would be good for me, or for us. I'm not sure what the point would be. I trust that you're sorry. I don't need to see you to believe you. I don't need to see you to forgive you. I'm not sure, but I think I've already forgiven you. Maybe I'm too quick to forgive? Maybe that's just another weakness of mine.

I need to protect myself. I need to move on. I need to make this place home.

I got the papers. I can't help but think this is all related, your sudden need to make things right. You said that you didn't care about the money. Maybe it was foolish of me to believe you? Maybe we all care about money more than we think?

Happy Thanksgiving, Liv.
T

He types the words fast, faster than he's ever written something. The sentences pour from him and appear, lines of black on a white screen. He reads it all over and he hovers the mouse over Send, but then closes his computer and heads to the kitchen to fetch a beer.

He stands there, alone in his top-of-the-line kitchen that needs cleaning, and drinks his beer. His mind wanders and he thinks of her, but it's a different her. Snippets of the day flash through his head. Smith, all concentration, flipping through a rack of dress shirts in the little boutique. Smith laughing. Smith watching that kid at the restaurant. He's never bought the bullshit about right place, right time, the crap about love at (second) first sight. He's too smart for that. And yet, what is this? He finally decides to put an end to his hibernation and go to the game and there she is, an enigmatic soul hiding behind her phone. And they talk. And he doesn't want their talking to end. And all he can think of is what it will be like to taste her perfect lips and be inside her. And now he is going to Thanksgiving with her family and escorting her to her sister's wedding. These things should feel onerous and overwhelming, but the thing is they don't. They don't at all. He wants to meet her family. He wants to get dressed up and dance.

But what about Olivia? What if she's really coming around? Shouldn't he slow the fuck down and really try to make sense of this all? If he really loved her, wouldn't he give her another shot? What does it mean that he's thinking so much of another girl? And the money? Does he even give a shit about the money? And maybe it's only fair that he owes her just what the lawyer says he owes her. She worked herself into the ground while he was building the app. She did help with the contracts and all the legal stuff.

Without much thought, he starts running Google searches, looking for Smith's ex. It's incredible what a few pieces of information can do. He types in "Asad, Pakistan, neurosurgeon, Mass General" and he is bombarded with words and images. He studies the pictures first. The guy seems tall. His shoulders are broad and his eyes are dark and he's seriously handsome. He wears a suit in each picture. Tate finds himself despising him for no good reason at all.

He clicks over to Instagram and Smith's feed. So many clean, careful images of candles and pillows and impeccable stacks of clothing. Interspersed are pictures she's taken of herself, and here, he focuses. That milky skin. Those blueberry eyes. That long dark hair he wants to yank.

He sees she posted a photo just moments ago. He can tell from the background that she's home, sitting in that big window in her living room. She's smiling and it's so close up that he can see her bare collarbone. She writes one word: *Onward.*

He texts her.

Tate: Onward.

Smith: You stalking me? ☺

Tate: Something like that. What are you doing?

Smith: Brushing my teeth. Going to bed.

Tate: Bed?

Smith: Bed.

Tate: Sounds like a plan.

Smith: I like a good plan.

Tate: You do, don't you?

Smith: Good night, Tate.

Tate: Good night, Smith.

Smith: Goodnight Moon

He puts his phone down. Opens his laptop again. Saves his e-mail to Olivia as a draft.

In his bedroom, he pulls his shirt over his head and steps out of his jeans. He folds both items and places them on top of his suitcase. Tomorrow he will unpack this suitcase and put things away. He will wash his underwear and his sheets. He will frame his favorite photographs and hang them on the wall.

Onward, indeed.

CLIO

Yet why not say what happened?

— Robert Lowell, "Epilogue"

FEAR OF FALLING

by Clio Eloise Marsh

FALL 1996

Essay for Application to Yale College

I have a 15–30 percent chance of being diagnosed with bipolar disorder in my lifetime because my mother has the disease. She was diagnosed in 1979, shortly after I was born.

For many years, I didn't know she was ill. I just thought she was very happy sometimes and very sad at others. I thought that it was just the way she was and I learned to read her moods the way farmers learn how to predict storms. Sometimes, she races around a mile a minute. This is mania. Sometimes, she spends weeks or months in bed. This is depression. She has words for it though, words I like better than the medical terms: ***flying*** and ***falling***.

I learned the truth about her illness when I was thirteen. She went on a trip to England without telling us. Her plan, we learned later, was to visit Charles Darwin's grave in Westminster Abbey. She needed to spend some time in the hospital when she came back and this is when I found out she was sick. I started to research everything I could about bipolar disorder. I learned that it usually presents around age twenty-five. I learned that more women than men suffer from it. I learned that children with at least one bipolar parent are far more likely to have it too.

Obviously, this scares me, but I'm trying to stay positive. I know that when carefully monitored and treated properly with medication, bipolar patients can succeed and flourish. I know that there is a good chance that I will be lucky and be okay. I know that I love my mother, and even though my childhood has not been easy, I would like to stay close to home for college. Yale is minutes away and it is my biggest dream to be able to study at such an excellent school and also remain close to my parents.

I think being my mother's child has made me thoughtful and resilient. I don't take life or good health for granted. I would like very much to study science, to learn more about genetics and evolution, because the topics are of great personal interest to me for reasons that are probably pretty clear.

I also love birds. My mother has encouraged this interest and we love to watch the birds in our backyard together. Two springs ago, we made a hummingbird feeder out of an empty Gatorade bottle, a salad dressing cap, tinfoil and artificial flowers. We mixed some sugar nectar and waited. One day, a little ruby-throat came and it was the most magical creature I've ever seen. I've learned a lot about hummingbirds now, including that they are the only birds that can fly backward.

Whatever the future holds, I look forward to leading a positive and productive life, to moving forward, hopefully beginning at Yale.

8:14AM

"It's over."

The phone call came at 10:47 p.m. last December 22.

Clio had just been named associate curator at the museum and Smith was on a mission to get over Asad, so they went downtown to Karaoke One 7 to celebrate/cope/let loose a bit.

When Clio's phone buzzed, a sake-bombed Smith was onstage delivering an embarrassingly shy rendition of Coldplay's "Fix You." When Clio saw that it was Jack calling, her stomach seized and her throat tightened. It was late. Jack was a dad to a toddler and an infant now, and their late-night calls, once a constant, were a thing of the past. Clio knew something must be very wrong.

And it was.

She dashed out to the street to answer and

stood in the blustery cold on Sixth Avenue while he told her the news she'd been consciously or unconsciously anticipating and fearing for years now.

Those moments were stark and surreal, grainy in retrospect, haunting like an antique film. She waited for Smith to finish her song and told her what happened and Smith, ever graceful and composed, turned ashen at the news and looked as if she might be sick. Clio said she would take a taxi straight to Grand Central, catch a train home to New Haven, and Smith insisted on coming with her. But Clio didn't let her; she pushed her away. She needed to do this alone.

Clio caught a cab and she sat there in the darkened backseat, her body limp, melting into the duct-taped fake leather, and it struck her as simply unfathomable that she was in a taxicab, traveling through the city she'd come to love, and her life had, in a matter of moments, just fallen apart. She was heartbroken, but she was also relieved. Two words floated in her head. Words that made her feel terribly guilty.

It's over.

When she arrived at Grand Central a mere eleven minutes later—why does that detail stick when more important ones have faded?—she teetered at the top of the big stairs, fixed her gaze on the small round clock in the center of the terminal and felt a deep vertigo, like she might tumble all the way down. Part of her wished this would happen, that she'd knock herself out. But it didn't happen. She held on. She held on to the railing and descended one shaky step at a time. She found the right track for her 11:22 p.m. train. Somehow she found it. She slipped onto the train just as the doors were closing.

When the conductor came around and asked for her ticket to New Haven her voice cracked and only then did she come close to crying. Not when she got the phone call from Jack. Not when Smith hugged her and then began to sob, wetting Clio's shoulders with tears. Not even when she saw her mother's pale and lifeless body in that quiet hospital room. Not when she gathered with her father and Jack's family in her living room to eat egg salad and say a silent good-bye. It was as if the tears were stuck or perhaps all cried out. They hadn't been a picnic, her thirty-three years.

But that conductor of that late-night train? His face stays inked in her mind, his features crisp, the butterscotch hue of his eyes etched in her memory. He was a wonderfully nice man and asked Clio if she was okay. Maybe he could see she was rattled and racing and Clio nodded yes, that she was fine, even though part of her wanted to tell him everything. Even in that tattered and tortured moment, she resisted the urge to do this. Even then, she knew you don't do this, this is not something that's okay to do, to tell unsuspecting people deeply dark confessions, that your mother has just hanged herself on your childhood swing set.

The memories come flooding back as she stands in the great hall of Grand Central for the first time since that tragic night. She's early this time. At the entrance, she takes in the familiar sight, the awe-inspiring details of the cavernous space, the big American flag that went up right after 9/11, the tie-dye swirl of human beings in transit. She steps slowly down the stairs, studies people as they pass. She wanders through small coffee shops and newspaper stands, all of them fancy and seemingly new, but buys nothing. She's tempted to scoop up a *New Yorker* to escape and pass the time on the train, but this is exactly what she can't let herself do. She needs to be alert and aware and *think* about how all of this is going to go down, with her father preparing to vacate his home of more than thirty years.

Her mind snags on the question that's pressed her for months now: how do you tell the man you love that your mother committed suicide? She tells herself that her mother's death has nothing to do with her, but the shame she feels has been paralyzing. At the museum, she's told only Greta, the grad student she supervises, a girl with her own grisly stories, a girl with whom she's grown close, but everyone else thinks her mother was simply ill and passed.

She boards her train. She has her choice of seats, picks one in the middle of the car, facing the right way, the direction the train will travel. She looks around, wondering suddenly if this was the exact car she was on. She has no way of knowing, but much comes back now. The quality of the artificial light that fateful night, fluorescent and eerie; the cloying smell of sweat and newspaper mixed with industrial grease; the rattling clunk of the train making its way; the snips of drunken banter floating from fellow passengers; minutes passing in a soft, cinematic blur, a stretch of time during which she was neither asleep nor awake, her mind mottled with dreamlike images of her mother from over the years, a haunting highlight reel.

She's right back to that night again. On December 23, two days before Christmas, the train pulled into the New Haven station on time at 1:17 a.m. Clio got off and floated almost unconsciously through the dim tunnel she'd walked so many times before and climbed the stairs to the main level and frantically looked for her father. She felt panic rising, but then she spotted Jack walking through the doors of the station. His eyes were an angry red, swollen no doubt from crying. He wrapped her in one of his perfect hugs.

I'm so sorry, he said. *Your dad sent me to pick you up*. Later, she'd learn that her father had disappeared from the hospital and no one could find him. It was not lost on her that he picked the one time she needed him most in her life to check out.

She and Jack climbed into his old beat-up Chevy. Just sat there for a while.

Do you want to go to the hospital? he asked.

Is that what I should do? Is she still there?

Yes, he said. *I think so*.

The time of death, Clio would learn, was called at 10:41 p.m. Cause of death: asphyxia. Just six minutes before Jack called with the news. This detail pierced her more than others and guilt spiraled within her. What if she had called Eloise that afternoon to talk about birds? Bird talk was their secret language and always livened up her mother. She knew all the Latin species names and loved uttering them. What if Clio had gone home earlier for Christmas instead of staying in the city to put in more work at the museum? What if she hadn't gone to

Costa Rica the month before to do fieldwork instead of going home for Thanksgiving? Why did her father call Jack before he called his own daughter?

The train moves now. Soon Clio hears the conductor coming on through. She holds her ticket in her hand, nervously tracing its edges, and waits for her turn. When she looks up, she longs to see the man from last year, but it isn't him. It's a new man. He's tall and thin and balding and he looks so tired.

He punches her ticket and disappears.

Her phone rings. A blocked number. She comes close to answering but doesn't. There isn't a voice mail.

Her phone rings again. She looks and sees that it's Henry. Her heart flutters as she answers.

"Hello?"

"Clio, love, I have some good news."

She waits, feels her pulse quicken. "What?"

"I'm coming. I rearranged things. This is more important than a few PR meetings. I can only stay for the afternoon, but I want to get there. My train is due in at 1:05."

She smiles into the phone but also notices how badly her hands are shaking. This is what she wanted, what she asked for, and yet part of her was relieved that he couldn't come. She has no idea how this will go. "I'll pick you up at the station then," she says.

"Wonderful."

"Henry?"

"Yes, Clio?"

"Thank you. I know this isn't easy," she says.

"No, Clio, thank you for inviting me. My meeting's starting, so I must run, but I will see you very soon."

She hangs up just as the train is pulling into the station. She gets off and makes her way to the concourse, where her father waits at the top of the steps. For a moment she doesn't recognize him. His hair is almost white and he seems hunched, much older. But it's him.

"Hi, Clio," he says stiffly, throwing an awkward arm around her shoulder. He takes her bag to carry to the car. To *his* car (this is how Clio now thinks of things—*his* car, *his* house), which smells definitively of cigarettes. He's been smoking again. He quit many years ago; both of her parents did. She looks over at him but says nothing. If he smokes, he smokes. He's *alive*.

She planned to come back frequently, maybe even once a month. Her father deserved this. To lay eyes on his only child, to have someone with him at the house, to help do the wash, stock the fridge. But she couldn't bring herself to do it. The thought of being in that house filled her with foreboding, a pervasive dread, and she felt paralyzed. Time rolled by. She drummed up all kinds of excuses: she was busy writing grants and doing her own research and planning expeditions in the field and also teaching an undergrad course at Columbia and leading her Sunday tours. And then she was getting to know Henry.

Her father took the train to the city a couple of times instead. And they were fine days, quiet but fine, and Clio would give him tours of the museum and the neighborhood and they'd go to the park, to the Ramble, and even though it was hard to see him, it meant something that he was there, in the tangle of her life.

The engine makes a worrisome sound.

"Is there something wrong with the car?"

"Possibly. I'll have to get it checked after the move."

The move. *The move*. Her father is moving out of their house. It was her idea. She brought it up last year and he was resistant at first, but then realized it would be good to downsize, to get some distance from the memories.

The enormity of this begins to hit her and she feels a catch in her throat. This is exactly what she's wanted for him to do and yet now it's happening and she's feeling shaken. She reminds herself of the practicality of this transition; it's too much for him to maintain the place. It wouldn't be good for him to stay there.

"How's the house?" Clio says.

"Pretty much packed up. Didn't touch your room. Left your mother's dresses in the closets, in case you want anything. Shouldn't take long. You can turn around tonight if you want. Spend Thanksgiving with Henry."

"Henry's Northern Irish. He doesn't care about Thanksgiving," she says, hesitating, tracing the chrome door handle on the passenger side. "He's coming."

"Coming?" Her father turns toward her. His eyebrows arch in confusion.

"Here," she says. "Today."

"What do you mean today? When?"

"Around one. I'm going to take him around campus and then we'll head back to the house. When will you get off work?"

"Six," he says.

Her father nods and drives, winding them through familiar streets toward their home. "I wish you would have given me some warning, Clio," he says huffily.

"I just found out myself, Dad. He didn't think he could get away from the hotel in its first week, but he's coming. He can't stay long, but even if you just get to say hello, I figure that's better than not meeting him, right?"

"I guess."

Her dad has never been a fan of surprises. This makes sense. All those years with Eloise, all that ferocious unpredictability. She flips on the radio. They listen to a weather report, learn that Thanksgiving travelers are scrambling to book earlier flights to avoid the big storm bearing down on the East Coast. A messy mix of snow, rain and wind threatens to complicate the busy travel day and ground the giant balloons at the Macy's parade. Forecasts call for sustained winds of twenty miles per hour and gusts of thirty-six miles per hour.

When the small house comes into view, Clio feels a shiver travel through her body from her ears to her toes. She tastes vomit in her mouth. Her hands tremble and her palms grow slick. After this weekend, she's concerned that she might be at the edge of another panic attack. She must eat something. She forgot to eat earlier. She looks over at Jack's house next door. A small pink bike sits outside it. He has daughters now. A three-year-old named Maddy and an eighteen-month-old named Gabby. They live in Chicago but are back here visiting his parents for Thanksgiving, just as they were last year.

Her father stops the car. The drum of the engine fades into an evocative silence. Sunshine blasts in on them.

"Clio," her father says, grabbing her hand, then taking her chin to turn her face toward him. "You were busy moving on. You're here now. I'm happy you're here."

Clio nods. Tears come, but she won't let them fall. It's a familiar feeling, this welling up. All of those years of stuffing it down, of wanting to let go or lash out, but resisting because she knew her role: to be a buffer, to support them with her meekness and invisibility, to quietly navigate the turbulence. There was enough drama. She couldn't add to it.

She looks over at her father and feels an intense mixture of empathy and anger. He's been through hell, a hell only she knows, but he never once put Clio first. He never pulled her aside and asked her how *she* was doing. It was always about Eloise, her cycles, her depressions and episodes. It was a given that Clio would hold it together and she did, but the resentment built.

And the house. There it is. The small home that could have been charming had it been cared for, but it wasn't cared for and so it wasn't charming. The exterior paint is rudely chipped, the roof a constellation of angry leaks, and the walls inside are zebra striped with brown water stains. Every now and then, Eloise would energetically scamper about, proclaiming a desire to "fix it up," to beautify. She'd do her little dance, collecting carpet and paint samples, but these little squares would meet their predictable fate on the tiny kitchen table Clio's father built in their backyard, gathering dust. They'd sit there next to the unopened bills and her father's crushed cigarette packs.

She follows her father inside.

Everything is the same. Everything is different.

The same flickering lights. The same damp, musty smell. The same old fridge that makes the angry humming sound. The same stained linoleum floors. The same water-damaged walls. But all else is gone, all the colorful clutter and knickknacks of their onetime life. Big boxes sit in the center of each room, boxes labeled in her father's clumsy scrawl, the antithesis of her mother's meticulous handwriting. She remembers them well, those minuscule, precise cursive letters that filled the margins of her books, the pages of her journals.

After it happened, Clio stayed at home for a week. She and her father went to church on Christmas Eve as the three of them had always done. Over the years, her mother had grown deeply religious, more and more inclined to speak of Jesus and the devil and whether the three of them would be saved, all of this starkly inconsistent with her longtime devotion to Darwin and his theory of evolution. Clio sat in a pew at the back of the church last year and thought of her mother and wondered where she'd gone. They had heeded her wishes and buried her body at the Grove Street Cemetery near campus.

"I'll see you tonight," her father says now. "I'll leave you the car. The site's not too far; I could use the walk."

"Thanks," Clio says, and nods. Her father still works as a supervisor for a construction company. When her mother was alive, he often worked several jobs at once just to make up for her mother's destructive spending. There were weeks when he would barely sleep, juggling construction shifts and stints at Yale–New Haven Hospital disposing of medical waste.

Clio watches him go, wishes he wouldn't leave, though; it's unsettling to be here alone. She walks through the house, empty room by empty room. Memories flicker like fireflies. In the living room, she recalls that afternoon sitting with her mother on the beige couch as Eloise lectured her on the principles of natural selection. She was only six or seven and found it pretty boring, but she knew her mother would quiz her, so she paid close attention.

In the kitchen, she recalls so many silent and strained meals, the three of them sitting around, the air dense with things they couldn't say.

Her parents' bedroom. The bed in which Eloise spent the bulk of Clio's childhood. The bed Clio would climb into when she was feeling lost and brave. The bed where her mother had loud sex with her father. And with other men, too. Promiscuity, Clio would learn when conducting her obsessive research, is a hallmark of the disease. She opens the closet door and there they are, all the beautiful dresses her mother wore when she was feeling well enough. Clio would walk through the door after school each day and brace herself. Would Eloise be in a bathrobe or one of these ethereal frocks? She reaches out and touches them, one by one. Silks and laces and wool. She holds the rust-colored gown up to her nose, inhales. She can almost smell the cinnamon from her mother's Christmas apple pie. She steps back, closes the closet door.

Clio's bedroom is just as she left it. Books spill from the shelves. The birds she carved out of wood with her father rest on the windowsill. Stuff everywhere, cluttered and dusty, and she doesn't know where to begin.

She calls Smith.

"Hi. I'm walking through the house and I don't know what to do. Talk me through this. *Please.*"

"Okay. First, *breathe*. Remember: they are just things. It is up to you what you keep and what you toss. You're going keep things that are associated with memories you *want* to have. If something makes you feel negative, leave it behind and don't feel guilty about it. Keep books you read and loved, but you don't need to keep everything. It's not a betrayal to throw things out. Grab a garbage bag and a box. The bag gets the junk. The box gets the treasures. I wish I could be there to help. If not for this Thanksgiving/wedding double punch . . ."

"Me too," Clio says. "I'm scared, Smith. Henry's coming. He'll be here soon. He's going to see this place. I'm going to tell him."

"Clio, he wouldn't be coming there if he didn't care about you already. It will be fine and I'm proud of you for opening up to him, for showing him your past. It's a giant step."

It is a giant step. Clio remembers how nervous she was to bring Smith here for the first time. Smith is the only one other than Jack who's been in this home, and it took Clio a long time to muster the courage to invite her. What would this shiny girl with her fancy designer dorm-room sheets and silver-framed photographs think of her depressing and decrepit childhood home? It turned out that she was silly to be worried; Eloise was on her best behavior that day and Smith came and marveled at the trinkets from Clio's childhood.

When she hangs up with Smith, everything feels slightly less sinister. Smith's words ring in her ears. *They are just things. It is up to you what you keep and what you toss.* Nothing revolutionary, but hearing her voice helped. It always does. She pulls open a drawer. It's filled with pencils that smell like fruit, sketches of birds, loose-leaf papers with bubble-letter doodles of her name.

She grabs the big black garbage bag and dumps the contents of the whole drawer in. Only dust remains. She runs her fingers along its surface, feels a sense of satisfaction. She begins to attack the rest of the room. She finds all of her old chapter books—paperbacks of *The Baby-Sitters Club* and *Nancy Drew*—and decides she will give them to Jack's girls.

There are some books she will take with her. Books she read with her mother and alone, almost all of them about birds. She places them gingerly in the box. Scribbles her name on the outside.

Her phone rings again. That number. She picks up and hears a man's voice.

"Is this Clio?"

"Yes," she says, but then she loses the call.

She texts Jack.

Clio: Did u just call from a blocked number?

Jack: No. Why? When do I get to see you?

Clio: Getting strange calls. Tonight?

Jack: Looking forward! The girls can't wait to see Auntie C.

Hours pass. She loses track of time and realizes with a start that she must get Henry from the train.

1:02PM

"We never *do know about anything, do we?"*

At the New Haven station again, people wait and mill about, most of them lost in their smartphones. It's hard to remember life before these things. Clio keeps an eye on the time, waits at the top of the stairs just as her father did this morning. Her pulse quickens and a fluttering fills her. She spoke to Henry just this morning and felt pretty good about things, remarkably calm about his impending visit, but now she's a tangle of nerves. When her breath grows shallow and her chin starts its tingling, she fishes in her pocket for the Xanax. She swallows it without water, the powdery residue leaving an awful taste in her mouth. She hates to take these pills—they remind her grimly of

Eloise—but this afternoon is too important to have it derailed by another panic attack.

Soon it's clear a train has arrived from the sudden throng of people riding up the escalator, hefting bags up the stairs. She doesn't see him. A wave of panic pummels her, but then there he is at the bottom of the steps, looking up at her. He wears his favorite sweater again, and jeans, and his hat. He looks young.

"I'm here," he says when he reaches her, and wraps her in a hug. "On your turf."

"My turf," she says, the two words strange, stiff on her lips. She walks him to her dad's Ford, and as they approach it, the dusty rust-colored car her parents have had forever, she feels ashamed of it. It's not just a car. It's more. As if he can tell where her mind is going, he says something.

"Look at this charming relic," he says.

"I learned to drive in this car, you know."

They get in. Clio sits in the driver's seat and looks at him. Her throat tightens and she's aware of the thinning of her breath. She can't do it yet. She needs more time. "Have you eaten? Why don't we grab a bite? And then we can walk around campus and head back to the house. My dad doesn't get off work until six, but he will race back to say hello before I take you back to the station."

"Sounds lovely," Henry says, shooting her a quizzical glance and then casting his gaze out the window. "What a lovely ride that was. I haven't been on a train in an eternity. Something wonderfully soothing about traveling that way."

Clio drives, that word he always uses on a loop in her head—*lovely, lovely, lovely*—and he puts his hand on her knee and squeezes. In her mind, she goes over her plan. They will eat. She will tell him everything. She will not get overly emotional. She will be matter-of-fact and cool in her delivery. It will be *fine*. They will share dessert, something chocolate and rich, and then go for a walk around campus.

At Union League Café, a brasserie on Chapel Street, the maître d' shows them to a sun-blanched table by the window. They sit.

"I haven't been here since graduation," Clio says, draping her napkin on her lap, looking around. "I came here with my parents and Smith's family. I think we drank four bottles of champagne between us."

She remembers how painful that night was, how awkward. Smith's perfectly polished parents presented their daughter with a glossy brochure for the pristine San Remo apartment, her graduation gift. Clio's parents just sat there, nervous, quiet and stunned. She felt it too, out of her league, in the fine restaurant with its glorious beaux arts atmosphere and endless wine list. These kinds of places don't intimidate her as much now; she's had plenty of time to grow accustomed to them, particularly since Henry.

Today it's not the restaurant that makes her anxious but what she has brought him here to say. She sips her water, spills some of it down the front of her shirt. He blots it with his napkin.

"Are you okay, Clio?" he says, genuine concern plain in his eyes. "Deep breaths, darling."

The waiter comes. Hands them menus. The words are blurry on the page. *Confit de Canard. Homard Roti. Bouillabaisse.* Her head feels light. Her chin tingles. Her tongue feels leaden in her mouth. She wills the Xanax to kick in.

"Are you okay?" Henry says again.

She nods, squints at the menu. He takes her hand, lifts her chin to look at him.

"I'm going to ask you once more. Are you okay?"

Met with his unyielding gaze, she answers. "I don't know, Henry. That's the thing. That's what I haven't been able to tell you. I don't *know* if I'm okay. That's what I've been worried about all these years, whether I'm okay, whether I'm sick like she was, what's going to happen."

Words are just spilling from her and it's clear that he's confused.

"Okay, slow down. Why are we at this restaurant?" he whispers, then stands. "I don't need an elaborate meal. I'm here to see *you*."

Henry takes charge, talks with the waiter, puts a protective arm around Clio and guides her out of the restaurant and back out to the street.

"Take your time," he says. "Tell me what's going on."

She looks at him and suddenly she knows she must tell him everything. She *wants* to tell him everything. It's time.

"Do you mind if we walk?" she says. "I want you to take you somewhere."

He takes her hand and they walk. She just starts talking, the floodgates opening. She tells him everything.

That she was thirteen when she found out her mother was sick. That Eloise fell into a depression soon after Clio was born and was diagnosed with bipolar disorder. That her parents hid the diagnosis from her, or tried to. Clio always knew something was wrong. She told herself that her mother was just moody, but she was a smart kid and she knew it was more. But then Eloise disappeared one day. She was gone for days and she finally turned up in a hospital in England. They got her home and she was in the hospital for weeks while they figured out her meds and gave her electroshock therapy. Eloise didn't believe anything was wrong with her. No, it was all a conspiracy hatched by the big bad pharmaceutical companies and her depressions were the work of the devil. Clio's father told her about Eloise's illness and Clio spent those weeks researching this disease she'd never heard of. She learned everything she could. Including that she could be sick one day too. That her chances were pretty high. *Are* pretty high.

Jack was the only person she told. She told him the very day she found out, racing over to his house, letting herself in through the kitchen door, settling down next to him on the couch. He looked up from his comic books and listened as she talked and then as she cried, and he told her that she would be okay. Their talks became ritual, true medicine; this is where Clio went when she couldn't be at home, which was often. Clio also confided in Jack's mom, Katherine, who worked at the Planned Parenthood in town not far from them and had some fluency in medical speak.

Henry squeezes her hand. "But you're fine, right?" he says, smiling. A question. "Look at you. You're *fine*." Now a statement.

She hears his words, but they don't sink in. They are wispy, almost imaginary. Is he minimizing what she's been through? Doesn't he understand the gravity of what she's saying? Her mother was very sick and she might be too. This is no small thing, but she can't expect him to understand. Just because she looks fine doesn't mean she is. To the outside world, Eloise managed to hide her illness pretty well; everyone was always remarking on how beautiful and intelligent she was. You couldn't always know from looking at her that there was so much turmoil under the surface.

"It was pretty awful. She was either in bed for long stretches or flying around our house in a rage, completely manic. I learned how to navigate, when to hide, but it wasn't easy. The summer before I went to college, she tried to kill herself. It didn't work that time."

"That time?" Henry says, and she watches the shock register in his face.

Clio doesn't answer. She gets an idea. She will take him.

Her body begins to tremble as she walks him down Chapel Street. They turn right at High Street. She leads him past Elm and Wall until they hit Grove and the entrance to the cemetery. She looks over at Henry and his face remains calm. He looks down at her and smiles.

"The Grove Street Cemetery," she says, her head light, leading him in. "My mother used to bring me here as a girl and I thought nothing of it. She often talked about death but didn't make it scary. She was always pointing out dead beetles and spiders and she brought me here and we'd just walk around and she'd give me little history lessons on all of the famous people who've been buried here. All these famous Yale and New Haven folks. Eli Whitney and Samuel Johnson and Timothy Dwight. She had an odd fascination with this place. She left instructions to call the superintendent here and we learned that she'd purchased a plot. She had even picked out a quote for her headstone."

Clio leads him along the grass, clutching his arm tightly. She feels as if she might faint. Tears begin to rise as they reach it. She bends down to trace the etched letters of her mother's name. *Eloise Marsh. July 3, 1961–December 22, 2012.* As she begins to read Darwin's words, her body convulses and she begins to sob. She collapses to the grass. *As buds give rise by growth to fresh buds, and these, if vigorous, branch out and overtop on all sides many a feebler branch, so by generation I believe it has been with the great Tree of Life . . .*

Henry pulls her up and holds her to him, wrapping her tightly. She buries her face in the wool of his sweater.

"I've got you," he says. "I've got you."

The three words repeat in her head like a heartbeat, *I've got you I've got you I've got you,* and time passes and she feels herself breathing again. She looks up at him.

"I'm so sorry," she says.

"No," he says. "I'm so sorry."

She takes his hand and they retrace their steps to leave.

"December of 2012?" he says, his eyes wide but kind.

"She killed herself before Christmas last year, Henry," Clio says, stopping, looking at him.

"My God, Clio," he says, pulling her to him, wrapping his arms around her. "I'm so sorry. I wish you would've told me," he says. "You could have, you know."

"I was so scared," she says, and the relief of allowing the tears to come warms her.

Henry holds her for a long time. She waits for the panic to come, waits for her brain to scream, *Run,* but miraculously it is silent. Her mind doesn't race. Her heart doesn't seize and then quicken. She can feel herself grounded in her body. As if in a trance, she sinks deeper into his arms.

"Why didn't you tell me?" he says, and she can see now that his eyes are wet, his features soft and sad.

"I liked you. I liked you even though it was so soon after. I was worried it would frighten you away. I can barely handle it and I have no choice. Why choose to deal with this?"

After it happened, after she was back in the city, she holed up in her office at the museum, and instead of working on her bird research and grant proposals, she spent hours and hours researching suicide. She swam in statistics—that more people in the U.S. now commit suicide each year than die in car accidents, one every fourteen minutes or so. She developed a morbid fascination with all the famous writers and artists who had killed themselves or tried to: Ernest Hemingway and Virginia Woolf and David Foster Wallace. She learned that it's likely that Beethoven was bipolar. But the most harrowing statistic of all would linger and haunt her: children of a parent who has committed suicide have a one-in-five chance of committing suicide themselves. She doesn't tell Henry this last fact; she knows better.

"I understand why you were afraid," Henry says, nodding. "But you needn't be, okay? I'm here and I want you to tell me as much as you're comfortable telling me. Now I feel like a bastard for talking about missing my mother, God. I can't imagine what it would be like. Clio, I'm sorry."

No, he can't imagine. That's the thing. That's the hard part, the loneliest part. Death is natural, her mother taught her that, but this isn't. This is more than grief, more than loss. This is mystery and heartbreak and harrowing regret. This is shame blended with sadness, fear with the most ferocious anger. This is the opposite of closure. It's an open wound that will never heal. What she would give to experience a purer grief, a cleaner breed of longing. What she would give to not lose so many moments trying to understand why, wondering what she could have done. What she would give not to feel the unannounced spikes of anger, the showers of guilt, the haunting howl of questions she'll never be able to answer. What she would give to visit her mother's grave and cry simple tears.

She walks him back toward campus. A silence shrouds them and she feels a faint lifting, a sharp sense of relief. He holds her hand tight. She pulls him onto Old Campus, where she lived freshman year. "So, anyway, Mr. Kildare," she says, laughing nervously, "this is Yale. My escape hatch."

She thinks back. To those first days of school, to that time of keen flailing when her mother, in the throes of mania, would show up unannounced on campus. Smith stepped in and took charge. She had this magical way of intervening, of escorting Eloise back home. Clio remembers the first time Eloise appeared in nothing but a red lace nightgown and a garish face full of makeup. It was October of their freshman year. She barged into their dorm room and started moving things around. *Who is that?* Smith asked, because how was she to know? Clio didn't have any pictures up. She didn't talk about her mother at all.

It's my mother, Clio said, panicked, feeling frozen. But Smith was all action; she waltzed over to Eloise and held out her hand. *Hello, Mrs. Marsh, so lovely to finally meet you. I'm Smith, Clio's roommate. Why don't we take a walk? There's a great coffee place nearby.* Clio stared in disbelief as Smith efficiently extracted her babbling mother from the dorm. She watched from the window as Smith led Eloise out, down the small set of stairs, and out of view. Smith returned an hour later as if nothing had happened. Clio thanked her, still stunned. And then she explained. *My mother is crazy,* Clio said, even though she tried not to use that word. They talked for hours and hours that afternoon, just as they'd done a mere month before when Smith found out she was pregnant. What a wild relief it was to finally open up, to have someone listen and not judge. It was more than tit for tat. It was friendship. Swiftly formed, swiftly cemented.

Clio looks around at the glorious green campus, the place that once intimidated her. "Sometimes, I'm still dumbfounded that I managed to get myself out of that broken house in good enough shape to come here."

"Were your parents proud of you? They must have been, right?" he says, rolling with the abrupt topic change. "I mean, it's Yale."

"Yes and no," she says. "I think they wanted to be, but it was never that simple."

School was a salvation for Clio, a place that felt safe and normal, and she worked hard and got good grades and this got her mother's attention. A science teacher encouraged her to apply and shepherded her through the process, reading all of her application materials, with the exception of her personal essay. "It's just sort of private," Clio had said. Her teacher had nodded in understanding. She got in. And then she hatched this foolish plan to come here and start over and forge a normal life.

The plan, at its most cellular level, was to get out. To climb in the backseat of her parents' battered Ford wagon one final time and travel the measly few miles to campus, to walk with them, maybe even between them, through that big fancy gate. They would help carry her things. They would climb together the steps of her assigned dorm and watch as Clio quite literally kicked open the door to her future. They would help her unpack, get settled.

It didn't happen this way.

She arrived alone. She walked through the door of her dorm and there was Smith, glamorous and tall, all tanned legs in a pair of white shorts and a blue floral blouse. She wore her dark hair in a ponytail and flashed a beatific smile. In the background, Smith's crisply coiffed parents hovered. Bitsy snapped tags from fancy tasseled throw pillows. Thatcher fixed Clio with his squinty, judgmental eyes and pinned her with that cruel question that's stayed with her.

Where are your parents?

Oh, they couldn't be here today.

Clio left it at that, but what more was she supposed to say? That her mother had tried to kill herself days before? That she was all drugged up in a small room in the psych ward at Yale–New Haven Hospital, that her father wouldn't tear himself away from his wife even for an hour to take his only child to college?

"I remember that April day when I got my acceptance letter. And I just thought it would be a happy thing, that we'd celebrate, but it wasn't that simple. I hate to admit it, but I was so relieved to be getting out of there and then so guilty about my own relief. When I got here, I was so overwhelmed, Henry. So excited, but I also felt like an impostor."

She remembers now those flutters of optimism she felt standing on this grass for the first time as a student. Yale. A world she'd glimpsed from the little coffee shop where she'd sit with Jack as he worked shifts in high school, stacking napkins, refilling stirrers, watching college students come and go, students lugging big books that would lift them up in some poetic and heralded way, students brimming with easy laughter, students who were on their way to a species of greatness well beyond what she herself could hope for.

She remembers the dizziness and awe and gratitude and respect and mostly fear, always fear, that it would all be taken away. And so she worked very, very hard to make sure it wasn't, to prove that she in fact belonged. And yet she never quite did feel that she did. She always felt fringe, peripheral, like an observer studying an exotic breed of bird, taking notes, doing research. It astonished her how many of her classmates seemed to take it all for granted, these four years, this tremendous opportunity. They skipped classes and got drunk night after night and many of them, like Smith, managed somehow to pull off near-perfect grades. Their nonchalance was a badge of sorts, something Clio both envied and felt sickened by.

"I had this interesting optimism. Told myself it would all work out," she says to Henry. "I had these vivid recurring dreams. They were really simple. My parents just turned around and told me they loved me." She plays it out in her head now, this hopeful story. Eloise and William Marsh said they were proud of their only child, Clio; they owned up to their shortcomings and apologized, noting how overwhelmed they were by life and circumstance. There was always a happy ending where they told Clio how much they loved her.

But they were only dreams.

"I just wanted to be normal, Henry," she says. "That's all I wanted. I didn't want to break any records or win any prizes. I just wanted to fit in."

Even then, she knew normal was a chimera, that, if anything, normal is a pejorative, boring, anti-Tolstoyan term. Clio knew that smart kids, Yale kids, would shun normal and embrace oddity, originality, wildness, whimsy, that if anything darkness and deepness would be championed over light and surface and ease, but those were the things she wanted: light and surface and ease.

From across the campus, Clio eyes Vanderbilt Hall, where she and Smith went freshman year for a party. Clio's first college party. Before it all went black that night, the details were sharp. She was just another freshman girl and she trailed behind Smith and a group of other freshmen along High Street. They all seemed to know each other. They were giddy, skipping, tripping, already drunk, or maybe just happy. Clio hung back, watched her own feet plod along, progressing on the pavement where so many great people had walked in their day, one foot and then the next, and she wondered if she would ever catch up, whether she'd ever be one of them, those who led the way. They all filed upstairs, swam into a crowded room. Bodies bumped, hands flailed, pretty lips were curled into victorious Ivy League smiles. The revelry was full throttle and red cups were everywhere, dotting the darkened scene—in fingers, on heads, on mantels, on ledges and sofa cushions. She drank a cup of punch and then another and felt like she was floating, like she was *fine*. She had more.

The next morning, she woke up in a hospital room at Yale–New Haven and learned that she'd come in with a .12 blood alcohol level, that her stomach had been pumped.

"There was this one night just a few weeks into college," Clio says, holding Henry's hand between both of hers. "I was so frightened, Henry. I was so sure it was my time. I went to a party with Smith and I felt so anxious in that room with all those kids, so out of place. And I drank and loosened up and the next thing I knew I was waking up in a hospital room and I was convinced that the disease was there, just lurking in my genes, waiting to pop. I'm still anxious about it."

The memories of that one night continue to haunt her all these years later. She was all alone, tucked into a hospital bed. Her arm had fresh scratches and was tethered to an IV bag. She tried to hide her tears, but the room was menacing in its brightness and they were big, her tears, tumbling down, streaking salt on her cheeks. The nurse looked away, said nothing. The black sky outside veered gray, and morning came. They called her parents, but there was no answer.

"I actually requested a psych consult and this young doctor comes and I tell him all about my mother, about her illness, and I want to know if I have it. And this poor guy starts asking me these questions about how I sleep and whether I talk fast sometimes and whether I ever feel my mind racing. And these questions make me even more nervous, but he releases me. He tells me he thinks I'm fine, a wait-and-see kind of thing."

"But *look at you,*" he says again, optimistically. "You're okay."

Is she though? Is she okay? Wasn't she the one on a street corner in a bathrobe and heels, what, seventy-two hours ago? Bipolar usually presents in adolescence or in one's early twenties, often during college years. For Clio's mother, it emerged soon after she gave birth to Clio—at eighteen—and there Clio was, her age at onset, and all she could feel was fear. She learned to deal with the fear—maybe she internalized it—but it was always there, in the corner. And when she graduated, it was so hard for her to go to New York even though it was all she wanted to do. Though the guilt she felt for leaving, for not sticking close, was acute.

"Yes. *Maybe,*" she says. "Maybe now I'm okay. But I wasn't. I was a mess. I joined this awful suicide support group in midtown. I had this horrifying recurring dream where I found my mother and she wasn't breathing and I did nothing to help her. But then something happened, and these things got better."

"What happened?" he says.

"I met you, Henry. And I began having moments where I wouldn't think of her and you and I have had so much fun, but then the other night when I saw the apartment and you said all those wonderful things, I felt like this big liar, you know? I felt you needed to know about all of this. To know what you're getting. I come with a lot of baggage. It didn't seem fair. And then you mentioned wanting us to have a life together. To be a family. And this was incredible, Henry, but you know something? I haven't allowed myself to even consider having kids. Even if I'm spared in this game of genetic roulette, what's to say my kids will be? I'm not sure I'm willing to risk that."

He takes her face in his hands. "And what's to say I won't be hit by the M79 next week crossing the street going to get my *New York Times*? Or that I won't wake up with bloody cancer all over my body like my poor mum did? Or that you won't discover some brand-new species of hummer in some remote isle or some much younger and better man and leave me? Clio, we *never* do know about anything, do we?"

She has a sudden urge to grab him tightly and hold on for dear life. So she does.

We never do know about anything.

"No," she says. "I guess we don't."

3:47PM

"I've never wanted you more."

So, this is it," Clio says, walking Henry through the front door of the house. Somehow, it looks different, and feels different, with him here.

"I'm picturing you as a little girl," he says, looking around. "Bouncing around here in your pigtails."

There wasn't much bouncing. Or pigtails. There was tiptoeing and sneaking and she did her own hair and learned to cook her own meals.

"Sorry it's nothing fancy," Clio says, ashamed of the humble surroundings.

"Don't apologize," Henry says, standing still, surveying the space. "This is the kitchen, I see?"

"Yes," Clio says. "We spent a lot of time in this room. Mostly at this little table my father built. Had all of our meals here."

She had many breakfasts alone. Her father often worked odd hours and frequently slept through until noon, and her mother was either in bed too or up and about, buzzing with energy, cooking up some elaborate meal she would never finish. Often the ingredients would end up thrown on the floor.

"And the living room through there," Henry says, walking into the dimly lit wood-paneled room.

Clio nods and follows him into the room, the room Eloise never called a living room. Living was done in every room. "She called it Darwin's Parlor," Clio surprises herself by saying. After all this time avoiding the topic, it feels strange to talk about her mother.

Henry reaches into an open box and pulls out a few books. "All Darwin," he says, studying them. "My God, you weren't kidding around."

Eloise had a manic fixation with Charles Darwin. She'd spend thousands of dollars, blowing through money they didn't have, buying books and artifacts en masse. Packages would arrive daily and her elation was wild when they did; she'd rip into the boxes and stockpile her treasures in the room off the kitchen, Darwin's Parlor, leaving the shelves ominously empty, stacking books into precarious towers that would invariably tumble, flipping an internal switch to black rages or brooding depressions. To make up for her epic sprees, her exhausted father took extra shifts at work. There were times when they only ate ramen or leftovers Jack's mom, Katherine, brought over. On more than one occasion, Eloise insisted she saw Darwin in their small yard. Clio and her father learned quickly to play along; questioning her claims was too risky.

Clio meets Henry's eye, shakes her head, forces a smile. She joins him in sifting through the boxes. She finds it, holds it up. "And here we have the pièce de résistance, an expensive early edition of *On the Origin of Species*. My childhood Bible. Other kids learned about princesses and pirates and I learned about natural selection."

Henry takes the book from her and studies it.

When it came in the mail, Eloise called Clio in and sat her down and presented it like it was a new puppy. She let Clio hold it, run her fingers along the spine. *You should know it's actually called* On the Origin of Species by Means of Natural Selection; or, The Preservation of Favoured Races in the Struggle for Life.

"I'm thinking all this Darwin material served you pretty well, though," Henry says, a twinkle in his eye. "A bird guru, curator at one of the best museums in the world, professor at an elite university."

"I suppose," Clio says quietly.

What she does not say: Eloise practically locked Clio, her sole student, in this room to conduct her "lectures" on Darwin's life and work. *He was nearly forbidden from sailing on the* Beagle *because of the shape of his nose, Clio! He once ate an owl while in the Glutton Club at Cambridge, Clio! He would have been a doctor but couldn't stand the sight of blood. He was a backgammon fiend! Had a mountain named after him by age twenty-five! Remember: he didn't actually coin "survival of the fittest"; that was Herbert Spencer! He married his first cousin! He lost faith in Christianity when he witnessed slavery and lost his beloved daughter Annie to scarlet fever when she was only ten. His wife, Emma, filled a small box with Annie's treasures and kept it with her until her own death.*

"Would you put the Christmas tree in here?" Henry says, squinting, snapping her from the sluice of memories.

"One of them, yes."

There were always several trees. Leading up to the holidays, Eloise talked fast and made grandiose plans and proclamations, but several days of this and she'd be fully manic, ablaze with a cutting desire to make everything *perfect*. It was always a depressing portrait of excess. Seven pumpkin pies. Four nativity scenes. A tree in every room, decorated with homemade ornaments.

"What were your Christmases like as a girl?"

There is a sense of wonder in his eyes and Clio can tell that he's simply curious, but she finds herself bristling; this simple question makes her recoil.

"I'm sorry," he says, seeming to sense her discomfort. "I just want to know things."

"It's okay," she says. "I want to tell you, but it's hard." Telling is reliving in a way; telling makes it more real. "An example? One Christmas, I took my gifts up to my room and she ducked her head in and told me to clean my room because there was wrapping paper and boxes everywhere. And I was a kid and I stalled and then I heard her coming and without a word, she dumped everything, every single gift and other things too, into a giant garbage bag and took it out to the lawn and burned it in front of me."

"My Lord," Henry says. "You went through hell, Clio."

She nods, fighting tears that want to come. "And now she's gone and now I get to worry about my dad. Lucky me."

"What's he like? You haven't said much about him."

"He's a good man," she says, thinking about this, "but it's been so hard for him. They met in high school. She got pregnant when they were seniors. They had me. They stayed together. And I know he was doing his best, working all those jobs, tending to her impossible needs, but he also enabled her."

Even as a girl, Clio was amazed that her father didn't leave. All of those fights, the howling screams and shattered glasses and delusions of grandeur and bleak months in bed and constant threats of suicide and attempts to burn down this house. Eloise would disappear for days at a time and they'd find her in odd places with odd men, and he just took it. He was her punching bag and Clio had a front-row seat when she wasn't in the ring herself. And that was the worst, when Eloise turned her aggression on Clio and her father did *nothing*. He was supposed to protect her, right? But he just treated Clio like this unlucky partner in crime, like they were in this bad situation together.

His refrain: *We'll have to talk to the doctor about tweaking her meds.* But the problem was that most of the time she wouldn't even take her meds. And Clio could handle it, but it devastated her that her father was never present for the other stuff. The science fairs and school plays and soccer games. She didn't want her mother on the sidelines, but he could have found a way to be there. He made his priority clear; he was always working or tending to the ever-unpredictable Eloise.

"Did you have a service?" he says.

"A small one," Clio says. "Just my father and me and Jack and his parents. We went to the cemetery for the burial and came back here to the house. I made egg salad because it was her favorite."

"Did she leave a note?" he asks, and then backpedals. "I'm sorry. Am I asking too many questions?"

Clio shakes her head no. It surprises her that his questions are welcome, that she wants to tell him these things. "She didn't leave a note, but trust me, I tore this place up looking for one."

"Of course you did," he says, taking her hand and holding it.

"Even now," she says, looking around, "I wonder if there's some place I haven't looked. I find myself holding out for this secret letter of apology. It's really pathetic."

"It's not pathetic," he says, taking her shoulders, pinning her with his eyes. "It's *human*. It only makes sense that you want to understand."

Clio nods. Leads the way to her bedroom. She hears a sound. And it takes a good minute to register that the sound is coming from her. She's weeping. Huge, heaving sobs shake her entire body. Henry grabs her from behind, drapes his hands around her, kisses the top of her head again and again.

"I'm just so angry," she says, her words weak, her eyes brimming with tears. "I know she was sick and in pain, but how selfish is it to end your life? And I'm angry because it's always been about her. I'm so tired of this. I'm sorry to unload all of this on you. It's just a lot to be back here."

She catches her breath, startled that she's telling him all of this. Henry spins her around to face him, pulls her down to sit on the bed. She looks at him, his gently lined, handsome face, the silvery shadow of stubble on his chin, the endless blue of his Irish eyes. She kisses him, pulls away.

"*Stop* apologizing," he says, putting his forefinger to her lips. She opens her mouth and takes his finger in. Looks at him. He pulls his finger from her lips and traces a line down to her chin, then to her neck, and lower and lower, until he's tugging at the button of her shirt.

"I've never wanted you more," she says.

Clio unbuttons her own shirt and peels it off. Henry buries his head between her breasts. She pushes him back on the little bed and climbs on top of him. He's hard beneath her; she can feel it through his jeans. He scrambles to unbuckle his belt as she kisses his neck, bites his earlobe. It only takes a moment or two and he's inside her and it occurs to her that the window is open, that someone might see, that Jack might see, but this only turns her on more. She rocks back and forth fast and hears him moan and he holds his hand to her mouth and she kisses it again and again and again and she screams out, louder than she's ever screamed maybe, and he pinches her side as he does when he finishes and when she stops screaming she opens her eyes and looks down at him and smiles.

They lie there. Pressed against each other in the tiny bed.

He points at the ceiling. "Tell me about the stars," he says, his voice still husky.

"Eloise and I put them up," she says. "I remember that day. She stood on my father's ladder. She knew everything about every constellation. That was a good day."

"So there were good days?"

"There were," she says, thankful for the reminder. Eloise could be magically present: humorous, ebullient, deeply curious about the smallest details. Nothing, to her, was meaningless. Everything was of consequence, worth learning about. *Let's look it up,* she'd say about the odd-shaped cloud in the sky, the dead bug on the driveway. These were characters and stories, part and parcel of an ineffably ordered cosmos. When she was flying, her enthusiasm would ripple through everything. She'd present gifts from tag sales, she'd pontificate about her latest *theory* about self and world.

"I've noticed that sometimes you call her Eloise and sometimes your mother."

"Yeah," Clio says. "Depends on the memory. If it's a tough one, it's easier if she's Eloise."

A sound comes from downstairs.

"Shit," she says. "My dad."

"Shit!" he says, shooting up.

And they are laughing like kids, scrambling for their clothes. She slips into the bathroom and fixes herself in the mirror.

"Pull yourself together, Mr. Kildare, and come say hello," she says, kissing him once more, running off.

6:11PM

"This is Henry, Dad."

In the kitchen, her father takes off his coat and drapes it over the back of a chair. He walks to the fridge and grabs a bottle of beer.

"Hey, Dad," she says.

He turns and smiles and Clio can see it in his face that he's nervous.

"Henry will be down in a minute," she says, but Henry is right behind her. She meets his eye and his face relaxes and wordlessly she ushers him over.

"This is Henry, Dad," Clio says. The word *Dad* sounds strange as she says it. She hasn't called him this in a long time. *William* or *my father,* yes, but not *Dad*. A therapist once said this is what children do to distance themselves from their parents. "And, Henry, this is my father."

"It's great to meet you," Henry says, his voice firm, filled with confidence.

"You too," her father says, and nods.

They shake hands.

Clio hangs back and watches and as she does, she appreciates that this is a sight she never truly expected to see. They are both tall, almost exactly the same height—a touch more than six feet two—and they have similar builds. Wiry but strong. She realizes how on edge she is, how much she cares, that this is probably a good sign.

"Quick beer before you go?" her father says.

"That would be lovely," Henry says, taking a seat at the small kitchen table. He catches Clio's eye and she smiles.

So far, so good.

Her father returns with the beers and they all sit.

"Clio says you work in construction?" Henry says.

"For more than thirty years," her father says, and takes a long swig of his beer. "Since I was practically a kid."

"What are you working on now?" Henry asks.

"We're remodeling an old building not far from here to create an ambulatory care center for Yale–New Haven Hospital. It's fast-track project and there's a watertight budget, so it's been a bit crazy at times but also kind of interesting. There will be a radiology center and a lab. One of those jobs where I feel like I'm doing some good."

Henry smiles. "Well, I must say I have a great deal of admiration for the work you do. Just finished construction on my hotel and am floored by the amount of intense coordination and skill that goes into these projects. We had a million hiccups, but the windows alone nearly killed me. We were hoping to salvage the old ones, but we were inspected and needed to retrofit."

"Which ones did you end up installing?"

"We went with the Marvin double-hung Magnums," Henry says. "They look great but cost us a pretty penny."

"They're good, though," her father says, nodding. "Tried and true."

Clio sinks deeper into her chair and feels the rise and fall of her own breath. For a brief moment, the tangle of voices becomes muted and distant and she thinks to herself: *They are talking shop. They are discussing windows. This is going okay.*

Clio checks her watch. It's 6:31. "Henry, I need to get you to the train."

Henry smiles. "Oh, how I'd prefer to stay, but duty calls." He takes a final sip of his beer and shakes her father's hand. "It was good to meet you. I hope we have more than fifteen minutes next time."

"So do I," her father says, standing and taking the beer bottles to the counter. "It's probably a good thing you're getting out of here anyway. Otherwise, I might have gotten you all liquored up and grilled you about your intentions for my daughter."

A lifting. Clio hears herself laughing, feels her body relaxing even more. When's the last time she heard her father crack a joke? And where did this protectiveness come from? It's something she's always longed for, to have a parent look out for her. Maybe it's not too late. She looks at her father, catches his eye, and grins.

"Ah, I look forward to my day of pickling and grilling," Henry says. "Soon, I hope."

"Soon," her father says.

At the station, Clio parks and walks Henry inside.

"Thank you," she says, "for coming here. It means so much that you did this."

He takes her face in his hands. "I'm so happy I came. That you opened up to me, that you took me to the cemetery, to the house, that I met your old man."

Clio laughs. "If he's old, you're old, Henry. He isn't that much older than you."

"Well then, I'm old. Old and madly in love with a certain irresistible young thing. I love you, Clio. I love you even more than I did this morning. I didn't know that was possible."

Clio feels herself smile. His words are needed and she feels thankful for them; her body literally relaxes with relief. It's another one of those moments; this man, this thoughtful man, is saying these things to her.

"What's my Christmas present?" he begs her playfully. "Now I'm the one who can't handle surprises."

She shakes her head. "You and me both. You'll have to wait and see."

A baby cries. It's not a soft cry but a shrill, desperate howling, and Clio follows the sound. The baby is blond, wears pink. She wriggles in her mother's arm, flails madly to get down. The mother holds tight to her child, keeps her cool and kisses her daughter's head again and again, but the tantrum continues. Clio is transfixed. She stares at the scene, her body tightening with each shriek. Henry stands next to her as she feels herself fraying. She's dizzy. She grabs on to him.

"Clio? You were fine a moment ago."

And she was. He holds her up. She stares at the mother and child. She's six again. Six or seven. Sobbing on the cold floor of a grocery aisle. Eloise has left her clutching the box of chocolate chip cookies. She finds Eloise examining fat green watermelons, her eyes angry. *What's wrong with you, Clio?* she says. *Stop crying right now. You're making a scene.*

"Clio," Henry says, snapping her back. "*Clio.*"

"I can't do this to you, Henry," she says. "You deserve someone who doesn't fall apart like this. You deserve someone who can give you kids. You deserve better."

"Clio," he says, taking her face between his hands. "I want *you.*"

She pulls away, shakes him off her. "I just don't know if I can do this."

"You are not your mother, Clio," Henry says, his words loud now. People are watching. The baby stops crying. "How the hell do you think I feel knowing my mother died of bloody cancer at sixty-one? That she was suffering for months on end and couldn't even eat and died in terrible, crippling pain? None of us is immune to suffering, Clio. You can't go through life putting up walls to protect yourself from pain or grief. I've been around long enough to tell you there's no use."

She looks up at him. He's shaking now. His pale blue eyes are glossed with tears.

"I know," Clio says.

He waits. He waits for her to say something more, but she can't. The words are stuck inside her.

"I need to make my train," he says. "You know exactly where to find me."

Clio nods. And she waits for him to say *I love you,* but he doesn't this time.

And like that, he's gone. She's alone again. Her heart thumps wildly in her chest and she stands there frozen, the world swirling around her, the muted sounds of people going places a grating static in her ears.

8:04PM

"You'll figure it out as you go."

She drives and drives, her hands gripping the wheel, the world blurry through a curtain of fresh tears. More than an hour slips by as she makes her way through the streets of her hometown, her college town, her past.

When she pulls up back at the house, she thinks she sees something, a flutter of movement, a shadowy figure by the swing set, and her heart drops. She squints in the darkness, walks over. No one's there. Just the three swings, one for each of them. The center one is the one her mother chose. It's still broken, the rope cut and looped, dragging in the grass. Clio sits on the swing she always thought of as hers.

Eloise hanged herself here, inches from where Clio sits now, swinging like a child. Why couldn't it have been pills like the first time? Why did she have to go and ruin this, this one happy object from growing up? This is the closest Clio's gotten to it since it happened. She takes the rope and holds it, runs her hands over it, memorizes its roughness.

She swings. She cries. Thinks about how her father has been too sad, too paralyzed probably, to tear the swing set down, how he must look at it every single day.

She sends Henry a text.

Clio: I'm sorry. I'm so sorry. I love you. I hope you know that.

He doesn't respond. She doesn't blame him.

She swings, her cold hand wrapped around the rope. Her father has always loved building things. This was his first of many swing sets. An accidental side business was born. He made swing sets for Yale professors and their families, and sometimes Clio would tag along as he went to install them, glimpsing big homes and charmed lives and kids with different childhoods. It was work that made her father happy; Clio could see this, and that it heartened him to bring in some extra cash for the family, which they sorely needed once her mother could no longer teach and started going on her spending sprees. In doing her research, Clio would learn that financial irresponsibility was a hallmark of the disease, a telltale symptom of mania. They'd inherited the house from her grandmother June, but it cost something to maintain and it was always a question whether they'd be able to hold on to it.

She looks up. In the darkness, she sees Jack approaching on the lawn. He appears beside her, clutching an extra coat and a steaming mug. He wraps the coat around her and hands her the mug. He lowers to sit on the other swing.

Clio takes a sip. It's hot chocolate. Her childhood favorite. Jack's mother used to make them hot chocolate every winter and they'd pass the plastic bag of mini-marshmallows back and forth between them, refilling and refilling, making themselves sick.

"Spiked," he says. "I saw you out here and figured you could use it."

"You figured right," she says. "Kids asleep?"

"Yes," he says. "For now. I hope you'll come by and see all of us tomorrow?"

"Absolutely," she says, staring up at the sky. Stars twinkle. Beside her, he swings, pumping his legs, his feet skimming the grass.

"Where's Henry?"

"He had to get back to the hotel. You'll meet him next time."

If there is a next time, she thinks.

Jack nods. "You hanging in?"

Clio shoots him with a punitive look. "Not funny." Jack and Jack alone is the only person who gets to make a suicide joke.

"Kind of funny?" he says. "Maybe we are allowed to be funny now?"

"How are the girls?" Clio says.

"They're good," Jack says, looking toward his house. It amazes her that he has kids. "Maddy fought her nap for more than an hour and then passed out on the carpet, and Gabby is miserable cutting a tooth, but all's fair in love and war, eh? I'm fried."

"But no regrets?"

His eyes brighten as he looks at her. "Are you kidding me? It's a wild ride, this parenthood thing. Hardest thing I've done in my life and by far the best."

"What's it like?" Clio says, well aware that this is a ridiculous question.

"It's like yanking your own heart out of your chest and handing it over to these tiny humans. It's like falling in love again every day."

"Wow," Clio says, smiling at him. "What happened to my macho Jack?"

He grins. "Your macho Jack is a dad now. Total game changer."

"He wants a family, Jack. Henry does."

Jack doesn't seem surprised by this. "Do you? Is that what you want?"

"I don't know."

Clio shoves her hands in her pockets and looks down at the grass. She imagines Henry sitting on the train, probably fiddling away on his phone, getting things done, always getting things done. She still can't believe he came, that he met her father, that everything was fine.

The wind picks up and makes a murmuring, whistling sound. Clio snaps back into the present, looks over at Jack, Jack who was there for everything, who held her as she cried her way through childhood. It was the portrait of innocence, of platonic affection, until that one night the summer before college when it tipped into more. There was beer and laughter, a tangle of young lust and limbs in her floral-sheeted twin bed. It was each of their first time, a simple, sweet foray until Eloise walked in on them. Clio remembers her mother's eyes in that cruel moment, how they glowed in the dark, the rage-filled words she sputtered as she flipped on the light, the keen panic she and Jack shared. He scrambled for his things and escaped.

In the weeks that followed, Clio wondered what might have been if Eloise hadn't ruined that night, whether she and Jack would have found a way to be together, but even back then, Clio knew that it would never work. She loved him and would always love him in an abiding, brotherly way, but he'd seen too much and he knew too much. In August, she went to Yale and he went off to Wake Forest. They promised they'd speak on the phone and they did. Almost every evening of freshman year, less so as time went on, particularly after he met Jessica, an English major, now his wife and the mother of his girls.

She looks over at him, Jack, a new iteration of the boy next door. His eyes are bleary, his forehead showing faint wrinkles. His hair is beginning to thin, but only slightly. She can see that he's happy, content. His contentment, though palpable, is not of the simple, saccharine variety. She can see this. It's a complex breed, edged in effort and exhaustion, an elegy of real life. It inspires her.

"What if it is, though?" Clio says. "What if this is something I want? What if I do want kids with him?"

"Then you'll do it," Jack says, smiling. "You'll do it and you'll figure it out as you go. That's all any of us can do."

Clio hears this and feels an odd surge of optimism. *You'll figure it out as you go.* This coming from the one guy who knows *everything* she's been through, who saw it all unfold harrowing scene by scene, who knew her then and knows her now, who knew her mother. *You'll figure it out as you go.*

"He met Henry. And it was *fine,* Jack. They just sat there with their beers and talked construction. I don't know why I've been so afraid. I know it's not that easy, that it was just fifteen minutes, that it's bound to be more complicated, but I was kind of shocked. How do you think my dad seems anyway? Do you think he's handling this move okay?"

"Have you asked him?" Jack says. "Have you asked him how he's doing?"

Clio shoots him a punitive look. "You know how it is with us. The fine art of avoidance."

"You need to talk to him, Clio."

Clio nods, looks down at the grass. He's right.

"You going to miss this place?" he says.

"Yeah. More than I thought."

"This better not mean I won't ever see you," he says. He stands and walks over to her and reaches out his hand. Clio drags her feet in the grass to stop the swing. She lets Jack pull her to stand. He smiles down at her and throws both arms around her, pulls her into a hug. It's cold and she's shivering. He kisses her lips very lightly, but there's nothing to this kiss but simple affection, history. As if he's reading her mind, he says, "Not that my opinion matters anymore, but I think you would make a terrific mother. I always have. She's gone now, Clio. It's your time to live."

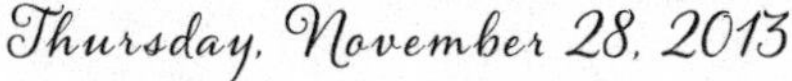

TATE

There is a creative fraction of a second when you are taking a picture. Your eye must see a composition or an expression that life itself offers you, and you must know with intuition when to click the camera. That is the moment the photographer is creative. Oop! The Moment! Once you miss it, it is gone forever.

—Henri Cartier-Bresson, in a 1957 interview with *The Washington Post*

INTERNATIONAL SCHOOL OF PHOTOGRAPHY

MFA (Photography) Application 2014

Statement of Interest and Intentions: Please outline your reasons for applying to this graduate program. Articulate how you envision contributing to the program. Make sure to include a description of your academic/professional background, a tentative plan of study or area of inquiry in the field, and your professional goals, and indicate how you see this program helping you reach those particular goals. If you have not been a student in the past five years, it is recommended that you address challenges and opportunities you might predict facing in pursuing the degree as well as the career possibilities you foresee upon completing the program.

The truth: I can finally afford to do what I want to do. I have long loved photography, ever since I was a small boy with a bowl cut in St. Louis, Missouri. My parents gave me a Polaroid for Christmas when I was eleven. My father probably regretted this; he harbored hopes that I might be a jock, that he could live vicariously through anticipated athletic triumphs, but, sorry, Pops, I've always been more drawn to the arts, to the lights and shadows of life in this world. What it came down to was this: My parents worked hard to send me to Yale. They were loving, but firm in their love. My mandate was clear: I was to choose a practical major, a major that would lead to a lucrative career.

Unenthusiastically, I chose economics. I enjoyed it well enough. I graduated; worked on Wall Street; started PhotoPoet, a software company, and then sold it. At the age of thirty-four, I now have financial means I never expected to have.

This is not to boast or brag; it is simply to explain. Finally, I feel free to pursue my passion. I've taken many courses over the past fifteen years, in college and beyond, and I'm comfortable with my technical skills. That said, I know I have a lot to learn and I've never been more eager to learn it. I'm most interested in street photography, in people, real ordinary people, and New Yorkers in particular. There is something feral and utterly unique about this city and the individuals it attracts. It's all in the eyes. Degrees of solemnity and soul, of ambition and artifice, of exhaustion and euphoria, of panic and purpose. It's my aim to collect slices of unself-conscious and unrehearsed life. My hope is to contribute in my own humble way to the history of street photography in this country, to continue to take portraits à la Henri Cartier-Bresson, to capture moments that are decisive and fleeting, filled with the grit and glory of everyday life.

I haven't been a student for thirteen years, but I do not see this as a negative. I'm eager to get back in the game, to return to a life of questions and creativity. I will also say that after too many years of doing what's been expected of me, I feel a tremendous energy to take a crack at the work I've always dreamed of doing. To put it simply: I'm ready to live my own life with my eyes wide open. I'm hungry.

7:14AM

"Well, mercy me, that's the first time you've used that word in a while."

She fiddles with her panties. They are chocolate brown, lace, barely there. She bends over, mumbles something about a missing boot. She's on the floor now, crawling around like an animal, looking under the bed, ass in the air. He's hard again. As she contorts her arms behind her to clasp her bra, he presses himself against her back. *Let me help with that,* he says, grabbing the straps and pulling the whole thing away. He kisses her neck and she turns to him. He reaches between her legs. In clumsy unison, they topple back. He pulls her on top of him. This time he doesn't bother with a rubber and she doesn't say anything. It's fast, too fast, far too fast. He pulls out, makes a mess all over, and she takes the final dregs in her mouth. She swallows. Licks her lips. Swallows again. They rest briefly, in his bed, tangled in sheets. She stands, puts on her blue cowboy hat. *This time,* she says, *I'm really leaving. Good,* he thinks. *Fucking go.*

A crooning sound. A phone ringing. Tate startles, shoots up in bed, opens his eyes.

Fuck.

It was only a dream. Was it about Olivia? Smith? He can't conjure a face. Just pale skin, breasts, long dark hair . . . all of which they both have. Disappointment and relief fill him, but everything fades as he talks to his mother. It's good to hear her voice this morning, the steady cadence of her reasonable thoughts, her chirpy, cheerful tone. The connection is bad because she's calling from the cruise ship, but he's able to piece it together: his dad is terribly seasick and has spent most of the trip in bed, his mother has won a whopping $78 playing blackjack. The mundane details buoy him.

He checks the clock in his room. It's not even eight. He can't remember the last time he was up this early.

"Well, anyway, happy Thanksgiving," she says. "I've made a deal with myself not to worry too much about you today."

"I'm telling you I'm fine, Mom," he says. "I'm good, actually."

Good. For the first time in a long while, it doesn't feel like a lie. He actually does feel good. A little groggy and out of it, yes, but decent. His hangover is on the mild side today, just a dull ache at his temples and a dry tongue, but nothing major.

"Well, mercy me, that's the first time you've used that word in a while," his mom says. "I just spoke with Emily. She says she's going to call you, so keep a listen out. What do you have planned for the day?"

"I'll keep myself busy."

Tate smiles into the receiver and thinks of the day ahead. He will spend the majority of it with Smith. They will watch the parade from her apartment and then head to the Hamptons. "Happy Thanksgiving, Mom. Give my best to Dad. Love you both."

They mutter quiet good-byes, a mother-son melody they've had years to practice and perfect.

He hangs up. Sits there on his bed for a minute to think. When's the last time he paused to reflect on himself and his life? He can't remember. He's never been very good at this, he's always thrived on constant motion and activity, on avoidance, but it's gotten worse since Olivia. It's the moments where he's left alone with his thoughts—and regrets—that are the hardest, so he's fled them like the plague, drowned them with alcohol. He knows this. Hey, whatever works.

But here he sits, in no hurry, just looking around. What's up with the dreams? He hasn't remembered his dreams in ages, but now they linger, and crisply too. What does this mean? And what does it mean that his dreams have been consistently hypersexual, near pornographic? He's not complaining, there are worse things, but this is new. Is this because he's sleeping better? Or is this about Smith? About his ridiculous attraction to her, the fact that he feels he can't act on it?

It's too soon to make a move and he knows this, but the thought that he might slip up tonight excites him. It's downright bizarre that he cares enough already to worry about messing this up, but he does. He will meet her parents and they might take one look at him and disapprove. From everything Smith's said, they're a tough crowd, and it's clear that she loves them and despite ambitions of independence, she's all about her family.

He thinks back to meeting Olivia's parents at graduation, how he felt not a twinge of nervousness. Why is this so different? Is it just that he was young, that he didn't know enough to worry?

What's clear is that he will have to behave himself and, if necessary, put on a good show. He knows how to be the résumé guy, how to turn on the Ivy League charm, how to tweak his accent to attain that affected privileged drawl, to drop it into conversation that he stinted at Goldman and started his own multimillion-dollar company. Truth is, he hates talking about this stuff; these conversations are dreadfully pretentious and banal, but he will rise to the occasion and do what he has to do. And no, he will not lay a hand on Smith even though that's all he wants to do.

In the bathroom, he splashes cold water on his face and then cups some water in his hands to drink. *New York City's finest,* he thinks. He brushes his teeth.

He settles in on the toilet for his morning dump and loses himself in his latest favorite book: *Bystander: A History of Street Photography*, a thick tome surveying the evolution of the kind of photography that intrigues him most. He overnighted an extra copy to give Smith's parents when he visits them in the Hamptons tonight. It cost $200 and he wonders if it's too much, if it will seem that he's trying too hard.

The phone rings and he adjourns. He runs into the bedroom to pick up. A London number appears on the caller ID. His sister.

"Em."

"Tater," she says. Hearing her voice, he remembers how much he's missed her. She's younger but far wiser, and it was her long e-mails that helped most in the aftermath of Olivia's betrayal. He's always told her everything about his life and he's never once felt judged by her.

"Hey, Em. I don't suppose Mom made you call?"

She laughs. "She's worried about you, Tate. All by your lonesome in that big, bad city. She's allowed to be concerned. I'm not saying she should be, but it's kind of her job to worry about us. She's also fretting about me being pregnant here, like I'm in some third-world country or something. I'm in *London*. What do you have on tap today?"

"I'll bum around with my camera this morning and then . . ." He pauses. "I didn't tell Mom, but I met someone, Em. I'm spending the afternoon with her. I'm going to her sister's wedding on Saturday."

"I *knew* it. Tell me everything," she says. "I told you. I told you you'd meet someone. Who is she?"

"She went to Yale with me. My year. A buddy convinced me to go back to Yale on Saturday for the game and I was at the tailgates and I brought my cameras and there was this girl and she was . . . I can't explain it . . . but she had such an expressive face and I didn't even think about it. I just started snapping away, getting closer and closer. She wasn't paying attention. She was with friends, but kind of on the edge of the group and lost in her phone. I got incredibly close and we started talking, Em, like really talking. I've seen her twice this week. I'm going with her to her sister's wedding this weekend. I'm spending *Thanksgiving* with her family in the Hamptons. Fuck, it sounds so nuts saying these things out loud. I know what you're going to say."

"What am I going to say?" Emily says, laughing. "Educate me. What exactly am I going to say?"

"That this is too fast. That I should be careful. That I'm still hurting from Olivia and I should slow down."

"Nope," Emily says. "I wasn't going to say any of those things."

"No?"

Maybe these are *his* thoughts. His fears. His hesitations.

"I think you deserve this, whatever it is or whatever it isn't, and I think you know just what you're doing. You're smart, Tate. I haven't heard this kind of energy in your voice in ages. Have an adventure. And, for what it's worth, I don't think it's an accident that you met this girl while taking pictures. I think passion begets passion."

Tate laughs. "Is that what you think? Passion begets passion?"

"Yes," she says. "It is. I think when you take steps to do what you want to do and be who you want to be, then the rest starts falling into place."

"Okay, now you are sounding like Oprah Winfrey meets fortune cookie."

"I'll take that as a compliment, actually," she says, laughing into the receiver.

"I miss you, Em. Mom says you've been feeling the baby kick?"

"Yeah. It's the coolest, most surreal feeling, Tate. Like a butterfly flapping around inside me. Kind of mind-blowing, really."

"That's rad," he says, thinking about this little life growing inside his sister. "You going to find out what it is?"

"It's a baby," she says, laughing. "The rest will remain a mystery. There are so few mysteries in life, you know?"

"I do. I like a little mystery, too. Well, I can't to meet this little guy or gal. And the awesome thing is that you already have a hot New York City baby photographer raring to go."

"Happy Thanksgiving, Tater. Go for it, okay? I don't even know what that means, but look, you've been hurt and you've stumbled through that and if that's the worst that can happen, that you get hurt again, then so be it. Be smart, but do what you want to do. You are finally on your own. And, no, I will not tell Mom. My lips are sealed."

He hangs up but can't stop smiling. In the kitchen, he makes coffee. He doesn't use his Keurig, the easy pop-it-in-and-press-a-button machine, but instead tries something new, a pour-over coffee. He read about this somewhere and thought it sounded pretty cool. He grinds his own beans, measures them out, puts the paper filter into a brew basket, adds the grounds and takes his time pouring water over it. Slowly, the coffee drips through. It takes forever, but his coffee tastes richer at the end.

He drinks it. Lingers quietly in the threshold between the kitchen and his living room. He notices things. Things he doesn't normally take the time to see. The crooked stacks of photography books he's been collecting and neglecting, the strewn piles of unopened mail, the plastic bags full of new cameras and lenses, the orchid his mother sent him that died more than a week ago, the settlement papers from Olivia. Sun streams in from the big window, blasting the dusty, espresso-hued floors with brilliant stripes of light. He walks to his desk and sits, places his mug beside him. He taps the keyboard and the screen lights up.

8:56AM

"Tell me more, Professor Pennington."

The door is propped open. Tate walks through and pulls his boots off, places them by the door. He hasn't seen the place in daylight before this.

"Hello?" he calls out.

"In here!" she says. He follows her voice and finds her in the living room.

Smith sits in the bay window, surrounded by piles. "I'm making the hotel welcome bags for the out-of-towners. Can't believe everyone arrives tomorrow."

"Can I help?" he asks, perching beside her.

"Sure," she says. "Each bag needs one of these welcome letters from Sally and Briggs, one of these lists of local sights and restaurants, a pre-filled MetroCard, packets of frozen hot chocolate mix from Serendipity, one of these little boxes of miniature black-and-white cookies, a little thing of jelly beans—oh, and Advil. People will need the Advil. Oh, and we should look out in a minute. The parade should go by soon. It starts up on Seventy-Seventh at nine and doesn't take all that long to get down this way."

"Good thing Mother Nature cooperated," he says. "There was a lot of chatter about canceling the floats because of the wind. Apparently, they have wind gauges set up along the route."

"Ah, I had a feeling it would work out," she says casually, optimistically.

He gets to work, steals glances out the window. Soon enough, the Thanksgiving Day Parade inches by, the titanic floats coming within yards of her window. He doesn't recognize all of them, but some are familiar, and he trains his lens out the window and snaps away, capturing the big balloons that almost press against the glass. Spider-Man. Hello Kitty. Ronald McDonald. Buzz Lightyear. SpongeBob.

She joins him to watch, seems completely unimpressed.

"This is so old news to you, huh?" he says. "You know, most of us have only seen this on television. Wait, what's this? An elf?"

She laughs. "You haven't heard of the Elf on the Shelf?"

"Can't say that I have."

"It's this elf doll that shows up on the first of December and hides in a new spot each day of the month leading up to Christmas. The kids need to find it each morning and the gist is that the elf is watching on behalf of Santa to ensure some solid holiday-time behavior."

"That's really kind of creepy . . . and genius," he says. "I'll have to get my sister one at some point. She's having a baby this summer."

"You looking forward to being Uncle Tate?" she says.

"I am," he says. "I really am. I'm going to spoil that kid."

She smiles. Her hair is still damp and tied back off her face. She wears a loose sweatshirt without a bra and leggings. Her feet are bare and he studies her toes. Her second toe is crooked, bigger than the big one.

"Looking forward to tonight?" he asks, watching her. He can't peel his eyes from her. He prefers her this way, unpolished, slightly disheveled.

She rolls her eyes. "I've never really liked Thanksgiving. Too much room for drama. My mom gets worked into a froth about making the perfect meal and then ends up catering it all anyway, and my father always sees it as an occasion to drink too much and be obnoxious. And then there's the pie. I have a small pie problem and I always end up eating way too much of it. And last Thanksgiving was crappy. Asad came out to the house and my parents were on their best behavior and it was fine, but then he couldn't sleep and felt sick and I worried he'd gotten food poisoning. When we got back to the city, something was off. I told him he was acting strange. We broke up a week later. Anyway," she says. "What about you? You stoked?"

"Absolutely," he says. "I've only been to the Hamptons once and it was many years ago."

He and Olivia went for a weekend the summer after college, to stay with one of her friends' families. It was a big, fancy home in East Hampton and Tate was put off by the conspicuous displays of wealth everywhere. The tennis whites and fast cars and glittering pools. It was a different world, for sure.

"It's kind of an abhorrent place," she says, looking at him, eyes softening. "So much money. So much privilege. So much posturing. But it's also really pretty and peaceful. I kind of have this love-hate thing going with the Hamptons and I'm probably not alone in that."

"I did a little research last night on the literary history of the Hamptons. Learned some pretty cool things. Apparently, there's this plaque dedicated to Truman Capote in Sagaponack? He's one of my favorites. Maybe we can make a little detour on the way back tomorrow? I'd love to see it and get some photographs of the pond."

She stops what she's doing. "You know what? Help me finish these last few and then let's go. I can't believe I'm saying this because I'm the last person in the world to do an impromptu excursion, but let's go today, to find your little literary plaque and hang in Sagaponack. I'll call down and have them pull the car around. It'll be a little adventure. You said you need adventure, eh?"

"Really?" Tate says, feeling a charge.

"Sure," Smith says, hopping up. "Give me a few minutes to freshen up."

As she disappears into her bedroom, Tate looks around. The place is sparingly decorated in soft, safe colors. A few candles and photographs, but not much else. He ducks into the kitchen, peeks in the fridge. It's full of glass Tupperware containers, all carefully labeled. Kale. Green apple. Grapes. Fennel.

"Ready?" she says, reappearing in the kitchen door. Her eyes are beguilingly wide.

He carries their bags, follows her down the hall. They wait for the elevator.

She's an atrocious driver. Her foot is fidgety on the gas pedal. The car is not what he expects. A beat-up, dusty white Prius, plenty old. She turns on some music. Mumford and Sons.

"I have a confession," he says as she brakes to a stop at a red light.

She turns toward him, fear in her eyes. "Is this something I want to know?"

"I Googled your father," he says, and waits for a reaction.

A few efficient clicks and Tate learned that Thatcher was named one of the top ten wealthiest real estate investors on CNNMoney. One thing was clear: this man is a force to be reckoned with.

"Oh dear," she says, laughing. "That must have been fun for you. Rest assured, only ninety-five percent of it's true. And the other five percent is basically true."

They continue on. The traffic isn't as bad as he imagined it would be. They drive along at a good clip, talking, but also enduring stretches of intimate silence. He watches her most of the time, how her thin fingers curl around the steering wheel, how her legs bounce to the beat of the music, how she bites her lip at stoplights.

At a red light, Smith gets a text. "Sally. Wondering when we're arriving. She's been all over me since our fight. I think she gets how wrong it was not to tell me about Asad."

"Did you forgive her?" Tate says.

"Yeah," Smith says, smiling. "It's hard to stay mad at her, but I'm making her think she needs to work for it."

"She's younger?" he asks.

"Yeah, but not by much. My parents had a hard time having me. They tried for years. My mother had several miscarriages but then got pregnant with me when she was almost forty. And after me, she was convinced she'd never get pregnant again, and what happens? Sally. Not much more than a year later."

"If this is too personal, just tell me to stop, but do you think that's why you didn't tell your parents about the abortion? Because of what your parents went through fertility-wise?"

She nods. Considers this. "I've never thought about that, but yeah, it probably had something to do with it. But it's mainly their politics. Thatcher is a pretty rabid Republican. A daughter having an abortion wouldn't work for him. My mom would have handled it better, but she wouldn't have been able to keep it from Thatch and she would've probably encouraged me to keep it and would have probably offered to raise the baby while I finished school. I think about that sometimes, you know? What if? What if I had an almost *seventeen*-year-old? I can't even wrap my mind around it, but things would be so wildly different. I probably wouldn't be meeting brooding artistic types at tailgates or taking Thanksgiving detours to check out literary plaques."

"Butterfly effect for you, eh?" he says.

She nods.

"You ever regret it?"

That question again.

"No," she says automatically, but then she pauses. "Maybe. Shit, I swore I was over it, but now I'm not sure. What if I made the wrong call? What if that was my chance to be a mom? It makes me a little bit sad. And now my sister will have a kid soon and I hate that I'm always comparing myself to her, but I can't help it. I'm the slightly older, less decisive, highly neurotic sister. Alas. Sally has always been the trailblazer, the one who knows what she wants and how to get it. Career? 'I've always gotten a kick out of math and science. I'll be a doctor!' Men? 'I like that handsome investment banker from Texas over there at the keg. I think I'll say hello and introduce myself.' Done and done."

"They meet in school? Sally and Briggs?"

"No," Smith says. "They reconnected at their ten-year reunion a few years back and I should warn you that this wedding will practically be one big ode to Princeton, which tickles old Thatcher big-time. He's a Princeton man through and through. His father was a Princeton man. My going to Yale was this big rebellion. They're naming the wedding tables after Princeton landmarks. I'm half expecting a Tiger to bust out on the dance floor as they're cutting the cake. Our Bulldog pride might surge uncontrollably." She laughs. "Where did you say this Capote plaque was? We're approaching Sag now."

Tate checks the GPS on his phone. "We're not too far. And I think we're like a mile from Peter Matthiessen's place."

"The *Paris Review* guy?" she says.

"The one. I read this piece in *Vanity Fair* this summer and apparently, he bought like six acres around here in 1959 and this was all a farm community with small, unassuming wood-frame houses and fields, and it was all writers and artists and musicians. Peter would come out here with Coast Guard buddies and he'd write on bad-weather days and then work as a scalloper and a fisherman. He kicked it with artists like Jackson Pollock and did his share of duck hunting and drinking. And what I love is that the dude is, what, eighty-six, and he just published a novel, and his best buddy, James Salter, just published his first book in thirty years and he's *eighty-eight*. How fucking cool is that?

That's what I want, you know? To chill with interesting people, to be doing something I love when I'm old as dirt."

Smith smiles. "You're pretty jazzed about all of this. Maybe you can become a Hamptons historian on the side. You seem to know everything. And I've been coming here my whole life and I'm totally ignorant. I appreciate the education though. Tell me more, Professor Pennington."

He *is* getting jazzed. This is all fucking cool, to be out here in this land that has such amazing history, where so many of the artists he admired spent time. And it's fun to share this stuff with her; she seems to actually be interested.

"I might be getting this wrong, but I think Steinbeck was the original and then Peter and then a bunch of others—Doctorow, Plimpton, Vonnegut. The houses were cheap and the isolation was the appeal. The place was practically deserted from Labor Day to Memorial Day. I read that Capote came to escape the social enticements of the city."

"And now look at this place: Norman Jaffe monstrosities and McMansions galore," Smith says. "It's kind of tragic if you ask me. Jaffe's son Miles is quite the card. Has this insane website called Nuke the Hamptons or something where he goes on these indignant Holden Caulfield–style rants about the lack of values here. It's kind of disturbing but also kind of right on."

Smith parks and they walk together down an unassuming path off Widow Gavits Road into a broad clearing with a straight-on view of Crooked Pond.

Only now does it occur to Tate that this has all been something of an unconscious test, this little detour they're taking on Thanksgiving Day. He didn't think of it this way when he mentioned the plaque, it was just a detail, a conversational snippet, but now he realizes, in part, his intentions. He wants to suss her out, discern out how flexible Smith is, how married she is to routine, because this was one of the things that doomed his relationship with Olivia. She always had a meticulous plan, an unwavering sense of how things should go, and Tate was more interested in winging it sometimes, in having impromptu adventures. She felt this was immature and juvenile, this taste for spontaneity, and incommensurate with a responsible adult existence, but Tate wasn't wholly interested in a responsible adult existence. He wanted to go surfing on a whim or make a late-night grocery run to gather ingredients for a spur-of-the-moment picnic or have sex in the parking lot of the movie theater.

"What do you know about this spot?" she says, eyes twinkling. "I'm sure you have a pint-sized lecture prepared given your lively performance in the car."

"There should be a bench right up here and a granite marker with the plaque. It was all put here in 1992 to honor Capote and his partner Jack Dunphy. I think their ashes were scattered over the water. I might be getting this wrong, but before he died, Capote stipulated that the proceeds from the sale of his estate around here should go to the Nature Conservancy and that the charity would use the funds to buy and protect this land, the Long Pond Greenbelt, which has a ton of biological diversity. I guess they did this 'Black and White' hike here in the fall in honor of Capote's birthday a couple years back and the walk was named after the 1966 Black and White Ball in Manhattan. The walk ended with a reception that includes a reading of some of his work, a display of memorabilia and samplings of Cousin Sook's fruitcake from his famous short story 'A Christmas Memory.' "

Smith walks ahead on the path and Tate trails her, takes a few photographs of her from behind. She doesn't seem to notice. The bench comes into view and she bends down and squints. When he is in earshot, she begins to read.

" 'The brain may take advice, but not the heart, and love, having no geography, knows no boundaries.' Oh my, I love that," she says. "Maybe I should rustle up some Capote. I read *In Cold Blood* and it haunted the hell out of me."

"It's one of my favorite books of all time," Tate says. "The original true crime. The idea of life being one way, leading this life of a farmer with your family, and then enter these devils and everything changes. What about this, from Dunphy? This is good too . . . 'I was grieving the way the earth seems to grieve for spring in the dead of winter, but I wasn't afraid, because nothing, I told myself, can take our halcyon days away.' I read somewhere that *halcyon* is the Latin name for belted kingfishers. Legend has it that on that day, as Capote's ashes were being scattered, this belted kingfisher came flying around from the end of the pond."

"Pretty incredible," Smith says, looking around.

Tate stands, lifts his camera to his eye, starts snapping the pond, the sky, the bench, the plaque. He trains his lens on her and waits for permission. It comes, and swiftly too, in the form of a shy smile. She's incredibly photogenic, but this doesn't surprise him.

"Fuck, it feels good to be out here, doesn't it? I've been slaving away on these precious MFA applications, writing up these quaint little statements of interest, explaining myself, justifying my absence from the academic world, but I'm standing here and feel suddenly convinced the idea of school is all wrong. I need to be out here, *doing* it, you know? Just wear these babies around the world and figure it out myself," he says, fingering the straps of his two cameras, a Leica M3 and a Leica M9, both of which he bought the afternoon the acquisition money came in. The purchases cost a fortune and made him feel sick to his stomach, but he's been putting them to good use.

"You going to wear your cameras for Thanksgiving dinner? You'll be poised to capture the robust dysfunction," Smith says.

He laughs. Feels thankful for her timely humor, for the fact that she didn't challenge his statement about not going to school. Olivia would have brandished her prosecutorial skills and argued for the practicality of obtaining a degree. Maybe it's not fair comparing them; he's just met Smith. But he can't help himself.

"So, what did you tell your folks about me?" he asks.

"Not a ton," she says, smiling. "I've kind of learned my lesson to keep it simple until there's a reason to provide details. They're so wrapped up in the wedding hoopla anyway. They barely have time for me."

"Anything else I should know before I meet them?" Tate says. "How about a quick and dirty crash course."

She chews her gum and looks at him. "Okay, you will very likely love my mom. Everyone adores Bitsy. Ditto Sally. She's sweet and harmless and fun. But Thatch? He's a wild card at best and a raging asshole at worst. I tell myself he's a good man deep down, a real teddy bear, but I don't know. It depends on how you catch him. He can be kind and lovely and full of great stories, or he can be an acerbic and unapologetic thug. It will probably depend on the cocktail quotient, but just steel yourself because it might not be pretty."

"I consider myself warned," Tate says.

"Then again, he might be on his very best Bitsy-mandated behavior around Briggs's family. They're churchgoing folk from Fort Worth, Texas. Mark my words. Bitsy will insist upon grace before we eat—which we never do—and you guys will be relegated to the guesthouse even though there are plenty of bedrooms in the main house. Just for the appearance of propriety. I'll bet I'm right. Speaking of which, we should get going," Smith says, checking her watch. "Bitsy will have my head if we're even a minute late for cocktails. I bailed on dinner last week when I was out with you and you don't even know the drama it caused."

They begin to retrace their steps to head back to the car, but Smith stops and turns to him. She flashes a winning smile, looks around, up at the blue sky, but then settles her gaze on him.

"What?" he says.

"Thank you," she says.

"For what?"

"I don't know. For bringing me here. For going to the game. For getting me drunk enough to puke noodles and *wake up*. For this week. I've been in a pretty shitty, cynical place, Tate, but I think I'm finally beginning to climb out."

"Well, you're welcome," he says, taking her hand. They keep walking. "I could say similar words, but you said it better than I ever could."

She links her arm in his.

"Where is this Meadow Lane anyway?" Tate says.

Smith turns to him. Smiles. "I never said anything about Meadow Lane. A little fruit of your illicit searches?"

"Guilty as charged," he says, feeling embarrassed. It's one thing to spend a night researching the family of a girl you've just met and it's another thing entirely to cop to doing this. When he ended up bleary eyed in the early morning hours reading a half-baked piece-of-crap article called "Ten Proven Ways to Ace Meeting Her Parents," he knew it was time to cut himself off and go to bed.

"Tonight will be fine," Smith says, clearly sensing his building nerves. "And if it's not, we will drink copiously and just push on through. Deal?"

"Deal."

5:37PM

"You've got some balls"

When they reach the grounds, Smith rolls down her window, snakes her arm through it and taps a security code. An ornate metal gate swings opens slowly and she drives through. It's getting dark, but the property is generously lit and glows against the horizon. Tate carries their bags along the stone path that leads to the house. With each step, his nerves grow. Why he is so anxious? What's the worst that can happen?

The pictures he found on the Internet don't do it justice; the estate is a fucking joke. Enormous and in-your-face grand. There's an artificial quality to it, like it's part of a Woody Allen movie set.

"Welcome to our humble abode," Smith says through a smile as they reach the front door. "There used to be this charming, understated old house here, but it wasn't flashy enough for Thatch. He knocked it down and created this beast. Eleven thousand square feet. Five-plus acres. Four-thousand-square-foot guesthouse—where I bet they'll park you. Eleven bedrooms. Fourteen bathrooms. Nine fireplaces. Infinity pool, Jacuzzi, twin tennis courts, a helipad, a thousand-square-foot wine cellar, a gym, a screening room, a koi pond, a bakery. Wait until you see it in the daylight."

She opens the front door and they walk through. The front hall is austere and quiet, lit with crystal sconces and a handful of votive candles. A uniformed maid scurries in to greet them. Her name is Esmeralda and Smith captures her in a hug. A man appears, too, Samson, and whisks away their luggage. "Mrs. Anderson has Mr. Pennington with Mr. McGee in the guest quarters."

"Told you," Smith whispers through a laugh.

Muted laughter and classical music float from a distant room and Smith leads him toward its source. They walk through room after room full of formal furniture and art that seems important and they end up in a sprawling living room with several seating areas. Everyone is gathered around a roaring fire, dressed for dinner, clutching sparkling cocktails.

A woman, tall and regal with a short haircut, and a squat red-faced man peel off from the others and come to greet Smith and Tate. Smith hugs them both and then makes introductions.

"Tate, meet my mother and father, Bitsy and Thatcher. Mom and Dad, this is Tate Pennington."

"Nice to meet you both," Tate says, extending his hand. "Thank you for having me."

"Welcome," Bitsy says. "Come have a cocktail. We'll be sitting for dinner soon. I hope you brought your appetite."

Thatcher surrenders the faintest of smiles, but that's all.

Sally pushes through the group and captures Smith in an enormous hug. "I'm so happy you're here," she says, a frank giddiness in her

voice, and then turns to Tate, hesitates only briefly before hugging him too.

The others gather around and Tate meets them too. Sally and Briggs. Briggs's parents. Briggs's older brother and his wife. He can't stop staring at Sally. It surprises him how much she looks like Smith. Her hair is a caramel blond and she wears more makeup than Smith, but none of these details distract from the deep, almost uncanny resemblance.

Time passes in an innocuous blur of small talk and smiles. Appetizers are passed on silver trays. Classical music pumps through the space. Tate stays by Smith's side and feels far quieter than usual. He looks around, zeroing in on details, silently berating himself for worrying so much. At best, he is peripheral to this night, an extra body to feed. There is endless talk of the wedding, of the conundrum of the seating chart, of last-minute details that must be ironed out. Smith is quiet too. She sips her drink and plays nice, chiming in when asked a question but not offering much else.

They sit for dinner in the oval-shaped dining room. The walls are blanketed in a mural, maybe even a famous scene by a famous artist he should know. The settings are formal—good china, shimmering silver, several crystal wineglasses lined up at each seat. Thatcher settles at the head of the table and Bitsy sits opposite him. The rest of them fill in the sides. There are little name cards at each seat. Tate is seated between Sally and Briggs's mother.

Bitsy straightens in her chair and smiles. "Shall we begin with grace?"

Tate steals a glance at Smith.

"Told you," she mouths.

"Come, Lord Jesus," Bitsy says, eyes closed, hands laced on her lap. "Be our guest. Let thy gifts to us be blessed. Amen."

A chorus of amens.

Uniformed staff breeze in and out wielding silver trays of rich-smelling food. Traditional Thanksgiving fare taken up a conspicuous notch. Thatcher asks whether everyone can taste the white truffles in the potatoes. Everyone says yes, including Tate, even though they just taste like potatoes.

Smith sits between Briggs and his father and gracefully alternates between talking to each. She takes small bites of her food and big gulps of her wine. She catches Tate's eye over the table again and again and smiles.

Tate turns to Sally. "Are you excited about the wedding?" he asks.

It's a lame softball of a question, but he asks it anyway and she seems happy to answer it.

"I *am* excited," she says, authentic joy plain in her voice. "I was that stereotypical little girl who loved princesses and fairy tales and I've long dreamed of my wedding. Maybe that's silly, but it's true."

"It's not silly at all," Tate says, thinking back to that week before his own wedding, the adrenaline and anticipation he felt in spades. It was such a good, busy week. He ran all over doing last-minute things, but he remembers vividly how excited he was, how purely excited, to make it official.

"I'm glad you'll be there," Sally says, lowering her voice. "My sister can be so serious about everything. She deserves to have a little fun."

"I'll do my best to make sure she does," Tate says, heaping more stuffing onto his plate. He takes seconds of everything even though he's full. He looks around the table. The scene could not be more different from his modest Thanksgivings in Missouri with his parents or in San Francisco with Olivia's. Tonight is all politeness and pleasantries and even the light is surreal, almost antique and sepia in tone.

By the time pie comes around, he's stuffed, but he takes a slice of each kind anyway—pumpkin, pecan, apple. Bitsy announces that she hand-whipped the cream and that everyone must sample it. And so he does. It's not very sweet at all, actually rather tasteless, but he eats it too.

Thatcher stands, and as he does, he rings a small silver bell indicating the meal is over.

Everyone stands, leaves cloth napkins by empty plates. Staff slip through a door and begin to clear.

"Join us in the library, Tate?" Thatcher says. It's more command than question.

"Sure," Tate says, nodding, suddenly feeling impossibly insecure and unsophisticated. He smiles at Smith as he leaves the room and follows the other men. He can't shake the feeling that he's about to be grilled.

"Tell me, Trey. Do you remember that charming old bar at the Essex House? The one that was there before those big renovations?" Thatcher asks, lighting a cigar. He offers one to Tate, but he declines.

"No," Tate says. "I can't say that I do."

Trey. What the hell?

"Well, I loved that place. I used to go there with the fellas after work and we'd blaze through a bottle of good bourbon and sit by the fire during the winter. Anyway, that was one of my very favorite rooms in Manhattan and inspired this little library."

It's not a little library. It's a grand, wood-paneled space with thick navy drapes and endless shelves of what seem to be rare books. Tate squints to try to read the spines. Several oil paintings hang on the walls. Another fire blazes in a hearth framed in a rich mahogany marble. A silver tray of cocktails rests on a brown leather ottoman between them. Thatcher hands one to each man. All but Tate smoke a cigar and he finds himself regretting his choice to abstain. One cigar wouldn't hurt.

"You like it?" Thatcher says, pointing to Tate's glass.

"I do," Tate lies. It's too sweet, too strong. "What is it?"

"A Manhattan. Rye whiskey, sweet vermouth and bitters. Pretty tasty, no?"

Tate nods. Briggs and his father stand by, puffing and sipping.

"So," Thatcher says, squinting, appraising Tate. "Twenty million pretax. Not a bad start."

Tate startles at the sudden proclamation, looks over to Briggs & Co. They wear matching bemused smiles and appear genuinely unfazed.

"Thanks, sir."

So, they looked each other up. Fitting.

"I hear something about you being married?"

"Yes," he says. "A few loose ends I'm dealing with. Settlement details. Should all be tied up soon."

Thatcher inches closer to him and his voice dips into a scratchy whisper. "Whatever you do, hang on to the money, son. I know that might sound ruthless, but you've got to be ruthless in this world. It takes a pretty penny to get by and don't go throwing away your hard-earned cash to a starter wife."

Tate is taken aback by his energy, his insistence. Also, by the fact that the two other men in the room, Briggs and his dad, remain totally silent. They've been around longer and perhaps they've learned an important lesson.

"Look. It seems I've gained a reputation for being a shark. You might not know this, Trey, but during the crash in 2008, I made a fucking fortune by shorting the derivatives of risky companies. I literally watched the world around me crumble, and I *profited*. I'd seen the crash coming and I made money off it, so much cash that I bought this land and built this place. And you know what? Smith sat me down, Trey, and you know what she said? *I don't like who you've become, Dad.* Smith can be rather high-minded, I'm sure you've noticed as much, but you know something? I've worked my tail off to provide for my family. I grew up with very little and I'm proud of this house. I'm proud of the fact that I can throw my baby girl the wedding of her dreams."

"Cheers to that," Briggs's father says, raising his glass. "I think I'm going to call it a night. The flight and all that decadent food have left me fried."

"I'll head out with you," Briggs says, standing. He and his father make for the door and mutter good night. Tate is tempted to follow suit, but something compels him to stay.

Now it's just the two of them. A sinister quiet falls over the darkened room. The fire spits and roars. They sip their drinks.

Thatcher looks over at Tate, scrutinizes him. "So, now what? Smith said something about photography? Thank you for the book, by the way. Will make a winning doorstop. I kid." He chuckles. "Actually, I don't. Not a big book guy. Don't have the attention span. Sue me."

"Yes, photography," Tate says. "I've always loved it. Now I can afford to do it."

"But how will you *make a living* by taking pictures? What with all the new technology, that ridiculous Instaframe thing Smith's all taken by? Isn't everyone a photographer these days anyhow?"

Tate hesitates before answering. "I'm not sure I will make a living doing it. I'm doing it because I love it, and for the moment, I'm not interested in making any more money. I'm trying to focus on being happy."

Thatcher looks as if he's been struck but then smiles. "This all sounds very familiar. What is it with your generation, all hell-bent on happiness? I suppose Sally will rub a few pennies together as a doctor, but Smith, with her organization business? She's spent hours trying to explain the importance of her work, but I continue to struggle with the fact that I paid for a Yale education and my exceedingly intelligent daughter has opted to be a glorified maid for the privileged Manhattan set. And on top of that, she's taking whatever paltry money she's earning and giving it away. My bleeding-heart progeny. Cheerio."

Tate feels his body stiffening, bites his lip. Breathes. He takes a giant swig of his fancy drink and sits back in his chair. Tells himself that this man is not an evil soul but a father. A father who cares about his kids and wants to see them thrive. He feels an odd kinship with this fellow whose belly hangs over his belt and threatens to bust open his custom shirt. This could have been Tate. He too went from college straight to Wall Street. He too had dollar signs in his young eyes. He too grew up hearing whispered conversations and arguments about there not being enough money for this, for that. The message, intentional or accidental, was that money would fix things, solve problems. At twenty-two, Tate genuinely believed this. When he walked onto that trading floor for the first time and saw the glowing flat-screen TVs, the high-tech computer monitors and phone turrets with enough knobs, buttons and dials to approximate the cockpit of a fighter plane, he felt that insidious electric charge. It felt as if they were all playing an elaborate video game.

If Olivia hadn't insisted on their move west, Tate would never have quit his job. He would have stayed. He would have worked hard—he's always worked very hard—and he would have been sucked into the life he sees so many of his friends leading. Lives fueled by an addiction to affluence. One of Jeff's buddies got a $2.3 million bonus last year and he was pissed because it wasn't fat enough. And what's to say that wouldn't have been him? He was on his way. Still a kid, he could get a table at any restaurant in Manhattan—Per Se, Le Bernardin, Daniel—and use one of his unlimited expense accounts. He could get good seats at whatever sporting event he chose. It wasn't just about money. It was about power.

Thatcher sips his drink and fiddles with the dark laces of his dress shoe. In this one man, Tate's able to see the limitations of unlimited wealth. Is this man happier because he has all of this? It doesn't seem so. And yet he is not a bad guy.

"By the way, my name is not Trey. It's Tate."

Thatcher cackles. "Shit, you've got some balls on you, young man. I already like you better than the Paki."

The Paki. This guy is a bigot.

"Now, this is between us, son," Thatcher says, his voice lower, "but the truth is, I've been holding out hope that she'd find someone like you, a good-hearted Midwestern chap with an ounce of bite, and here you are. I can see past the tattoo nonsense; you are at heart a straight arrow. My kind of kid."

Tate traces the small tattoo of a camera on the inside of his wrist, doesn't know what to say to this. He smiles, sips his drinks, aware that there will be more.

"Want to know something?" Thatcher says, eyes blazing, moving to the edge of the chair. His voice dips into a scratchy whisper. "I stood right here in this room one year ago and I told him in no uncertain terms that he wasn't going to marry her. The whole thing was absolutely ludicrous. My little girl converting to Islam? I wasn't just going to stand by and watch this madness. I told him that I loved her far too much to let it happen. I gave him a week to end it. I was clear that if he didn't do it, I'd have to resort to plan B and send his family a little note about how pleased my wife and I were that our kids would be getting married. He stood his ground and refused to part ways—I give him credit for that—but I had to do what I had to do and here we are, in a better place."

Disgust pulses through Tate's veins.

"She's brilliant, my Smith. I've told her again and again that I'd love for her to come work for me, but she scoffs at the idea. She seems intent on remaining a contrarian. I should've had sons. Maybe then I'd have someone to take over my business. Instead, I'm stuck with my girls, and I love them, but it isn't the same. And Smith, I swear she's out to ruffle my feathers. I'm just waiting for her to throw in the towel on this foolish 'business' of hers and get some sort of new 'idea.' " He makes air quotes, scoffs, drinks more.

"Sir, with all due respect, she's passionate about what she does. You should be proud," Tate says. The moment the words are out, his pulse quickens and he wonders what the hell he is doing testing this man.

"Is that so?" Thatcher says, blue eyes glinting, a bemused smile spreading over his face. He pours himself another drink, swallows half of it immediately. Tate can see it in his eyes, how gone he is. "How do you think this following of passion was possible in the first place? Do you think the seed money for this precious company of hers fell from the big blue sky? No, it didn't. I wrote her a check because I love her and I want my girls to be happy, but that doesn't mean I have to be pleased with the bullshit. I'm allowed my opinions, Trent."

"I suppose you are, but I think you should celebrate the fact that your daughter hasn't tethered herself to a miserable quintessentially prestigious job just for the sake of it and isn't frittering away her days like many people in her position would do. She's working hard at something she cares about. And she's giving back, too. Personally, I find it inspiring. And it's *Tate*."

"Balls," Thatcher says, chuckling.

Tate looks toward the door and startles when he sees Smith standing there, leaning against its frame. She's barefoot and her hair is pulled back. She clutches a glass of white wine and smiles.

"I'm going to steal Tate, Daddy," she says softly. How long has she been standing there? It's clear from the wistful expression on her face, from the affection in her voice, that she did not overhear her father's ugly confession. Tate feels thankful for this, a sudden urge to protect her. He will not tell her what he's just learned. Not yet, at least. He knows how this information would destroy her. *Shit,* he thinks, wishing he'd gone to bed an hour ago.

9:45PM

"I'm hard."

"Don't say I didn't warn you," Smith says, walking Tate along the path to the guesthouse.

"Wow. You weren't kidding around. He's a piece of work," Tate says. Thatcher's bombshell explodes again and again in his mind. What kind of father would do this to his own daughter? No wonder she's confused about what happened. He feels a newfound respect for Asad for not telling her how it went down. It would have poisoned her relationship with her father.

"I still love him though. I still love him even though he's hard-nosed and doesn't get it at all and is so unbelievably tone-deaf. I personally think he gets a kick out of giving me shit, but thank you for sticking up for me back there," she says. "I've brought a few guys around here at this point and not a one has had the guts to put Thatcher in his place."

"I'm not sure I put him in his place," Tate says. "But I couldn't help myself."

"Well, I like that. Here we are," she says. "El Guesthouse. I called it, didn't I? I'm sure Bitsy went all out stocking the kitchen for you boys."

"After that feast, I don't think I'll need to eat for weeks," he says.

"It wasn't torture, was it?" she says. "You survived okay?"

He nods. "It appears so. We'll have to see if there's any fallout tomorrow."

Smith puts her hand on the doorknob but pauses, stands on her tiptoes and kisses his cheek. It's all very fast and innocent, but just feeling her skin against his fires him up. She opens the door and walks inside. Another extravagant space, no expense spared. Endless furniture and books and art. The soothing hum of heat being vented through the ceilings and floors. She walks him to a bedroom past the kitchen and flicks on the light. His suitcase has been unpacked.

"Will this do?" she says with a smirk.

"Oh, I think it will."

"Okay, I'm going to head back and deal with my wedding speech. I've never in my life procrastinated like this."

"Good luck," he says, taking her hand.

She squeezes it. Looks straight into his eyes. "Good night, Tate."

He watches her leave, her body moving slowly toward the door, slipping through. He plops down on the bed and looks around. Just another bedroom. No big deal. He changes out of his clothes into a T-shirt and a pair of boxers and heads to the kitchen to see if he can find another beer. Briggs is there. He's also changed out of his dinner clothes.

"Hey," Tate says.

"Hey."

He's buzzed and riled. It takes every ounce of restraint not to tell

Briggs what just happened with Thatcher. "Where the fuck are we?" he says, laughing, opening the fridge. "It's three times bigger than my childhood home. I'm not sure what's going on."

"This, my friend, is what happens when old money meets new money," Briggs explains. "Bitsy comes from this flush New York family, blue, blue blood in that one. Miss Porter's, Sarah Lawrence, Colony Club. And then you get Thatch, the son of a Midwestern salesman and a nurse, who works his ass off and makes it to Princeton and then lands Bitsy and then strikes gold and can't stop spending to save himself. An interesting combo. He can be a dick, but I've been around long enough to know that they're a good family. Sally and Smith are amazing girls."

"They look so much alike. It's crazy. They even have the same mannerisms."

"Yup," Briggs says, taking a long swig of his beer. "Absolutely. Feel free to fantasize about the two of them. I do."

Tate laughs. "You ready for this, man? This marriage thing?"

"Yeah," Briggs says. "I'm ready. I'm pumped."

"Good, man. Good."

"Sally said your ex was playing around?" Briggs says, a serious look on his face.

Tate sips his beer. "Indeed," he says, matter-of-factly, surprised that he's feeling less and less embarrassed about admitting this detail.

"She ruin you? Or would you do it all over again?"

"I'd do it again, man. I'm an idiot. I'd do it all again in a heartbeat."

Back in his bedroom, Tate grabs for his camera and starts photographing everything. *Still lifes of a foreign land*, he thinks. In the bathroom, he takes a piss, stares at the white wicker basket full of magazines and catalogs: *Town & Country*, *Hamptons* magazine, and *Scully & Scully*. He hears his phone buzz in the other room.

Smith: They like you.

Tate: Who's they?

Smith: Bits & Sally. Thatch too.

Tate: Big thumbs up. Now I'll actually sleep. Phew. ☺

Smith: If B weren't there . . .

Tate: Yes?

Smith: I'd sneak over barefoot in my nightgown and let you warm me up.

Holy shit. Where is this coming from? He certainly felt she was flirting earlier, in the car and at the pond, but it was all subtle and he wondered if it was even all in his head. This now is the opposite of subtle. This is fucking hot. A dream. His pulse picks up as he types . . .

Tate: I would warm you up. What else would you do?

Smith: I'd sit on the edge of your bed and tease you.

Tate: Tease me?

Smith: Yes. You'd try to touch me, but I wouldn't let you.

Tate: Why?

Smith: Because it isn't time.

Tate: FYI, I'm hard.

Smith: Did I need to know that? ☺

Tate: Yes. You did . . .

Smith: I'm wet . . .

Tate: Fuck.

Smith: I can't believe I just wrote that.

Tate: Believe it.

Smith: What are we doing?

Tate: ???

Smith: Happy Thanksgiving, Tate.

Tate: Happy TG, S.

Hand on his cock, he closes his eyes and imagines her. She's in a nightgown. It's short and sheer, a soft see-through pink. She's barefoot even though it's cold, running in the grass toward him. She appears at his door shivering, teeth chattering, nipples hard as hell, hair a fucking mess. She gets under the covers with him. *Relax,* she says, and he lies back. Her hands are frozen . . . She grabs him . . . puts him in her mouth . . .

Fuck. He hops up. Runs to the bathroom, finishes in the toilet. He's not about to make a mess of those fancy sheets. He doesn't want to do *anything* to fuck this up.

He likes this girl.

CLIO

"Life can only be understood backwards; but it must be lived forwards."

— Søren Kierkegaard, *Journals IV A 164*

Dearest Clio,

I'm thinking of your name. Clio Eloise Marsh. Clio is, as you know, the Muse of history. History is everything and it is nothing. It's important, but it need not define you. I'm your mother. Your MOTHER and I've been a lousy mother and a brilliant mother maybe too but you've always been my bright light, my greatest LOVE. Love can be paper light, paper white, and love can be a monster, a dreaded darkness, a tempest of regret and discovery and islands, so many islands with jutting rocks and creatures and you are in the boat, sailing along and it's up to you and it's not up to you because you're not the CAPTAIN, but just a passenger. I want you to go, GO, have a good life, full, crammed with passion and purpose and questions and forgiveness—so important to forgive—and curiosity and GOD and birds, you love them so and I love that you love them, and big books and the little nothing books nobody knows too, and clues and laughter. We haven't laughed enough yet. We will. We will laugh at it all. And you will understand, it will make sense, AHA, AHA, you will say, yes, yes, you will be a mother one day, and see what it's like to crack open with hope and worry and desire and pain and most of all love. But it's not simple. It's hellos and good-byes, nevers and forevers, and go away and come back, please come back, forgive me, I'm flying, I'm falling. The world is big and bad and good too, ancient riddles, chaos, phenotypes and genotypes and survival and death and life and loss and energy and voyages forward and back and inside. Remember when Charles lost his daughter Annie? Remember how sick he was, how sorrowful? I cried for him, I cry for him, because there's nothing worse than losing that kind of love. But she was in pain, she was not well, she was not meant to linger. Poor little Annie. Poor Charles. You are loved, my muse.

Mama

8:15AM

"Why don't we ever talk about her?"

The last time.

The three words tumble through her head, over and over, as Clio opens her eyes. She stares up at the ceiling, fixing on those plastic stars that caught Henry's attention, those stars that have lost their glow. This is the last time she will wake up in this bed, in this room, in this part of her life.

Clio stays in bed, her body peaceful and limp, and she feels it: the mournfulness fading, draining from her pores. That she will leave these stars behind, this room behind, this house behind, is nothing but right.

It's finally time.

Last night. Remarkably, Thanksgiving dinner was fine, far better than she expected it would be. She and her father crunched through the snow to get to Jack's house and it was the two of them and Jack and his wife, Jessica, and their adorable girls, and Jack's parents, whom Clio hadn't seen since last year. She'd worried that the reunion would be awkward, but it wasn't. It relieved her that there was no talk of Eloise. The kids took center stage. Maddy sped around wielding toys and books, and Gabby toddled about, pulling things from shelves. It was chaos, but a joyful, hopeful chaos.

When she and her father came back here, there was this moment when they stood together in the darkened hall outside the bedrooms, this swollen moment when it seemed like he might say something. He had this look on his face, this sheen in his eyes, and he put his hand on Clio's shoulder and looked into her eyes and she felt as if she might burst. She waited for him to say something. Something meaningful. *I love you* maybe. Or *I'm sorry*. But he looked at her and then he looked down and said just two words. *Good night*. And with these two simple, cowardly words, a familiar pulse of disappointment shot through her and she watched him disappear into his room and close the door. She just stood in the hallway and listened to the cadence of her own breath in the silence.

Back in her bedroom, her phone rang. She hoped it was Henry. She wanted to hear his voice, but it wasn't him. They'd agreed not to talk until she returned to the city. This was his idea; it was clear, he said, that she needed some space. But as soon as she had it, this space, all she wanted was to go back, to rewind to those moments before that baby cried in the station, to those moments when they were joking about Christmas presents. Instead of speaking, a string of texts, none of it immensely assuring.

Henry: Enjoy your time with your dad,

Clio: I will try. I miss you though. I'm sorry. All I am is sorry.

Henry: You must stop saying that word.

Clio: I know, Henry.

The phone call was instead from Smith. Clio felt a lifting as her friend spoke; the mere rumble of Smith's voice was soothing and just what she needed. Clio could detect a different texture in this voice, a palpable lightness. Smith rambled on and on about the day she'd enjoyed with Tate, how they'd visited some magical crooked pond to find some sort of poetry plaque, how dinner was surprisingly innocuous, how Tate held his ground with Thatcher, how she thinks she might really like him.

I feel like I've known him forever, Smith said, a quasi-giddiness coating her words. *I feel like you and I are finally getting our lives together, Clio. Isn't that an exciting thought? Like we've been stumbling along, but now we're finding our footing?*

Smith didn't ask how things were at home for Clio and this was an anomaly—Smith was typically dutiful in soliciting such information—but Clio found herself thankful for the lapse. She relished Smith's telling.

And she stayed up late. Packing, going through old things, figuring out what was worth saving. As she tossed things into boxes and garbage bags, she remembered an old, silly television show she and her mother used to watch together from her mother's bed. *Supermarket Sweep,* where a shopper had to fill her basket with the most valuable items in a limited time. In the end, they'd ring up all the contents and see what it added up to. On the show it was a sum of money. Here, now, a childhood. A life.

As Clio did it, this impossible thing that felt easier than she'd imagined it would be, this literal boxing up of her past, words Smith once said echoed in her mind, a balm. *It is just a physical place. Walls and floors and a roof. They are just things. It is your past. Take with you only the parts of it that you want. Create room for your future.*

She sits up now, tosses her legs over the side of the bed, buries her toes in the carpet. She lingers, looks around the small space, which is now almost entirely bare but for the boxes. Boxes for donation. Boxes to store with her father for now. And a box she's marked "Jack's Girls."

She smells bacon. It's a purely happy smell. Growing up, every Sunday morning, her father would get up and make breakfast, and it was always bacon and eggs. His eggs were good, laden with dill, but it was the bacon that was her favorite and his. The crispier, the more blackened and burned, the better. Her mother, if she felt well enough, would make something sweet. But most of the time, Eloise would just sit there, eyes vacant, and drink coffee from a mug Clio made at school for one Mother's Day that said *Best Mom in the World* with a sloppy approximation of a globe.

On the way to the bathroom, Clio stops at the window, presses her palm to the glass, traces her finger around the wooden frame, the frame littered with smudged pencil notations of birds she's seen and the dates. *Baltimore Oriole 4/2/94. House Finch 5/13/95. Mourning Dove 5/27/95.*

In the bathroom, she washes her face and brushes her teeth, stares into the mirror for a final time. She eyes the duct tape in the uppermost corner of the mirror, where her mother punched it. She remembers that day with haunting clarity, her mother flying into a rage with no warning, spouting paranoid thoughts, slicing her hand up, leaving blood everywhere and young Clio to pick up the pieces.

She pops open the plastic disc that contains her birth control pills, slips one from its clear cocoon, stares at the tiny white dot in the center of her palm. She tosses it to the back of her throat and washes it down with water from the tap. Will she stop doing this at some point? Soon? The thought excites her and scares her in equal measure.

She zips up her cosmetic kit. Scans the contents of the small white cabinet. It's all junk—ancient deodorants and yellowing lotions—but she pauses when she sees her mother's perfume. She lifts it to her nose and smells. The aroma brings her back. She carries the bottle with her, places it next to her book bag. Gets dressed for the day.

"Clio! Breakfast!" her father calls, his voice robust. It's as if nothing has happened.

Downstairs, the table is set. Heaping plates of food and large cups of coffee wait. Her father sits and Clio sits across from him. The third chair, her mother's chair, sits empty between them.

Clio tries the eggs. They taste just as they always have. Her father is particularly quiet this morning, but there's a peaceful quality to his face. She takes a few more bites, a couple big swigs of coffee, and watches him. Silence shrouds them, as it so often does, but it feels heavier today, dense. She puts her fork down.

"My last meal here," she hears herself say. The words come from her without her permission. They are hers but less than conscious. Her head feels lighter than it should.

He nods but says nothing. He shovels large forkfuls of food into his mouth. Clio watches his Adam's apple bulge as he swallows. There is a speck of red by his upper lip. Blood. He has cut himself shaving, Clio deduces, and without warning, she's hurtled back to Easter Sunday when she was eleven. She sat in this chair at this table. Eloise was manic, flying around the kitchen in a loosely tied robe. Her father played along with his wife's elaborate breakfast orchestrations, making fried eggs into bunny faces, adding M&M's eyes and bacon ears. Clio fixated on the crimson dot of blood on her father's cheek, how it kept growing before he'd dab it with a square of paper towel. She ate everything they put in front of her even though it didn't taste good and she wasn't hungry. When her father's face stopped actively bleeding, she felt a surprising pang of relief. Somewhere along the way, she'd forgotten that he could hurt too.

"The eggs are good," Clio says because she can't bring herself to say anything else, because it's an easy and true sentence, because it fills the silence, but adrenaline starts to cruise through her veins and panic builds. There are things she needs to say and ask and she can't keep waiting for the right moment. There will be no right moment.

"I have a talent or two," he says.

She pushes her plate away from her, takes a deep breath. "We need to talk, Dad," she says.

He looks up from his plate.

"We never talk about her. Why don't we ever talk about her?"

He stares past her and it's clear he's thinking. "I don't know why, Clio."

"Our lives were flipped upside down last year and we just sit here carrying on, eating eggs. Isn't there something wrong with this?"

He looks at her again. His glance is sharp. "It seems you think there is. Go ahead. Diagnose what's wrong with this. You're good at that. I don't know what you want from me, Clio."

"I want you to look at me for once," she says. "*Look at me.*"

He looks up, fear and rage in his eyes. He says nothing. Anger rises like steam inside her. She grips the edge of the table. The shell cracks. The armor is gone. She is just a daughter. "What do I want? I want us to take a moment from the lives we are so intent on piecing back together and talk about what the hell happened to both of us a year ago. She hanged herself, Dad, on my swing set, the swing set you built. She's gone. She left us. I want us to *talk*."

His face reddens and he looks down. Shreds his paper napkin. "You've made it hard to talk, Clio."

"What's that supposed to mean?"

He hesitates. "Are we really doing this?"

"Yes," she says emphatically, her spine stiffening. "We are."

9:31AM

"Me too."

She feels dizzy, impossibly nauseated, but wills herself to focus. What if she's having a panic attack? She feels some relief when she remembers the bottle of pills stashed upstairs.

"Do you know how sad and angry I've been for all of these years? All I wanted was for you to be there for me for one minute, for you to look at me."

"I've gotten the distinct impression that you do not need me," he says. "You've made that pretty clear."

"Are you kidding me, Dad? I've needed for you for more than thirty years. I've taught myself not to need you, I've convinced myself that I don't need you, but it's all bullshit. I've always needed you."

"Well, I'm sorry I've been an awful, absentee father. That was never my plan. I did my best, Clio," he says, resignation in his voice. "But let me tell you something: we—and that includes me—must have done an okay job because look at you, right? You are successful and strong, tough as nails, feisty as all get-out with your poor old man. I think you turned out just fine, Clio, and I'm going to claim an ounce of credit for that. Maybe most of it was *despite* our bungled efforts, but let me believe I had a small something to do with this."

"Believe what you want to believe," she says. "But, tell me, is it outlandish that I actually want to talk about what happened? Is it that crazy that I want to have a conversation?"

"It's a two-way street, Clio," he says, looking down. "I'll be the first to admit I've messed plenty of things up, that I haven't been the best father, but I'm not so sure you've given me a chance to be. You come home when she dies and then you run away. You promise to visit, but you don't. And shit, Clio, I get it. I'd do the same thing in your shoes. I don't blame you, but you can't have it both ways. You can't fault me for shutting down and avoiding everything when you've done the exact same thing."

She listens. There is something painfully true about what he says, something that slices her. "But this is not just about her, Dad. It's always been about her, yes, but what about me? I was the kid, the daughter, and you never even saw me. All I wanted was for you to see me, to notice me, to ask me questions. I felt invisible, Dad. I just wanted you to come to my plays and my games and take me for a walk or a meal at the diner or take me to college. Shit, Dad, you could have taken an hour. *Something*."

He nods. Looks down at the floor. "I'm just saying it's a two-way street," he says again. "You call for a few minutes each week and we talk about bullshit and I'm the one not noticing you? How about asking me how I'm doing? I lost my wife, Clio, and maybe this is impossible for you to understand, but I loved her."

He stands abruptly and yanks their dishes away. A fork falls to the floor. He escapes to the sink, drops everything inside. Braces himself against the counter. She hears something. He's crying.

"Dad," she says, walking up behind him, guilt pulsing under her skin. She puts her hand on his shoulder. "*Dad.*"

He turns slowly to face her. There's a familiar quality to his eyes, a gloss of fear, of shame, of regret. "Look," he says, his voice calm. "I have no idea how to do any of this."

A lone tear snakes down her cheek. "Neither do I."

He throws his arm around Clio and pulls her into his chest. Hugs her tightly. She weeps into his shirt. They stand there like this for several minutes before separating and wiping their eyes dry.

"Can we sit and talk for a minute?" Clio says. Much of the anger and anxiety has washed away; something has shaken loose.

He nods. Takes her hand and walks her through the door into the living room.

"Let's talk," he says, lowering to sit on the big tattered beige sofa. Her parents found it at the Salvation Army.

She sits beside him. Looks at him and then down at her lap. This is her chance. All those years and they never really discussed things. They reacted to Eloise, weathered her brutal storms, but there was a dearth of actual conversation about what was going on. Clio felt shut out of most of what was happening, relegated to the proverbial sidelines, a mere bystander. She worked to absorb what she could, to glean clues from her parents' cryptic, anger-laced exchanges. She scribbled the names of the swarm of doctors they visited, worried about the arguments she witnessed on a daily basis. She was left to piece together what she could, to guess when her mother was taking her medicine and when she'd stopped.

"I've been really lonely, Dad," she says, biting her lower lip, willing herself to keep breathing. *Lonely*. The word catches in her throat. "When she was alive, I felt peripheral, like I was getting in your way, maybe even making everything worse. I just wanted you guys. I wanted you to see me and notice me. I'm dredging all this up now because I want so badly to move on, Dad, to have a normal life, but there's so much I haven't processed and we haven't talked about and I think it's been getting in the way."

He nods. "I know."

She looks at him. Braces herself. Swallows. Takes a deep breath. Asks the question she's been wanting to ask, the question she knows is terrible to ask, the question she's vowed never to ask anyone who has been through what she's been through. "Did you see it coming?"

He pauses for a beat and then looks at her. "Yes and no. She was terribly depressed, but you and I both know there were plenty of times when she was that way. I keep going over it in my head, wondering if I missed something, a clue, if there was something I could've done."

Clio nods. "Me too. Maybe if I had come home for Thanksgiving instead of going to Costa Rica? Maybe if I had called that day . . ."

Her father puts his hand on her knee. "We can't do this to ourselves. She was sick, Clio. She was so incredibly sick. This wasn't our doing, but I am sorry that I was so focused on her, on how she was doing, on keeping her alive, that I wasn't there for you like I should have been. I can see that now. And I'm sorry. I was trying to protect you and then I couldn't anymore. All of a sudden you knew everything and there was nothing I could do to give you your innocence back."

Innocence. What a foolish, quaint word. Is this something she ever had?

"I want you to have them," he says, pointing at the boxes of books in the center of the room. "But only if you'd like to have them. I can store them for a while. You can think about it," he says, backpedaling.

"I think I'd like them," she says, picturing that big empty shelf at Henry's hotel.

"She'd want you to have them."

"What's in the little box?" she says, pointing to the one smaller box by the larger ones.

He stands, walks over to it and picks it up and carries it back to Clio. Hands it to her. "I found this while I was packing up our closet a few days ago. It was shoved way back on the upper shelf of her side. Take a look inside."

Clio peers inside. It's a jumble of unfamiliar items. She pulls a small plastic circle from it. There are words. Her name. *Clio Marsh. Baby Girl.*

"Your hospital bracelet," her father says.

Something in her comes alive. She pulls a larger bracelet from the box.

"Hers," he says. Her name—*Eloise Marsh, Mother*—is printed in matching type.

Clio reaches in again. Pulls out a Ziploc bag with her first lock of hair. She was almost white blond. Then a photograph of Clio and her mother on her first Easter. Clio wears a frilly white bonnet and is barefoot. There are papers at the bottom, and Clio lifts them out and studies them. They are her school reports from each year since kindergarten. Her Yale acceptance letter. Printouts of some e-mails Clio sent her mother.

"I can't believe she kept all this," Clio says.

"You were her pride and joy," he says. "She loved you more than anything in the world, Clio. She talked about you all the time."

This is a different story than the one Clio has told herself all these years. In Clio's version, she's the Mistake, the fruit of an accidental pregnancy that caused an unwanted marriage and an unwanted life.

Clio closes the box, sees that her hands are shaking as she places the lid back on top. She will have plenty of time to sift through the rest of the contents. This is her time with her father. This is a morning she will not get back, this last morning in her childhood home. She looks up at him, smiles.

"You know something?" he says, standing, walking toward the far end of the room, gesturing toward some green crayon marks on the wall. "She loved it when you did this."

"She did?" Clio says, surprised, standing to join him.

"Yes," he says. "She was proud of you. Decided that you were a little visionary. A note taker like she was. For your first birthday, she gave you a package of index cards and a box of crayons. She wrapped them in newspaper and I remember thinking how odd it all was, but that's it, I just thought she was odd and eccentric and I loved that about her."

Clio imagines herself as a toddler, taking to the wall with a crayon, scribbling on the wall, her mother different than many others would be. Most mothers would race over and grab a wrist and chide their child. Instead, she had the wild and offbeat mom, lingering in the background, a portrait of shifting smiles. Maybe for her mother, Clio's young scrawls were tiny bits of genius, hieroglyphics, budding shreds of communication. That she didn't try to scrub them away, but instead rearranged the furniture—what little there was of it—to afford a better view of these mini masterpieces, offers some ineffable solace in this moment so many years later.

"What was she like when you guys were young?"

At this question, her father's face lightens. He smiles. "She was gorgeous. Wild. Lit up every room. When things got bad later on, I would imagine this version of her and that would help. I'd remind myself that I landed Eloise Marsh. She was quite the catch, you know. I would have never imagined the turn things took."

"I guess that's what scares me," Clio says.

"What does?"

She meets her father's eye. "I love Henry, Dad. I want to be with him."

"That's great," her father says.

"Yes," she says, "but what will things look like a year from now, or five or ten? You and I know better than most how everything can change on a dime."

He nods, grows pensive. "True, but you know something, Clio? Even after everything, even after her diagnosis and all the nightmares and heartache, I wouldn't change a thing. I'd do it all over again because I have you."

I'd do it all over again because I have you. The words stun her and she feels an internal shift, a shaking loose, a thawing. She looks over at him and smiles. "You don't need to say that, Dad."

"I know I don't need to, but it's true and I apparently need to get better at saying these things," he says. "I loved her to her last day, Clio. I loved that woman. I still love her. And she's not here anymore and I'm still making sense of that, but you are here. And so am I. And now it's my turn to figure out how to be a better dad to you. And you're going to have to help me."

Clio nods, thinks about this. "And you're going to have to help me figure out how to be a better daughter."

He smiles. "Sounds like a plan. So, are you going to give Henry a chance?"

"I want to," she says, suddenly feeling a drifty, almost pleasant light-headedness. There's something surreal about these moments, the finality of them, the symbolism. She looks around and around, a dizziness descending, and throws her arm around her father. He clutches it and they stand together in silence.

"He wants us to live together," Clio says. "He's even mentioned having a family."

"Is that what you want?" he asks.

"I don't know," Clio says. "I think so maybe. Do you think Mom would've liked him? He's a lot older than I am."

He laughs. "Mom would have loved him. A smart, successful, suave Irishman courting her little princess. She would have called him delightful. She would have swooned over the slight accent and flirted up a storm. She'd want this for you, Clio. She was always enormously proud of you and wanted you to have a happy life."

Clio wants nothing more than to believe everything her father's saying, and though her doubts rise quickly and her cynicism stings from within, though this sounds nothing like Eloise, she looks over at her father, the openness in his cerulean eyes, and she decides to believe him. Maybe because she wants to, because she needs to, because she's exhausted from questioning every little thing, because believing him will make moving forward easier, but it really doesn't matter.

There is a freedom in this. In deciding to believe. In deciding to take a chance and move on.

Clio looks around the room, the room that will soon bear witness to another imperfect family, and she feels something, a twinkling of gems that have long eluded her, that have seemed fictive: peace, progress, closure.

"I'm so sorry, Clio," her father says, pulling her to him. When her head meets his chest, she hears the refrain of his tears once more.

And through fresh tears of her own, she mouths words. *Me too.*

11:21AM

"I'll be fine."

"I'll be fine, Dad," Clio says at the station, even though there's no way for her to know this.

He kisses her forehead like she remembers him doing when she was a little girl before she'd run into school for the day. Or maybe she doesn't remember this at all. Maybe it's something she made up because she needed to, because it couldn't all be so sad. It's hard to believe that she was a little girl at all, but that's just how she feels right now, small and scared. She doesn't show her father this though. She protects him. She does something she's grown skilled at: she pretends, finding a smile.

She hugs him. "I'd really love to see your new place," she says. "I can get a later train."

"No," he says. "Let me get settled in. You'll see it at Christmas."

"Okay," she says, hugging him once more, descending the escalator to the tracks.

At the bottom, she looks up. He's still there, waving.

She rides the train with the box on her lap. She sifts through it, examining each item as if it were one of her specimens, as if she were gathering data, and the truth is she is.

Time passes. The world blurs. The train hurtles toward home. Home. That's how she thinks of it. New York City. Home. When did this happen?

At some point, she drifts off. She's never been one to nod off on a train, but the lulling motion and the weight of what she's just weathered catch up with her and she surrenders to a stretch of surprisingly peaceful rest. She even dreams. In her reverie, she's on the swing set with her parents. Her mother's in the middle, barefoot. She's laughing her infectious, tinkling laugh and her hair is long and tangled, flying behind her.

Clio startles awake as the train pulls into Grand Central. Disoriented, she looks around her, down at the box she cradles on her lap. She lifts the lid and fingers the treasures inside. This is when she sees it, resting at the very bottom of the box.

An envelope.

Nothing's written on it, but she holds it up to the light and through it she can see her mother's handwriting. A note. It must be a note, *the* note, she decides. All these months and she's been hoping for some kind of note, some kind of something, an explanation or words she could mold into an explanation. Anything. Anything but this crippling confusion and silence. Oh, the hours she wasted on the Internet trying to determine whether suicide notes were common in situations like this. The answers were mixed. Some people found notes, notes that were surprisingly articulate or utterly nonsensical. Some people never found a single clue. All this time and she's held on to a sliver of hope that she'd be a note finder, but now that she possibly has it, she's incredibly afraid. What if her mother has taken one last opportunity to hurt her with words, to break her heart?

When she gets off the train, she's carried by a tide of Black Friday strangers into the station. She clutches the letter, fantasizes for a moment about letting it go to be trampled by all these feet. She looks up at the clock.

All of these people swarming under one clock, one time. So much life. Noise. The mosaic of faces, of heartbreak and happiness, of apathy and ambition, of history and future. She stands for a moment in the midst of it, people whizzing by, brows furrowed, bags swinging, the sound almost too much to bear.

She needs to be alone to read this letter. Somewhere tucked away and safe. Smith is at the apartment. Henry is at the hotel. She looks around, focuses on her breath. It suddenly hits her. She knows where she will go.

3:08PM

"I've been trying to call you."

Clio stands on Central Park West and looks up at the façade of the American Museum of Natural History. She enters through the security entrance under the stairs, flashes her badge to the guard and fights through the hefty holiday crowds to get to the elevator. This is one of the busiest days of the year and the place is wall-to-wall with visitors. She waits a while for the elevator and then squishes on and rides it to the fifth floor.

She hasn't been here for weeks and this always feels strange; for years now, she's come here almost every day when she's not in the field. She often comes on weekends even, logging endless hours doing her research, writing articles and grants, overseeing her grad students. After undergrad biology work at Yale, she came to start her PhD at Columbia and got a graduate-student affiliation in the ornithology department. Her dissertation was on the evolution of hummingbirds, their phylogenetic relationships and historical biogeography in relation to the formation of the Andes.*

Looking back, she can't believe how perfectly it all came together, that she was able to do work she loved and live so close by with Smith, who was not just a friend but almost a sister. The years piled up, blurred by, and Clio worked hard to finish her PhD and do a postdoctoral fellowship, before moving on to teach and become a curator.

She uses her key to enter the private ornithology hall and heads to the collection. It's quiet and dim; no one is around today and she has the place to herself. As she enters the chilly space, which smells of mothballs, she feels an immediate wave of calm roll over her. It's meant to feel like a library and it does; it reminds her of the stacks at Yale.

She's spent so many hours here in the past thirteen years. It's the largest bird collection in the world, numbering nearly one million specimens, including skins, skeletons, alcoholic preparations, eggs, nests, and tissue samples for molecular biochemical studies. They also have a large number of type specimens and rare or extinct species. The specimens here represent all continents and oceans and nearly 99 percent of all species.

All those years of head-down research, losing herself in data and questions, working with and among so many with interests like hers, studying higher-level phylogenetics of birds, studies of speciation and species status, and the description of patterns of geographic variation.

She walks to her own specimens, gingerly pulls out one of her steel trays and looks at them, all the tiny hummingbirds she's collected over many years, those miraculous little bodies, the study skins with the small white labels attached, with her careful notes.

She takes out her first bird, holds it in the palm of her hand, stares at

---

* Based on the work of Jim McGuire et al., "A higher-level taxonomy for hummingbirds," *Journal of Ornithology* 150.1 (2008) 155–165, doi: 10.1007/s10336-008-0330x.

the little body, lifeless and beautiful, and thinks back to her first field trip as a collection assistant. This was the first bird she killed with her own two hands. She asphyxiated the creature through thoracic compression, or "squeezing," by pinching the bird's rib cage very hard between her thumb and forefinger. The memory of this moment remains sharp, imbued now with new, tragic meaning. This little bird and her mother died in the same way. The only difference: her mother held her own wings down.

She sits on the cold linoleum floor. She looks around even though there is no one here but her and these little birds. She grips the envelope, sealed and unmarked, and brims with hope, a foolish and staggering hope, that this is it. The Note. The Explanation. The Final Good-bye.

She runs her finger under the flap, pulls out the single, folded page. She opens it and there they are, her mother's words. Her heart gallops in her chest and her throat tightens as she begins to read.

Dearest Clio.

She cries. Fittingly, it's a jumble. A jumble of brilliance and madness, love and gloom. There is no date. No real indication at all of when her mother wrote this letter. It must have been a while ago because her handwriting was still relatively smooth; in the end, she was too hazy, too shaky, to write. This is not closure. Here, there are no final answers, but she does have these words, words from the woman who brought her into the world. Seven words in particular stand out:

You will be a mother one day.

A sentence. A simple sentence that's not simple at all. A sentence that grabs her.

And you will understand, it will make sense, AHA, AHA, you will say, yes, yes, you will be a mother one day, and see what it's like to crack open with hope and worry and desire and pain and most of all love. But it's not simple. It's hellos and good-byes, nevers and forevers, and go away and come back, please come back. . .

She reads it again and again, tears streaming down her face, thousands of lifeless birds her abiding witnesses. She pulls out her phone and texts Henry.

Clio: Finishing up some work at the museum. Will head to the hotel in 10 min or so.

Before leaving the museum, she stops by her wood-paneled office on the fifth floor. When she unlocks the door and walks in, she trips over something. A package. She picks it up, studies the return address. She smiles, realizing what it is. She tears it open, pulls out the card on top.

Ms. Marsh, I've been trying to call you to arrange delivery and discuss care of the enclosed cuttings, but your assistant said I could go ahead and send these. If you plant them now, they should make a decent seedling by Christmas. Please call me if you have any questions. Bob Leland.

Clio reaches her hand inside and feels the dampness. She smiles. They're here.

She walks over to her desk. A tidy stack of papers sits as she left it and she begins to flip through them. They are papers about recent hummingbird fossil discoveries, a possible new species, a comprehensive Smithsonian review of the special and unique features of the hummingbird skeleton, a paper describing the mites found in hummingbirds and an article about hummingbird entrapments in spiderwebs. She thinks of all the work she and her team must do with the new specimens they found in the Andes, how in the past she would have wasted no time diving into this work.

But not today.

She stands to go, more eager than ever to see Henry.

5:37PM

"I have a surprise for you too."

Clio exits the museum and walks uphill along the concrete path, past the subway entrance. When she reaches the street, she feels her phone buzz. A text.

Henry: Look toward Teddy.

She turns and casts her gaze up at the big equestrian statue at the entrance, the statue of Theodore Roosevelt on horseback. Next to the onetime governor of the state and twenty-sixth president, ardent naturalist and visionary conservationist, Henry sits waiting. She walks toward him, climbs the steps. He holds two big salted pretzels, one in each hand. He hands her a pretzel and empties a pocket full of mustard packets. She takes a large bite and feels now how hungry she is. It's almost evening and she hasn't eaten anything since her father's eggs this morning. They sit and eat side by side on the long steps leading to the museum, Central Park across from them, fat chunks of salt scattering around them.

"How long have you been here?" she says.

"A while," he says, kissing her cheek. "Doesn't matter. God, did I miss you."

"I missed you, too."

"Did you get some good work done?" he says.

"She wrote me a letter, Henry," she blurts out, looking at him.

His eyes widen. "She did?"

Clio nods. "I'm not sure when. Probably years ago. I'm not even sure I understood what she wrote, but she wrote me a letter, Henry."

Clio smiles, and he pulls her to his lap. He doesn't ask. He doesn't ask what it said, how she is feeling. It's as if he knows that she doesn't want him to pry, that what she needs is to be held. They eat their pretzels.

"I was thinking we could have a low-key night," he says. "Tomorrow's the wedding, so maybe a burger and beer at the Dublin House like old times?"

"Sounds perfect," Clio says. And it does.

They sit for a while longer and then he takes her hand and leads her down the steps. They walk west, dodging people and strollers and dogs. At Columbus and Eighty-First, the Christmas tree stand is already up. A scruffy, bearded guy in plaid waits, arms crossed, in front of a dusty blue van.

"Mum was enthralled by Christmas," Henry says, a twinkle in his eye. "She collected all these fragile glass ornaments and we'd break a slew of them every year and she'd lose it. She'd put a tree up as soon as it was November."

Clio smiles. "Which explains the early-bird tree at the hotel. Eloise used to buy her first tree this weekend every year. The weekend after Thanksgiving. She'd scope out the ugliest little runt she could find."

At this, Henry smiles. It feels nice to open up. When they approach the hotel, she and Henry wave at the bellhop who's carrying a family's luggage in from a taxi. Henry grabs Clio's things and runs them inside. He returns, smiling, rubbing his hands. "Shall we?" he says. "I'm oddly excited for our evening."

She is too. She places her hand in Henry's as they walk the length of the block toward the little pub. She fixes her gaze on the neon yellow and red Celtic harp that hangs outside. It flickers and glows. They climb the small set of steps and enter the slender, wood-paneled taproom, which, according to Henry, hasn't closed for a single day since Prohibition.

Mike, the chatty and charming white-haired bartender, greets them fondly, and they settle into two stools at the bar. "What'll it be for yous two?"

"Two Smithwicks and two cheeseburgers, please," Henry says.

Mike handles the food order for them even though most patrons must use their cell phones to call the number printed on the little menus to place their orders.

Henry points to the phone booth and dips into a history lesson. "There used to be a dumbwaiter there," he says. "Story goes that Mum's father knew Carway, the bloke who first rented this place in 1921. Prohibition started a year before, so from the outside they kept it looking like a home, but they had arrangements with local authorities; this whole level was a bar and upstairs was a restaurant, and there was a kitchen in the back. My man Carway here bought the whole building in the thirties and put up the famous harp. That brilliant blinking light was the first thing sailors saw when they docked at the Boat Basin, and this joint opens at eight a.m. every day but Sunday because some people need a nip or two before heading to work."

Clio looks around, appreciating the history of the place, but more the man who's so passionately sharing it. The pub is not full, but they are not alone. There are other patrons and many of them speak with Irish accents.

Henry wipes his eyes and sits up straighter on his stool. "So, my dear." He taps her gently on the nose. "You've barely told me a thing about your trip."

There's so much to tell him. About the early mornings sipping coffee by the mist nets, untangling non-hummingbirds and setting them free. About their trips into town to buy chocolate ice cream and check e-mail at the dusty little Internet café. About all of the exquisite species they had a chance to see close up.

She pulls out her phone and shows him the photos she took, photos that are incredible and yet still don't do justice to the beauty of the birds themselves. She flips through, pointing out some of the birds they saw at various elevations, rattling off their exotic names. *Tyrian Metaltail. Buff-winged Starfrontlet. Mountain Velvetbreast. Sparkling Violetear.* And of course the *Ecuadorian Hillstar.*

"And what did your research tell you? I'm embarrassed to say that I still don't have a clue what you were doing there," he says.

"Do you really want to know?" she says, sipping her beer.

"I do," he says.

And she believes him.

"Well, we are exploring some angles of the work pioneered by an ornithologist named Christopher Witt and a geneticist named Jay Storz, and what we are examining is that there are all of these hummers that fare far better with the altitude than we humans do, and we are looking into why. On a gram-to-gram basis, hovering hummingbirds burn ten times as much energy as a very fit human, so the question is why these little creatures thrive in the Andes when we can barely breathe there. It turns out that hummingbird species living at high altitudes have evolved hemoglobin with enhanced oxygen-binding properties so they can thrive in oxygen-poor environments. If the research pans out, and I really think it will, this will be one of the most breathtaking examples of parallel evolution. It's exciting."

"Parallel evolution, huh?" Henry says, laughing. "It's as if you're speaking in a foreign language, I'm afraid."

Clio smiles. "Let me put it more simply: these little creatures are evolving so they can live in extreme environments."

His eyes are focused and it's plain that he's thinking hard. "That's quite wonderful."

"I'm impressed that you're not glazing over like most people do when I talk about this stuff."

"I'm not most people, Clio."

"No," she says, grabbing his knee, "you're not."

"Hearing you talk about your work is an incredible turn-on, if you must know."

"Noted," Clio says. "The upsetting thing, though, is what this all means for conservation. The escalator-to-extinction hypothesis is that global warming is forcing some species to migrate even higher in search of cooler climates, but the concern is that certain species might die out before adapting."

"Shit," Henry says. "What do we do? Maybe we should run off to the Andes and build ourselves a little hotel at four thousand meters above sea level and all profits will go to saving the hummingbirds."

Clio laughs. "Now you're talking."

All of this feels so good. Telling him about work that matters so deeply to her. Laughing with him. Sitting next to him in a charming old city pub. She looks at him, really looks at him, studies his smile. It is the smile of the man she loves, the man she wants nothing more than to know. It's still a bit of a mystery why he's here at nearly fifty, why he hasn't settled down before now. Surely, he has his own stuff, his own memories, his own fears. In time, she will learn about all of it, and there is no rush. This is the way it works. No one emerges from childhood totally unscathed. You do the best you can. And, if you are lucky, you find someone to do the best you can with.

"My mother said something in her letter that I can't stop thinking about," Clio says, suddenly pensive, the taste of beer on her tongue, her head blissfully light.

"What's that?"

"She said *you will be a mother . . .* She imagined me as a mother, Henry."

Henry grins. "Are you saying that you're entertaining the notion?"

Clio shrugs. "I think I might be saying that."

She still doesn't know whether a mother is something she can, or wants to, take the leap to be, but it's a leap she's thinking about now, and that's something, an enormous something.

Mike refills their beers. Clio takes a big swallow and puts her hand on Henry's knee.

Be Obscure Clearly.

A few hours and a few beers later, back at the hotel, Clio reads these three words, which are etched on the glass shower door of the hotel bathroom, traces them with her index finger. They are E. B. White's words. Once, Clio thought these words were cryptic and pretentious, but she feels differently now. These words speak to her now. *Be obscure clearly.* This is what she's done, she's embraced obscurity, not in an effort to deceive, never in an effort to deceive, but in an effort to give things a chance.

She steps into the shower. The hot water feels good on her body. She shampoos her hair, applies conditioner to the ends, examines the bottle in her hand. It is Henry's conditioner, organic. The price tag is coming off, but she can see that it cost thirty-something dollars. How has she slipped into the world of thirty-dollar hair products?

Clio hears something. She sees Henry standing there, the silhouette of his frame through the fogged shower door. He opens it and steps in. It is the same body she's seen hundreds of times now, a body she's all but memorized, but suddenly it's deliciously foreign and new. He puts two fingers under her chin and lifts her face, looks into her eyes, wraps himself around her, steals a bar of soap from the shelf. Cleans her again, the redundancy welcome, needed somehow. Traces slow circles around her small breasts, between her legs. Her mind empties to nothing. She reaches for him. He lifts her, slips himself inside.

After, through the sound of the water and their mingled breath, she hears his words. The words she needs to hear.

"I love you so much," he says.

Out of the shower, they stand, side by side, toweling off. At the twin sinks, they get ready for bed.

He turns toward her. Pulls her into him, and she rests her head on his chest. His heartbeat is steady and strong. She listens.

"Will you come back to the museum with me? I need to get something."

"Now?"

"Now," she says, her pulse quickening. She's going to do this. She doesn't want to wait.

"All right, let's go," he says, clearly confused. In silence, they dress. On the street, she takes his hand and leads him along at a swift clip toward the museum.

"I'm not sure what it is that you could so desperately need at this hour," he says. "It's almost midnight."

"You'll see," she says, looking over at him. "I have a surprise for you too."

In the moonlight, his eyes sparkle. His face is calm, free of anxiety, and in this moment she appreciates how different they are. A week ago, she stood in that small elevator filled with panic. The idea of a surprise unmoored her entirely, but here he is, serene and pensive as they walk.

She retraces her steps from earlier today and he follows, his hand linked in hers. She's done this many times, but there's something exhilarating about being here after hours. As they ride up in the elevator, her palms begin to sweat and she focuses on her breath. Her lips shake as she smiles.

He waits behind her as she unlocks her office door and then pushes it open to walk inside. She flips the light switch. He paces around, walks to the window, looks out. "Bloody good view," he says, looking back at her.

She bends down and lifts the box and carries it toward him.

"Here," she says, handing it to him. *Here*. The single word echoes.

He looks at her and smiles and sits in the leather chair to open it. He pulls them out, the two green cuttings, each about ten inches long, the ends wrapped in moist paper towels. He holds them up.

"Do you know what they are?"

He laughs. "I haven't a bloody clue."

"They are cuttings from E. B. White's old willow tree in Turtle Bay. Your favorite tree in the world, Henry."

The excitement that takes over his face is that of a little boy. "Are you bloody kidding me?" he says, running his hand along the length of the green cuttings, looking at her, standing. "I don't understand. How did you get these? Oh my goodness."

"It's a long story, but I tracked down this guy in Brooklyn who was the one who cut down the original willow in 2009, and when he did, he saved a few cuttings and planted them and they are now about eight feet tall. These cuttings are from his trees. I thought we could plant them in the garden behind the hotel."

He captures her in the most enormous hug. His breath is heavy. She feels his heart pounding. When he pulls away, he's grinning from ear to ear. Tears fill his eyes. "I can't believe you did this for me."

She smiles. "This is your Christmas gift, but I didn't want to wait."

"Are you saying that you want to set down some roots with me, Clio?"

She pauses. Smiles. Nods. "That's exactly what I'm saying." And then she repeats those words, his words from the very beginning. "HK, you might just be my thing."

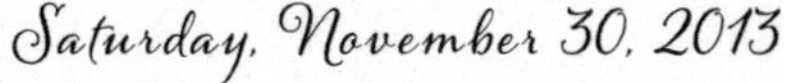

SMITH

The deeper that sorrow carves into your being,
the more joy you can contain.
Is not the cup that holds your wine the very cup
that was burned in the potter's oven?

—Kahlil Gibran, *The Prophet*

Client Name: Smith Anderson
Coach's Name: Laura Newman
DATE: AUGUST 21, 2013

CONSCIOUS GOALS

Please list your conscious goals of our coaching relationship, ***and*** *how you would define "success" by the time we finish working together.*

CONSCIOUS GOAL #1:
I will move on from my breakup with Asad.

Success Defined:

1. I will give myself 6 months and then start dating again;
2. I will forgive Asad for the decision he made;
3. I will forgive my parents for the fact that they never approved of our being together.

CONSCIOUS GOAL #2:
I will take far better care of my mind and body.

Success Defined:

1. I will do yoga 1–4 times a week;
2. I will experiment with transcendental meditation;

3. I I will eat a mostly vegan diet;
4. I will be moderate in my intake of caffeine and alcohol;
5. I will not drink from plastic water bottles;
6. I will train for the New York Marathon;
7. I will read good books;
8. I will get at least 7 hours of sleep a night;
9. I will see a maximum of 12 clients per week;
10. I will watch a maximum one hour of reality television per week.

CONSCIOUS GOAL #3:
I will forgive my sister for getting engaged while I was at rock-bottom.

Success Defined:

1. I will help her & Mom with the wedding planning;
2. I will make a genuine effort to get to know Briggs better;
3. I will remember that life is not a zero-sum game.

CONSCIOUS GOAL #4:
Write a book.

Success Defined:

1. I will sit for 5 hours a week and write;
2. I will have a workable draft and query possible agents by May.

8:41AM

"It's you."

Smith opens her eyes. Looks around. Realizes that she's not home but at Tate's place downtown. It was his idea to take a walk after the rehearsal dinner in midtown. He snapped photos as they walked and walked. Even though she was wearing heels, and high ones at that, they never started to hurt as they normally do. Soon they were close to his place. He suggested one last drink at the White Horse Tavern, where she'd been once or twice before. He was full of stories about writers who'd frequented the bar in their day—Dylan Thomas and Norman Mailer and Jack Kerouac, who, per folklore, got kicked out a handful of times.

At one point, he sneaked her into the men's bathroom and showed her where it says "JACK GO HOME!" on the wall.

Tate ordered one of the famous bloody burgers for them to share. One drink became a few and it grew late and they were just around the corner from his place and he invited her up and even in her intoxicated state, she knew better, but then said screw it and up they went into his charming prewar building on West Eleventh between Bleecker and Hudson, up two flights of stairs into his newly renovated floor-through.

The space is modern but filled with prewar details—tall ceilings, a wood-burning fireplace, three oversized windows with traditional moldings overlooking Bleecker Playground. They stayed up late talking in his living room.

My parents are worried about me, he said. *And I understand why. I'd be worried about me. You know, I've wanted to tell my mother about you. She'd like you a lot.*

He poured them tall glasses of ice water and they sobered up some.

She looks over at him now, lying on the bed beside her. His eyes are closed, his lashes long. His pajama bottoms, a red Christmas tartan flannel, make her smile, and she suddenly remembers last night's drunken deal: she would crash here if and only if he promised to behave himself. He would, he promised, snapping the Lands' End tags from the drawstring pants, affectionately mocking his mother, who apparently loves sending him things. With just these pants slung low around his hips, he climbed into bed next to her. It was past four a.m. when he drifted off, just a few moments before she did.

So, less than five hours of sleep the night before Sally's wedding. Far from ideal, but the crazy thing is that she doesn't even feel tired. She thinks back on the week—it's only been a week—running into him at the game just last Saturday, and here they are, in bed together, on the verge of something maybe. She's vowed not to get ahead of herself, to take it a step at a time, and she believes she's doing a decent job of this. Sure, there was that highly erotic text exchange in the Hamptons, but it was really nothing but evidence of tension, a pulse, a possibility that they might at least click sexually.

She looks at him and marvels at the fact that he's the polar opposite of what she's always seen as her type: tall, dark, handsome, exotic, macho. Here he is, Midwestern and fair, with his artist's soul and his textbook rebellion tattoos. (She just saw for the first time his Walt Whitman *I contain multitudes* ink wrapping around his right shoulder.) She's only seen so much, but she can tell already that he's a thinker like she is, equally intent on finding himself and aware of how clichéd this search is. She studies him now, listens to the rhythmic purr of his breath, grows tempted to reach under the covers and stroke him awake, but she hesitates, resists. There will be a chance for this, she hopes.

She has to pee. She slips off her side of the bed and tiptoes into the en suite bathroom, a modern space blanketed in crisp white Carrara marble. As she sits on the toilet, she studies the mess: a razor and a stick of Old Spice deodorant and an odorous pile of dirty socks. There are books and magazines on the floor by her feet. She stacks them into a tidy pile. Flushes and washes her hands. She walks out into the living room and looks around. It's hard not to; she's curious about this guy and also, this is what she does, what she loves to do and is paid to do, imagine order by examining chaos, understand people through their physical places.

His photographs are everywhere, on every surface, in messy piles. She sifts through, studies them. The images are stark and powerful and, as far as she's concerned, stunning. Most of them are black and white, a tad grainy, with people in them.

She opens the shutters and the space fills with morning light. More details snap into focus. Precarious towers of photography tomes dog-eared with yellow Post-its, a stack of brochures for local photography programs, a few empty beer cans. The walls are neutral and bare.

In the kitchen, she opens the fridge. It's practically barren. A near-empty bottle of Heinz ketchup lies on its side. One last lonely beer stands upright in the back. She imagines filling this fridge with good things, fresh produce, organic omega-3 eggs, distilled water.

"Hungry?"

Smith turns. He stands in kitchen doorway, his hair mussed from sleep. She tries not to stare at his bare chest, slim, muscled, tan for November.

She looks at him and smiles. "Sweet dreams?"

"Yes, actually," he says.

He squeezes past her and starts coffee. "So how do you like it?" he asks, his question faintly sexual.

"With almond milk and stevia," she says, and his forehead wrinkles in confusion.

"I don't even think I know what those things are," he says, and shrugs.

"You have a lot to learn," Smith says, lightly flirting. "This place is great."

He scoops coffee grounds into the filter. "Well, it's no San Remo classic six, but hey, gotta start somewhere."

"It's *yours*, though. You can do what you like with it. No parents breathing down your neck, no doorman watching your every move, no sister next door. All of this sounds quite appealing to me right now."

"It could use a little love," he says. "I'm suddenly feeling motivated to get it together. Maybe you could help me?"

"I'd love to," she says, walking into the living room. "You could definitely use some window treatments. Maybe three of your photos blown up on the wall behind the couch." She walks to his desk. "What are these again?" she says, holding up a stack of pages with small images.

"Contact sheets," Tate says, joining her. "Some of the most famous photographers argue that they're more important than prints because they show the actual process of getting to the final product. Cartier-Bresson said something great about how you can see the photographer in the contact sheets, how hardworking he is, how much effort he took to work the scene. He talked about the 'decisive moment,' but the deal is that even the best photographers don't take just one shot but 'work the scene'—from different angles, perspectives, by crouching, getting closer, and using horizontal versus vertical orientations. Shit, am I boring you?"

"Not at all," she says, and this is the truth. There's something wonderful about hearing the passion in his voice, how much he cares. "Are all your photos digital or do you develop some the old-fashioned way?"

"Both," he says. "Come."

She follows him and he opens a door off the living room. It's the apartment's second bathroom, but he's transformed it into a darkroom that has a distinct chemical smell. Basins of solution rest in a large sink. Photographs hang from the shower bar.

"Wow," she says, looking around at the prints he's developed. She pauses when she sees something. "Wait. Is that . . . ?"

"Yes," he says. "It's you. Last Saturday. At the game."

She moves closer. There she is, standing in the grass, her face obscured by her giant tortoiseshell sunglasses. In the image, she looks down at the screen of her phone. There are several shots, a whole series of them, the differences between them subtle.

"I didn't notice you taking these," she says, looking at him.

"I know. I'm getting better at the surreptitious portrait. I love these, though," he says, admiring his own work. "And I love what they led to. I did it on purpose, you know."

"Did what?"

"Spilled my beer on you," he says. "I needed to find a way to talk to you. Pathetic perhaps, but it worked. I wasn't sure you'd remember me. I don't think I was on your radar in college."

"You are now," she says, and smiles, recalling that he did spill his beer. Not much of it, but enough to annoy her. It soaked her blue jeans but dried as she talked to him. Hours later, they were still talking and sipping drinks and she forgot all about the inaugural mishap.

They head back out to the living room. Tate disappears to pour their coffees, leaving her alone for just a few moments. She sits in his desk chair and spins around in it, checks her phone, but it has died and she doesn't have a charger. "Do you mind if I quickly check my e-mail on your computer?"

"Go ahead," he says.

She moves the mouse and the screen lights up. He has several windows open and she takes it upon herself to reduce them. She pauses when she sees Olivia's name.

An e-mail.

From Tuesday morning.

Smith peers back over her shoulder, sees that Tate's still busy in the kitchen. Furtively, she skims.

I'm worried I made a big mistake. I think I was going through something. 13 years. Are we really just throwing that away?

He lied to her. At Balthazar. He said he hadn't heard from Olivia, but he'd heard from her that very morning. A faint nausea takes hold and Smith feels light-headed. She closes the computer and stands.

She hears him approaching and looks away from the computer, meets his eye. He hands her a cup of coffee.

"Black today, but I'll make sure to snag some of, what was it, nut milk and . . ."

"Stevia," she says, forcing a smile. "An all-natural plant extract."

He's joking around. He's insinuating a next time. This is all good, but she can't shake this feeling, this foreboding feeling that she's jumped the gun, gotten her hopes up. She shouldn't be here right now. She should be in her own place getting ready for the day. What is she doing here? It's clear he's not ready to move on.

She takes a small sip of her coffee, places it down on the desk. "I should get going. I need to be at the hotel in just a few hours for hair and makeup and pictures. Big day."

"That's right," he says. "You ready for tonight?"

Smith nods, grabs her things.

"Everything okay?" he says, putting his hand on her arm.

"Sure," she says, pulling away. "One too many cocktails. Not enough sleep."

"Okay," he says, retreating, concern plain on his face. "Let me walk you out?"

She lets him. Waits for him to pull on some jeans and find his shoes. In the landing outside his place, she waits some more as he pulls the door closed. They silently make their way down to the street. Outside, he hugs her. It's a friendly hug, platonic in hue, the kind of hug a brother would give.

"See you tonight?" he says.

"Yup," she says.

She turns to go and walks to the corner and gets into a taxi. From the backseat, she looks through the window and watches him. He stands in front of his building, hands in the pockets of his jeans, his sandy hair blanched by sun. She tells herself a story: He didn't lie because he wants to get back together with Olivia. He lied because they were having a good time and he didn't want to get sidetracked talking about his past. She will ask him about Olivia again, make sure to figure out where he stands. She has plenty of time to get to the bottom of this. There's no rush. And if he's still hung up on his past, Smith will be fine. If nothing else, it's good to know she can feel hopeful again.

9:45AM

"It could be a true disaster."

A long shower. Far longer than usual. Scalding water pummels her back, rushes over her body. Smith exfoliates her skin vigorously with a peppermint scrub. Her fingertips soften and wrinkle, and her mind releases and roams.

None of this is about Tate, she decides. He is just a person, a good and interesting person from what she can tell, and he, like she, is recovering from something hard. It's clear now; this is why they clicked so intensely, because they have both been trying to push through pain, because they have that common ground of hurt and hope, because they have been able to remind each other what it is to like someone.

She likes him. That's all. And that's okay. She's allowed to like someone. Seeing that e-mail from his ex? It was just a moment. Nothing more. If anything, it was a reminder to slow down, to stay strong. She's fine. She's better than she's been in a long time.

The uncertainty and the confusion are just part of the deal, part of life, gentle, benign constants. Insecurity will always flare and fade out, make joy seem better. She thinks of him now, a new *him*, of the peace plain on his sleeping face this morning, of his bare chest, his tapered waist, that smile.

She steps out of the shower, turns the water off, towels dry and stares at herself in the mirror. She's thinner than she's ever been, also stronger. Her hair's grown long.

In the kitchen, she unloads the dishwasher and steeps some green tea. When it's ready, she sits with her tea in the bay window of her living room and looks out at the park. She hears the front door open and turns to see Clio. Smith called her on the way uptown, in the middle of her spiral about the e-mail. Clio listened; Clio always listens. She said she'd come by.

"I brought scones from Alice's Tea Cup," she says, walking in. "Pumpkin."

"Thank you," Smith says.

Clio smiles and sits beside her. "So, what happened?"

"The strange thing is that I don't think *anything* happened. I was with him at his apartment. Things were really comfortable and nice and we were joking around and then I was checking my e-mail on his computer because my phone died and I saw a message from his ex saying she wants him back and I panicked. I don't even know why. I've known him for *a week*. Yes, I like spending time with him, but I don't even know how I feel about him. The e-mail felt like a red flag. A warning not to get involved with another unavailable man."

Clio pinches the edge from a scone and drops it in her mouth. Her brow furrows as it does when she's thinking hard. "Can I ask you something, though? Are you even available?"

Smith looks at her friend and smiles. Leave it to Clio, smart Clio, to turn this around. This is one of the many reasons she loves her, because she really thinks about things, because she's able to see nuances that Smith often misses.

"I guess I don't know," Smith says. "I think I am?"

"Think about it from his perspective for a minute. He meets you and you are this stunning girl with your own business and a gorgeous apartment and you are admittedly still getting over a relationship that you believed was going to be *it*. He's had his heart stomped on. So have you. He's reeling. You're reeling. You're both gun-shy about getting involved again. You're both thoughtful people. That's only a good thing."

Smith nods as Clio continues. "You haven't cared about anyone since Asad and I know it's scary. I get it. We were sitting here just last weekend and you were encouraging me to trust that things with Henry would be okay and I'm beginning to believe you were right, and now it's my turn. From what I can tell, you like Tate and he likes you. He's a good guy. He's doing everything in his power to spend time with you. Thanksgiving dinner with your family? Your sister's wedding? If he were just playing around and didn't like you, he wouldn't in a million years be doing these things."

"Right," Smith says, nodding. She always feels so much better after talking to Clio. She has this way of breaking everything down to its elements, offering translations. She looks at her friend, her friend who has been through so much, who has come so far. "How was the trip home?" She remembers the little home blocks from campus, escorting Eloise back there several times when she showed up in their dorm.

"It was really good, I think," Clio says, and Smith can see a gloss of tears in her eyes. "I brought him to Eloise's grave. I didn't plan to, but then we were there and I wanted to. Poor man handled it well. It was heavy but good. I had this huge conversation with my father. It was kind of ugly at first, but then we were able to really talk. And he gave me this box of items my mother saved. My hospital bracelets, my school reports, a letter."

"A letter?" Smith says, expectation in her voice.

"Not *the* letter, but a letter all the same. It was brilliant and totally nuts and I'm not sure it answered any of my questions, but I'm so thankful to have it. And guess what?"

"What?" Smith says. "There's more?"

"There is," Clio says. "I'm doing it, Smith. I'm moving in with him."

Smith smiles. Nods. Takes her friend's hand. "I'm happy for you."

"You know how you asked me what I wanted?" Clio says. "You know how I had no idea how to answer you? I've been thinking about that question all week, here and when I went home, and I think I've figured it out. What I want is *peace,* Smith. Happiness would be nice. I'm not going to turn down happiness, but the one thing I've never ever had is peace. Not when she was alive. Not in the past year. I want to breathe and sleep and read the newspaper and go for walks and do my work and hang out with you and Henry and not spend so much energy worrying what catastrophe might crop up next. I want peace."

Smith nods. "And that's just what you deserve."

"You ready for tonight? Want to practice your speech?"

"I didn't write it," Smith says.

"What do you mean?" Clio says, panic in her eyes.

"It's not like me at all. God knows, I sat down to write it a million times, but it just didn't come, and that stressed me out enormously, but it just occurred to me that I need to just get up there and keep this real."

"You'll be fine," Clio says, remembering college. How Smith did everything last-minute, cramming for finals, whipping up ten-page papers the night before, still managing to get straight A's. It bothered Clio some, that it all seemed to come so easily to her friend, that Clio had to work so hard to get good grades, but in time, envy gave way to admiration.

"I hope so. It's entirely possible that I'll get up there and clam up and not be able to utter a word. It could be a true disaster."

"It won't be," Clio says, looking at Smith. "It won't be. It will be perfect."

"Clio?"

Her friend looks up. Waits.

"Thank you," Smith says.

"For what?" Clio says, nibbling her pumpkin scone.

"For calling Jack's mom at the clinic, for walking me there that day and waiting with me and walking me back to the dorm. For being there. For keeping my secret all these years. I'm realizing now that it's been weighing on me and I just feel lucky that I had you then. That I have you now."

"You're welcome," Clio says. "And thank *you*."

Smith laughs, slips off the window seat, disappears into the bedroom and returns with a plastic-wrapped gown. The black dress Clio will borrow for the wedding. "Thank you for what?"

Clio smiles, tears filling her eyes. "For taking a chance on a quiet, broken girl from New Haven."

Smith feels her own tears now. They rise in her eyes and burn as she blinks. Through the salty blur, she fixes her gaze on her friend. "Shit, we're all a tiny bit broken, aren't we?" Clio nods and grabs Smith's hand. A meaningful silence cloaks them. Smith watches as Clio scans the room, a wondrous look on her face. "I'm going to miss this place," Clio says, "but it's time for me to move on. That really sounds so clichéd—*moving on*—but it's true."

"I know," Smith says, nodding. "I know. I think it's time for me to move on, too."

"Wait. What?" Clio's eyes widen.

"After the wedding, I think I'm going to look for a new place. Maybe downtown or even Brooklyn. Being on top of my family twenty-four/seven isn't healthy for me. I think I've known this for a while, but it's time I do something about it. I need to live my life. *My* life."

"That sounds like a good plan," Clio says, eyes twinkling.

They sit together as they've done countless times before, two friends nibbling on crumbling scones, the green trees across the way witnesses in the wind. The sky is clear, a deep, promising blue.

10:35AM

"Aap khubsurat hain."

Smith will walk. The Waldorf is not close by any means, but she has plenty of time and it's nice out and she does her best thinking while walking anyway. Her hope? That her speech will take shape in her mind as she strolls. She heads down Central Park West all the way to the Time Warner Center to cut over to Central Park South. She waits for a light and checks her phone, keeps walking. She bumps into something. Someone.

Startled, she looks up. First, all she sees are the scrubs, the caramel skin. She keeps looking up and nearly stops breathing.

Asad.

No, not Asad.

It's not him. This isn't the way life works. It's a guy who only vaguely resembles Asad, a guy who now stares at her in the middle of this crosswalk. Cars honk. She snaps out of it, dashes to the sidewalk by the big gold statue of Columbus. She peers up at the two glass towers, up to the windows of the third floor, where she last saw Asad, almost exactly a year ago, for the final time.

They sat at Bouchon Bakery, at one of the tall tables. He bought her a croissant and a cappuccino. She touched neither. She reached into her bag and pulled out the ring, placed it in the center of the round table. He stared at it, the small black box, a keen despair evident in his dark eyes.

I told you I don't want it back. I got it for you.

You got it for me because we were getting married. Now we're not. I don't want it, Asad.

I want you to keep it, he said, looking up at her.

I don't understand what happened.

A long silence. Then words. Words that didn't sound like him at all.

I love you too much to continue this.

I don't understand.

My family knows, he said.

You told them? The plan wasn't to tell them until after.

They know.

Because you broke down and told them? Why couldn't you wait?

Silence. He began to cry. She'd never seen him cry before; cruelly, seeing him crumble made her love him more. He looked up at her and she was convinced that he was about to say something, but then he must have changed his mind. Regular life continued around them. People held hands. Chased kids. Talked on phones. Shopped for Christmas.

I just don't understand, she said again. She waited for him to say something, but he didn't. He just sat there with his bloodshot eyes, periodically looking at her, and it was clear, blazingly clear, that he still loved her, that whatever this was, it wasn't about love. She had a piercing intuition that her father had something to do with this, but she pushed it away.

She stood. She had no choice but to walk away. She did it slowly, wordlessly offering him the breakfast she couldn't stomach, collecting her bag from the floor, leaving the ring on the table.

Good-bye, Asad, Smith said, taking his hand one last time. He lifted it to his mouth and kissed it.

She felt as if she might faint, but she didn't. She made it to the escalator, but before she stepped on, he grabbed her.

"*Aap khubsurat hain,*" he said, his voice shaking.

You are beautiful in Urdu.

As she walks toward the hotel, she thinks back to that afternoon. It feels like ages ago, but also like yesterday. She feels for that girl, that girl whose world was turned upside down, that girl who had no choice but to fall to pieces and then do the work to pick them up. And that's what she's done. There's still progress to be made, that's obvious, but she's doing it, pulling herself together, more or less, and here she is, walking past those big buildings, the mere sight of which made her cry for months. But there are no tears today, just slices of memory, dregs of a devastation that's thinning with time, the keen sense that things will be okay.

11:25AM

"What in the heavens is transpiring in here?"

Smith rides the elevator to the forty-second floor of the Waldorf Astoria. She walks down the hall and knocks on the door of the Royal Suite. Sally answers. Her fresh-scrubbed face is flawless and glowing and she's wrapped in a white robe with the word *bride* scrawled on the front in gray cursive letters. Her hair is up in curlers. Smith hugs her, hugs her hard, and doesn't let go for at least a minute.

"What was that about?" Sally says, smiling, her eyes twinkling.

"Nothing," Smith says. "It's just that I love you and it's your wedding day and I'm so fucking excited for you. That's all."

Sally beams. She takes Smith's hand and pulls her toward a grand sitting room, which glows with sunlight. "This place is *insane*. Two bedrooms, two and a half bathrooms, and check out these views."

Smith walks to the window and looks out. The sweeping views of Manhattan are divine, and though not her taste, the space is objectively exquisite, decorated with antiques and lush period furniture. She walks to the dining room. It overlooks Park Avenue and St. Bart's.

"Help yourself," Sally says, pointing to an impressive spread of breakfast on the table. "The food is delicious and Bitsy went overboard."

"Bitsy going overboard? You don't say," Smith says, laughing.

Sally grins. "She's in the other room getting started with makeup."

"Must prioritize caffeine," Smith says. "I need it after last night. I made the genius move of practically staying up all night talking to Tate. Wondering how wise that was now."

"Tate," Sally says. "Gee, Smith, I *like* him. I really like him. I can't explain it, but when you walked in with him on Thanksgiving, there was this incredibly positive energy around you guys. It was like you'd known each other for a long time and were so comfortable with each other. I don't know, but I just got this really good feeling."

"Thanks," Smith says. "I like him too, Sal. Probably more than I should after seven days, but I need to take a breath and not lose my wits over a guy who is still *married*."

"Briggs thinks it's just a matter of time."

"Briggs?"

"I guess they bonded in the Hamptons when they were sequestered in the guesthouse. He said Tate wouldn't shut up about you. I think he might have used the word *whipped*. And apparently Dad went on some horrific diatribe about how Tate should protect every hard-earned penny and Tate told Briggs it made him want to just sign the damn papers. So maybe you'll have Thatch to thank if this thing works out."

Smith smiles. Naturally, these snatches of gossip serve to lift her spirits, but she implores herself to remain cautious, to focus on her sister.

"Today is about *you,* Sal. How are you feeling? Can you believe it?"

Sally grins, sips her coffee. "I'm so excited. Can you believe this mild weather? Snowing last week and now it's positively springlike."

Smith studies her sister. There's a palpable calm to her face, a true serenity and joy that Smith has missed because she's been so wrapped up in her own narcissistic nonsense, because she's been getting in her own way. All the plotting and planning and grasping for control and maybe what she's needed most was to just breathe and let go. Wordlessly, they sit together on the floral sofa.

"I'm sorry, Sal," Smith says, looking her sister straight in the eye.

"For what, silly?" Sally says, arching her eyebrows.

Smith's throat tightens. "I know I haven't been the best. I know it's so ridiculous, but I've been feeling really stalled and left behind. It's not easy for me to admit these things, but it's true."

Sally smiles and nods. "It's okay. I understand," she says. "I felt the exact same way when you got engaged to Asad."

"You did?"

Sally nods. "I was with Briggs, so the blow was cushioned, but even so, I felt left behind, too. I get it."

Smith remembers the night last winter when Sally called. The phone rang and for a split second she hoped that it was Asad, but it wasn't, it was Sally, and she just knew; she knew what was happening. Smith picked up and heard her sister's saccharine voice, but its tone was detectably different, even lighter. She said two words. Just two words. *He asked.* And all Smith could think was, *Shit,* and the moment hardened in her mind, emblazoning itself. She remembers all of it: that she wore her pink nightgown, that she was half-asleep, that as she sat there in her dark, exquisitely appointed and lonely bedroom listening to her younger sister gush, a new kind of sadness swaddled her. She didn't sleep that night. Not a wink. She lay there in her bed and her mind filled with a million memories from their childhood. Halloweens and trips to *The Nutcracker* and their birthday parties and their Brearley graduations and the first time they sneaked a beer when they were thirteen and fourteen. It was like this strange movie playing in her head.

"I don't know," Smith continues, fixing her gaze on a lone flower on the wallpaper. "I've been so *lost* and I've missed so much of this time. Look at you. I've never seen you so happy. You are glowing, Sal, and you love him so much and he adores you, and you are going to have this gorgeous life together and the most ridiculously stunning children, I just know it, and I've felt envious and resentful and mostly just really scared that you're leaving, but you're not really leaving, are you?"

"I'm not, Smith," Sally says, her eyes glossed with tears. "I'm not going anywhere. We are so desperate to stay put that we might offer an astronomical sum of money to buy the apartment on the other side of us. I've already warned Briggs that you're an important part of the package."

"Good," Smith says, tears snaking down her cheeks.

"What in the heavens is transpiring in here? An after-school special?" Bitsy says, floating into the room, her face made up like a doll's.

Smith and Sally laugh. Leave it to Bitsy to inject a dose of timely humor.

"How are you, Bits? Did the dinner last night pass muster?" Smith says, kissing Bitsy on the cheek hello.

"Honestly, dear? I'm losing my marbles. Briggs's mother. Did you see the blouse she was wearing? The plunging neckline? She's seventy! With a colt's tooth! There should be rules written about what one can and cannot wear. And the cash bar after the dinner? Beyond tacky. But what did I do? I bit my tongue. I'm not going to come to points with this woman over something as inane as a bar tab. But this tongue? I tell you it's going to bleed. I'm fine with the father. Just a harmless, coxy-loxy fellow. A few drinks in him and he's in prime twig. He'll fit right in. The apple doesn't fall far. But she is a veritable fruitcake. I can't fathom how you will put up with her, Sally. We must tolerate them for another week, but Sally's got decades ahead."

"That's the idea, yes," Sally says, laughing.

"Anyhoo, you're up for makeup, Smith," Bitsy says. "Chop-chop. We've got pictures in less than two hours."

Pictures. She thinks of Tate, of his cameras and books and photos everywhere, of the fact that he saw something in her last weekend and trained his camera on her. She can't help but wonder what will happen with them. She's never been good with not knowing, but there's something exciting about the uncertainty, the anticipation. She refills her coffee and carries it with her to the other room to get her makeup done.

She unzips the garment bag and pulls the dress from it. Remarkably, the dry cleaner was able to remove the stain. She lays it on the bed. The blue silk shines in the sunlight and it surprises her that she actually looks forward to putting it on.

6:27PM

"You may kiss the bride."

One step at a time. That's all Smith needs to do. She positions her flowers near her belly button as the wedding planner instructed. She concentrates on going slowly, but this proves a challenge; she's far more nervous than she ever expected to be. All along, she's seen this wedding as a hurdle to clear, as something to get through; not once did she seriously consider that it would shake her up like this. Her lips quiver as she smiles and approaches the front of the church.

She didn't shed a tear yesterday afternoon at the rehearsal. It was all business, a logistical puzzling of who stands where and who walks when and who says what, but today is a different story. When her father and Sally are halfway down the aisle at the vast St. Bart's Church, Smith feels herself welling up. It could be the music. Church music—its haunting, echoing innocence—has always moved her, but whatever the true cause, she's crying. She tries to keep the tears from falling, worries about her makeup running, but surrenders; it's not up to her. Eyes wet, she peers down at her maid-of-honor bouquet, a stunning spray of white orchids tied with blush-colored ribbons.

She locks eyes with some cousins in from Boston, spies a few of Sally and Briggs's preppy classmates from Princeton, spots Clio and Henry. As she reaches her spot near the altar, she does her duty, crouching down to fan out Sally's lace train on the floor. She takes Sally's bridal bouquet, a more robust version of her own, to hold. She looks around the enormous church, taking in the stained glass and carved wood, and then fixes her gaze on her parents in the front row. Her father is stuffed into his tuxedo and her mother looks positively regal in her navy gown. Smith notices something; they are holding hands. Not lightly, but tightly. They are clutching each other hard, veins popping from their hands. They both have tears in their eyes.

Smith peers out at the sea of guests—the final count was over three hundred—her eyes scanning row by row, but she can't find Tate. The pastor begins the ceremony, welcoming everyone to this happy, blessed occasion. Words rise from him like smoke, familiar words, words Smith's had occasion to hear dozens of times in the past several years. So many friends have gotten married, so many friends have asked her to be a bridesmaid, and she knows that she's become jaded about it all, maybe a drop bitter, but what bitterness has built up is gone now as she stands here. She's thankful for this.

Sally's best friend, Gemma, another Princeton grad and a junior partner at a law firm, stands to give a reading. Sally was willing to get married in a church—an absolute must for Briggs's family—as long as Sally could select at least one nonreligious reading. She and Smith spent hours huddled together on Sally's bed, books splayed open all around them, a laptop cracked for searches, sifting through potential passages, interpreting them, and narrowed it down to an excerpt from

Rilke's *Letters to a Young Poet*. Gemma, a stunning and petite redhead, reads now.

> **For one human being to love another human being: that is perhaps the most difficult task that has been entrusted to us, the ultimate task, the final test and proof, the work for which all other work is merely preparation . . . Loving does not at first mean merging, surrendering, and uniting with another person . . . it is a high inducement for the individual to ripen, to become something in himself, to become world, to become world in himself for the sake of another person; it is a great, demanding claim on him, something that chooses him and calls him to vast distances . . .**
>
> **But once the realization is accepted that even between the closest people infinite distances exists, a marvelous living side-by-side can grow up for them, if they succeed in loving the expanse between them, which gives them the possibility of always seeing each other as a whole before an immense sky.**

Smith listens to the tumble of words. The interesting thing, the inspiring thing, is that today they have new meaning. Today, as she stands here at this altar bursting with flowers, wearing her bridesmaid dress, the words feel fresh and she rolls them over in her mind. Love as ultimate task. Loving as inducement for self-actualization. The persistence of an infinite distance between people who love each other. Wholeness before an immense sky.

It is the words that hit her more than the music, more than the portrait of her parents' abiding and complicated affection, these words that are perfect and well chosen, reflective of the complexity and realness of love, of commitment. She catches Sally's eye. They exchange quick sister smiles. The pastor carries on, his words ephemeral and fuzzy, but then sharp.

"You may kiss the bride."

Smith watches her sister throw her arms up around Briggs's neck. The kiss is neither safe nor scripted. It is real and lingering and they carry on as if they've forgotten their audience, as if they are not in a holy place.

Everyone erupts. Clapping, hooting, hollering. And this is when Smith spots Tate. He's toward the back, off to the right, in the suit they picked together. His Leica—she's learning some photography language—hangs around his neck. He catches her looking and even from the distance, she can make out his wry smile. She gives a small wave.

Clio jogs over, hugs Smith quickly before the wedding guests are ushered back to the Waldorf for cocktails before the reception, but Smith stays put at the church with her family and the wedding party for more pictures. Tate waits with her. She catches him snapping some pictures of his own. When it's time for them to head to the hotel, he inserts himself in the inner circle and links his arm in hers.

"Solid job up there," he says.

"Thanks. The hard part is yet to come, though."

Her speech. The thing that she's worried about on and off for the better part of a year, a writing assignment that's rattled her far more than even the prospect of writing an entire book.

"I have a hunch it will go just fine," he says as they walk. "I'm not sure I've met a smarter person."

"No need for the superlatives, buddy."

"It's only the truth."

"You're embarrassing me," she says, feeling her cheeks redden. She's got to admit that it's nice to hear these things.

"About earlier," he says. "I think I know—"

"I don't want to talk about this morning," Smith says, cutting him off, feeling embarrassed. "Not now."

They walk ahead of the group and arrive at the Waldorf's main entrance on Park Avenue before the rest of them.

"It's wild that my parents got married here so many years ago," she says, looking up at the lit-up brick and limestone façade of this historic hotel that occupies an entire city block.

He grins, peers down at the sidewalk. "There's an abandoned train platform—track sixty-one—under us. I guess it was built to carry freight from Grand Central and then it became an underground station for VIPs to secretly enter the hotel. There was this enormous elevator big enough to hold FDR's bulletproof car. And there's a train car down there. I read that Warhol hosted a famous video art exhibition down there in the sixties."

"Is that so?" she says, laughing.

"Tell me that's not cool."

"It's cool."

"Did you know that this is one of the largest art deco structures still standing? An official city landmark. One thousand four hundred thirteen guest rooms, no two alike; forty-seven stories; first choice of the presidents. This was the first hotel to ever offer room service. The Waldorf salad was invented here by a chef named Oscar and it is rumored that he came up with eggs Benedict too, to cure some VIP's raging hangover."

"You and your city architecture obsession," she says.

"There's nothing wrong with being obsessed," he says.

Inside, they climb the plush carpeted steps.

He points down at the mosaic floor. "Here we have the famous *Wheel of Life*. Up there on the terrace, that was Cole Porter's piano."

When her mother pushed Sally to get married here, Smith thought it was totally narcissistic and egotistical, but now she thinks it's kind of cool, in a full-circle way. Sally didn't want the Grand Ballroom, though. She picked the younger, hipper spot on the top floor with the blazing blue retractable roof.

They walk past the big clock tower.

"It was once at the Empire State Building. Nine feet tall, two tons, made of bronze, created for the Chicago World's Fair in 1893."

They reach the elevator bank, where the rest of the wedding party catches up with them.

"You going to make sure my daughter behaves herself?" Thatcher says, pounding Tate on the back.

Tate grins. "Quite the opposite, actually."

Thatcher guffaws.

They all pile in and ride the elevator to the top floor. When they step out, they spill out into a hallway lined in black and white photos of the "good old days." Photos of celebrities—Lana Turner, Gene Kelly, and more. Tate pauses to inspect them.

"In its heyday, this place was a high-society supper club," Smith says. "Everyone came. Diplomats. Presidents. Sheiks. Endless celebrities. People came to eat and drink and listen to music."

"Pretty rad," he says. And this word makes her chuckle. It's such a surfer word.

They keep walking and see that the cocktail hour is in full swing. Smith spies the artisanal cocktail bar next to the champagne bar and leads Tate over. "I don't suppose you want to try lavender-infused champagne?"

"Why not?" he says.

A live musician plays along with a DJ. Sally and Briggs make their rounds. She's taken her hair down and it cascades in natural curls around her face. Guests flock to an enormous seafood bar. Smith takes Tate's hand and leads him over. He loads a plate with shellfish.

"You willing to part with one of your slimy old oysters?"

"Really?" he says.

"Really."

He lifts the shell and tilts it over her open mouth, watches it slide down. She swallows, cringes slightly, but recovers.

"Was it that bad?" he says.

"Kind of," she says, laughing, dabbing her mouth with a cloth napkin.

When they all walk into the Starlight Roof, Smith feels as if she's been transported to another time and place.

"Holy crap," Tate says, sipping his drink.

"Exactly," she says, looking around. She's only been in the space once before—last year when Sally was scouting locations—but it's been utterly transformed into a Sally-and-Briggs wonderland. Long banquet tables flank the central dance floor for the younger folks. Big, romantic candelabras sit on draped pale gold silk, surrounded by collars of white flowers—orchids, hydrangeas, dahlias. The older set—friends of the parents—are seated at round tables around the periphery of the room, closer to the wall-to-wall windows boasting sweeping views of Manhattan. Tall branches burst from the center of each table, creating a subtle forest effect. A twelve-piece band starts playing on a balcony above. But the ceiling—a cobalt art deco installation—is, by far, the pièce de résistance.

"I've never in my life seen anything like this," Tate says, looking around, lifting his camera to take photographs.

"We're not in Missouri anymore, Toto."

"A monogrammed dance floor? Is that normal?"

"None of this is normal, Tate." Smith laughs. "But we might as well enjoy it."

They walk around, cocktails in hand. Low-profile white lounge chairs and couches line the outermost edges of the room, by the windows. There are two old-fashioned photo booths.

"What's a selfie station?" Tate says, pointing to a cordoned-off area with an open laptop.

"You don't even want to know. Basically you pose in front of that screen and hit Confirm and it is automatically sent to Instagram under the hashtag sallyandbriggs."

"They have a wedding hashtag?" he says, laughing. "Smith, this is nuts."

A voice comes over a microphone. "Let's all welcome, for the first time as a married couple, Sally and Briggs!"

Everyone gathers around the dance floor and looks toward the entrance. Briggs glides Sally over and they slip through a break in the crowd onto the floor. She can tell her sister is nervous because she can't stop laughing.

Everyone waits. The band begins playing the instrumental intro to Frank Sinatra's "The Way You Look Tonight."

Smith fixes her gaze on the balcony, on the barely visible door. And then it happens. The door opens and Harry Connick Jr. walks through in his trademark dark suit and shirt. She grabs Tate's arm and points up.

"Holy. Fucking. Shit. Are you kidding me?" he says, looking at her, eyes wide.

"Nope. Thatcher pulled it off. I knew he was trying, but I didn't know it would actually happen."

Harry begins crooning, his unmistakable voice filling the cavernous space. "Some day, when I'm awfully low / When the world is cold / I will feel a glow just thinking of you / And the way you look tonight."

Smith watches her sister's head swing up toward the balcony and she nearly melts into Briggs. She looks around the dance floor, catches Smith's eye. "What in the world?" she mouths.

Smith watches her parents. They beam. It's plain that they are proud. The crowd goes absolutely wild, many people singing along. Sally can barely dance, she's so beside herself. So much for all those dance lessons. Her smile has never been bigger. Briggs steps on her dress over and over and they continue to dissolve into ebullient laughter, pausing only to kiss.

When the song is over, he stands there, *Harry Connick Jr.* stands there—this is pretty hard to wrap her mind around—and waves down to Sally and Briggs. "Congratulations, you two," he says. And then he is gone, through that door again, and everyone seems rightfully stunned.

"So. That just happened," Smith says.

"What the fuck?" Tate says. "Come on, let's get another drink. That was insane."

He leads her to the bar, where she orders another champagne and knocks it back. She must get up there soon for her toast. She's suddenly a bad bundle of nerves. Her inner monologue grows sharp. What was she thinking, not writing a speech? Who is she to think she can pull this off? Look at all these people. *Harry Connick Jr.* just sang. This is no joke.

They sit for the first course, a locally sourced organic fall-vegetable terrine composed by celebrity chef Rocco DiSpirito. Smith pushes it around her plate. She can't bring herself to eat right now. She drinks her water and tries to keep breathing. Her parents stand and deliver their remarks. Their words are plenty loud, but Smith can't really hear them. She's stuck in her own head right now, deeply worried that she might not be able to pull this off after all. She looks over at Sally, over-the-moon Sally, Sally who glows like the star she is. And then she looks over at Tate, Tate who is oblivious to her swelling panic, Tate who devours his food and seems to hang on her parents' every word.

She startles when she feels someone tapping her shoulder and turns to see who it is.

9:17PM

"Slow down, cowgirl."

It's Clio. Clio whom she's barely seen tonight, Clio who is not wearing the black gown Smith lent her, but a belted loden-green dress. Smith grabs the hem, smiles.

"Um, what's this insanely gorgeous thing?"

Clio squats down by Smith's chair. "I found it when Henry and I walked back to the hotel this morning, in the window of that little vintage store on Columbus. The color reminded me of Central Park in springtime and I decided I needed to have it."

"You, Clio Marsh, bought yourself a dress? My goodness, you are changing."

Clio smiles.

"You look exquisite, Clio."

"So do you, Smith. Are you all right?" Clio whispers. "I took one look at you and I could tell that you were panicking a little. I guess I'm something of an anxiety aficionado."

"I'm freaking out. It's true."

"All you have to do is get up there and say that you love your sister and you want her to be happy. That's really all anyone expects. You'll be fine. You'll be great."

Smith pulls Clio in for a hug, whispers thank you in her ear. She feels better.

When it's time, Smith stands on the dance floor, clutches the microphone in one hand and an old-fashioned champagne saucer in the other. She squints into the bright light that's trained on her. Her dizziness is acute and she finds herself wondering if this is how Clio feels when she's on the verge of a panic attack. Smith has thankfully never had one but worries there's a first time for everything.

She bends down and places her glass on the floor and stands back up. She wraps both hands around the microphone, takes a deep breath, and begins.

"If it's not clear for some reason, I'm Sally's sister. Her older and less wise sister."

She pauses, and the laughter comes as she hoped it would. It's a robust, encouraging sound and it buoys her to continue. She looks straight at Sally and thinks of something simple that might just save her: All she must do is speak to Sally. She's been speaking to Sally for more than thirty years. There just happen to be a few people listening. She's got this.

"So, I'm going to do something I've never done before. Something that's always horrified me. I'm going to make this up as I go. Wing it. And I've decided this is appropriate because Sally's always been on me to stop planning every little inch of my life. This is not easy for me; I'm a control freak. But this is for you, Sal.

"Sal, do you remember our trip to Europe during college? Well, we had very, um, different approaches to international travel. I got on that plane with a dozen travel guides, detailed lists and maps, and you had a *Star* magazine and a stash of gummy bears—Briggs, know that gummy bears can solve most anything—and a passport and all the trust in the world that we'd figure it out, that we'd have fun, that we'd be totally fine. And you were right, Sal. We were. Your optimism about the world has served you so annoyingly well at times. Look at the guy next to you. For those of you not privy to the story of how they met, it went a little like this. Sally goes back to her tenth Princeton reunion. She's with her friends, many of whom are here tonight, and she spots this guy at the keg at Tiger Inn and he's doing a *keg stand* at age, what, thirty-one? And Sally, my genius *doctor* sister, is like, *That looks like fun, I'm going to do one of those*. And she marches on over and lets everyone lift her legs so she's upside down funneling beer. And then they talk and, bam, love."

Smith looks over and sees Tate and thinks of something. Keeps going.

"I stumbled upon this quote just a few days ago, on Thanksgiving actually," she says, catching Tate's eye. "Truman Capote said these words, and I hope I'm not butchering them too badly, but he said, 'The brain may take advice, but not the heart, and love, having no geography, knows no boundaries.' I love this because I'm realizing that Sally has been trying to teach me that love is not something we can map out but must stumble into, and when we do, if we are lucky to, it has no limits. That's what I see when I look at Sally and Briggs. Something limitless. It's inspiring.

"Oh, and Briggs, for you. One final thing. That fateful summer in Europe when we were in college? We sat on this bench in Amsterdam one day, feeling very grown-up drinking our sludgy black coffees, and your wife asked me something. *What kind of guys do you think we will marry?* And we thought about this and I said I didn't know and clearly I still don't know"—she pauses for the crowd's laughter—"but she had these stars in her eyes, Briggs, and she said, *I'm going to marry the greatest guy. And I'm going to wait for him*. And she did. Let's all raise a glass of something good. To my sister and to Briggs and to a love worth the wait."

Smith exhales. She reaches down to collect her glass and lift it high into the air. The applause is thunderous and she feels gripped with joy, almost as if she's floating. As she makes her way back to her table, to Sally, she's overcome with a deep sense of relief, but also with the sense that what she said, however imperfect, however unpolished, was utterly honest and real. Sally stands and meets her halfway. The wedding photographer lowers himself by them and snaps furiously, capturing this moment of two sisters wrapped up in a hug.

Briggs waits for his turn. He hugs Smith. "I think we are going to have to find a way to get some keg stands going at the after-party."

The band starts playing "We Are Family" and Smith dances with Sally, and is wonderfully surprised when her parents join them. Bitsy has let down her immaculate guard and twirls with abandon. Thatcher has loosened his bow tie and smiles earnestly, his forehead glistening with sweat. Guests spill onto the floor to surround them. She spins Sally around and around. When the song is over, Tate stands waiting, an enormous smile splayed on his face. He pulls her toward him. "That was perfect, you know," he says, leading her toward the bar.

"I need a cocktail," Smith says, bouncing almost. "I need six cocktails."

"Slow down, cowgirl," he says, smiling.

But she doesn't slow down. She speeds up. She drinks and she dances and she talks to people. She flits about. She and Tate take goofy photos together in the photo booth. They even pose for some ridiculous selfies, participating in the hashtag nonsense. They spend the remainder of the evening with Clio and Henry, bouncing between the bar and the dance floor, taking periodic pauses to stand by the windows and look out at the city.

At one point, Tate takes Clio to dance and Smith hangs back with Henry. She looks at him, really looks at him. His alabaster skin and brilliant blue eyes, his black hair. He sips his whiskey, seems far younger than his fifty years.

"You having fun, Henry?"

"Absolutely," he says, looking around. "This is a lovely party, Smith. I consider myself lucky to be included in this important night for your family."

"Thanks, Henry," she says, staring at him. He's a very good man, this Henry, and Smith will make a point of getting to know him even better. He's brought out the best in her friend; Clio is a different person with him. So solid. So strong. Happy. She must tell him this. The alcohol pushes her along. "Thank you," she says, "for making Clio so happy. As you now know, she's been through hell, and just to see her smiling again . . . The point is, well, you better take care of her or I'll, oh, I don't know what I'll do, I'll organize your shoes or something, but take care of her, okay?"

Henry beams. Laughs heartily. Drains his drink. "That's my intention."

"Well, good then," Smith says, taking his hand. They weave in and out of tables and make their way onto the parquet floor. Song after song, the four of them dance. The band plays Coldplay's "Yellow." Smith smiles when she looks over and sees Clio and Henry in an embrace by the bar. Her friend is smiling, singing along. *Look at the stars, look how they shine for you*, she mouths at Henry.

It dawns on Smith that she's drunk. Totally, blissfully gone. High as a kite. Free as a fucking bird.

She pulls Briggs aside and hugs him. "Do you know how lucky you are to have her?"

He grins. "I know."

"No, I mean it. You better not ever fucking take her for granted," she says, waving her finger jokingly in his face. "She's the best girl in the world. You know that, I trust?"

Briggs laughs. "She feels the same way about you. You know she's always been a little envious of you?"

"What?" Smith says.

He nods.

"What is all of this?" Sally says, appearing seemingly from nowhere, draping her arms around Briggs.

"Your sister is just reminding me of my good fortune," he says.

A crashing sound from across the room interrupts them. One of the enormous arrangements of branches has toppled over, first causing shrieks and then howling laughter. Things are, as they should be, taking a turn toward wildness. Some of the older guests start sneaking out. But Smith and Tate and the rest of them stay until the bitter end, drinking and dancing.

As it does during the best and brightest moments in life, time zips by, and just like that, the wedding is over. Hotel staffers shuffle the drunkards through a black and white marble foyer into the regal two-story Conrad Suite, which awaits for the equally over-the-top after-party. David Guetta spins at a DJ booth. The space is utter opulence, embellished with silver and gold leaf and rich jewel-toned fabrics, etched mirrored paneling, lavish multitiered crystal chandeliers and a vast marble fireplace. Waiters circle with trays full of late-night bites: cones of herbed French fries, tiny pots of mac and cheese, mini pizzas and Kobe beef sliders.

After twenty or so minutes, Sally and Briggs enter. She has changed out of her wedding dress and now wears a short, flirty white number, her hair swept into a topknot. Everyone gathers around them. The music is loud and thumping. Candles flicker everywhere.

"So, look, I have something to tell you," Tate says, grabbing Smith's arm. His voice shakes. His eyes are wide, bleary from booze. A frank seriousness falls over his face. Through the haze of alcohol and euphoria, Smith feels herself beginning to panic.

"What is it?" she says.

"Get some air with me?"

MIDNIGHT

"I like the sound of that."

Tate holds Smith's hand and drags her through the lobby. They stumble past the big clock. It chimes midnight.

He pulls her along the famous mosaic floor at the entry, past Cole Porter's Steinway piano on the Cocktail Terrace, down the plush carpeted stairs, through the glass doors and out onto Park Avenue. Smith looks up at the hotel's grand brick and limestone façade, which is lit with bright lights.

It's cold enough now that she's shivering. Tate peels off his jacket and drapes it around her. He fiddles nervously with his camera, his fingers looping and unlooping the strap, fidgeting with the gears. He kicks anxiously at the sidewalk and then looks up at her. Smiles. His eyes are big and bright under the lamplights. "How are you doing? This is quite the event. You seem to be surviving pretty well."

"I am. I think the vats of champagne are helping, but I feel better about things than I have in the longest time, Tate. I've been moping around, all woe-is-me, but tonight, I don't know . . . Tonight, I feel okay, optimistic even. So what about Asad and broken hearts and all that garbage, right? The past is the past."

"Yes!" Tate says, taking her shoulders. "The past is the past and I mean, I'm sorry to say, but that Asad didn't deserve you. He could have married you, Smith. He's a grown man. A *doctor*. He doesn't need anyone's approval. You deserve a guy who's going to stand up for you."

Like you? she wonders.

She nods, galvanized. "You're right. He could have stood up to his family. If they love him, they would have come around. I know that. It's just hard to admit. It's easier to blame these people I never had the chance to meet."

"It wasn't just his family, Smith," Tate says.

It's clear from the look on his face that he's censoring himself, that he knows something more.

"I'm not totally oblivious," Smith says. "I wouldn't be surprised if Thatch said or did something to make Asad leave."

"Smith, when we were in the Hamptons and I was having drinks with your father in the library, he told me that—"

She holds up her hand to stop this confession. It's been a good night, all about family. "That's okay. I don't need details. I know who my father is. Besides, like I said, the past is the past . . ."

"Well, speaking of the past, I'm guessing you saw the e-mail from Olivia this morning?"

"Was it that obvious when I stomped out of your apartment?" Smith laughs sheepishly.

"Pretty much," he says. "And I'm sorry. You shouldn't be in the middle of this crap."

"Are you going to see her when she comes?" Smith asks, and then wishes she hadn't. Her insides lurch as she waits for his reply.

"I don't know," he says, shaking his head, looking down at the sidewalk. "I'm not sure I can figure any of this out if I'm with you right now, Smith. I don't even know who I am anymore and I don't want to drag you through this. I need to be alone. I haven't been single since I was a freshman in college, which is insane, and I need time to process the shit I've been through."

"I get it," Smith says sincerely. "Believe me, I get it." She finds a smile even as a quiet sadness spreads inside her. But he is right. They've both been burned. They both know better than to jump into something serious now. Time. Space. Solitude. Freedom. They both need all these clichéd things people talk about.

After a beat she breaks the silence. "You said that you don't even know who you are anymore. The messed-up thing, Tate, is that I'm not sure I've ever known. I've been so close with my parents and my sister and Clio, I haven't even needed to figure it out. But Sally is married now and Clio and Henry are moving in together and I need to find out who I am on my own, without them. I'm going to get my own apartment. Something I can afford on my own. I will still see my family, of course, but not every day."

As she stands on the blustery sidewalk in front of the grand hotel, Smith begins to truly feel the enormity of what's to come, of the steps she's now vowing to take. Yes, she's a bit sauced, but that doesn't matter. This courage is not liquid; this resolve is real. All of this is incredibly, inspiringly clear to her now, what she must do, what she *will* do. She thinks of her family and Clio tucked inside, celebrating, and she loves them and knows how lucky she is to have them and love them as much as she does, but finally, after thirty-four years in this world, she's ready to strike out on her own.

It's time.

"How about this," Tate says, rubbing his hands together, his breath forming clouds in the air. "You'll find your own place, maybe even downtown where all of us cool kids live, and I will figure shit out with Olivia and get in a good groove with my photography and we can meet again . . . for a tailgate in New Haven or Cambridge or a stroll through the park or a noon Bloody at the Boathouse? Or for a mind-erasing bender around the city?"

"I like the sound of that." And she does. She really does.

Tate pulls her into him, throws his arms around her. "Look," he says, pointing up at the sky, and Smith sees it: the moon, a barely there crescent of white against the inky expanse. "Our goodnight moon."

Her mind snags on one word, a hopeful word: *our.*

And then he does it. What she's been imagining, what she's been waiting for. He places his cold hands on her cheeks, frames her face, pauses and then pulls her toward him. He kisses her. And he keeps on kissing her. He doesn't stop. She tries to pull away—there are people around, they are on the street—but he won't let her. And so she surrenders, allows her body to fall into his. His camera is bulky between them, but he tosses it around behind his back. He playfully bites her bottom lip.

Minutes pass and the whole world falls away.

It just falls away.

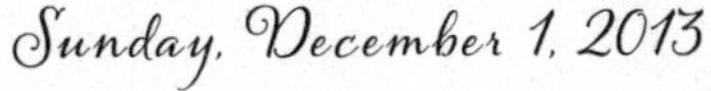

CLIO

A block or two west of the new City of Man in Turtle Bay there is an old willow that presides over an interior garden. It is a battered tree, long suffering and much climbed, held together by strands of wire but beloved of those who know it. In a way it symbolizes the city: life under difficulties, growth against odds, sap-rise in the midst of concrete, and the steady reaching for the sun.

— E.B. White, *Here Is New York*

NOTES/FACTS FOR RAMBLE WALK*:

SEPTEMBER 30, 2001

HISTORY: Designed by Frederick Law Olmsted & Calvert Vaux and completed in 1859. 38-acre area running between 73rd and 78th streets. Originally an expanse of rock outcrops running along a large swamp, it was transformed into a tranquil and lush woodland or "wild garden." Per Olmsted, the area was created to "excite the childish playfulness and profuse careless utterance of Nature."

LANDMARKS: Azalea Pond, Balcony Bridge, Loeb Boathouse, Evodia Field, the Gill, Hernshead, Humming Tombstone, Indian Cave, the Lake, Maintenance Field, Mugger's Woods, Oven/Willow Rock, the Point, Rustic Shelter, Riviera, the Swampy Pin Oak, Tupelo Meadow, Upper Lobe, Warbler Rock.

THE RAMBLE'S BIRDS: Central Park is situated on the Atlantic Flyway (favored migration route for many birds); more than 250 species of birds have been spotted in the Ramble and people come from all over the world to see them. Common sightings: pigeons, warblers, hawks, egrets, woodpeckers, ducks, vireos, cuckoos,

---

* Many of these details have been culled from *The Ramble in Central Park: A Wilderness West of Fifth* by Robert A. McCabe.

sandpipers, flycatchers. Also, many species pass through during spring and fall migration. Park has become magnet for migrating Neotropical songbirds and other species that winter in the south.

MIGRANT SPECIES: Eastern Phoebe (mid-March through late May), wood warblers (small, brightly plumed Neotropical songbirds) including Prothonotary, Cape May, Yellow-throated, Hooded, Worm-eating. Also: Solitary and Spotted Sandpipers. American Woodcocks and a variety of sparrows.

BREEDING SPECIES: Thirty-plus species (per Audubon), including: American Robin, Starling, Common Grackle, Song Sparrow, House Wren, Gray Catbird, Tufted Titmice, Downy Woodpecker, Warbling Vireo, Wood Thrush, Cedar Waxwing, Eastern Kingbird, Northern Flicker, Mallard, Green Heron, Eastern Screech-Owl, Red-tailed Hawk (two or three per year).

HUMMINGBIRDS: Ruby-throated Hummingbirds visit in spring and fall and are attracted to deep-throated flowering plants. Extract nectar from flowers with long, thin bills and are very active feeders.

CELEBRITY BIRD: Red-tailed Hawk Pale Male (named for his fair coloring) kicked out of nest it built on Fifth Avenue building. Celebrity protest brought nest back.

POINT IS TO GET LOST?: In an 1860 essay, an NYT reporter had two complaints about the Ramble: (1) not enough benches, and (2) there were absolutely no signs indicating how to get out of the Ramble. Today, a few benches, but there are still no signs. Apparently, it was the designers' goal to make this intimate area seem big and complex through the use of winding paths, shrubbery and rock hills to block visibility. The result: no logical way to organize a tour of this place or give easy directions to someone who is lost in the Ramble. Maybe that is the point after all. To be lost.

8:24AM

"What will happen?"

All she remembers from her dream: The harp, fluorescent, flickering fitfully in a grainy darkness. Under it, a single word, all caps, a conspicuous exhortation, lit up, blinding in its cartoon cast: *FORGIVENESS*. All other details are lost. The dream, she decides, was neither nightmare nor fairy tale.

When she opens her eyes, the world is befuddling in its sameness and strangeness. The hotel room is just as it has always been, arrestingly white, ever generic and pristine, but it's as if the quality of the air has been tweaked just so. The light is brilliant and lacelike; there's an almost viscous serenity to the space. Clio feels as if she's floating. She hears the faint rumblings of Henry puttering on the other side of the cracked-open bathroom door. He hums opera. He runs the tap.

She sits up. Swings her legs over the side of the bed. Without thinking, she reaches to open the bedside drawer. Her mother's letter sits there, quiet and crisply folded, just as she left it last night. Clio retrieves it, smooths it open, the single page of paper, the cryptic swirl of her mother's head and heart a transfixing blur before it all grows sharp.

She reads it again, the words whirring through her, awakening her veins, better than caffeine. A curious thing happens. Anger doesn't alight. It will again, Clio knows this, but these moments, as they tumble past, don't contain vitriol and bitterness. Just longing. Now it's soothingly simple: she's just a daughter who has lost her mother and misses her deeply.

Clio looks up. Henry comes toward her wrapped up in his robe, his hair glistening wet and dark, carefully combed. His blue eyes beam as he sits on the edge of the bed next to her. "You slept hard," he says, sweeping a strand of hair from her eyes.

She smiles. "I did. I can't remember the last time I slept that well."

"Good," he says. One word. *Good.*

A knock on the door.

"Breakfast," he says, popping up. "Hope you're hungry."

She is. She's more ravenous than she's been in many months. She slips into the bathroom but watches through the crack as silver steaming trays float by and through the other door, *their* door. The empty shelf is tucked into the corner of the room, where it will stay. She will fill it with Eloise's books.

She throws cold water on her face and blots it dry. Dregs of makeup from the wedding linger defiantly on her lashes and under her eyes. She wraps up in her own robe, the one that matches his. She knots the sash tightly and looks in the mirror again. She sees something: a true smile.

In the new place—what will be their home—Henry stands by the triplet windows, his silhouette framed by sunshine that spills in from the street. She walks over and stands with him for a moment. Looks out. The trees sway in a slight wind.

It's December again.

He turns to her. "Good morning, my Clio."

"Good morning, my Henry," she says.

Plates upon plates of food await them. Eggs and bacon and French toast and exotic fruit, and it all looks good, worth tasting. There are plenty of chairs, but Clio settles on a square of carpet by the coffee table and begins to eat. He sits with her on the floor, feeds her cubes of cantaloupe.

Side by side, they sit like this and eat in silence, trading sections of the Sunday *New York Times*. Over the pages of her newspaper, she steals glances at him to remember that this is real.

It is.

She stands and walks around the place, the place she didn't really see a week ago because she was so stunned, so scared, so riddled with panic. On the wall hangs a Currier and Ives print of Central Park.

Henry comes up behind her, drapes his arms around her chest.

"I was hoping you might give me a private tour," he whispers in her ear.

"Let's go," Clio says, grabbing his hand. They dress.

Outside the hotel entrance, pigeons peck at a piece of poppy-seed bagel.

"So," he says. "What are our thoughts on pigeons?"

"Our thought is that despite conventional wisdom and widespread disgust, they are brilliant birds. Considered to be among the most intelligent. They can do things only humans and primates were thought to be able to do. They can pass the mirror test."

"The mirror test?" Henry asks eagerly.

"A pigeon can recognize its own reflection in a mirror. It's the only non-mammal species that can do this. They can also recognize all twenty-six letters in the alphabet."

"Incredible."

She nods.

Say hello hello to the pigeons.

They hold hands as they walk toward the park. They enter on Eighty-First Street and pass the Delacorte Theater, where they saw Shakespeare in the Park in August, then wind along the Great Lawn toward Turtle Pond. She leads him to the dock, to the spot where she meets her walkers each week, and they stand together gazing out over the water. In the distance, a pair of Mallards swims, leaving behind them a gentle wake.

Then the Ramble, the labyrinthine heart of the park. She thinks of the passion-filled, metaphor-laden journal notes she wrote so many years ago. Hiding and seeking. Lost and found. City and wild. Humans and nature. It was about these things and so much more: getting out here, experiencing something, seeing, feeling.

Rambling.

"So what's the scoop for winter in these parts? Pretty quiet birding time?" Henry says.

"A little quiet, but maybe my favorite season here. When there are no leaves on the trees, it's easy to spot the owls and the hawks. And there are these thistle and sunflower feeders in Evodia Field that attract lots of birds . . . Hairy and Downy Woodpeckers, White-breasted Nuthatches, Carolina Wrens, Fox Sparrows, Blue Jays, Northern Cardinals, Common Redpolls, Black-capped Chickadees, Tufted Titmice. And on the Harlem Meer and the Lake, you'll see Hooded Mergansers and Pied-billed Grebes and Ruddy Ducks and Wood Ducks. And it's pretty remarkable to see this place in a snowstorm."

She points at the walkway near Bow Bridge. "Years ago, five Long-eared Owls perched in that tree right there. They stayed for weeks. Huge crowds gathered. It was pretty incredible. Rumor has it there's a crew this year too."

She leads him to her bench. *Their bench.* They sit for a while. They don't say much even though there's much to say. They just sit, their legs touching, dappled by sun. People pass, kind-faced strangers who clutch coffees and papers and phones and dreams. People somewhere between here and there, then and when.

"Oh, that day. That first day on this good, green bench," he says. "I was a world-class wreck, wasn't I?"

Clio nods, remembers. "There's poetry in the wreckage."

Henry laughs. "Indeed there is."

The sun continues to shine. Birds sing. Sirens croon in the distance.

For Clio, a singular thought alights, bold, quiet, unbidden: *I'm home.*

The air is fresh and full. She breathes it in and out and looks up at the San Remo, the austere and brooding building where she's lived all these years, these complex and important years, and wonders what it will be like to move on, to have a fresh view of the world. She thinks of Smith. As Clio and Henry left the wedding last night, they walked by Smith and Tate on the street. The two were lost in an embrace, blind to the world. Clio wonders if he's up there this morning, next to Smith in bed. The thought makes her smile.

Friends. A dance of moments and memories, a tumble of years and tears and talks and walks, of sameness and difference, closeness and distance, words and silence, secrets and survivals big and small, a swirl of *I'm okay* and *I'm a mess* and *It is what it is*. And it is.

Time passes, as it does. An uncertain amount. Wordlessly Clio stands, pulls Henry up too.

"Let's go home," she says.

"Home, huh?" he says, beaming. "I like the sound of that."

And she leads him along, under her trees and through her birds. Her mind tangles with memories and questions and then she feels it, the subtle but also unmistakable sensation of emptying, of letting go. Hand in his hand, one foot in front of the other, she is going forward for once.

They exit the park where they entered. Wait for the green light to cross.

She leads Henry along her shortcut by the planetarium, and this is when she sees it: the blurry object near the foliage that flanks the ground-level entrance to the Rose Center.

"Wait. What was that?" she says, dropping Henry's hand, sneaking toward to the blooming *Mahonia japonica* plant to take a closer look. "What in the world?"

"What is it?" Henry says. "What do you see?"

"Come," Clio whispers emphatically, waving him over. "*Come.*"

He comes to her and she points at the small blur hovering over the bushes.

"A *hummingbird*, Henry. On the first of *December.*"

She studies the tiny creature. It's no more than four inches long, with its rapierlike bill. It hovers insectlike, remaining stationary in midair. Then it flies backward, straight up and down, side to side. Its colors are grand: kelly green above, white below, strongly washed with red on its sides, flanks and under-tail coverts. The center of its throat is a pure, unmarked white, which suggests she's an immature female.

"You see the bright plumage?" she whispers. "It's often a trick of the sun. In some species, the coloring doesn't actually derive from pigmentation in the feather structure, but rather from these prismlike cells found in the topmost layers of the feathers. When sunlight hits these cells, it breaks into wavelengths that reflect to us in various degrees of intensity. So, if we change position, a muted-looking bird might suddenly look fire-engine red or bright green."

"So, it's all about the light we see things in. All about perspective," he says.

"Exactly."

Clio snaps a quick photo with her phone, sends it to her museum colleagues.

Clio: Probable immature female rufous spotted in shrubbery at AMNH 81st Street entrance. Confirm ID. Could also be Allen's or broad-tailed?

She looks up at the blue sky and then into Henry's blue eyes. And then she settles her gaze back on the bird, the bird that buzzes around the nectar-filled plant. She's careful to keep enough distance, not to disturb the small creature. She knows how quickly word will spread, but for now, it's just the three of them.

"As far as I know, this is the first vagrant in a while to show up in New York State. She was probably on the way to Mexico and miscalculated the angle of her southern flight path and ended up here. A small navigational error can amount to a big mistake."

"So, she got lost?" Henry says, breaking it down.

"Yes," Clio says, and laughs.

He laughs with her.

We haven't laughed enough yet. We will. We will laugh at it all.

She thinks of her mother, feels with every bit of her being that Eloise is behind this. Around them, the world goes on.

"Can you believe it?" she whispers, looking up at him.

"I can," he says through a smile, throwing his arm around her. "What will happen? Do you think she'll survive?"

Clio leans into him. Buries her face in his chest. Inhales.

"I do," she says. "I think she'll make it. She'll do what she has to do."

ACKNOWLEDGMENTS

First, I must thank three brilliant women who read multiple drafts of this book and whose encouragement kept me going: Brettne Bloom, Lucia Macro, and Christine Pride. This book would not exist without their imaginative guidance.

I am indebted to Lucia's wonderful team at William Morrow, especially Liate Stehlik, Kelly Rudolph, Kaitlin Harri, Nicole Fischer, Leah Carlson-Stanisic, Serena Wang, and Aja Pollock. Thanks also to Sarah Burningham of Little Bird Publicity, Brettne's lovely assistant Dana Murphy at The Book Group, and to Jenny Meyer.

I'm enormously grateful to the experts I consulted with while researching this book. Eleanor Sterling at the glorious American Museum of Natural History in New York was generous with her time and connected me with Ana Luz Porzecanski and Paul Sweet, who enlightened me about the ornithology world. Philippe Cheng shared the intricacies and wonders of photography with me. Libby Nelson educated me about the intriguing modern space of Co-Active Life Coaching. Rachel Yehaskel of Resourceful Consultants, LLC shed light on the work of a professional organizer. Gareth Russell helped me bring to life my dear Northern Irishman Henry Kildare. Jes Gordon lent me her party planning skills, this time for a fictional wedding. Durre Nabi and Lindsay Choudry talked with me about Pakistani culture and customs. Jennie Tarr Coyne and Patsy Tarr graciously welcomed me into their San Remo homes.

I wish to thank all of you who shared your firsthand experiences of bipolar disorder and other mental illnesses with me. You will remain anonymous here, but please know that I'm tremendoulsy grateful for your personal stories and hard-earned insights. I am also indebted to Dr. Lauren Weinstock and Dr. Brian Kurtz for their medical expertise.

Thank you to all of the wildly talented writers I've come to know over the past six years, both online and in real life, and to all the women who have joined me for my Happier Hours Literary Salons. Your friendship means the world to me.

Thank you to the wonderful Rowley family for your love and support. I lucked out in the in-law department. You are the best.

Thank you, Yolanda and Pat, for taking such tremendous care of our girls and our home while I'm writing.

Thank you to my favorite Donnelley women. To my sisters Inanna, Naomi, Ceara and Tegan and your families. To Mom, for teaching me to write and encouraging me to read and, above all, for showing me how to be a good mom to girls in this amazing urban jungle. To Dad, who read me *Charlotte's Web* when I was a little girl, kindling my longtime affection for E. B. White. Many years later, I encountered White's *Here Is New York*, a brilliant portrait of this city of mine, and an inspiration for this book. Dad, you are now fishing in distant waters, but your spirit infuses *The Ramblers*.

Finally, thank you to my husband and to my daughters. Bryan, you are my rock, my world, my rambler. My Rowlets, my sweet petites, there are no words to describe my love for you. You inspire me. You light a little fire under me. You fill my days with laughter and light. Everything I write is for you.

ABOUT THE AUTHOR

Born and raised in New York City, Aidan Donnelley Rowley graduated from Yale University and received her law degree from Columbia University. She is the author of a previous novel, *Life After Yes*, and the creator of the Happier Hours Literary Salons. She lives in Manhattan with her husband and three daughters.